**ALSO BY DAVID RILEY BERTSCH**

*Death Canyon*

# RIVER
## OF NO
# RETURN

### A JAKE TRENT NOVEL

# DAVID RILEY BERTSCH

SCRIBNER
New York   London   Toronto   Sydney   New Delhi

Scribner
A Division of Simon & Schuster, Inc.
1230 Avenue of the Americas
New York, NY 10020

First Scribner hardcover edition January 2015

SCRIBNER and design are registered trademarks of The Gale Group, Inc., used under license by Simon & Schuster, Inc., the publisher of this work.

For information about special discounts for bulk purchases, please contact Simon & Schuster Special Sales at 1-866-506-1949 or business@simonandschuster.com.

The Simon & Schuster Speakers Bureau can bring authors to your live event. For more information or to book an event, contact the Simon & Schuster Speakers Bureau at 1-866-248-3049 or visit our website at www.simonspeakers.com.

Interior design by Jill Putorti
Jacket design by Laurie Carkeet
Jacket photographs: Sign © Shutterstock; Landscape © Alterndo Nature/Alterndo/Getty Images; Helicopter © Chris Tobin/Digital Vision/Getty Images

Manufactured in the United States of America

10  9  8  7  6  5  4  3  2  1

Library of Congress Cataloging-in-Publication Data

Bertsch, David Riley.
River of no return : a Jake Trent novel / David Riley Bertsch. — First Scribner hardcover edition.
pages ; cm
1. Fishing guides—Fiction. 2. Missing persons—Fiction. I. Title.
PS3602.E7688R59 2015
813'.6—dc23
2014030186

ISBN 978-1-4516-9803-9
ISBN 978-1-4516-9805-3 (ebook)

*This book is dedicated to all those who enjoy open spaces; to my wife, Katie; and to my family.*

*It's a bugged and drugged world . . .*

—Alfred Bester, *The Computer Connection*, 1974

# RIVER
## OF NO
# RETURN

*The power of population is indefinitely greater than the power in the earth to produce subsistence for man.*

—Thomas Robert Malthus (1766–1834)

**KOWLOON WALLED CITY, CHINA. SUMMER1960.**
**5:30 P.M., HONG KONG TIME.**

*The boy, Xiao, tottered from one foot to the other. He had been standing in the water line for hours without a single step of progress. Hundreds of people were in front of him. Pain seized his ankles. The summer heat made him sweat, and he swatted at biting flies.*

*His breaths came shallow and fast. Dry. He'd not had a drink in almost twenty-four hours. No food either, but that wasn't even on his mind. Other needs had to be fulfilled first.*

*Shoddy apartment towers littered Kowloon City. In contrast to the immodest skyline of Hong Kong, the precarious gray sentinels stood as a memento of hard times following the Japanese occupation during World War II, twisted obelisks teeming with the destitute and the depraved.*

*The new water main had been installed by Hong Kong's Social*

*Welfare Department the previous summer. It provided a critical resource, but exposed human behavior at its most ruthless.*

*As dusk fell, when the water was being shut off, the crowd began to push. The Welfare Department knew better than to operate at night. It was too dangerous. Dusk wasn't much better. Several yards ahead of him, Xiao saw a commotion: a man pulling a blade from his belt; another man trying to wrestle it away. The fray morphed into a swarm of thirsty beasts, pulsing with energy. A riot. With only seventy-five pounds to his ten-year-old frame, Xiao didn't stand a chance in the chaos. Gazing one last time at the queue ahead, he took his jug and ran.*

*Xiao caught his breath and walked home along the gutter stream, past the floating plastic bottles, bags of waste, and dead birds. These things made no impression on Xiao. It was the only world he'd ever known.*

*A few hundred yards from his family's building, Xiao dunked the jug and retrieved a liter of greenish-brown water from the stream. It would have to do.*

*His family lived in a second-story room, separated from another clan by moldy plywood. When he arrived, his mother, Niu, was breathing but still feverish. Sweat dripped from her hair and onto the dust floor; in this heat she wouldn't last long without water. His older brother, Shui, had been asleep, but woke upon Xiao's entrance.*

*Shui took the jug and opened their mother's mouth. She drank eagerly. Then she fell back onto her mat.*

*Shui grabbed their mother and shouted. "You have water, mama! You'll be okay now!" Her face was pale and waxy. It showed no signs of life. Eventually, Shui gave up and sat down on his mat. He reached for the jug, looked at the dirty water, and then turned to Xiao.*

*"The gutter? You bastard."*

*Shui stood and backhanded his younger brother hard across the face. Xiao sat still for a moment, then picked up the railroad spike the family used for self-defense. He turned to Shui and stabbed his brother until he stopped moving.*

*"There's never enough," he said to his brother's raw body.*

*Xiao took the soda bottle and guzzled the rest of the water.*

*Xiao sweated and vomited for three days in the stench of his family's death. Mother and brother gone, and a father he'd never known. He wanted to die, yearned for it, but his fever subsided.*

*On the fourth day, he gathered every bit of strength he could and wandered outside. He remembered a building where his mother had said boys and girls went when they had no mother or father. So he went there.*

*Once he was showered and fed, they began the tests.*

**WEST BANK, SNAKE RIVER. OCTOBER 15, 2013.**
**3 P.M. MOUNTAIN STANDARD TIME.**

*"You sneaky little bastard!"* Jake Trent hissed under his breath. Talking to himself. A sure sign of obsession.

The object of his disdain wasn't *that* little. Seventeen or eighteen inches at least. A good-size fish. Big enough to be a worthy adversary, if he could ever get the size 18 cinnamon ant where it needed to be.

It was a tough shot: forty-five feet across Trout Creek, upstream of the tree roots and ten inches in under the willow. It would require a big mend, but without submerging the ant, which would prevent Jake from seeing the strike. He was on river right, looking upstream and across to river left, where the king sat in his castle.

The mend, the upstream flip of the fly line meant to preserve the dry fly's natural drift, had been the problem. Jake had made the proper cast a few times, but his mend pulled the fly under the surface, where the big guy couldn't see it. On the last cast, Jake had seen his quarry, with its butter-yellow underbelly, trail the sunken fly, considering it. But the fish sensed something was awry. Back to the castle.

Jake had a few more casts at most. The fish was onto him. It had slowed its feeding rhythm considerably, wary of an imitation. The wind wasn't helping. It was picking up as the afternoon wore on, rustling the sparsely dressed willows. With it came a cold blast, a herald of the approaching winter.

Jake switched the rod to his left hand to make the cast. He found the mend easier with his upstream hand. The first cast fell embarrassingly short. A small fish pecked at the ant, but Jake pulled it away. He didn't want a small-time tussle to spook the one he was really after.

His second attempt was spot-on. The fly drifted right over the fish. The king of the trout rose, and his mouth enveloped the fly.

Jake pulled up to set the hook, but his left hand lacked the coordination of his right. It was too much. He felt the weight of the fish for only a second before the fly tore free. The fish splashed in a fury, wondering what the hell had just pricked him in the mouth. King Cutty was gone, looking for a new kingdom to call home, where stinging cinnamon ants wouldn't bother him.

"Damn!" More talking to himself. "Only been working him for a month now."

If they were all easy, it wouldn't be any fun. Jake relished the smart ones. They challenged him. Right now, he needed that. A restless feeling engulfed him every autumn; the tourists were all but gone, and the best fishing was behind him. Little to no business for the bed-and-breakfast. *I need a vacation,* he thought. *But to where?*

Jake bit through the tippet and stuck the fly in his hat for next time. He walked through the high grass back to the front door of the "guesthouse," Jake's own residence on the property he owned—a little irony he enjoyed—broke down the three-piece rod, and slid it back in its case. He could leave it conveniently assembled for his next walkabout, likely tomorrow, but Jake liked to put everything back in its place: the reel in its faux-velvet bag, and the eight-foot, four-weight Winston back in its PVC tube.

After his equipment was stashed, he grabbed a diet soda from the fridge and shuffled over to an old cowhide sofa by the wood-burning stove. The flames from the morning were withering, and the pile outside was diminished. Jake made a mental note to pick up the cord of wood that J.P.—his occasional employee—had chopped for the bed-and-breakfast, the Fin and Feather.

Jake's cell phone was buzzing on the side table. Area code 202. Jake flew through old associations. DC. Who could be calling from Washington?

"Hello?"

"Jake?" A woman's voice.

"Who am I speaking with?"

"It's Divya."

Momentary confusion, then a bolt of recognition. "Divya Navaysam?"

"How many Divyas do you know?" A sweet, flirty tone.

He thought he'd recognized the voice, but it had been so long. *What in the world does she want?*

"I'm calling to ask you a favor. It's about a legal issue—a civil rights issue, actually. Influencing Washington away from some scary legislation. Speaking truth to power—your sort of thing." Divya went silent for a moment, allowing her words to sink in. "I think you'll want to hear what I have to say."

"I'm not a lobbyist."

"It's not a lobby. Just listen."

*Sounds like a lobby*, he thought. But Divya had slyly employed that damned quote. *Speaking truth to power.* One of his favorites. The keystone of legal scholar Robert Cover's avant-garde critiques on the state of twentieth-century law. Long before Cover, it was a Quaker maxim, as meaningful now as ever: to stand strong against totalitarianism.

Jake looked out the window at the woods behind the guest-house. A breeze blew brown shells of life from the streamside willows. Fall was here. He was looking at a month or more of reading and fire stoking before there was too much snow to do anything.

"Well, go ahead."

# 2

A dead-end day at a dead-end job; J.P. had been in the damned shop for too long without a single customer. And he missed his girl. He was bouncing a tennis ball against the wall, thinking. The ball's bright fur under the fluorescent lights offended his senses, like catching sight of the Vegas strip when you're hungover. Still, there was nothing better to do, so he kept on bouncing.

He could inspect the rental fleet again, but that was pointless. Fat chance anyone was going to come in. The tourists had all left in September.

J.P.'s thoughts turned to Esma. How serious had their fight really been? J.P. wondered if the language barrier made it seem worse than it actually was. But he also suspected that his inability to completely grasp Esma's motivations was exactly what she was pissed off about. J.P. liked to think of himself as easygoing, but

9

she saw him differently. In her view, he was incapable of taking anything seriously.

Esma had come to Jackson for the same reasons many did—better wages and more opportunity. She and J.P. met at the Teton County Fair. It took some convincing, but J.P. eventually succeeded in wooing her. Now she had moved back to Mexico for the winter, where she was going to clear her head. They weren't broken up, she'd said, but they weren't together. *Whatever that means.*

For all his shortcomings as a boyfriend, J.P. didn't lack patience. He was upset when she left, but he'd stopped short of blowing up. If she wanted time, he'd give it to her. He could wait her out. It was worth it.

He smelled the tennis ball and curled his lips in disgust. It stank of the can and the dog's slobber. Curiosity and the cat, and so on. He tossed it back in the drawer, walked over to the ancient radio, and fiddled with the dial. A new station came in clearer than the last one, which was a small improvement in his day.

*"She said you're pretty good with words, but words won't save your life . . ."*

J.P. turned up the volume. Somehow, the song seemed to be coming straight from Tlaxcala, intended for his ears only.

If he cared, why didn't he do anything to show it? In her nebulous English, Esma had expressed that sentiment to him daily for the last few weeks.

*What does she want? I'm not husband material, if that's what she's thinking.* Though maybe that's what he was hoping for.

The bike shop didn't have any windows. That was one of the problems. J.P. looked at the blank white walls around him, bearers of the harsh report from the ceiling fixtures. He'd read about sick building syndrome, which afflicted people who spent all day indoors with stale air and light, and figured this was what it must be like.

Chayote was curled up in the corner, half-awake. His ears perked up and his eyes opened every time J.P. looked at him.

"How does he know?" J.P. wondered aloud.

The dog closed his eyes again. J.P. looked away and then glanced back. Up went the ears. J.P. tested him a few more times, then moved on to other variations: watching out of his peripheral vision and waving his hands in the air. Could he trick the pup by sending invisible sonic waves toward him? The dog snored.

J.P. finally turned his head toward him. The big satellite-dish ears rose.

"C'mon buddy, I'm just messing with you." The mottled young heeler sleepily lumbered over, sat on J.P.'s feet, and gave him a solemn look. "Sorry, dude." J.P. scratched his ear. The dog leaned into his petting and let out a sigh. Chayote was bored too.

"Poor thing. We're not cut out for this, are we?"

The hound only cocked his head.

Without warning, the bell rang. Someone was coming into the shop.

"Best behavior, Chayote." The dog rebelled immediately and yipped at the intruders, but settled back into slumber when J.P. glared at him.

When he looked up, J.P. was surprised at his luck.

The women were both tall, one blond and the other brunette. *Probably dyed*, J. P. thought; her skin was so pale. They wore dark pantsuits that were perfectly tailored to their bodies. They were all lipstick-red lips and long legs. J.P. bent over and feebly tried to wipe the dog hair off his pants. "How can I help you ladies?"

The light-haired woman spoke with what sounded like a Scandinavian accent, but her English was confident.

"Just looking, thanks."

J.P. couldn't think of anything witty, so he simply nodded, pretending to punch something into the register.

The women looked at the merchandise on the walls: bike-tire levers, pumps, and a few kitschy hats and T-shirts. J.P. watched them out of the corner of his eye. They didn't stay for long.

"Thank you!" the brunette said as they turned to leave.

When they opened the door, Chayote bolted for freedom from behind the counter. "Hey! No!" J.P. ran after him, but it was too late. *Dammit.* The dog was looking for Jake again.

J.P. quickly caught up and found Chayote on his hind legs, front paws planted on the brunette's toned stomach. She was giggling and petting his head while trying to avoid his tongue.

"Chayote, down!" The dog obeyed, which shocked J.P. Still, he stayed by his new friend, his tail wagging with enough momentum to make his rear end wiggle.

"No, no. It's okay. He's adorable. What do you call him—coyote?"

"Chayote, actually." J.P. felt sheepish. A classy woman in a classy outfit, and Chayote had jumped all over her.

"Well that's an unusual name, huh, Chayote?" The woman never looked up from the dog.

"Yeah, he's not mine." The woman looked up at J.P., a tinge of disappointment in her face. "I mean, he kind of is, I guess. But my buddy named him."

"Does he know any tricks?" The other woman asked.

"Yeah. Quite a few, in fact." J.P.'s voice regained a note of confidence. He reminded himself to thank Chayote for the favor with a pig's ear.

"Chayote, come." The dog obeyed.

"Sit." He moved his hand in an upward sweep as Jake had shown him. Again the dog obeyed. This was going surprisingly well. One of the women clapped briefly, but it didn't distract the hound. Not now. Not Chayote the Wonder Dog. He was staring intently at J.P., waiting for the next command.

"Good dog. Now for the grand finale!"

J.P. put his hand behind his back and made it into the shape of a pistol. "Okay, Chayote . . ." The dog focused, his tail wagging slowly in anticipation, like a metronome about to kick off a grand symphony.

"Bang!" J.P. shouted, pointing the faux weapon at the dog. The women watched eagerly. Chayote didn't move.

"Bang!"

Nothing. J.P. put his hand behind his back and started from the beginning.

"Bang!" This time he shouted it even louder, startling the women.

He started again with his hand behind his back, but the brunette shook her head at him.

"It's okay," she said again. Chayote ran over to her when she did. She bent down to pat him on the head. "You're still a good dog!"

"We should get back to the conference," the blonde interjected. They smiled at J.P. one last time.

"He's supposed to play dead!" J.P. shouted after them, then quieted down and spoke half to himself. "It's not *that* weird."

J.P. opened the door for Chayote, who walked back into the shop without being asked.

"What? You forgot 'bang'?"

Upon hearing the magic word, Chayote dropped to the floor and rolled over onto his back, dead.

"Never could perform under pressure, could you?"


At 4 p.m., J.P. put up the CLOSED sign, even though the shop was supposed to stay open until six.

Outside, the October air felt warm and dry like early September. It had snowed in the high country overnight, but only a few centimeters. Most of it had melted on the south-facing peaks. A few of the north faces were still dashed in white. The leaves were past their prime, and it wouldn't be long before the harsh winter set in.

J.P. got to his bike and rolled up one leg of his baggy jeans so it wouldn't catch in the drivetrain. He whistled for Chayote, who was off sniffing God-knows-what at the back entrance of the restaurant next door.

# 3

**CHICAGO O'HARE INTERNATIONAL AIRPORT. OCTOBER 16.**
**12 P.M. CENTRAL STANDARD TIME.**

Jake was finally boarding the plane after a long layover. The frenetic hustle of the airport irritated him. Loud and stuffy. Hot. Too much energy for one place. He imagined the innards of a combustion engine. *No, that's too orderly. More like a contemporary* Animal Farm.

Herds of cattle hemmed and hawed in different parlances about shared nuisances: slow Wi-Fi, flight delays, lousy food. Atrocious shortcomings in the modern world.

The agent announced boarding for first class. A horde of men— why were they all men?—was hovering near the doorway like kids waiting by their parents' room on Christmas morning. *Ready for their free cocktails.*

Jake stood up and got in the back of the line. He felt awkward in the presence of these well-fed men and their shiny watches and shoes. He was only flying first class thanks to Divya.

He settled into the third row next to a plump, brown-skinned man adorned with gold bracelets and rings. Already trying to sleep, he ignored Jake's greeting.

When first class was seated and their drinks were delivered—ginger ale for Jake—the coach contingent began to board. They moseyed by, eyes darting from seat to seat, hoping to catch a glimpse of a celebrity. Their prolonged gazes made him feel like a fish in a bowl.

Jake wanted to break out of this caged existence, even though he'd left Jackson only a few hours earlier. But he was restless there too, and in need of a distraction. Things with Noelle—the park ranger Jake had dated for the past thirteen months—had gone sharply south. The circumstances of their meeting were far from normal. They'd been through too much early on—murder, natural disaster, and government conspiracy—and the flame had burned hot, but only briefly. The pace of the affair scared Jake off.

He was longing for something, but he wasn't sure what. He'd worked plenty over the summer, sixtysomething guided fishing trips. His back was tired and his hands calloused, but his intellect begged for a new challenge.

He had to admit that, true to form, Divya made a convincing case. She'd cunningly engaged him with her words and reminded him that his past profession still *required something* of him.

In law school, Jake's professors always spoke of justice and fairness, while in the real world it was all fees and billable hours. Jake preferred the idealistic perspective, when he could convince himself of its legitimacy. In this instance, maybe he could.

This was his biggest weakness, and he knew it—he searched for meaning in life by fighting high-stakes battles. Sadly, those quests had been more destructive than he cared to admit. He'd sacrificed much over the years: friends, coworkers, a chance at monetary success. And, occasionally, a clear conscience.

And for what? He used to ponder that question more. To keep his own devils at bay by fighting a tangible evil? To slay the restlessness that plagued him?

Life in Wyoming had been his escape. He found solace in the mountains, his fears allayed.

But the last few autumns, when the leaves fell and the pace of life slowed, the burden had snuck back in under the cover of darkness. In his bed, alone, Jake wondered whether extant happiness was enough, whether the tranquilizing effect of the pines and rivers and peaks was permanent or fleeting.

He'd find out soon enough. The pilot was on the PA. *Flight time to Dulles, one hour and fifty minutes.*

From his carry-on—a sky-blue Mammut day pack—Jake grabbed the two-inch-thick stack of papers that Divya had FedExed him and put it on his lap. Then he closed his eyes.

After a few minutes of trying, Jake gave up on sleep. He took the black binder clip off his stack of papers. On the first page was a short handwritten note from Divya. "Jake—Welcome to For a Free America! We're lucky to have you."

He positioned the air vent above him so it was blowing on his face and began reading. The next page was a photocopy of a newspaper article with the headline "Senator Canart Stirs the Melting Pot":

> Where's Waldo? Senator Rick Canart of Idaho wants to
> know. He has sponsored a bill to provide federal fund-

ing for the development of "human tracking" technology. The grant is earmarked in part for the joint venture dubbed "SafeTrak," a collaboration between InfoTech and Catalyst Technologies, where Canart was CEO before winning election to the Senate. Since its inception the company has focused on researching and developing nano-GPS technology for various markets "from household to the whole world," according to the company's mission statement.

"I think it's important to develop all technologies that could lend a hand in our nation's progress," said the freshman lawmaker in a CNN interview on Tuesday. "Do I think all illegal immigrants should be tracked? Of course not. But I do believe there may be a time when this technology will be useful not only for individuals but also in managing our nation's immigration and criminal issues."

The proposed legislation has provoked outrage among citizen-democrats and legal immigrants alike. New York University law professor and Cuban émigré Arin Helva says we shouldn't buy into Canart's hype. "It's doomsday this, doomsday that. The only thing that Senator Canart should be worrying about is whether his own policies will cause a doomsday scenario. That, and obvious conflicts of interest."

Critics contend that using technology to track illegal aliens could be a slippery slope to tracking the activities of the entire population. Political correspondent Renee Williams doesn't think such a scenario is likely in the short term, but says the legislation opens that door. "We are years away from any tracking program 'hitting

the shelves,' as it were. That being said, any victory for
Senator Canart will be seen by his camp as public support for his views."

"Jesus." Jake had read snippets of Canart's stratagem in Wyoming newspapers, but nothing so blunt.

He moved deeper into the stack, looking over some case law
Divvya had pulled. Fourth Amendment cases, right-to-privacy
stuff. Cases on thermal imaging, illegal search and seizure, and so
on. Basic first year con law.

But the first year was when they hooked you with fairy tales of
heroic advocacy, starring noble martyrs who gave it all up for the
common good, men and women who found the underdog and bet
it all. Jake had always been one to romanticize the underdog.

Divya knew it. She was shrewd, and had made dragging Jake
out of Jackson look easy. It helped that the town of Jackson's Envi-
ronmental Subcommittee, whose board Jake was on, was on hiatus
until January.

Divya had gushed about Jake's skills of persuasion, his Honest
Abe reputation, his considerable pro bono work (far exceeding the
required fifty hours) on projects ranging from local HUD cases to
his recurring advisory role for the Southern Poverty Law Center's
Hatewatch Program. She was using his own sensibilities against
him, and he was smart enough to realize it. Still, those traits were
his, and he decided there was no use in fighting himself.

She promised to cover all expenses, which Jake didn't doubt.
There was enough cash forgotten in pockets at DC dry cleaners to
fly a thousand washed-up lawyers back to Dulles.

He leafed through the remainder of the pages. A few years back,
certain uses of RFID (Radio Frequency Identification) technology

had been banned by the Supreme Court of the Philippines. Interesting, but not a precedent for US jurisdiction.

Jake went back to reading. A few minutes later, the pilot announced that they were beginning their descent into Dulles.

It couldn't come soon enough. Jake longed for fresh air. It wouldn't be Wyoming, resplendent with sage and pine, but anything would be better than canned airplane air.

Jake thought about Divya's project. He agreed with her completely on the substance of the matter—a government tracking individuals, citizens or not, was unsettling at best, diabolical at worst. Forget the affront to the Fourth Amendment.

Still, he always found it helpful to deconstruct his thoughts—in case they were biased—and reason them out fully from beginning to end.

*What is the issue here? Control? Being tracked is not inherently offensive; it's what the people who collect that information might do with it.* It was, as Divya had said, "a blatant invasion of privacy for immigrants"; that much was certainly true—but it was more tangible than that. It was downright scary. *Information is control. If they know where you are, what you look like, where you are from, and what you are doing, the next step is total control. Playing God.*

Divya was right about another thing—there was a certain pride that was shattered when your every move was surveyed. It was like being invisibly chaperoned for the rest of your life. Back to being a kid.

What would the proponents of the GPSN (nano-GPS) proposition say? The old classic, of course—*If you aren't doing anything wrong, then what do you care if we're tracking you?*

Jake always found this argument callow, especially when it

would be the government deciding what was "right" and "wrong" for immigrants.

The plane bumped to the ground.

Dulles was crowded too. It was a Monday, and there were suits everywhere. Jake was able to avoid baggage claim. He had everything he needed in his small carry-on backpack.

When he walked out the sliding-glass doors, the humidity and heat struck him. It was October in DC, but it felt warmer than a mountain summer.

The rental sedan would have felt luxurious to a sheik, just as the agent had boasted. Jake thanked God for the AC and the cooled leather seat. He turned both to high and headed east.

The traffic was bad, even by DC standards. It took him more than an hour and a half to reach the Teddy Roosevelt Bridge. As he crossed it, he opened the windows. The stained current of the Potomac was moving imperceptibly, but he still got the feeling he always did on rivers—that the ambient flow was somehow washing him clean, circulating through and refreshing him. After crossing the bridge, he turned left and headed north along the river's east bank.

Jake appreciated the peculiar beauty of the urban environment, but more so its grandeur than its aesthetics. To think that man created all this—a whole world, a reality, from scratch—filled him with a sense of wonder.

It was 6:15 p.m. by the time Jake arrived at Divya's home in Georgetown, a beautiful Richardson Romanesque of pinkish stone. Its exterior looked newly renovated. He drove around the block for a few minutes, looking for parking.

Divya answered the door wearing a hip herringbone pantsuit with a silk scarf, barefoot and clutching a glass of red wine. She stood a thin five-foot-ten, just two inches shorter than Jake. Her skin had a light cinnamon tone. As she kissed Jake on the cheek, he caught a whiff of something exotic in her long black hair. Jake had to admit she still had her looks.

"I failed to warn you, but I've got some colleagues over for a dinner party." She paused. "Try not to look so overwhelmed."

"Just a bit tired." Which was a lie. He was slightly overwhelmed to see *her*. "Where can I put my bag?"

"Top of the stairs, straight ahead is yours. Bathroom is down the hall." He started up the stairs. "And Jake, what's with the coat?"

He looked down and noticed he was holding a puffy down jacket. "Oh, um, Wyoming." He held it up for her to see. "Makes a good pillow too." He balled it up and pretended to rest his head on it.

"Okay, cowboy. See you in a minute."


The guest room was ornate. Jake tossed his bag on the bed and ran his hand along the headboard. All of the furnishings were antique. Divya had won some big cases, sure, but the last time he'd seen her she was more bohemian than bourgeois.

Jake washed his face in the bathroom's porcelain bowl sink, listening to the distant voices of Divya's guests. He wasn't looking forward to mingling, but he couldn't hide in the bedroom all night. He looked at himself in the mirror. The little crow's-feet around his eyes didn't make him feel any more confident. He blamed the high-country sun.

Divya was waiting at the bottom of the stairs with a glass of wine. She was either still hung up on their decades-old fling, or trying hard to make him feel important. He took it, and the two clinked glasses.

"To old friends," she said.

She took Jake by the arm and pulled him into the chaos. A dozen well-dressed men and women were glued to a flat-screen: *Straight Up! with Sandy Hornan*, the fast-talk musings of a hambone political analyst. The topics of discussion on tonight's show were an Iowa senator's personal indiscretions, followed by population growth in Third World countries. Hornan swung for the fences on the changeup. "Speaking of spreading your seed . . ."

Divya cut in over the din. "Everyone, this is Jake Trent." Not everyone turned from the show. "A dear friend. He prosecuted war criminals. Then, he cleaned up the streets of Philly!" The confused guests turned and nodded. Divya was laying it on thick. "And now, Jake?"

"Now I need a refill." He held up his glass.

A short, dark-haired man in an expensive suit stood up and walked over with his hand in the air.

Jake gave him the awkward high five he seemed to want. "Scott, how are you?"

"I'm great, man; haven't seen you since graduation. How are *you*? Heard you're in Wisconsin now or something?"

"Wyoming, yeah. Been there several years."

"Right." He snapped his fingers as if trying to think. "Spencer, um, George Spencer, hell of a trial lawyer, man. The best. Are you working with him out there? I'd only assume . . ."

"Gerry Spence. No, I haven't practiced, I—"

Scott interrupted. "I called you when I got laid off way back; thought maybe the firm could use someone. You never called back."

"Yeah, I'm sorry about that. I should've—"

Another interruption. "Aw, no worries. I'm just fucking with you. You want a Scotch? I brought over a hell of a bottle."

Jake held up his wine glass. "I'm good."

"Suit yourself. More for me! Let's catch up later." Scott punched him hard in the arm and walked away.

Jake turned to Divya and rolled his eyes; the pace of the interaction had stunned him. She noticed the redness in his face.

"So, Scott hasn't changed," Jake said sternly.

"And neither have you." She smiled. "Let's find a seat."

Divya played the coquette and Jake the hesitant participant. Washed down with a few glasses of Stags' Leap SLV Cab, her flirting was palatable. But the moment was soon ruined. It wasn't more than an hour until a well-besotted Scott zeroed back in.

"I just don't get it. No offense."

"None taken." What Jake meant was he wouldn't bother acknowledging the slight.

"You give up all for what? To be a rancher?" Scott hee-hawed at his own repartee.

Divya tried to come to Jake's rescue. "It's beautiful there, from what I've heard."

Jake shrugged, not backing down, but unwilling to stoop to Scott's level. "Takes all kinds, I guess," he muttered.

"I get it!" Scott's epiphany made his face look like a surprised pig's. His balding head harbored beads of sweat from all the eating, drinking, and disparaging. "You couldn't take the pressure!"

*Keep it together,* Jake thought.

But it was too late. "The hell do you know about pressure?" Jake blurted out.

A moment-long stare down between the two men.

"Here." Divya to the rescue again. She interrupted and poured both of them more wine.

"I gotta take a piss." Scott stood and strode away.

When he returned, Jake changed the subject. He had no interest in a pissing contest, despite his opponent's empty bladder. "So, you're helping with the lobby?"

"It's not a lobby," Divya murmured.

Scott huffed. "No way. Can't take the time off. New wife wants a swimming pool. That's pressure." He rolled his eyes. "Seven figures last year, Jake. Corporate litigation. Better than I woulda done if you'd thrown me a bone back then. I guess I should thank you." He raised his glass, almost spilling the contents. So much for avoiding the pissing contest.

"Congrats." Jake gave Divya a smirk and then drained his just-filled glass.

"Speaking of, are government employees supposed to be lobbying, Divya? Sounds like a conflict of interest to me." Scott wagged his finger in her face.

"Government?" Jake's attention was piqued.

"Legal aid, he means." Like Jake, she adeptly changed the subject. "Let's play a game!"

Jake didn't get to bed until 12:30 a.m. The crowd had gotten worked up discussing politics and the law, and Scott remained ruthlessly acerbic. He stirred awake at 3:30 a.m. in a cold sweat, ran to the bathroom, and vomited.

*Welcome back to the real world*, he thought.

# 4

Going home was easy. For the first time she had the money to bus it rather than rely on a ride. When she'd moved to Jackson, Esma rode in a two-door '88 Honda Accord with five others—one pregnant and vomiting, two others chain-smoking harsh Vera Cruz tobacco. Thirty-six hours. She'd made the trip a half dozen more times: running money to her mother, and returning with the food and drink her friends in Wyoming missed from home. It was the least she could do.

*Never again,* she'd said.

The Border Patrol on the highway was probing and demeaning. They treated the commercial bus passengers marginally better; if they knew you had some money, they figured you were legit.

*Family* was a tricky word for Esma. Her father was a tyrant.

26

Angry and drunk, he made her mother's life miserable. Esma hadn't spoken to him since first going to the States. She preferred it that way.

Her mother couldn't see it so clearly. They'd never divorced; instead, they dragged out the troubled alliance. He came and went, bringing joy on arrival and leaving a trail of emotional destruction behind him. He sometimes disappeared for months at a time.

Esma and her mother had an unspoken rule. Papa was never mentioned, though she could hear in her mother's voice whether he was around. Manic or morose, never even-keeled.

Which is why it was such a shock when Arturo the Terrible opened the door. Her mother had given no hint over the phone that he might be around. Esma didn't see it coming. Her initial impulse was to curl up in a ball, submit. But she was better than that now, though it took a little forced moxie.

"*Señor*." She nodded her head and squeezed past him, holding her breath. He smelled of tequila and Te Amo cigars. In her peripheral vision, she glimpsed a crooked smile. He was happy to see her squirm.

Leticia. *Mamá.* The poor soul. Still beautiful at sixty-six, she was in the kitchen looking flustered.

Mother and daughter exchanged a short embrace. Esma wanted to look into Letty's eyes, search for any insight into why she still tortured herself. But Mamá was too smart for that. She eluded eye contact, muttering something about dinner.

Arturo had wandered into the *cocina*, bumping and brushing the relics hanging on the adobe arch. He fumbled with a bottled of off-color liquor. When it was opened, he poured an ample portion into a dingy cup and held it out for his daughter.

She didn't acknowledge the gesture.

"Try it." Leticia spoke in Spanish. "He makes it himself."

"Quite the accomplishment." English in return. An insult. Her parents didn't understand the words, but Arturo laughed, getting the gist. His teeth were as yellow as his eyes. They glowed against his puffy brown face.

"I thought we would go to church after dinner." Spanish again.

Esma responded to her mother in like tongue. "To repent for our sins?" Another laugh from Arturo. "I'm going to settle in."

The small house had a second story that had been added after the initial construction. The ceilings were low, and the floors were sloped and creaky.

Her childhood room remained much the same, aside from a few extra knickknacks that were being stored.

She could hear her father downstairs growling at her mother. "She's *always* been a bitch! She didn't even say hello! She can't stay in a hotel with all that money?"

*Dios mío.* Esma sat on her old twin bed and cried. She missed J.P. now. Arturo's reappearance put J.P.'s faults into perspective. She wanted out, and she had been there only for half an hour. *Poor Mamá.* Esma knew her presence was going to fuel Arturo's rage to rare heights. The grumbling from the kitchen had already turned into shouting and tears.

Esma wiped her eyes and opened the front zipper of her roller case. She took out her checkbook and emptied her modest savings in her mother's name.

"Dinner!" Her mother shouted from the bottom of the stairs. She could hear the fake cheerfulness. Feigned normalcy. *A perfect family dinner.*

Esma took her luggage and went back downstairs. Her mother did not look surprised.

Arturo was pouring another drink, wearing a shit-eating grin.

Esma handed her mother the check and turned to her father. "Keep it up. I hope it kills you." English.

*Never again,* she promised herself on her way through the door.

Boarding the bus, she felt ashamed. She had abandoned her homeland and the woman who raised her. But what solution was there? Arturo had plagued her mother for forty years, despite Esma's best efforts. She knew if she stayed, she would only make things worse.

Esma tried to make small talk with the other passengers, working-class women in their thirties and forties, but they were wary of her. Maybe her accent had changed over the years, giving away her Americanness. Or maybe it was her J.Crew slacks, peppered with the red dirt from the yard where she had once played as a child.

*Executive Housekeeper.* Esma loved that they added the "executive" to make it seem as though she were something other than the head of housekeeping. But the hotel *was* fancy—five stars—and it was, on its face, a good job: $45,000 a year, plus benefits. What more could a girl from the outskirts of Tlaxcala ask for?

Still, she knew what the management thought of her. Pretty? *Yep, the men even think I'm "sexy."* Hardworking? *Of course, like all beaners are.*

And she could speak Spanish! The only thing that really mattered. Was she smart? A good person? They had no idea; they'd never bothered to find out.

29

She spent the night at a little motel in Miguel Ahumada with five other women from the bus, who had slowly warmed up to her. She would cross the border in the morning, legally and with all the right papers. She knew that wouldn't be the case for some of the passengers.

Esma could sense their nerves, smell their anxiousness. But they wouldn't turn back; they were all headed to the States because they needed money, and not for trivial reasons. Most of the passengers were immigrating to the States to provide medical care and food for their families back home.

At about 1 a.m., some young men from the bus kicked in the door to their motel room, drunk on tequila. They woke the women up, laughing, propositioning them.

Esma wasn't afraid. She could see weakness in their faces and in the way they moved. As far as threats went, she'd faced much worse.

When one of the men grabbed her and tried to lead her away she hissed sharply in his ear in Spanish. *You don't have to do this. Your mother and father would be ashamed.*

The man slapped her hard across the face and called the rest of the gang out of the room. The other women quietly nodded at Esma, thanking her. Esma dabbed the blood from her nose in front of the bathroom mirror, half wishing her skin were another color. Then she lay down on the mildewed floor of the crowded room. From the bed above, someone tossed her a sheet and a pillow.

"*Gracias.*" Her accent sounded unfamiliar, even to herself.

In the morning, the passengers from the bus went in different directions to rendezvous with their *coyotes*, the smugglers who would help them into the States, if all went well. More often than not, aspiring immigrants weren't successful; they either got ripped off or were detained shortly after crossing the border. There were stories of women being kidnapped, force-fed heroin, and sold as sex slaves. All this after they'd handed over their life savings to fellow countrymen who had promised to help.

The border agent glanced up to see a striking young woman in a slightly dirty pantsuit standing in front of his window.

"You can't walk through this line; motor vehicles only." He gave her a confused look. Something about her confidence, her resolve, was off-putting. Behind her, a line of a dozen cars honked, their drivers agitated. She paid them no mind.

She looked bedraggled, but her beauty couldn't be disguised by things as relatively dull as dust and grime. She said nothing in response to the agent, just handed him a neatly paper-clipped stack of papers.

He looked them over, then reclipped them and handed them back.

"What the hell are you doing?" A gust rolled through the checkpoint, blowing sand across Esma's face. She didn't flinch. The agent slid his door shut momentarily to protect himself.

When he opened it, he spoke again. "You've gotta be careful out here. A woman who looks like you, I mean."

Esma huffed. "Am I free to go?" She tucked a few disheveled strands of black silky hair behind her ear, still staring squarely at him.

"Where are you going? For how long?"

"Home," she said obstinately.

He looked around to make sure a supervisor wasn't watching and then swiped his hand through the air, left to right, from Mexico to the States.

"Be careful."

Esma shuffled through the checkpoint, catching a few curious stares from the contraband-search team as she passed. A man on the team whispered to his female coworker, who snickered. Esma kept walking fast, afraid to look back. She had no desire to be questioned or detained.

In a few minutes she was a quarter mile past the border. Here she turned around and found no one following her. She took a deep breath and stuck her thumb in the air. She'd left herself only a few dollars, giving the rest to her mother.

It wasn't long until a recent-model Volvo station wagon pulled over. The family took her as far as Santa Fe. They pulled into the plaza and offered to buy her dinner, but she declined. For a moment, she stood in front of the luxury hotel and watched the man and his wife check in, while the kids ran around the lobby, looking for a swimming pool or vending machine.

*Life must be good.*

The pueblo-style plaza, while mostly authentic, looked like a mockery to Esma in the fading evening light. The plaza here featured tourists and expensive German cars parked in valet lots. That familiar conflict arose within Esma—irritation at the vanity of the American lifestyle versus the urge to indulge in it.

Esma walked several miles along the highway, almost to Española, before she got picked up again. This time, her company was more country music than country club. Esma didn't mind; she just wanted to get back to J.P.—to get back home.

The Dodge pickup truck had recently been washed. Its black glitter coat, complete with chrome trim accents, reflected the harsh lights from the run-down roadside casinos. The two gringo men were quiet well into Colorado. The only thing they had asked was *Where to?* The driver's response worried Esma a bit: "Jackson? Us too."

*What are the chances?*

Esma tried not to think about the coincidence. She was happy to be escaping Tlaxcala.

She awoke at 5 a.m., surprised that she'd been able to fall asleep. The driver and the rear-seat passenger had swapped spots sometime during the night. Her new partner in the backseat was staring at her with a wry smile.

"Morning, *chica*." His breath reeked of wintergreen chewing tobacco, his teeth brown.

The man's hair was short, blond, and unevenly cut. The right side of his head bore a long scar where no hair grew.

Before Esma could look away, the man acknowledged her stare.

"Name's Ax."

*Jesus,* Esma thought.

She concentrated her attention out the window so as not to stir up any more unwanted information.

A roadside sign read: BAGGS, WY—41 MI.

*Well, that's a relief.* The vessel, despite its dubious crew, appeared to be going in the right direction.

She drifted back to sleep.

Esma woke up to her ears popping from altitude and loud country music. She looked out the window, trying to figure out how much progress they'd made during her slumber.

Verdant, groomed fields dominated the landscape—potatoes and barley, not hay. At the junction of the highway and a small dirt road, she saw a familiar sign: GRUPO MODELO BREWING. She knew she was in neither Mexico nor Wyoming. They were somewhere in Bumfuck, Idaho, where the brewery owned massive tracts of land.

*What the hell?*

She closed her eyes again so she wouldn't attract attention. Over the music, she heard one of the men say, "Twenty grand, man! What the hell would *we* do with her anyway?"

# 5

WASHINGTON, DC. OCTOBER 17.

8:30 A.M. EASTERN STANDARD TIME.

Pounding on Jake's bedroom door. He bolted awake. The early morning hours had been miserable, and he had just drifted to sleep, finally comfortable. He mumbled something resembling *C'mon in.*

Divya entered carrying a silver tray, upon which stood a silver carafe, two small mugs, and a ceramic kettle. Tea-party-sized cream and sugar vessels in her left hand. She fumbled finding room for the platter on the bedside table, and Jake moved the alarm clock and lamp to the floor.

"That wasn't as graceful as I imagined. Tea or espresso?"

"Wow." Jake's compliment came out more like a groan. He cleared his throat. "The coffee, please."

She poured him a cup, then motioned to the cream and sugar, which he declined. "You look like shit."

Divya was wearing a violet silk nightgown that was sheer

enough to reveal every detail of her breasts. As always, she smelled like something wonderful and exotic. Clove and fenugreek and sweet mango.

"Guess I overdid it last night." Jake sipped his coffee. It was strong and bitter—expensive, no doubt.

"You kinda wandered off to bed." She sat down on the bed and started pouring herself a cup of tea. "I was disappointed."

Jake smiled accommodatingly and took another sip. Anyone else and he might have wondered if she was referring to something sexual, but with Divya, he had no doubt. Sure enough, she pushed the hair gently from his forehead and felt for a fever with the back of her hand.

*What a flirt.*

"Do hangovers come with a fever?"

She took her hand back. "Guess not." She stood up. "I'm gonna get in the shower." Again the innuendo. Jake ignored it, though he might have been tempted if his stomach didn't feel as if he'd been at sea for six weeks.

"Ready in thirty minutes?"

"Sure."

Jake dawdled for a bit, a little unsure if he could go through with it the way he was feeling. *Get it together, man. It's just a hangover.* He tried to drink more coffee to wake up, but its effect on his stomach offset any bump gained in energy.

The shower turned on, and the sound made Jake regret his decision. His former relationship with Divya had been passionate, to say the least. Most of their dates had started with sex—they couldn't help it—then moved on to dinner, a show, whatever, punctuated by sex again when they got home. Their split had had nothing to do with lack of desire.

Still feeling familiar enough, Jake opened the door to the master bathroom and hung a dress shirt on the towel rack to lose its travel wrinkles. He saw his ex-lover's curves and color through the frosted glass.

"Just putting a shirt in here for a minute."

She turned toward him, still mostly obscured by the shower door, but now the dark circles of her nipples were visible, if blurred.

"There's an iron in my bedroom."

"This'll be fine."

He retreated to his room and pulled on socks and gray pants, found a white T-shirt in his bag and threw that on too. He looked in the mirror above the dresser. Thankfully, his hair was still short enough that a shower wasn't required to wrestle it into submission. He opened his mouth wide and stretched his face. Divya was right—he looked like shit.

The water stopped and Divya came in, wearing only a towel, with Jake's dress shirt. He thanked her and turned away before she could make any more out of it.

"Gimme fifteen more minutes. The car's not gonna be here till nine fifteen."

"I can drive," Jake replied toward the bedroom that she'd withdrawn to. "Got the rental."

"It's already arranged."

He buttoned his shirt, gave himself one last look, and then headed to the foggy bathroom to brush his teeth. Next, to the kitchen, stopping at the front door to grab the *Washington Post* on the way.

He mixed a little bit of orange juice with cold water, hoping to rehydrate himself and spark a little energy. The concoction went down much easier than the coffee. Standing, he read the paper at the counter. There wasn't much going on: murder in the ghettos, bickering on the Hill, Capitals on an early six-game losing streak. No mention of the GPSN issue.

Divya came down at exactly 9:15 looking gorgeous. This was how Jake remembered her: scrambled, frenetic, yet elegant. Strangely self-assured, at least on the surface.

They walked out to the curb and loaded into the black town car. It was early but already humid, and the air conditioner was pumping inside.

"Oh," Divya said.

"What?"

"I was gonna ask you for your jacket, but I just realized you're not wearing one."

Classic Divya. "You said everything was going to be informal."

"It's fine." She put her hand on his wrist and left it there, as if she were some debutante with her suitor.

The car came to a stop outside an all-glass building behind the United States Botanic Garden. A slick brass sign read OLSEN WILLIAMS LAW.

"Running with the big dogs again," Jake muttered.

"Oh, shhh! You ready for this?"

"Hey, I was born ready," Jake said, putting on his professional face, then a smile. Divya laughed.

"It's not like that, I told you!"

"But I should have worn a suit?"

Divya sighed, and Jake opened the door. They walked into the lobby toward the security console, where Divya signed in. The click-a-clack of dress shoes on a marble floor took Jake back to various courtrooms. A disturbing rhythm.

In the elevator, the occupants were checking their watches and iPhones, tapping their feet. Dreading whatever was in store for them at the office. Jake looked at their faces. The deportment of joy was missing from each one, muted by something deemed more pressing.

They got off on the eleventh floor. Jake followed as Divya walked purposefully through a glass door and checked in at another security desk. When they got to the conference room, a murmuring crowd of suits awaited them. On Divya's arrival, people shuffled around and found seats.

She began to speak.

"First of all, thanks to everyone for coming. This is the first time we've had all the major players together, so let's start at the beginning. Welcome to the For a Free America campaign. Our goal is to inform lawmakers and the American public about the dangers of Senator Canart's human-tracking proposals."

*Sounds an awful lot like a lobby,* Jake thought.

"We're first concerned with image, because that's the most important facet of the groundwork of this campaign. We need to get a message out there, clear and simple.

"So, I know some of you have emailed me with your ideas for casting this thing in a light that's most favorable to our position, but let's voice those ideas to the whole crew. Tom, let's start with yours."

Divya sat down. Tom began to speak. Jake recognized him from the party, but they hadn't talked.

"China." He paused. "That's it, really. Americans are scared of the Chinese, their government, their success, the whole idea of it. So, we compare this proposal to some of the societal-control issues that exist over there. Paint it that way. No American wants to be compared to the Chinese. China is the new Russia. We can produce a few national segments that compare the two and really hammer that into people's heads."

A young-looking lawyer spoke up with confidence. "I'm sorry, what commonalities exactly are we talking about here, Tom? You kind of lost me."

Tom gave a cold stare back to the young associate. "In ninety-nine the Chinese government, reeling over staggering population growth, implemented a covert program they'd had in their books for a while. Silly as it sounds, the operation was called Shar-Pei. The dog, the program's namesake, is considered a guard dog. 'The guardian of the herd.'"

"What does a guard dog have to do with GPSN?" The young man again.

"'The guardian of the herd,' remember, not 'guard dog.'" The distinction was lost on Tom's dissenter, who shrugged. Divya was staring Tom down, telling him to get on with it.

"Shar-Pei was implemented to track and eventually control China's population. The military descended on rural towns one April evening and took ten thousand 'sample citizens' back to regional bases where they were implanted with GPSN chips. For nearly a year, the government watched their movements, even toyed with the notion of upgrading their hardware so they could disable individuals remotely, should that become necessary."

Jake looked up, interested. "Remote-controlled killing? Is that what you're saying?"

Tom looked pleased. "Exactly. Never came to that, fortunately. They chose the rural folks because they didn't think those people would go public. Even if they did, the government figured no one would believe them. Unfortunately for the government, there was an American expat stationed in one of the towns. When he figured out what was going on, he immediately went to the US embassy."

"I never heard of Shar-Pei. Why wasn't it in the news?" While Jake spoke, Divya was rigging up her laptop with the projection system.

"Never left the mouths of our government. China gave us some intel on North Korea's missile program, and we kept it quiet."

"How did you become aware of it?"

"Ever heard of a locker room? My old squash partner is counselor to our embassy in China."

"Can he help us?"

"He'd lose his job."

"Does that mean Senator Canart has access to the formula for this same type of GPSN? The killer GPSN?" Jake grasped for the answer everyone was after.

The room buzzed.

"That's possible, yes. But I'd imagine its security clearance would put it far out of the reach of someone like Senator Canart."

This did little to assuage Jake's concern. "Hasn't he done some work on Department of Defense matters? Do we know his security clearance?" He shuffled through the research that Divya had provided him.

"DOD, that's right, but more on the legislative side."

Divya gave Jake a nod and spoke. "Tom—send me as much information as you have on this Chinese program, and we'll discuss it next time."

"What reasons did the Chinese provide for wanting to kill its citizens with the push of a button?" Jake wasn't done with the subject.

"Allegedly, they were concerned with communicable disease. They wanted the option to stop an outbreak before it really exploded. That and terrorist threats. Of course, it's not a big leap of the imagination to consider its potential to monitor and kill dissidents."

Jake rubbed his chin, thinking.

# 6

Jackson Chief of Police Roger Terrell was looking out of the plane window at Bejing's sprawl, wondering what the hell he was doing. The city below him appeared cloaked in an evening fog, but Terrell knew better. The grayish billow was pure smog, particulates from factory emissions. He glanced at his wife, Charlotte, beside him. Her face was lit with a smile. He forced one himself, then turned again to the window. His bogus simper faded.

Visiting China hadn't exactly been at the top of Terrell's bucket list, but how often do you get invited to a foreign country for free? Or so his wife had pleaded. This was more a concession to her than anything else. *We never travel, honey.* On and on.

Of course, Terrell reminded himself, he wasn't the one invited in the first place. It was supposed to be a junket for the mayor, Camp Winston, but he'd begged Terrell to replace him on account

42

of his bad heart. The mayor was nearly as adamant about Terrell's attendance as Charlotte was, seeing that Tram Village, LLC, had offered to contribute funding for a badly needed new wing in the Jackson Hole airport.

So it would be Chief Roger Terrell who was now the main character in a phony grand opening—Terrell, the demure civil servant, whose history of public appearances consisted mostly of the annual toast at the department's holiday dinner. But the resort's owner, Xiao, was eager to have him. They talked staging shoot-outs and bank robberies in the dusty streets of Tram Village. Real Jackson Hole police chief saves the day. That sort of thing. A few good photo ops.

Tram Village was an homage to Jackson, as far as Terrell could tell from the articles in the *Jackson Hole News & Guide*. An over-the-top amusement park with real animals and true-to-life lumber and stone. A tribute to the Wild West, set in a country where natural places were hard to come by. An escape for the elite.

Terrell wasn't an overly analytical man, but the whole deal seemed incongruous to him. Find a genuine place, re-create it, and cash in on the upper-crusters who longed to be out of the smoggy city. That wasn't what Wyoming meant to him, though he sometimes worried his own Jackson Hole was on a similar path.


Baggage claim was crowded. Terrell wondered if he would be able to pierce the barricade of sweaty, sardine-packed travelers to get to the belt.

It turned out to be moot—by the time he spotted his wife's bag, more than an hour had gone by, and with it, most of the passengers.

Terrell looked back at his wife, who waved enthusiastically, unfazed by the wait, and clutched the *Wiley Traveler's Guide to China* in her other hand. He forced a smile again and dragged the bags toward her.

"Honey, it says we should write down the name of our hotel on our hands in Chinese characters in case our driver doesn't speak English."

Terrell frowned. "The driver knows where we're going. Besides, I have the info on my phone."

"What if he doesn't know? Or your phone dies?"

"Trust me. Let's just find the driver. I'm exhausted."

With that, Terrell started toward the tall cerulean glass wall of windows that looked out on the transit lanes. The street was busy with buses, Korean-made taxis, and the tiny Smart Cars of locals. Standing in parallel queues on either side of the sliding-glass doors were limo drivers holding placards, most of them featuring Anglo surnames. They soon spotted one with their name.

The smog started to clear as they left the city heading north, toward Duolun County and Inner Mongolia. The driver, who insisted they call him "Bullet," sported a wide-brimmed ten-gallon hat, a button-down with turquoise buttons, and chaps over blue jeans. The Super Duty F-250 King Ranch towered over the surrounding compact vehicles, which were more suited to the country's narrow streets.

DVD screens on the headrests looped through Tram Village advertisements, and every leather surface that was big enough was embroidered with a bucking bronco, Wyoming's state symbol. Terrell traced the outline of the horse on the door panel with his pointer finger, longing to be home.

He dug his prepaid international cell out of his backpack and powered it up. Ignoring the excited conversation between his wife and Bullet—the driver was enthralled to have real "cowboys" in his company—Terrell checked for voice mails.

On any other vacation, the urgent message from his deputy, Layle Statler, would have irked him. Now, he savored the opportunity to be temporarily transported back to his real life.

Chief, little bit of a problem. Male wolf just got hit up by Moran. Park Service ran the wand over and got an ID, but it wasn't a number in their system. They pawned the damned thing off on me because they think it might have been someone's pet, probably illegal. I ran it through the animal shelter's database, but there wasn't a match. Anyway, call me back. I've got this carcass here and I don't really know how to proceed, given the Endangered Species Act and so forth.

*A new twist on roadkill,* Terrell thought as he powered down the phone. He tapped his right hip out of habit, but the pistol that normally rested there was thousands of miles away, locked up in his desk.

"Almost there!" Terrell heard Bullet say in the background. "You will be pleased with lodging."

"He's talking to you, honey."

"I'm sorry. Yes, I'm sure we will be." He smiled so Bullet could see it in the mirror. Despite his discomfort, Terrell didn't abandon his western manners.

He was looking out of the window with more interest now. The sea of buildings and people and automobiles had given way to waves of grain and wide grass flats, not unlike the American West. He opened his window and the air was cleaner, dry and cool.

For a moment, Terrell found the landscape genuinely interesting— locals in traditional garb worked the occasional farm, and birds unknown to him flitted through the air from the branches of shrubs he couldn't recognize. Then something out of place appeared on the horizon.

"Bullet?" Terrell winced while saying the name. "These are *American* bison. Why are these bison here?"

"Oh, yes, beautiful lot, okay? Idea is to give genuine feeling. We are very close to Tram Village now. Also, it is fully functioning sustainable farm for bison meats."

"There are no fences."

"Yes, correct, good eyes. Implant administers humane shock if they leave the grid. No fences is better for aesthetics, survey says."

"I see." Terrell frowned, disturbed at the plight of the symbols of freedom and unspoiled wilderness, now subjected to the intrusion of an invisible electric fence whenever they followed their wild whims.

Before long, the paved road turned to manicured gravel, then a suspiciously smooth dirt two-track. More "aesthetics," Terrell assumed.

The pickup rolled through reddish dust, which Terrell correctly guessed out loud had been imported for authenticity's sake, then finally under a large elk-antler archway identical to the ones in Jackson's town square. It came to a stop under a stone-and-cedar portico that adorned an ornate western-motif lodge.

"Newspaper," Bullet said in response to Terrell's quizzical look. Outside the truck, a cluster of men and women stood, cameras and notepads at the ready, waiting for the guests of honor to unload. "This is the most grand undertaking by Chinese tourism industry in some time."

Terrell was peeved. He knew that the opening of Tram Village was a big deal; the mayor had told him as much. But he was in no way prepared to offer statements to the press about it.

"We must go now, everyone is waiting."

The chief opened his door to a firestorm of questions and flash-bulbs. Ignoring the reporters, Terrell crossed behind the car and opened the door for Charlotte, who was beaming. He felt like his wife's bodyguard.

"Isn't this wonderful?" she asked, oblivious to her husband's uneasiness.

"Kinda creepy if you ask me." Terrell whispered in her ear, then led her to the tailgate of the truck.

"No, no! I insist!" Bullet shouted at them when they reached for their own luggage.

Terrell waved him off. He didn't need any damned help with a few bags. But Charlotte pulled at his sleeve. "Honey, look!"

"Please, regard them." Bullet motioned to the sea of reporters.

Terrell turned and faced the crowd, which fell silent instantly. A tall and lanky Chinese man emerged from the group with a note-book. He spoke in confident English.

"Yuan Chen, sir. *Morning Post.* What do you think of Tram Village?"

The silence intensified, if that was possible. The reporters were eagerly awaiting a reply from the "real" cowboy.

Terrell looked around, trying to inspire words. The surrounding buildings looked more like Disneyland than Jackson. Ornate, grandiose, and sparkling new.

More silence.

"It's . . . uh—"

"It's wonderful!" his wife interrupted, saving him from looming embarrassment. The reporters jotted this down and then clapped, appreciative of her approval.

"Yes, and . . ." Terrell thought back to what Bullet had said. "And, very . . . very . . . grand!"

More applause. Then the crowd fell silent again, hoping for Terrell to elaborate on his statement. Luckily, Bullet had loaded their bags onto a luggage cart and was ready to go inside. He shouted something in Chinese to the reporters that was met with grumbling and then turned to Terrell.

"Please, follow me."

Inside the hotel, the atmosphere was serene, a welcome change. Quiet Native American flute music floated through the lobby, and cowhide dressings hung everywhere. *A bit over the top,* Terrell thought. *Jackson Hole, meet Caesar's Palace.*

Terrell poured himself a long-awaited drink from a pitcher of ice water at the reception desk. He took a sip and his face immediately contorted.

"It is cucumber water," the front-desk agent said.

"It's good," Terrell lied. He knocked back the remainder of the water like a strong shot of whiskey, knowing he was likely dehydrated from traveling, then tossed the paper cup into an Aspen-bark-and-leather-lace trash bin.

The agent was thin and lovely. Her black hair reflected the LED track lighting so that she appeared covered by a tranquil glow.

"Here are your keys, sir. We have been expecting you."

"Thank you." Terrell bowed slightly and then was filled with a rush of embarrassment. *Is that a Japanese or Chinese gesture? Or both?! Moron!*

The agent only smiled.

"I will show you to your room," Bullet said, waving them toward him.

Charlotte punched Terrell in the arm as they walked toward the elevator. The spell the woman had cast upon him hadn't gone unnoticed.

In the elevator, Bullet was rattling off their itinerary, but Terrell wasn't listening. A fog was settling inside him, no doubt from the hours upon hours of travel. He wasn't even sure what time it was. The cool temperature and scent of sage and pine in the elevator acted like a tranquilizer. Suddenly, he longed for sleep as he never had before. He leaned his head against the back wall of the elevator and closed his eyes for just a second.

"Here we are. Eighth floor, penthouse level. Remember, you must slide key to have access here."

Terrell nodded at Bullet, showing him he understood.

"Your room is the Wapiti Suite. Please follow me."

The suite was lavish, though not enormous by American standards. An elk rack spanned the wall above the headboard. A vivid depiction of a Native American battle hung next to the bathroom door. The tall wood-framed windows looked out over "Main Street," abounding with saloons, western boutiques, and gift shops. The "American Western Museum," which spotlighted a large white bison mounted on wheels, sat directly across from the lodge.

"Is there anything else you will be needing?"

Terrell shook his head.

"Then I will leave you until dinner. Please be ready in half an hour."

"Uh, Bullet, gimme a second . . ." Terrell was scrambling to find cash, while his wife had already begun drawing water for a bath.

"Yes, sir?"

"Here, for your trouble."

"I cannot accept gratuity, sir."

Terrell looked sheepish. "Ahh, I'm sorry—"

"May I have a word?" Bullet glanced to ensure that Charlotte was out of listening range. She had closed the bathroom door.

In a low voice, he said: "I know that you think our resort is silly; that it is a bad replicate of your home, built for profit. But there is something you should know."

Terrell started to shake his head, but Bullet stopped him by raising a hand.

"Xiao has a daughter, Meirong—just like you have perhaps? There was trouble at home, you understand? So he sent her to California, where she could attend university."

Terrell was trying hard not to look bewildered at the man's narrative. "Okay," he said, nodding.

"This was ten years ago, more. When she finished university, Xiao went to visit. She had moved to your Jackson Hole to study the forestry and the wildlife. Xiao enjoyed his visit very much, but when he told his daughter she must return home, she rebelled. He came back empty-handed and has not heard from her since. You can imagine, I am sure, how difficult this was for Xiao."

"Yes."

"His daughter, she loved the open space of your country, the forests and plains and clean air. Xiao has created this place for his daughter and for the Chinese people. Our country is a very crowded one. And he desires to draw her back to him, you see? His strategy follows an ancient Chinese fable.

"So he abandoned his very fruitful career in the technology industry and used his fortune to make Tram Village. And we are very lucky to have such a place so close to the smog and the big cities."

"I think I understand. I am sorry," Terrell said, trying to sound genuinely apologetic.

"Not necessary. But you would do well to remember something my grandfather told me: 'Things are not always as they seem.' Do you have similar saying?"

Terrell nodded.

Bullet bid him good-bye. Terrell closed the door and flopped onto the king bed. Why had the man told him all this? His mind wandered, searching for meaning in Bullet's statement, then thinking about his deputy and the dead wolf at the police station.

# 7

Beyond the Grand Teton National Park's eastern boundary, where the valley floor began to incline slightly toward Togwotee Pass, the Youst cabin sat in its perpetual state of disrepair.

Dr. Eric Youst and his partner, Susan, were distraught. Over the loss of not only their pet but also their pet project.

Now it was just the alpha female, Luna, and her pup—a heart-breaking sight. To make things worse, the wolf was inconsolable. Wouldn't eat. Barely slept. She spent most of her time pacing around and whimpering, wondering where her mate was.

"It's almost a poetic analogy, how it happened. The pup was just born." Eric wore a sullen smile. That was true, but it didn't ease Susan's mind. Plus, she hated when he sounded like such a smart-ass.

"We should have kept better track of him. He'd been snacking on roadkill there for three days. It was just a matter of time until he got hit."

Eric shrugged and threw a bone to Luna, who sniffed it and let it lie.

They were eccentrics, wandering into town only occasionally to buy a truckload of groceries, mainly canned goods and organic dog food. They farmed what they could from their own land, but the harsh climate of Jackson Hole meant they never got enough to eat. To the folks in town, the word *scarecrow* came to mind. The reticent way they floated up and down the grocery-store aisles brought another word to mind: cagey. Rumors abounded. They were called communists, radicals, crazies, but the truth was that nobody really knew what they were all about.

Susan smiled from time to time, acknowledging strangers, but Eric only scowled. The townsfolk could feel his judgment upon them through that one simple facial expression.

"Are you sure this won't come back to us?" Susan had asked Eric over and over again for the first twelve hours or so. She was a nervous, neurotic woman.

There was no way it could, he'd assured her. The hardware gave an identical signal to the tags used throughout the world. Unless someone decided to actually crack the device open and examine its innards, it was impossible to tell the difference.

"It was a victory for us, albeit in a morbid way. It shows that the programming and the hardware work. Plus, we were able to put Alfie out of his misery; that is a gift."

# 8

"Can we just drop it?"

Jake still felt hungover. Combine that with rush-hour traffic and a particularly maddening version of Divya and out came one of the rudest things he'd said in a while. He didn't apologize, though, because he knew she could take it. And she deserved it.

"Of course we can." Her hand on his wrist again and a smile. "I was just curious as to your understanding of why things between us fizzled out."

Jake dodged the question.

"Your conference room there is rigged, you know." Jake changed the subject.

"Rigged?" Divya bit on the new topic. Jake was relieved.

"Rigged, yeah. There's some kind of recording device under or inside your table. It interfered with your computer there."

"Bugged, right. I know, darling."

"I figured you did; you moved your computer. What's the deal?"

Jake could see that Divya was enthralled by playing spy, and even more enthralled that she had somehow piqued his interest.

"Nothing, really. Our backers are keeping tabs on us, that's all."

"Backers?"

"Backers, supporters, yeah. Agriculture, tech companies . . . hell—even BigMart."

*It's a goddamned lobby!* "BigMart? What about the Fourth Amendment? 'The house of every one is to him as his castle and fortress, as well for his defence against injury and violence as for his repose,' that whole thing? I thought this was a human rights campaign. It's called For a Free America, for God's sake."

"It is, yes," she said, looking at him, thrilled to have his attention. "But this is DC; you know that people with similar interests tend to align. American business needs foreign workers. We need their money to further our cause."

"You're getting paid?"

"I said it was support. Our costs are being covered. You thought I was paying for all this?"

"You said it wasn't a lobby." Jake scowled at her.

"Can we just drop it?" Divya said, mocking him. She bent forward in the town car and directed an air vent at herself. Then she took off her silk scarf and unbuttoned her blouse so that the tops of her laced bra cups were exposed.

"This heat is awful."

Jake shook his head and looked out the window. The avoidance maneuver made her more aggressive. She motioned for the driver to put the divider up.

"You really mean to tell me that if I propositioned you to make love to me on my cool satin sheets like old times, you would reject me?"

She was leaning over him with both hands on his thigh.

"You lied to me," Jake grumbled.

"No. I care about this as much as anyone else. My parents were immigrants. Sometimes you have to make compromises."

"You played me, then." Jake looked back out the window.

After a few seconds passed, Divya pulled back.

"When did you become such a gentleman?"

Jake shook his head more noticeably now and looked her in the eyes.

"And what have *you* become?"

The rest of the ride back to Georgetown was silent, except for the hum of the AC.


"We have dinner in two hours," Divya said flatly as she dropped her keys into a porcelain dish in the entryway. She looked momentarily dejected, not a mask that suited her.

"Might just skip it." Jake was already headed upstairs to change out of his dress clothes. "Stomach is still bothering me."

"It's *Karma*!" She was agitated.

"I don't know what that means, Divya."

A smirk. "It's only the best restaurant in DC. Come on, I'll make you a gin and tonic right now. It will help. Hair of the dog." She was turning her mood around, just like that. Turning on the charm.

"Let me lie down for a bit."

\*     \*     \*

Jake stirred awake at the clinking of ice cubes on crystal, but didn't open his eyes.

*How long was I out?*

He felt breath on his neck, but his senses hadn't awoken enough to register what was happening. When he opened his eyes he was facing the window. It was dark outside. He must have overslept.

"Shit," he said aloud.

"It's okay. I moved Karma back."

This jogged his memory.

He turned to face the voice and let his eyes focus. There was Divya, perched atop him, gin and tonic in hand. She wore a daisy-yellow chemise and her hair was up, out of the way.

She took a sip of the drink and started kissing his chest. Jake let his eyes close.

"Jake!" She said his name as she kissed her way down to his navel.

"Hey! Jake!"

His eyes snapped open. He was facing the window again. It was daylight.

Divya was standing next to the bed, fully clothed, which was more than Jake could say for himself. He had kicked off his clothes before crashing.

"You stayed in pretty good shape." Divya was looking at his stomach and chest. She glanced lower. "Good dream?" She laughed. "You really wear boxers with *fish* on them these days?"

"Shit!" Jake tried to cover up with the duvet.

"Seen it before." Divya walked toward the door, still laughing. "You have ten minutes."

*Jesus Christ.*

Jake hopped out of bed, got dressed, and went to wash his face.

*I've gotta get out of here.*

# 9

"Where the hell is she, Chayote?"

The dog looked at J.P., then looked at the tennis ball lying at his feet, and then back at J.P.

"Fine! Shit!"

He opened the back door toward the creek and threw the ball. The cattle dog went after it in an explosion of acceleration, knocking against the modest CHECK-IN podium with his behind.

J.P. bent over and picked up the half-dozen pens that scattered in Chayote's wake. When he looked up, there was Chayote, staring at him through the screen door. The tennis ball was between his two front feet.

"Damn dog! Go play!"

Chayote cocked his head. J.P. slammed the heavy door, leaving the dog standing there alone.

58

J.P. checked his phone again for a new text message. Nothing. Just to be sure he wasn't losing his mind, he looked at her last message. At least he assumed it was from her; it was from a number he didn't know.

It's me. I'm almost back to you. Let's figure us out. I'll see you tomorrow morning. XO.

The message had come the previous day. J.P. wrote back several times with no further response. He'd even called, but the phone had been shut off or was out of service. Esma hadn't set up her voice mail yet.

He paced along the big picture window that looked out on the creek. Chayote paced with him, but on the other side of the glass.

"I can't take this," he finally said aloud, grabbing his keys. He jogged out the back door. Chayote bounced along in tow.

J.P. drove fast over the bridge, risking a ticket. The Snake River was a skeleton of its normal self this time of year, its flow lazy and low. It was a sign of things to come, the winter that would slow all Wyoming life, except for skiing, to a halt. He thought of the previous spring and of Esma with wildflowers in her black hair. The sense he had back then that something good was just beginning. He accelerated even more, wanting to get away from the dying river.

When he got to the *grocería* in Jackson, he slammed the shifter into park but left the engine running. Five minutes later he came back with a six-pack of watermelon Jarritos.

The apartment complex wasn't far from the *grocería*. J.P. parked on the street and walked up the exterior stairwell. Chayote followed behind. The young girl, Gaby, was sitting on the deck outside her unit. The Jarritos were her bribe. She sat playing a game of some kind on her smartphone and letting a red Popsicle melt on a plate beside her.

"Little cold for that, isn't it?"

The little girl just shrugged. Her dark hair was up in pigtails, tied with blue ribbon. She wore colorful pajamas. J.P. took a seat on the deck across from her, leaning his back against the railing structure. It flexed with his weight, which got Gaby's attention.

"Easy, big guy."

J.P. couldn't respond before a shout came through the door. *"¡Gabriela! ¡Hora de cenar!"*

Gaby ignored the call for dinner, but it pulled her attention away from the device long enough for her to finally notice the sodas next to J.P.

"Put them over here." She motioned toward the plate. J.P. pulled one of the drinks from the cardboard carrier and popped the cap on a rusty nail sticking out from the railing. Gaby gave him a disapproving look and went back to her game.

The door swung open. The smell of cumin and chili pepper floated out.

*"¡Gabriela! La cena esta . . ."* Gaby's mother stopped when she noticed J.P. She said something quickly to her daughter in Spanish.

Gaby replied in English. "No. Esma's boyfriend." She rolled her eyes, as if to say *Yep, this schlub.*

Another quick exchange, but now Gaby spoke Spanish too. Her mother was upset. J.P. stood to go, but before he could, Gaby grabbed his hand and led him inside. The kitchen table was crowded with a feast: tamales, pork, chicken, and a cucumber-and-jalapeño salad.

The middle-aged woman pulled out a seat for J.P. and then gave him a thoughtful look. "I sorry she make you sit outside."

"No problemo. Just looking for Esma."

The woman didn't seem surprised. She looked at Chayote, who had wiggled his way inside toward the smell when the door opened, with disdain. He sat and looked back at her, begging.

She frowned and threw him a piece of pork.

Gaby was Esma's goddaughter and their downstairs neighbor. Sometimes when her mother and father were at work for the dinner shift or wanted an evening alone, J.P. and Esma would take Gaby out for what the little fireball sarcastically called "fun nights."

The trio ate mainly in silence. When they were finished, J.P. tried to help clean up, but Gaby's mother waved him off. He sat back down at the table, where Gaby was playing on her phone again.

"Did you make her leave?" The child spoke without looking up.

"I, um, no. Of course not. She wanted to see her family."

Gaby was too sharp to fall for this. "Totally," she said sarcastically.

"Have you heard from her recently?"

"Nope. There's probably no reception down there." She turned to her mother and spoke in Spanish, then back to J.P. "She hasn't heard from her either."

"Did she get a new phone? I got a message from her, but it was a different number."

Gaby laughed. "I hope so. I've been bugging her to get an iPhone for like a year. She said she would when her phone died."

*It must be her! Her old prepaid wasn't holding its charge very well before she left.*

Gaby's mother brought in flan, made from scratch. Gaby pushed hers aside, but J.P. devoured his. He had barely eaten since he'd gotten Esma's message, and his hunger had caught up with him. Hearing that Esma might have gotten a new cell phone encouraged him. He was feeling better.

"When is she coming home?" Gaby asked. This time she paused the game and looked at J.P.

"I don't know, but I think soon. I have to go. I'll have Esma call you!"

He gave Gaby and her mother awkward hugs and sprinted out the door.

When he got in his truck, he immediately dialed the number again. The phone rang, which was the first time he had gotten that far. His excitement was building. Four rings. Five.

*C'mon. C'mon!*

J.P. dreaded the automated voice.

*C'mon. Please just pick up.*

"Hello?"

The voice shocked J.P.

"Hello? Who is this?"

"Whoa, who the hell is *this*?" A man's voice. American. From the background, he heard a scuffle and another voice, louder. "Put it down, idiot!"

"Hey! Is Esma there?"

Just laughter. Then, "I said put it down!" There was a loud thump and finally silence. Dead air.

"Hey!"

*What the fuck?*

J.P. dialed again. The phone rang but went straight to the automated voice mail. He dialed one more time. Nothing.

J.P. started the engine and swung the truck around in a U-turn, toward the police station. He fumbled to find a cigarette in the glove compartment, ran a few stop signs, then parked at the City/County complex. He jogged to the reception entrance, tossed the butt, and flung open the doors.

"Where's the chief?" he shouted. His voice was trembling.

The receptionist stood up to block him from walking back into the offices. An audience of officers stood up, ready to react if necessary.

"I know him," one of the detectives said. "It's okay." Mike, the ski-patroller-turned-cop. *Must have a hard-on for telling people what to do*, J.P. figured.

"Thanks, Mike." J.P. caught his breath, put his hands on his face, and sunk into one of the hard plastic chairs in the waiting area.

"What the hell is going on? You can't storm in here like that. You're gonna get yourself shot."

"I'm sorry. My lady is in trouble, man. We were having some issues, you know, and she left, but she said she was on her way back, was supposed to be here this morning. She never showed."

"Change of heart, maybe, J.P. Calm down." Mike gave him a sympathetic look.

"It's not like that. I called her phone, some guy picked up and somebody else was talking in the background."

Mike considered this for a moment. "Is this Liz Hingley all over again, J.P.?"

"What? Shit no! C'mon, man!"

Mike recited the facts: six years earlier, J.P. had come home to find his girlfriend of over a year in the shower with his closest friend. And another friend. So he drunkenly fashioned the horns of a cuckold out of paper-towel rolls and wandered around the square with a bottle of Jim Beam, bawling. The cops weren't far behind him.

"All right, I know the story, dude. Shut up." Mike was trying to keep a straight face while the receptionist guffawed. "I just know something's wrong."

63

Mike put on a straight face. "All right, c'mon back."

J.P. kept his head down while walking through the cubicles. Some of the officers kept their chuckles to themselves. Others weren't so kind. J.P. didn't look up until he sat down in front of Mike's desk.

"Let's start with her phone number. Sometimes if we call, they take it a bit more seriously."

"Her voice mail message isn't set up. It's a new phone. I'm not totally sure it's her, you know?"

"Not totally sure?"

"I think she got a new number."

Mike sighed. "Let me try the *maybe new* number."

J.P. reached into his sweatshirt pocket. He took out his phone and started pressing buttons.

Then he stopped. "Oh shit!"

"What is it?"

"Got a text."

"That says?"

"It says, 'I'm okay, see you soon.'" J.P. put his hand on his forehead, trying to think.

Mike flopped the notepad he had been writing on back onto the desk. He stood up and pushed his chair back in. "We're done, J.P. I've got shit to do. It's not our job to find your road-tripping girlfriend."

"But . . ."

"Look, if something happens, call us. You can't come in here like this."

"Where's the chief?"

"Business trip, buddy. Sorry."

"Shit!" J.P. slammed a closed fist on the detective's desk.

"All right, let's go!" Mike took him by the arm and pulled him toward the door. J.P. could hear snickers from the peanut gallery as he left.

J.P. staggered back to his truck. He looked at Chayote. "Something's not right." The heeler plopped into J.P.'s lap, muddying his pants. Then he settled down and licked J.P.'s face.

"You need a drink, buddy?" Chayote cocked his head.

J.P. nailed the concrete divider as he slid into the brew pub's small parking lot. *Goddammit!* A light sleet had started to fall, making the surface slick.

"Inside, now." The dog hesitated as if he knew better, but then followed J.P. inside. The pub was almost empty. Just a few locals having a beer.

Everyone stopped and looked at J.P., big and burly with his soft eyes looking wistful, and the dog, prancing around him as if to ask *Where we going next? Huh? Huh?*

"Whoa, whoa! He can't come in here, bro!"

J.P. beelined to the bartender who had just reprimanded him. The young man stepped back from the bar, intimidated.

"Listen . . ." J.P. didn't recognize the new employee, so he looked at his name tag. "*Skyler* from Connecticut. This is my anxiety dog. He comes with me everywhere, law says so. You want a lawyer up your ass? Get us two pale ales."

"Take it easy, man."

A particularly pickled local named John looked over. "You got that there anxiety, J.P.?" He giggled, showing his country teeth.

"Fuck off. Tonight I do."

J.P. drank half of his beer in one swig and then set the other

65

down for the dog, who drank eagerly too. He motioned for another from Skyler.

A woman appeared a moment later from the kitchen, smiling at J.P.

"Heard someone's threatening to sue us?" Melissa, the front-of-house manager, spoke with only a tinge of seriousness. "You think Jake would take the case? He likes our beer, doesn't he?"

*Shit.* J.P. chugged the rest of his second beer and prepared to be kicked out. He burped loudly.

"Impressive," Melissa said. "Well, let me see the little fella at least."

She walked casually around the bar, saying hello to the regulars. When she approached Chayote, he was wagging his tail so fast that he could hardly keep his body still.

"I think your anxiety dog needs an anxiety dog."

The new bartender was polishing glasses; their shiny glare matched the look he gave J.P., who thought in retort: *Fuck you, Connecticut!*

"I'll get out of here. Let my man finish his drink." J.P. motioned at Chayote, who had a third left and a bad case of the hiccups.

"Stay. Beer's on me. What's going on?" Melissa had a knack for knowing when a customer needed a shoulder to cry on. She walked back around the bar and rested her elbows on its surface, face low and close to his.

"What's bugging you?"

He looked at his beer glass like a starving orphan, and Melissa took it. "Pale ale, right?"

J.P. nodded. "You remember Esma? I had her in here for lunch couple times."

"How could I forget? Good-looking woman."

"Yeah, thanks. Well, we were having some issues, and . . ."

"You two were a *couple*?" John spoke up again. "That exotic-looking one? I had a dream once where she and I were stuck in the snow in my truck, and . . ."

"Better shut it, John." Melissa stopped the confrontation before it started.

"Jesus, man!" J.P. turned back to his drink. "So she went out of town, kinda upset you know, and I wasn't sure when or if she was coming back. Then yesterday I get this text from her saying she's coming back and wants to patch things up."

"That's great." Melissa was now pouring a beer for herself and a glass of water for John.

"But she never shows up, and I tried to call her and it's been just *weird*."

"How?"

"Some guy answered and then hung up."

"Don't let your imagination run like that. Probably a wrong number. You know what I think?"

J.P. shrugged as he took a swig.

"She probably wants you to come for her. Do something romantic, you know? Sweep her off her feet."

"I don't even know where she is."

"You could find her if you wanted to. She's playing hard to get."

"Wait. Maybe I can."

*Can't you trace a mobile phone?* He knew one person who ought to know. The last and best of J.P.'s resources remained untapped: Jake Trent.

# 10

*Schwack! Schwack!*

The rednecks were shooting stumps again. "No cable, can't even watch MMA, nothing," they said. So they shot stumps.

*Why don't you idiots wrestle each other?* Esma thought. *Maybe to the death?*

She had begun to grow accustomed to the noise, but she still jumped, imagining herself as one of the stumps.

*Schwack!* Then complete darkness. Or so she assumed. She'd become curious about death in the last few hours. First afraid, then curious.

*That's what people do when they kidnap you, right? Rape and kill you? Or try to use you to get something from somebody . . .*

She didn't believe they were trying for a ransom. She didn't know anybody who wanted her that badly, not to mention that

68

she didn't know anybody rich enough to make kidnapping her worthwhile.

So they'd kill her, more than likely. Violent crime was outside her expertise, but growing up in Mexico in the era of the drug cartels had taught her enough to know she wanted it to be quick. She hoped they would just kick in that shoddy old door and shoot her in the head. No pain. No fear.

Outside, the men didn't share the same frame of mind. They knew they couldn't kill her. But rape, torture—as long as it didn't put her life at risk—was okay, they figured. There were just two reasons that neither of the men had taken her already: First, they were both somewhat ashamed of their urge to do so; they weren't barbarians, after all. Second, neither of them wanted word getting out that he had boinked a beaner.

Randy, the more heavyset of the two, figured the only way to seal the secret was for both of them to do her, but he'd yet to propose this to his partner.

Tim, or Tinny, as they called him because of an old speech impediment, was lanky, medium height. His awkwardly long arms were marked with the sure signs of drug use—meth when money was low and heroin when he was down in Salt Lake and had some extra cash.

They only pretended to trust each other. They knew each other a bit, but this was the first time they had ever worked together. Their boss preferred to keep the relationship dubiously sterile— they didn't even know his name, had been given only the rough contours of the woman's fate.

But they had no qualms about being kept in the dark. They had their "subject," as the boss called her, and that, along with the tote bag stuffed with fifty-dollar bills, was good enough for them.

They continued to take out their rage on the lodgepole stumps. The ground around them was littered with spent shells and cigarette butts: off-brand menthols for Randy and hand rolled for Tinny.

The old hunting camp was pretty nice for two poor boys from Idaho. They guessed it belonged to some rich family from Boise. Who knew how their boss had found it?

The cabin was up on a bluff overlooking the river in the Salmon-Challis wilderness. The River of No Return, it was called. Randy liked the way that sounded, considering they were career criminals who'd just kidnapped someone. Tinny was oblivious to the kismet.

The structure was out in the open atop the hill, which would have been disconcerting if there were anyone around to see what they were doing. But there was no major road along this stretch of the river, only a few logging trails that provided access to the hunting camps in the hills. The occasional drift boat slipped down the inky current chasing steelhead, but that was two thousand feet down the steep bank. The fishermen were too focused on waiting for a twitch from their floats or the tips of their plugging rods to notice anything else around them.

"Let's get out of here," Randy said, taking his hands from his ears, where they had been protecting him from the percussion of the AR-15. "I'm sick of smoked salmon and jerky."

Tinny responded too loudly, his chainsaw-brand ear muffs still on: "Not 'posed to leave, 'member? Boss says so." He brought the rifle back up to his shoulder to fire again.

Randy yanked the muffs off his partner's head and pushed the barrel of the gun down. "Then you stay. I can't take it. I don't even like fish." He started toward the shed.

*Dammit!* Tinny ran to catch up with Randy, who was checking on Esma, making sure she couldn't fly the coop.

"I don't know if you not liking fish is an emergency." Tinny was referring to the boss's exception to the "never leave camp" rule.

"Shut up." Randy made tracks to the truck and turned the radio on. Raucous country music filled the cabin. Tinny jumped in.

When they got to the town of Salmon, they decided it would be prudent to stop throwing their empty beer cans and cigarette butts out the truck window. They didn't need any trouble from the cops.

Tinny pointed at an oversize bear statue on the east bank of the river, welcoming visitors crossing over from the west. "Look at them fish."

The bear was fishing for steelhead and salmon, represented in dull bronze at its feet. These fish kept the town alive through the fall and winter, bringing fishermen in from hundreds of miles around.

Randy gave his sidekick a dubious look. "Gimme a beer. I ain't gonna pay $3.50 down here before I get a buzz in the truck."

Tinny listened and obliged, as was becoming his way with Randy.

"You think maybe we oughta catch us some of those?" he asked, handing the beer over the center console.

"I 'ready told you I don't like fish."

"Sorry."

Randy wrenched the old pickup into a spot with a handicapped sign right in front of Bertram's Brewery. "We'll try this place." He appreciated the neon beer-mug sign.

"Looks fancy."

"You never had a microbrew?"

"Nope." Tinny wondered whether this was some small-portions bullshit like expensive restaurants did with their meals.

The two men hustled inside. The sun had set behind the high

bluff along the river in the west, and it was cold. Earlier that afternoon the wind had started to blow consistently from the Pacific, where the spawning salmonids came from, bringing with it an early snowstorm. The drift boats outside the small pub sported canvas covers to keep the precipitation out.

Their ragtag look turned some heads as the men walked through the dining room and back to the bar. Randy mean-mugged the other patrons in return, but Tinny, oblivious to their judgment, gave a goofy smile, revealing his tinged teeth.

"What can I get you boys?" The female bartender's warm smile betrayed no such judgment. She set down two cardboard coasters.

"A microbrew," Tinny answered eagerly, feeling all high-class.

"No, idiot, it's not like that. They got different kinds." Randy gave the bartender an apologetic smile.

"I'll give you a minute."

They buried their heads in the fold-over pamphlet that described the brews.

"Lookey, they got a nut-sac beer!"

Randy looked where his comrade was pointing. There was a blend of the Hazelnut Ale and the Sacajawea Stout for six bucks. He didn't laugh. "Something cheaper. You won't be able to appreciate that anyway."

The bartender returned. Tinny stuttered ordering his pale ale— he found the waitress rather endearing—and then he giggled when Randy asked for the nut-sac.

"Great. You'll like it." She smiled and turned to fill two mugs.

"Fuck is that 'posed to mean?" he mumbled when she was out of earshot.

Tinny just shrugged.

A cold blast accompanied the squeaking of the back door and

three armed men walked in wearing uniforms. It wasn't a kit that Tinny recognized, dark green and brown color scheme. Wool. Expensive. Like from a Barbour catalogue. They walked right by the bottling bucket and fermenters. Sat only ten feet away.

"Cops?" Tinny whispered.

"Shut it."

One of the men adjusted his sidearm as he sat down, nodding hello at the criminals. Randy's face turned red and that held the man's look for a second longer than usual.

"'Scuse me." Randy got up like a rocket and went to the bathroom. *Shit!* He'd been to jail once and never wanted to go back. He splashed cold water on his face and tried to relax. *It's fine, we'll just have a beer and get out of here.*

He pushed the hollow bathroom door open too hard and it banged against the pictures of other breweries on the wall. The men with guns stared, but their server finally distracted them with tonight's specials.

Randy sat back down and took a big swig of his beer. It was probably good, but he couldn't taste it.

After their first brew, Randy felt more comfortable. The high alcohol content of the microbrew finally gave him the buzz he was looking for. Tinny was watching *SportsCenter* and asking silly questions about sports rules.

"Haven't you never been exposed to *nothing*?"

"What, like nut-sac?"

Tinny was drunk too, and the men roared at the joke. The officers next to them stared, looking displeased.

"Sorry, fellas," Randy hollered with exaggerated sarcasm. The men nodded and went back to their food.

"Say, what is it you boys do?" Randy was pointing at one of the men's sidearm.

"IFG," a sturdy dark-haired man replied. He was trying to avoid a conversation.

Tinny and Randy laughed. "What the hell is that? Like CIA?" Randy backhanded Tinny on the shoulder as he spoke: *Get a load of these guys!*

"Idaho Fish and Game." The dark-haired man turned his broad shoulders to Randy. He pointed to the state IFG crest. Below it, a name tag: Agent Carlisle.

"Agent?" Randy asked. "Really?"

Carlisle stood and fully revealed his mountainous frame. He was clean shaven. Short hair. "Are you men driving anywhere tonight?"

"Hell no!" Randy finished his remaining half a beer. "Staying just down the street."

"Where at?"

"Hell if I know. Some shithole."

"Riverside." Tinny spoke up. "Called Riverside." He remembered the sign's artwork—a trout jumping over a rainbow—on the drive in.

"Don't get into any trouble on your way back," Carlisle said. Then he sat back down, apparently satisfied.

Randy kept on at him. "What do you do here?"

Carlisle sighed loudly. The other men at his table were chuckling. Pitying him for having to suffer such a fool.

"We're tagging steelhead. We monitor their numbers. See where they migrate. How they behave."

A pause.

Then Tinny spoke. "Oh?" He laughed and winked at Randy. "You hear that? Tagging *steelhead* . . ."

Randy glared at him.

The wardens were at attention now.

Randy laughed exaggeratedly. "You drunk fuck," he yelled loud enough for everyone in the bar to hear. Just two old pals yanking each other's chains.

He then turned to the wardens. "You gentlemen have a great evening," Randy said. He nodded at Tinny, threw down cash for the beers, and left.

Inside the shed next to the cabin, Esma had again tried to free herself. It was no use. It only bloodied her wrists and ankles. The restraints allowed her some movement, but the ten-foot shackles were a tease—all she could do was pace and walk in circles. Like a dog on a chain.

Gravel crunched. An engine sighed its final grumble and then died. The uneven cadence of their steps told Esma they were drunk. Their voices were muffled by the cedar planks and insulation of the shed, but she got most of it. *Girl. Shed. No one . . . find out. Ever.*

"¡*Gilipollas*!" she blurted out. They heard her. Went silent. Then snickered.

Esma whispered it this time. "¡*Gilipollas*!" *Not that these idiots would understand.* Now she yelled as loud as she could, her anger burning hotter than the desert sand.

"Assholes! Fools! Bastardos! I'll kill you!" Esma started to weep.

Her tone disarmed Tinny. "Maybe not tonight; she sounds like she might bite your dick off."

"Shut up and get the condoms; I don't wanna get the clap."

This Esma heard clearly. She looked toward the heavens, obstructed by her wooden prison, and crossed herself. Her chains clanged to the rhythm of the gesture.

75

**II**

A day-old *Washington Post* was tucked between the backseats of the car. Divya was busy on her phone, so Jake skimmed the paper, looking for something interesting. They were headed to another chichi restaurant after another day's work.

### "Overpopulation Viruses" in Slums
### Alarm African Officials

Nairobi, Kenya—Local health authorities are reporting a dramatic uptick in mortality rates from transmittable diseases among the poor. The outbreaks are attributed to crowded living conditions and lack of clean water.

Oyhed Ausim, chief physician at the nonprofit Kenyan Children's Clinic, called these new health statistics disturbing. "As the population continues to grow, we

76

will reach a critical mass, if we haven't already. From that point on, viruses will spread and mutate at an alarming rate, a rate that no nation in the world is prepared to cope with, especially Kenya. It's horrifying, really."

In Asia, where several nations are battling population-fueled disease outbreaks, government officials have convened to consider various proposals to stem the problem.

On Maryland Avenue, the driver stopped and opened the door for Jake, who walked around to the other side and opened Divya's. She was still sitting, waiting for him to do so. The driver was savvy, allowing Jake the opportunity to be gentlemanly.

*You're not helping!* Jake wanted to say.

"Thank you." Divya got out of the backseat.

"So what's this place all about?" Jake asked, referring to the restaurant.

"You'll have to wait and see." She winked. Flirty again.

Jake handed the driver a tip, likely not a very good one in this town.

Inside, cool-blue neon backlit the serpentine bar. Ice was packed in stainless-steel trays beneath the booze, chilling raw oysters from various regions, all marked with small slate boards and chalk. The room was bustling, and Jake could hardly absorb the frantic scene.

Their water glasses were filled. Crystal goblets. Within a minute, a server came by to ask for their drink order.

"Veuve, please," Divya requested.

The young man nodded. "And you, sir?"

"Old-fashioned." Jake felt as though he might need it to get through the evening.

"Yeah, you are." Divya brushed his slacks with her bare foot.

*Ugh.* "Champagne? What are you celebrating?"

"A reunion." A stunning, devilish smile.

They toasted with their water.

The drinks arrived just in time. Divya was asking Jake about his ex-flame Elspet. What happened? Not exactly Jake's favorite topic of conversation. Somehow his fumbling answer led to the recent drama surrounding Noelle, which wasn't any better. Jake ended that topic too when Divya said Noelle didn't deserve him anyway.

This made Jake miss Noelle immensely. He had no idea what type of woman Divya thought he deserved, but he knew the comment was a slight against Noelle. Something Noelle herself would never have said about anyone.

Jake's first old-fashioned went down easy, so he ordered a second. The tranquil azure lighting and clean steel decor—plus the bourbon—soothed his mood.

Still, all he could think about was going home.

After the two bourbon drinks and a glass of water, Jake excused himself to go to the bathroom. The door was heavy stainless, like an entrance to a walk-in freezer, and the attendant rushed from inside and pulled to help him.

"Thanks, got it," Jake said. He meant *Unnecessary*.

The stall doors and walls went floor to ceiling. Obviously, hearing another man's bowel movement wasn't in line with the "chic, upscale environs" the restaurant intended to create. Or whatever Divya had called it. Some silly phrase meaning *overpriced*.

Jake sidled up to the urinal.

"Not from here?" the attendant asked. Jake turned around, hoping the man wasn't talking to him. There were no other customers in the room.

Jake went to the sink, washed his hands, and avoided further conversation. "My oysters are getting cold." He accommodated the man with a smile.

They didn't get back to Divya's until 11 p.m. Jake was upstairs in the guest bedroom changing. He had a French 75 in his hand, a drink he wasn't familiar with but that Divya had forced on him. Not bad, really. Fancy gin and champagne. Better than a Pabst. Walking over to the bedside table, he took his cell phone from his pocket. He had forgotten to turn it back on after dinner.

It buzzed for a minute straight after he turned it on. Six voice mails, all from J.P. And two text messages. He read the texts first:

Dude—need you! Esma is missing. Something's wrong.

And,

Please call back! ASAP!

The messages had their intended effect. Without listening to the voice mails, Jake dialed J.P. It rang twice before he answered.

"Hello?" J.P. sounded foggy. Probably drunk.

"What's going on?" Divya peered in the room mischievously. Jake waved her away.

"Man, she's gone. Without a trace."

"Esma? You said she went home to Mexico."

"She did, yeah. Then she told me she was coming home. She missed me. Now she's missing. Kidnapped."

"How do you know?"

"She told me. Texted saying she was on her way. When I tried to call her, there was some dude's voice."

Jake immediately recalled Liz Hingley.

"That doesn't mean she's missing." Jake thought about how to word this. "Maybe she was just with a friend."

"No, Jake. I know you're smart, man. But I get this feeling. I've got some instincts too."

Jake knew this was true. Still, he couldn't help but think, *Yeah, instincts and about fifteen beers.*

"Did you call the police?"

"No help. They think I'm off my rocker. What's the next step?"

Jake thought on it. He hated to doubt his friend. If J.P. said Esma was kidnapped, Jake would believe him. "I'll look into it. Text me her cell number and I'll see what I can do."

"Thanks, man. I mean, God, thank you!"

"No problem."

"Jake, one more thing."

"Yeah?"

"When can you come home?"

In the doorway again, Divya stood. All five feet ten of her. Legs alone seemingly longer than that. Bronze-dark skin, fully nude, breasts befitting a woman half her age, her smooth skin glistening from her head down. Handcuffs dangled from her fingers.

"Let's play criminal investigator," she interrupted. Not asking.

"Soon, buddy." Jake hung up the phone.

Jake tried to stand up and stop her. Before he could, she was at the bed, gently pushing his shoulders, forcing him to lie down, whispering: "Relax, you're *only* under arrest."

He'd had enough. Enough of this town. Enough of Divya's constant advances that stemmed from God-knows-what psychological issues.

Still, something in his mind said *Go with it. Give in. What man rejects a model-caliber woman with no clothes on?* And she was familiar. It was all too easy.

Divya pulled his wrists between the hand-turned wooden dowels on the headboard and locked them with the cuffs.

"Do you remember the library bathroom during criminal procedure class?"

Jake could only nod, like a sex-crazed teenager. She started kissing his neck, her nipples bearing the mass of her breasts onto his own chest.

*I'm outta here tomorrow,* Jake thought. And pulled against the cuffs, straining to try to kiss her back.

# 12

Divya was quietly snoring. More like heavy breathing. Either way, Jake used to find it adorable, sexy somehow. Now it disgusted him. A *satisfied* snore. A reminder of the mistake he'd made the night before. *What the hell was I thinking?*

He got out of bed. Searching the floor for his boxers, he found them camouflaged against the peculiar pattern of the Persian rug. He got on his phone only after leaving the bedroom. Jake wanted to make a quick escape.

He felt like a caged animal, anxious and irritated. He rolled his neck and paced like a tiger on display while the phone rang. It was a dim, cloudy day. Out the hallway window, the fancy cars and brownstones glared back at him, moody fetishes of misguided ambition. Hungry desire. Wealth. The signatures of arrogance.

He gave the airline agent his name. Where he was.

"And where are you headed, sir?"

"Home. Jackson Hole. As soon as possible."

"No problem." The clatter of a keyboard sharpened by the amplifier of the phone. "Looks like the next available is 12:15 p.m. Dulles."

"What's the fare?"

"Let me see . . . $935. It's very last minute."

Flights to Jackson were always pricey, but $935 was egregious. "First class?" *Dumb question.*

"No, sir."

Jake silently weighed his options. "At least it's not $936."

"I'm very sorry, sir."

"Not your fault. Thanks."

Jake got in the shower. He wanted to wash off all of last night, along with the city and the convoluted arrangement of facts surrounding the GPSN campaign.

Yes, he wanted to help derail the plan to inject a microchip into every man, woman, and child that immigrated to this country. It was against everything he believed in.

*What will happen next if Canart's funding goes through?*

Although a mentor once convinced him that making the "slippery slope" argument was a fool's errand, he couldn't stop his mind from wandering down that road. The bow-tie wearing, musty tobacco–smelling old law professor had scolded him in front of the whole class. "Weak!" the curmudgeon had shouted, spit flying and pen pointing. "Every decision in the history of man could lead to unforeseen results. You slippery-slopers would hog-tie our decision makers if you had your way."

So Jake Trent, the attorney, never uttered the perfunctory phrase in a courtroom, and he was well prepared to argue against it.

\*       \*       \*

The hot shower left him wanting more. The humidity stuck to his body, even in the air-conditioned town house. He yearned for crisp, thin air. For immaculate white snow and effervescent mountain creeks. It would all rush in when he stepped off the jet and walked down the stairs, where the Tetons stood behind him. To the west.

Maybe give Noelle a ring. Tell her he had been afraid. That he had panicked when things got serious, convinced by his past that if something seemed too good to be true, it probably was. And he would confess to her, tell her how he really felt. That he loved her.

His confidence was coming back. The call from J.P. had put him squarely back in his element. He thought about Esma and how he would find her. That was his first priority.

He hoped J.P. was wrong and that Esma was simply incommunicado, but he knew it was a mistake to treat the situation as such before he could evaluate it. He had to be prepared for the worst.

After last summer's events, he had taken his Glock 30 Mariner Edition out of storage and cleaned it. The 110-lumen Streamlight TLR flashlight and aiming laser was dusty but spot-on. He'd tested it in a canyon a mile from the bed-and-breakfast. Put a cluster of three in a soda can from thirty-five yards. *Not bad for being out of practice.*

The Mariner had been a gift from a Mossad agent in the Philippines. It was waterproof and fired with deadly force after full submersion. He'd verified that. On its barrel was the acronym OSI. The Office of Special Investigations.

In the bathroom, Jake put on deodorant and did thirty quick push-ups to flush the adrenaline that was flowing through him. He hopped to his feet and wrapped a towel around his waist, which had seemingly become rounder in only a few days in DC. Then he took a deep breath and walked back into the bedroom to face the music.

"Are you fucking kidding me? Is this because of last night?"

*Not a very good start.* "No. My friend is in trouble."

"The whole country is in trouble, Jake!"

"Not like this." He was packing his bags.

A quick hug and he was out the door. The luxury rental had a parking ticket on its windshield. $170. Parked too far from the curb.

At the airport, Jake found a café kiosk and ordered a large coffee. He was beginning to feel normal again, although the acidic brew made his stomach turn. It hadn't seemed to recover from his first-day hangover.

By the time he reached the Dallas/Fort Worth airport, Jake was staggering, too sick to consider boarding his connecting flight. He checked into the airport Hyatt and dialed a doctor. The stomach cramps and nausea made it difficult for him to stand, so he lay in a crumpled ball on top of the bedding. Lights and TV off, he mulled the emergency room. No sleep. There was a physician's office close by, but they couldn't see him until the morning.

The night lasted an eternity. It was hellacious. Every object offended Jake: the blinking colon between the alarm's numbers, the surface of the bedspread. Even the small crack of light shining under the door from the hallway.

In the morning, he mustered up the strength to get into the

shower and brush his teeth so that the doctor wouldn't have to deal with the smell.

Downstairs, he hailed a cabbie, who told him he didn't look so hot.

*No shit. Pick up the pace.*

The nurse didn't finish her preexam before calling in the doctor.

"You're a tough son of a bitch," he commented, upon looking Jake over. "You're badly dehydrated. We need to put an IV in, then consider a visit to the emergency room, okay? I've got an anti-nausea drug that will help for a short time."

"What is it?" Jake mustered.

"Probably just stomach flu. A nasty one."

The medicine, along with the peace of mind that a doctor was nearby, allowed Jake to find sleep right there on the exam table. He woke to a jostling, not knowing how much later it might be.

"Sorry. We're gonna get you transported over to the hospital so you can recover. Nothing serious. But you'll be more comfortable over there."

Jake was too foggy to ask any questions. He drifted in and out of sleep during the ride to the hospital.

# 13

J.P. was crawling out of his skin. Jake had texted him in the morning, asking for a ride home from the airport at 7:30 p.m. That flight, United 721, had come and gone on time. Two hours later, J.P. was still sitting in the terminal.

He glanced at the flat-screen, which sat above the bronze relief of the Snake River, with its perplexing weave of meanders and side channels. No news of plane crashes or bad weather. J.P. tried Jake's phone again, but there was no answer. *Shit.*

J.P. stood and headed to the parking lot, unsure what to do next. *Where the hell is he?* It wasn't like Jake to no-show without calling ahead. Without Jake, he had no real hope of finding Esma. He tried her cell this time. No answer.

Coyotes howled as J.P. walked to his truck, fretting about the

87

imminent arrival of the high-country winter. When the snow covered the ground, the scavengers could only wander aimlessly, praying for a scent of field mice, pika, an elk carcass. They were hopeless but for luck. Like J.P. felt now.

Some would survive the ordeal. Many wouldn't.

# 14

Jake cleared his throat and opened his eyes. A blurry white room. No one around, at least not on his side of the curtain. Beyond it, he could hear the pained moans of another patient.

His stomach still ached, but he didn't feel as nauseated. At least he'd gotten some rest. The hit-by-a-truck feeling would pass soon enough. He closed his eyes again, imagining being home, the Indian summer sun on his skin. When he opened them, the fluorescent lights pierced through his brain. *A headache too.*

He sat up and cracked his neck. It was day outside, but not sunny. Thunderheads moved across the flat Texas landscape. The clouds could almost be mistaken for towering mountains.

He was dressed in the hospital's light-blue gown with rubber-grippy socks, and an IV was in his arm. Jake checked his own chart, but it was illegible. Doctors were no better than lawyers. He didn't seem to be on any medication at this point, so he carefully pulled the tube from his arm and stuck the medical tape over the hole. Then he dropped the gown and grabbed his clothes from the white plastic bag with his initials on it.

After dressing, Jake pulled the curtain aside and headed toward the door. The man he'd heard earlier looked up at him briefly, his face a disturbing yellow, and then vomited into a bedpan. Jake hustled out.

He was booting up his cell phone when he heard his name from behind.

"Mr. Trent! Please!"

A tall, handsome Indian man strode toward Jake.

"Back to the room, please."

Jake turned. "I'd rather not."

From the room, they could hear the other patient retching. The doctor looked enervated. "Fine. Follow me."

He led Jake into an exam room, quickly washed his hands, and then sat on a padded stool. Jake stayed standing. On the wall, a wide-eyed golden retriever puppy stood in front of a fireplace. Next to it was a poster about sexually transmitted diseases.

"Somewhere to be?" The doc was sharp. And not interested in hearing any bullshit.

"Stomach flu, right? I'll get over it," Jake said.

The doctor shook his head in frustration. Then he spoke, contradicting his gesture.

"Yes, stomach flu. You'll be fine, Mr. Trent. You had a norovirus, we suspect, and dehydration."

"And?" Jake paused and reconsidered his tone. "I'm not trying to cause any problems. I just need to go home. I have a friend who needs me."

"You are free to go. Stay hydrated and take it easy."

"Is that all?"

"You were hospitalized because your symptoms were so severe that the general practitioner was concerned. You're in the clear now; the virus has run its course."

"And my roommate?"

"I'm sorry?" The doctor looked up from his pad.

"The other person in the room with me. Norovirus too?"

"Yes. He'll be fine. There are many strains of norovirus, and they are always changing. Evolving. This one was formidable. Possibly a new strain. They come from all over and spread like wildfire."

"Is it a concern?"

"Probably not. You came through it fine."

Jake nodded, being careful not to wobble on his feet.


On the cab ride from the hospital to DFW, Jake arranged for a flight to Jackson. He explained his illness to the agent, who with some cajoling made an exception to the fare-change fee. Then he phoned J.P.

"Where the hell have you been?" It was afternoon, but it sounded as if J.P. had just woken up.

"I got sick on the way home. Had to stop for a night. I'm on my way."

J.P.'s tenor changed to sympathetic. "Oh. Got ya. I get nervous on flights if I don't hit the airport bar first."

Jake let it slide. "Right. Anyway, I get in at 5:45. Can you be there?"

"No worries."

Jake ended the call.

At the airport, Jake checked in and found the gate. He sat down and finally made the call he was dreading.

"Human Rights and Special Prosecutions." The Office had changed its name, but Jake recognized the voice.

In the main house of the Fin and Feather, J.P. was brewing coffee. There were no guests, which allowed J.P. free rein, but also made him lonely. And gave him time to obsess about Esma.

He fed Chayote, who'd been waiting by the food cabinet, probably since J.P. went to bed. When the coffee was done, he poured himself an oversize cup and walked over to the brown leather couch in the great room. To his right was the breakfast area, unused since the last guests in late September.

Through the big wood-framed picture window, J.P. could see out across Trout Run to the expansive ranch that bordered the far side. He felt lost. Looking for Esma was like looking for a needle in a haystack.

Worse yet, he had no clue where to start without Jake.

He dragged out the laptop from the office and sat watching TV and reading through old emails from her, more to reminisce than to find a trace of her.

When he clicked on his own user name to sign out, he noticed it. *No way.*

There, between his own name and Jake's, was Esma's email account. He clicked on her name. The password must have been saved, because a moment later J.P. was looking at her inbox.

Jake had paused too long.

"Identification number, please? Hello? You must have the wrong number."

*Here we go.*

"Nancy, it's Jake Trent." He was surprised to hear her voice, what with all the moaning she used to do about the Office. She'd stuck it out anyway. Her happiness was a sacrifice to superior government benefits and job security.

"Jake? How are you? Are you back in? What's your project ID number?" Enthusiastic, for her, but still a tinge of annoyance in her voice, like it was all so inconvenient. She preferred to talk about her children rather than her work.

"No, not back in. No ID number. I just need some help." Nancy was a ballbuster, but she liked Jake a lot more than she liked most guys at the Office. Over the intercom, the woman at the gate announced boarding for first class and premier members. Jake glanced at his boarding pass.

*Boarding Group five. That's what $935 gets you.*

"You know there's no way I can direct you without that number, Jake. Surely you remember."

"I do. And I'm sorry to ask this of you, but I need you to put me through to Schue without an ID. And before I forget, how are the kids?"

"All grown now. Do you believe it? And Ralph's wife is pregnant."

"Congrats." Jake couldn't honestly say he remembered which one Ralph was.

The phone went silent for a second.

*"Now boarding Group One, please."* The well-dressed passengers were all but boarded now, leaving a ragtag group in their seats.

"Well, anyway, no harm in running into his office and see if he'll take the call. What should I tell him it's about?"

"Just remind him of California."

"Okay."

The phone clicked back on.

"What the fuck, Jake? You can't just throw around 'California'! Unlike you, I still wanna work here." He was half-kidding.

*Same old Schue.*

"Figured it would get your attention."

"Whaddya want?" It was getting late in the day on the East Coast, almost after business hours.

"I need to locate a mobile. GPS if you can. Otherwise multilateration."

"Fuck. Does the phone even have GPS?"

"I don't know."

"Gonna take a few hours. Gimme the number."

"Thanks." Jake read the number to Schue, made small talk for a short moment, and hung up.

When boarding for Group Five was called, he headed to the gate. He finished his large bottle of water and took another one out of his pack as he headed down the Jetway.


J.P. searched through Esma's sent mail and found what he was looking for: an email back home to her mother. He copied the text and ran it through an online translator to English.

It had been sent from her phone four days earlier.

Mamá,

I am on my way out of New Mexico and toward Wyoming. I am sorry for leaving so abruptly. I will call when I get there.

Love,

Esma

The email meant she was somewhere in the States, and it meant she had indeed come back to see him. At least she hadn't been kidnapped by a cartel. What was disturbing was that she had never made it north to Jackson. And four days was plenty of time.

J.P. pulled up a map online. He magnified the Rocky Mountain West—in particular, the corridor between New Mexico and Wyoming. He hoped to see something, anything, that might give him a lead. Instead, the map only frustrated him, emphasizing the wide expanse of the region.

He looked at his watch. He was antsy to go pick up Jake. It was 3:30. He would just have to wait.


Jake had eaten at DFW, and the food digested well. Now, a mere four-hundred-some miles and he'd be back home. It would be a relief to be back, but the Esma issue was weighing heavily on him. He hoped her phone had functioning GPS, which would make Schue's job a lot easier.

Multilateration worked, but it would reveal only the general area of the phone. The technology relied on the fact that cell phones constantly check in with multiple cellular towers in the given area. By looking at the relative strength of those signals, it was possible to deduce the rough location of the phone. There was a catch, however: the phone would also have to be turned on and have service. If it was too far away to connect with any tower, there was no hope. But if Schue was successful, it would give Jake and J.P. a starting point.

The high plains surrounding Denver and southern Wyoming gave way to the towering alpine peaks of the Wind River Range. The sun hung on the western horizon. Jake watched the scenery for the last hundred miles or so into Jackson. There was a dusting of new snow at higher elevations.

As the plane banked hard to approach from the north, the town of Jackson came into view above Snow King, the town's ski hill. The plane bounced hard as it landed because of the short approach and small runway. Its rapid deceleration didn't affect Jake's stomach much. He was feeling almost 100 percent. As the plane taxied, he texted J.P. He looked for a message or missed call from Schue, but there was none.

The ski lodge–esque airport was tiny. Two baggage claims, though there were plans for more. More space for ever more visitors. October wasn't tourist season, so the building would be quiet today. Mostly families waiting to greet kids, brothers, or spouses. The "shoulder seasons" were when the locals traveled.

Jake descended the stairs out of the plane and onto the tarmac. There was a cold breeze, but the arid mountain air felt refreshing. It blew through his clothes, taking the swampiness of travel and overcrowded spaces away from him.

He set his backpack down and fished out his old Costa Del Mar Peninsula sunglasses. The Fin and Feather was a dozen miles to the west, and the setting sun was still bright above the Tetons.

After taking a long look at the Tetons, Jake followed the delineated path toward the terminal. Various animal tracks were painted on the tarmac trail: moose, bear, and wolf—a dash of whimsy for the children.

J.P. was waiting just sixty feet inside the entrance, as close as you could get. Jake smiled at him and gave him a nod. J.P. just stared back. He was nervously shifting his weight from foot to foot.

When Jake approached, he roughly took the backpack from him, eager to get going.

"Did you check a bag?"

"Probably already delivered to the Fin and Feather." This was one luxury of a small town.

"Perfect."

J.P. hurried out the front entrance, and Jake followed. J.P. had left his rusty old Ford pickup in the drop-off lane. Airport security was writing him a ticket, and upon seeing J. P., began berating him.

"You can't leave your vehicle here unattended, J.P. See the signs? What the hell? This isn't the brew pub; you have to respect me at work. It's a matter of national security."

"Fuck off, Mike, it's an emergency. You're a secret agent now? You Instagram pictures of your weed stash, you dumbass."

"Take the damned ticket." Mike looked around nervously.

"You stoner!" J.P. was shouting to make a scene.

"All right. Calm down." Jake walked up to the front of the truck and took the ticket. That made two in three days.

"Thanks, Jake," Mike said. "He can be a real ass."

Jake disagreed with that on principle, but didn't want to cause any more trouble.

"Sorry."

Jake climbed in, and J.P. pulled into the stream of taxi traffic by holding his left hand out of the window and signaling the taxi drivers to stop. They honked.

J.P. frantically recited the details about Esma as soon as they were moving. He explained the email he had read a few hours before.

"I knew she didn't ditch me, man—what we have is real. It's love. I've got to find her, Jake. I have a bad feeling about this."

"I'm on it. And it's probably nothing. Hopefully we will have some answers soon." Jake explained how he was trying to track the cell phone. J.P. seemed amazed by the technology.

"You never disappoint," he said.

They passed a sign: THANKS FOR VISITING GRAND TETON NATIONAL PARK. Jake thought of Noelle.

"I wish that were true."

# 15

The alarm buzzed and Terrell startled awake. It was 8 a.m. The night before, the chief and his wife had been treated to an elaborate feast. The chefs prepared buffalo rib eye, elk chops, and Colorado lamb, along with a myriad of traditional Chinese dishes: pickled cabbage called Suan Cai, Mongolian Hot Pot, and steamed buns. Terrell didn't care for the steamed buns, but his wife indulged.

Today was the day they would finally meet Xiao, at the ornate palace the owner called his ranch. More ceremony and more public speaking. More attention. Things Terrell didn't like.

He checked around the room for Charlotte, who was nowhere to been seen. Judging by her excitement during the first two days of the trip, he deduced that she was out sightseeing. He looked out across the way toward the white buffalo on wheels. The streets were empty, and smog had blown in from the city overnight.

Looking at the itinerary, Terrell decided the day ahead didn't look so bad. Meet in the lobby at 9 a.m. Walk down Main Street to breakfast and to meet Xiao. That was it. Seemed easy enough. Bullet had promised Terrell the night before that there wouldn't be any press this time. Nice and low-key.

After the meeting, Charlotte and Terrell would have some free time for lunch and exploring, and then their final dinner. He couldn't wait to get home, though he wasn't looking forward to the long flight or the mystery wolf carcass that was waiting for him.

Terrell grabbed the remote, which sat in a classy elk-tine holder, and clicked on the TV. The room was indeed very nice. *Grand*, as they had told him. He could get used to this level of luxury.

*But would it kill them to add some American channels?* The chief was a big fan of *Ax Men* on the History Channel.

He continued to flip through. Wacky game shows and news in a language he couldn't understand.

*Great.*

He phoned the front desk. The attractive woman answered; he recognized her silky tempo.

"Everything okay, Mr. Terrell?"

"Fine. I am just wondering if there is American news on the television."

"Of course, sir. My apologies, but no, not on the TV. Your best bet is to stream it from the business center."

"Stream?" He paused. "Oh, right. Thank you." He hung up.

*Stream?* The chief felt embarrassed. He knew basically what it meant—he did have teenaged children. But it dumbfounded him that a word he would never feel comfortable enough to use in normal conversation was commonplace for someone who spoke English as a second language.

He cycled through the channels again. Nothing. He looked at the remote to try to figure out how to turn on English closed captioning, but it was far too advanced. Too many buttons.

*Fucking technology.*

The chief hopped out of bed, brushed his teeth, and put his contacts in. Then he threw on a gray button-down with fake pearl buttons, jeans, and his turquoise and silver bolo tie. He took the stairs instead of the elevator. He felt out of shape from all the enormous meals he'd been served over the last couple of days.

Passing the front desk to get to the business center, he could manage only a sheepish smile at the beautiful front-desk agent.

Terrell had no intentions of streaming anything. Text news would do.

Finding nothing to steal his attention, he signed onto the police department's email server. There was plenty of spam, and a single email from Layle, his deputy.

Rog,

Wolf carcass is in the big fridge at game and fish. No leads and nothing suspicious, so we're just waiting for your approval to incinerate.

—Layle

Terrell responded, asking Layle to leave the carcass on ice for a day or two longer, in case any tips came in.

Charlotte was in the room straightening her hair when Terrell got back. She immediately noticed his pale demeanor.

"There you are. Everything okay?"

"Fine. Just tired. Still jet-lagged."

"We've got a few minutes, you know." She dropped her robe,

revealing her slim body, which, Terrell had to admit, was remarkably similar to its twentysomething version. She was a Nordic skier and a professional nutritionist, and it showed.

Terrell pondered her a moment, then bent and picked up her robe. He held it out and looked to the side. She huffed and grabbed it.

"I'm just exhausted, honey. Maybe coming down with something."

"It's fine." Her tone betrayed her.

*Doesn't sound like it.*

He lay down on the bed, thinking, while his wife continued to get ready for the day.

They headed down to the lobby a few minutes early. Neither was in a great mood now. Bullet was there to greet them, as enthusiastic as he'd been when he first picked them up. With him were two large and athletic Chinese men, whom Bullet didn't introduce.

Outside, Bullet filled the silence between the chief and his wife. The smog was starting to blow off with a north wind. "Weather is beautiful. We call this Golden October in China. Earlier in the month we celebrate National Day. By next year, Tram Village will be ready to have its own event."

As they walked down the main drag, Bullet pointed out the resort's attractions: a working replica of Jackson's Million Dollar Cowboy Bar, a "Cowboy Stage" for shoot-outs and country music, a gold-panning area for children, and a corral for small animals.

For the first time since their arrival in China, Charlotte was quiet. Not taking pictures. Terrell tried to hold her hand, but she pulled away. No visitors were in the village; the resort had just opened, and only a few of the lodge's weekend homes behind the main strip had been sold. The only people present were construction work-

ers, busy putting the final touches on the façades, and a few main-
tenance men who were sprinkling the imported dust with water so
it didn't blow away in the wind.

As they came to a stop outside an imitation clapboard saloon,
Bullet spoke again. "Best breakfast in the West!"

Charlotte giggled politely and Terrell forced a smile.

"Xiao is running late, I am afraid. My colleagues here will take
you on tour of the restaurant in the meantime." Bullet excused
himself and walked back toward the hotel, still without introduc-
ing the two men.

Charlotte spoke slowly and loudly to their new hosts. "He-
LLOOO. NICE TO MEET YOU."

The chief discreetly shook his head at his wife.

The gargantuan men looked at each other, but didn't smile or
respond. They turned and walked toward the front, where automatic glass doors led to an antiqued swinging saloon-style gate.
The men pushed through without holding the door for Terrell and
Charlotte.

They stood in the middle of a large dining room. The wooden
chairs had obviously been carefully chosen to mismatch just right,
and they were overturned and resting on picnic-style tables. Game
mounts were everywhere. They were regionally appropriate for the
most part, but a few exotics sprinkled the walls: dik-diks, a polar
bear, and even a rhino head.

The restaurant was empty except for the four of them. Smelling
sawdust and fresh paint, Terrell assumed the kitchen had never
been used.

After allowing them to wander for a few minutes, the men led
Terrell and Charlotte downstairs to the kitchen. The men's silence
was off-putting. In the kitchen, empty and devoid of utensils, the

giants stopped again, this time glancing at each other for a moment before one waved his hand in a semicircle, meaning *Look around*.

"Well, this is weird," Charlotte whispered to Terrell as they walked around equipment they didn't know and had no interest in learning about. Terrell just shrugged. He caught one of the giants looking at his watch.

"Somewhere to be, big guy?" Terrell broke the strange silence. He was getting annoyed with the bullshit tour. "What are we doing down here?"

"Shhhh. Honey!" Charlotte pleaded.

The men continued to look straight ahead.

"We're finished here. We'd like to go back up." The chief pointed up.

The slightly larger of the impressive men finally issued a thin smile and spoke. His English left something to be desired, and Terrell barely understood him.

"Private dining room." And motioned toward a back door in the kitchen.

He looked at Terrell and repeated the words in the exact same tone. "Private dining room."

Charlotte spoke up. "Just follow him."

The chief did as his wife asked, and they were led to a small room with cement-block walls that had been painted gray. Not the level of luxury they had been treated to thus far. Inside, a small aluminum table sat without a tablecloth or place settings. Two matching chairs sat on one side, and there was a single chair on the other.

The man spoke again. "Xiao." He motioned them to sit down.

Before Terrell could ask where they were and what the hell they were doing there, the men quickly stepped out, slammed the heavy door, and locked it.

# 16

It was 9 p.m. before Jake heard from Schue. The good news was that Esma's phone had been turned on. The bad news was that it apparently had no GPS and had been turned off shortly after Schuc determined its general location. Not only that, but it also appeared to Schue that the phone was transmitting from an extremely isolated area, because only one tower was receiving a signal. So much for multilateration. The best Schue could do was outline a thirteen-mile radius from the tower. He included two attachments with his message, both screen shots from the government version of Google Maps.

The first photo focused on the cellular tower, perched atop a high bluff overlooking a river. A highlighter-yellow hue showed the area where the phone could be, based on its signal strength. The tower was in a large expanse of wilderness intersected by a highway and the Salmon River. This didn't encourage Jake. It made it more likely that the phone had transmitted while passing through.

The second photo showed what Schue had labeled "Places of Interest." These were buildings where a person was likely to be, but there weren't many of them. A gas station attached to a home, an old tavern that was overgrown with grass, and four hunting camps up in the hills, away from the highway.

Jake walked out to his vehicle to get his *Idaho Gazetteer*. The low hoot of a great gray owl echoed around the property. Marking his territory.

Motioning J.P. over to the coffee table, Jake explained the satellite photos and then pointed out their location in the *Gazetteer*.

"Rough country?" J.P. asked.

"Very. These creeks are at about sixty-six-hundred feet." Jake traced the small blue veins that emptied into the Salmon River. "Gas station is here, right after the road crosses the river. That will be easy enough. The hunting camps are up high, though. Where the sheep are. This one is at nearly nine thousand feet, on the top of Mount Phelan. There's another peak, Mount Baldy, that has a couple of cabins near the summit. That's well over nine thousand feet. We're looking at a twenty-five-hundred-foot vertical ascent from the ends of these four-by-four roads to where Schue's places of interest are."

"Then we should go tonight."

"No use. It's four hours to Salmon, longer at night with the wildlife." Jake knew this from his many fishing trips to the Salmon River. The River of No Return, it was called, because of its isolation and the severity of its terrain. "And wandering around at night with headlamps only puts us in danger if your hunch about foul play is right. Believe it or not, nighttime is not the best time for a raid, especially without night-vision goggles."

"Fuck! Don't play know-it-all with me, man." J.P. was up and pacing.

"I'm trying to maximize our chances of getting Esma back." Jake shot his old friend a look.

J.P. nodded and sat back down. "What's our plan, then?"

"Sunrise is 7:38 a.m." Jake was on weather.gov. "We leave here at 4 a.m."

"Fine." J.P. didn't look pleased.

"Get a pack together tonight; we won't have time in the morning."


Jake fell fast asleep, only to be awakened by the growl of J.P.'s pickup leaving the driveway. He hopped out of bed and dialed J.P. Straight to voice mail. No reception on Teton Pass.

*Shit!*

Jake hurried back to his room, flipped on the light, and pulled on a pair of hiking pants. Then he ripped a quick-dry long-sleeve T-shirt from a hanger and put it on, adding a thick flannel over it. A mismatched pair of hiking socks would have to do.

The alarm clock read 1:15 a.m. *He left early. Damn.*

He opened the small safe in the bottom of his closet and pulled it into the light. The cold, matte black metal of the safe's contents leached a grave atmosphere into the room.

The Suunto Elementum Terra would be helpful for both its altimeter and digital compass. He strapped the timepiece on.

The Glock 30 Mariner felt lighter than he remembered. He set it down on the hardwood floor and looked through the rest of the contents. There were two magazines for the Mariner, a ten-shot that had come with the gun and a thirteen-shot from an older Glock 21. He chose the latter for its capacity.

The Blackhawk tactical holster felt stiff as he fastened it. Uncomfortable. After tossing a box of .45 caliber ammo into his pack, he slid the safe back into its hiding spot.

Already in Jake's backpack were extra warm clothes, a small inflatable sleeping pad, and his zero-degree sleeping bag, just in case the search lasted multiple days. He also had a one-liter aluminum water bottle, some iodine tablets, and enough dry food for three meals.

Jake's brain was racing. *What else?* His Costa sunglasses, down sweater, and waterproof shell were in the truck. Downstairs, he grabbed the printed email from Schue, the *Idaho Gazetteer*, and a topo map of the Frank Church Wilderness that surrounded the Salmon River. From the rack next to the front door of the guesthouse he grabbed his wool tuque and his fishing cap.

It was frigid outside. Twenty degrees at best. Small flakes fell from the sky, intermittently pushed by a cold, sharp gust. It took a few miles for Jake's SUV to warm up. He blasted the defroster to clear the windshield. Before he lost his cellular signal, he sent a text message to his neighbor.

Something came up. Please feed Chayote until you hear from me.

In reality, the doggie door in the back was probably enough; the cattle dog was an accomplished hunter of streamside voles. The remains were left for Jake at the back door, where magpies and ravens quarreled over them.

The convenience store at the foot of Teton Pass wasn't open yet, so Jake turned into the Stagecoach Bar to get some coffee. A few drunk patrons remained, playing pool and sad tunes on the juke-box. The bartender looked happy to see a sober face.

"Just a coffee to go, please." Jake pulled out his wallet.

"Early morning? It's on me; just the dregs anyway."

"Thanks."

A twentysomething woman winked at Jake through a horde of flashy skier types: flat-brimmed, ski-rep-giveaway hats and tattered skate shoes. Graphic T-shirts and tank tops that said things like *Live Simply* and *Send It!*

Jake sipped his coffee and let the engine warm in the parking lot. The bartender was right. Dregs. Oh well. He hoped the brew was as strong as it was bitter.

Driving at night was dangerous in the Tetons and the surrounding area. Elk, mule deer, moose, and large predators were active in the dark, and roads provided a travel option for them that they couldn't pass up. The man-made game paths attracted all sorts of fauna. It would be illegal and reckless to drive fast—the highways mostly had special night speed limits to protect animals—but Jake had no doubt that J.P. was speeding.

After Jake hit the summit of the pass at 8,431 feet, his cell phone would get only spotty reception. He called J.P., who was blasting some sad Eddie Vedder song.

J.P. apologized a few times, reiterating that he'd had a bad feeling about whatever was going on with Esma. Jake couldn't blame him. He remembered his concern for Noelle during last summer's escapade. Placating J.P. to the best of his ability, Jake told his friend to wait in the grocery-store parking lot in Salmon, where they could meet up and detail a plan.

For the remainder of the four-hour drive, Jake tried his best to analyze the day's mission through a sleepy head. He knew the basic strategy of a law-enforcement manhunt. But things were different when the target was a victim rather than a perpetrator, and most serious searches involved dozens of trained professionals. Jake and J.P. would have to do their best on their own. If the initial search turned up something that might convince the local police to take notice, the increase in manpower would provide a huge advantage.

There were some things Jake wasn't willing to share with J.P., like the fact that in a true missing-persons case two outcomes dominated the list of results: Most often the whole thing was a miscommunication and got cleared up during the first day. If that didn't happen, the search generally turned into a body recovery.

The other fact Jake was keeping from his old friend was that the hills of Idaho were a longtime haunt for white-supremacist and neo-Nazi groups. Only a hundred or so miles to the west, a small Idaho town called Bad Axe hosted a huge annual rock festival every October featuring neo-Nazi bands. These were the unusual and uncomfortable truths that Jake came to know at the Office of Special Investigations.

Jake stopped for coffee and a bathroom break in Mud Lake, Idaho, a two-hour drive from the area where Esma's cell phone had transmitted. It was 3:36 a.m. on an October Friday, and the fishermen in Mud Lake were having their coffee and cheap gas-station pastries before driving west to Salmon in pursuit of steelhead. Jake wished he were there to fish, rather than search for missing girlfriends.

Outside, a drift boat with high gunwales and a towering bow rested on its trailer. These boats were designed for the rowdy rivers where steelhead often swam. Unlike Jake's skiff, they were built to withstand serious white water.

Steelhead madness took over Idaho, Oregon, and Washington

every autumn. The fish, outsized rainbow trout that grew large in the Pacific Ocean before spawning in freshwater rivers, were revered as a sport fish because of their bulk, strength, and challenge on a hook and line.

To the fly fisherman, steelhead held a position of particularly high acclaim. Their fickle nature—they didn't actively feed when on a spawning run—meant that catching a fish a day was a success. Days and days of being skunked were punctuated by those magical hours when a few foolish fish indulged the angler. This was all part of the allure.

Once hooked, steelhead put up a frantic and acrobatic fight, launching their chrome, missile-like bodies toward the heavens in an attempt to escape the hook. Add the frothy, strong currents of the prototypical steelhead river to the mix, and it was inevitable that hooking a fish was only one small battle in the war. Landing rates on some steelhead rivers dipped below 50 percent.

In the most popular rivers, steelhead, gallivanting romantics from the sea, sneaked through a maze of lures, fly baits, and bare snagging hooks to their spawning grounds. Many never made it.

*Immigrants, really,* Jake thought. *Their survival instincts whisper to them,* Move or perish.

Jake's thought process was interrupted when he missed a right turn near the Idaho National Laboratory.

*Shit!* He swung the SUV around and joined the fishing traffic north toward Salmon.

J.P. was well ahead of Jake. He had just passed Diamond Peak and Scott Peak and was now on the final leg of the journey. Highway 28 rose gradually up toward Lemhi Pass, a modest hill compared with Teton Pass. But the flurries increased with elevation, and the road was slick with windblown snow.

Despite having consumed two energy drinks, J.P. was tired. Drained, really. He had run out of thinking, and he was anxious to act. The swirling winds blew the powdery snow around in psychedelic patterns like a storm cloud developing in a time-lapse sequence. It distracted him, tried to pull him toward sleep.

In the town of Leadore, J.P. pulled his old pickup into a convenience store. It was only 5:15 a.m., and the store was dark.

"Goddammit!" he shouted, to no one in particular. The sound was dampened by the falling snow.

J.P. looked around. There was a house about five hundred yards to the north of the store, but nothing else.

He picked up the thin doormat, a map of Leadore on Highway 28 with the caption *Leadore, Idaho: Ten Miles Past the End of the World*. He looked around one last time, wrapped the mat around his elbow, and smashed through the windowpane closest to the doorknob. No alarm.

*Only illegal if you get caught.*

He reached through the broken pane and unlocked the door. A bell rang when he opened it and startled him. He started to jog back to the truck, but stopped short.

*Fuck it.*

J.P. ran back inside, took a few Red Bulls from the cooler, and grabbed a carton of cigarettes from the rack behind the counter. Before leaving, he shuffled through his pockets and found a twenty-dollar bill, which he left on the counter.

"Sorry," he said, again to no one in particular.

J.P. was on cigarette number five by the time Jake's vehicle pulled into the parking lot. He stubbed it out prematurely and walked briskly to the driver's-side door. It was snowing harder. An inch of snow lay on the asphalt. Dawn was still a ways off, though the pines to the east were silhouetted against a slightly lightened sky. It was 5:20 a.m.

Around them, Jake noticed the sleepy-eyed fishing guides sitting in their rumbling diesel trucks, staying warm while waiting to meet their clients. The early season snow covered their boats. They sipped coffee, ate breakfast burritos, and chewed tobacco.

Steelhead guides had a name for inland trout guides: lucky. The anadromous rainbow trout had several discouraging traits, among them their tendency to stop chasing flies when the sun was high. A steelhead guide's normal day would start hours before dawn, when he would check river flows, read fishing reports, and ready the gear and boat. Then came the rush to beat the crowds to the most productive runs. It was important to be in a run and swinging your fly right at the magic hour before the sun came up. On a cloudless day, clients might be allowed to fish until an hour and a half after sunrise. If they were lucky enough to have a cloudy day, fishing would remain worthwhile longer.

When the sun was high, the guides tried to catch up on sleep on the riverbanks, while the clients buzzed them with questions and fiddled with their gear. Then, after what seemed like an eternity to the clients and a flash to the guides, the group would wander back down to the river and fish until after sunset. A good steelhead guide might spend fourteen or fifteen hours with his clients per day. Not to mention readying the gear before the trip and breaking it all down and cleaning the boat after.

Not that this effort was always reflected in their gratuities—

another reason steelhead guides called trout guides lucky. Often, the hard work resulted in nothing but a short tug, the pull of something that could have been a steelhead. No fish for a picture. No bragging rights. The clients, spoiled by trout-a-plenty, would decide the guide was to blame and leave him a measly forty bucks.

This day looked to be promising; fish numbers in the Salmon River were prime, and the snow-spewing clouds might very well have the steelhead in an aggressive mood.

"Why don't you get in?" Jake said. "We'll have plenty of time today to get wet and cold."

J.P. shrugged and got in the passenger seat. He cranked the defroster and held his hands near the windshield to thaw them.

"You have gloves?" Jake asked.

"Nah. You?"

"In my pack." Jake motioned to the backseat.

"I'll be all right."

"You'll get frostbite. We'll grab you some at a convenience store."

J.P. shrugged again.

"It's going to be tough going out there. We're going to find Esma, but our first priority needs to be ourselves. We can't help her if we're injured or dead."

"Affix your own oxygen mask first, before helping others around you?"

"Exactly."

Jake contorted around in the driver's seat to get the map and Schue's email from the back. When he twisted, J.P. noticed the gun.

"Jake?" He pointed at the weapon. "You think it's that bad?" J.P. looked afraid.

Jake covered the Mariner with his shirt again. "Just being cautious."

Jake unfolded the topo map and set it across his lap. He rested the email attachments depicting the signal area against the steering wheel so he could reference both. He took a short moment in silence to think.

"There's a bridge here, at the campsite." Jake traced a route from the grocery store into the center of Salmon, and then south along the river, to Forest Road 21. "We'll cross the river there, then head up into this network of logging roads. I don't know how passable they will be with this weather. When we can't go any farther, we'll get out and start our search."

"Weather really fucked us, huh?"

Jake looked out the window, contemplating the question.

"No. It will be a little uncomfortable, but easy to see tracks. And if there's a cabin up there, it will be burning a fire. They'll give away their position. Let's get moving."

# 17

It was now evening, and Terrell was still pounding on the door.

"Please, honey! Stop!" Charlotte's loud command startled the chief. He stopped pounding, but the metallic echo of his frantic attempts rang through the basement kitchen, a cruel reply.

"Nobody's coming," she said.

The chief went back to his wife and sat on the floor.

"I'm sure there's some misunderstanding."

"I'm not an idiot," Charlotte said bluntly. "Doesn't take a police chief to figure out that something's going on here."

"You were the one who wanted to come to China." Terrell immediately regretted the comment. "Look, honey, I don't know what's happening, but plenty of people know we're here. They can't do anything to us. It would bring too much trouble—the whole wrath of the United States government."

Charlotte gave him an unimpressed look. "I need water."

"Me too." Terrell stood up and rubbed his wife's shoulders. She started to cry.

"Shhh."

"I just can't take another minute of it in here."

"No, someone's coming."

The heavy steel door swung open. Charlotte instinctively backed into the corner of the room. The chief moved to shield his wife from whatever was coming. The same two outsized men from the morning entered first. Behind them strode a shorter sixtysomething man wearing an elegant three-piece suit. The giants parted, yielding him the stage.

"You're making a big mistake!" Terrell growled, looking Xiao straight in the eyes.

"Take a seat." Xiao spoke in confident English, but with a choppy cadence. The giants stepped away and each grabbed a chair, setting it next to the table. One approached Terrell and Charlotte, intending to guide them to their seats. The chief waved them off and walked toward the seats with his wife.

"Start talking." Terrell tried playing bad cop.

Xiao smirked. "May I get you anything? Tea?"

"Water. We need water. Please."

*Dammit, Charlotte.* Terrell glared at his wife. *Don't show weakness.*

"Of course, Mrs. Terrell." Xiao gestured and the men walked out.

He didn't speak until the men returned with the water. Charlotte downed the first glass quickly, and one of the giants poured her another. The chief took only a single long sip and then settled his eyes upon Xiao.

"Start talking," he repeated.

"In due time, Mr. Terrell. You haven't had anything to eat today. How rude of me. Invite you to breakfast and then starve you." Xiao looked entertained, not apologetic.

"We're fine. Why are we here?" Terrell stood up, causing the giants to close in a few steps.

Xiao said something to the men that Terrell couldn't understand. They took a step back. Then he turned again to the chief. "These men are animals." He laughed. "They don't understand Western hospitality. Take your seat, please." Terrell did as he said. "If you're not hungry . . ."

"Talk," Terrell demanded again.

"Okay. We can talk." Xiao paused for a moment, as if he didn't know where to start. "You know why you are here?"

"Publicity, mayor says. Though I can't imagine news of a kidnapping would bring in visitors."

"You are a smart man." Xiao laughed again. "But you have not been kidnapped. We are just . . . negotiating."

Before the giants could react, Terrell took hold of the lapels on Xiao's suit. "You son of a bitch!"

The bodyguards closed in, but their boss again uttered something that made them desist.

"This is good," Xiao said. "You are frightened. It will motivate you."

"I am *not* frightened. My wife . . ."

"Your wife? Do you think her coming was a . . ." He struggled for the word. "Coincidence?"

Terrell didn't follow.

"I know you better than you think, Roger. I knew you wouldn't cooperate if I didn't raise the stakes." Xiao motioned to Charlotte, who winced. The giants chuckled.

"The fuck do you want?"

"Some language! *Very* frightened, I see."

Terrell remained in Xiao's face.

"You do not have sense for the dramatic, do you, Mr. Terrell?" Xiao paused again. "Fine, we can get to it, if you insist."

Terrell finally backed off and went to his wife. "It's going to be okay, honey."

Xiao took off his shiny blue pinstriped jacket. Underneath was a tailored white shirt, suspenders, a vest, and a stylish turquoise-and-apple-red patterned tie.

"Where to start?" He paced back and forth. "Ah. The beginning is as good a place as any, I believe."

Xiao took a moment to prepare his soliloquy.

"You see, Mr. Terrell, I am very fortunate man. Have always been. My father was a vice-premier on the Guowuyuan—the state council. A very important man indeed. My mother was an engineering professor at Peking University—one of the first females to achieve renown in her field. My childhood was a dream—travel to foreign countries, exotic pets . . ."

"Good for you. I grew up on a tract of dirt and cow shit. I don't see how any of this matters to us," Terrell interrupted.

"Bear with me." Xiao's tone shifted, his face became grave. The levity with which he had treated their initial interaction was gone.

"At Peking, when I was young man, I met Mei Li. She was the most beautiful and graceful person I ever met. She still is." His dark eyes turned cloudy. "I wooed her as best I could. Fine dinners, beautiful flowers, clothes from New York, Milan, Paris."

He halted again, the memory obviously haunting him. He cleared his throat and started anew.

"None of it worked. She shunned me. She acted as though she was embarrassed by me. I was the laughingstock at university. I wasn't dissuaded by her scorn. Instead, I was enthralled. I knew she would be my wife; I just had to figure out how to court her.

"I enrolled in Tang poetry class, because I knew she had done it too. As the end of the school year approached, I recited for her a famous poem. It translates as 'Alone in Her Beauty':

*Who is lovelier than she?*
*Yet she lives alone in an empty valley.*

"I won't bore you with the rest, but after this recital, Mei Li soon became mine. We wed a year later to the day."

Terrell was thinking. This type of story was just what he needed. Exactly what any criminal negotiator would like to hear. It was an in. Xiao's weakness.

"Go on," Terrell urged. Xiao seemed pleased at his interest.

"She was . . . she *is* the love of my life. In the fall of 1981, we had our first and only child, Meirong. By that time, I had created my technology empire in China. We raised Meirong in the opulence of my heritage and the wisdom of Mei Li's. Meirong was an angel—smart, beautiful, and kind. You would say *special*.

"By sixteen, Meirong was ready for university. I wanted to send her to the States, where she could benefit from the best education. Mei Li disagreed. Thought it would be safer in China. She had fallen into a slump, become wrapped up in politics. Something inside her started to change after Tiananmen Square in '89.

"Her life became secretive. Because of her family's affiliation with Chairman Mao's wife, Jiang Qing, many speculated that she was part of an effort to revive the Gang of Four. She told me nothing."

"Gang of Four?" the chief asked.

"Communist hard-liners, according to Westerners."

Terrell only nodded, trying to guess where this drama would climax. He figured the story didn't end with Xiao feeling the love between China and the United States.

Xiao continued. "In 1999, while having coffee alone in our home, my wife was shot once through the temple. She died instantly. The investigation led nowhere. The only information we had was path of the bullet—from a neighbor's roof through our kitchen window and into my wife's brain. To this day, her death is mystery."

Charlotte wrapped her arms around herself and shuddered.

"I'm sorry," Terrell said. Seeing his own wife in danger now, he meant it. "So you are exacting your revenge on the US? Why?"

Xiao wiped a tear from his cheek and then laughed. "I am too old to be interested in revenge. And I have no reason to believe your country is responsible. My wife was troubled. Smart, but indignant. She may have made any number of enemies inside or outside China."

"Then what?"

"Ah." Xiao helped himself to a glass of water. "Then, we come to Meirong."

"Your daughter. She is in the States. Bullet told us. In Jackson, maybe." Terrell was trying to disarm Xiao with his knowledge of the situation.

"Yes."

"How do you know where she is?" Charlotte piped up. Terrell shot her another look.

"I have no doubt where she is." He spoke forcefully. "She loves your valley. There, she is free from the crowded streets of Beijing and the shadow of her mother."

"So you built Tram Village as a temple to her?"

"Temples are built on faith. I am much more pragmatic. Tram Village is a bait."

"You want to draw her back here with an amusement park?"

Xiao didn't seem insulted by Terrell's slight. "No. I aim to *take* her back, and *keep* her with my amusement park."

Xiao's intentions became clear to Terrell.

"In a few minutes, my men will bring you a telephone. You will inform your people of your situation. Do not attempt to give them our location. May I remind you that your wife's safety hangs in the balance. Do not let her meet the same fate as my wife."

One of the giants opened the door for Xiao, who stopped in the doorway and peered back. "When I see my daughter face-to-face, you will be free to go."

The heavy door slammed shut.

# 18

"Right here." Jake handed J.P. a pair of thick fingerless wool fishing gloves. Luckily, they'd found an open convenience store that carried basic supplies.

J.P. frowned.

"Here's your other option." Jake held up bright-yellow cleaning gloves made of latex.

"I'll take 'em both."

Jake paid for the gloves.

They left J.P.'s pickup in the parking lot and moved his gear into Jake's SUV. As they pulled away from the store, J.P. pulled on the latex gloves and then put the wool ones over them.

"Good look for you."

"Poor man's GORE-TEX."

As they crossed the river, Jake looked down at the swirling, leaden flow. This time he felt no relief. It moved along doggedly, stubborn like a mule. Nothing in this place gave away its secrets without a fight. Finding Esma was going to be like pursuing steelhead: frustrating and exhausting.

But harder. Finding a needle in a haystack? More like finding an honest man in Washington. At 4.3 million acres, the Salmon-Challis National Forest was one of the most massive pieces of wilderness south of Alaska.

After the bridge, Jake drove up the hill through Salmon's main residential area, turned left, and headed south, veering from the course of the river. The road was up and down as they left the flood plain and started their climb to the hamlet closest to the last known transmission from Esma's phone. Nothing but a few old buildings marked their arrival. Despite the infinitesimal size of the roadside quasi suburb, it was their best bet. They were ten miles outside the town.

They approached the first of the buildings, a concrete-block service station. An old Conoco sign hung crookedly from its moorings. Around its pedestal, a mound of snow enveloped a pad of thick grass. Jake pulled the SUV alongside the pumps. They had been raided for valuable parts. The office next door, connected to an old Craftsman bungalow home, was abandoned. There were no vehicles in working condition anywhere in sight.

"Great," J.P. said.

"I'm going to take a look around. Wait here."

For the first time in nearly a decade, Jake put a full clip in the Mariner with the distinct knowledge he might hurl one of its charges at something other than a target.

He left the attached flashlight turned off and returned the weapon to its holster. The light around the old house was still dim, but improving. As Jake walked, he looked for tracks. Nothing but filled-in rabbit tracks and frozen mule-deer droppings.

No interior lights shone in the complex—the station or the house. Jake removed his glove and held his bare hand against a window. No heat. No sign of anyone.

He rounded the back corner. Behind it, a sprawling pine forest remained stubbornly dark, still unlit by the early signs of sunrise. The back door was silently swinging in the wind. Jake kept moving, approaching the far corner of the structure.

A barely audible shuffle. A movement of feet. Jake pressed his back against the house and opened his coat to access the Mariner. He took two deep breaths. It was important to stay calm. Make quick but intelligent decisions. Pay attention. If he rounded that corner without a plan he would fall into adrenaline's trap—shoot first and ask questions later.

One more deep breath. The footfalls were getting closer, only five or ten feet from making the corner. Jake quickly pulled the Mariner, checked that the safety was off, and peeled off the wall, ready for whatever was coming. Few people knew that it was often easier to surprise foes by allowing them to come to you. That way you remained totally silent—no footsteps, no heavy breathing.

Jake took on a wide stance to ensure accuracy against the gun's recoil and waited.

In the dim light, the first thing Jake registered was a large, dark, and distinctly human shape. Next was the shout.

"Jesus Christ!"

The shape tried to turn around too fast, slipped, and fell into the snow.

"Put that thing away!" J.P. shouted again. This time from on his behind.

"I said to wait in the car!" Jake tucked the Mariner away and helped his friend up.

"I'm not just gonna sit around while you play cops and robbers! I can help."

"I didn't say you couldn't. *What* is going on with you?"

J.P lit a cigarette while still trying to catch his breath. "I'm just worried, man. Stressed. And do you think it makes me feel like a man to be Superman's sidekick?"

"It's not like that." Jake helped J.P. brush the snow off himself. "I couldn't do this alone, okay? Let's just communicate better."

J.P. looked down at the ground. "Deal. Sorry."

"All right, let's keep moving. This place is a bust."

"The bar?"

"Yeah. Let's check it out."

The Silver Doctor, a quarter-mile farther south, was in even worse shape than the gas station. Together, Jake and J.P. systematically checked the premises. No heat, no lights, and no signs in the newly fallen snow.

Before they left the parking lot, they rifled through their bags, checking items off out loud, so that nothing would be forgotten.

"You're expecting to spend the night, huh?" J.P. seemed discouraged by this.

"I'm expecting the unexpected."

The duo got back in the vehicle and cranked the heat. By now, a few other folks were up and about. Cars and pickup trucks passed by occasionally, their passengers undoubtedly wondering what two men with Wyoming plates were doing at the dilapidated tavern.

The abandoned buildings shed no light on Esma's whereabouts. The next most likely source of the signal was the hunting cabins in the hills. Jake pointed the truck past the Silver Doctor, continuing south. An intersecting road turned from asphalt to dirt just within their view. The snowfall had lessened in the valley, but a thick veil of white suggested that wasn't so at higher elevations.

"That's our logging-road network there. Access to the cabins. If anyone asks, we're hunters scouting around."

J.P. nodded.

The dirt road was passable for just over five miles from the tiny town. At that point, a mountain stream stopped their progress.

"This is it." Jake pulled the vehicle over.

"We can get through that, man."

"No. Not worth it. We can't search for Esma if we're down here trying to unstick the truck."

Jake put the SUV in park and headed to the tailgate. J.P. shrugged and pulled on his two pairs of new gloves, then joined Jake around back. Both men hoisted their heavy packs onto their shoulders.

"What's our plan of attack?"

"This two-track forks in two miles. Right goes to the base of Mount Baldy and left to Mount Phelan. I say we go right first—it's the longer ascent—while we have fresh legs."

J.P. nodded and began hopping his way across the creek, being careful to step only on dry rocks. Jake wore heavy-duty backcountry boots, completely waterproof, and he plodded through a shallow gravel bar.

As they rose in elevation, the forest was composed mainly of pure, dense stands of grand firs with low branches, which limited visibility. Jake climbed the occasional rocky outcropping to try to gain perspective on their progress. Even from the perches, they saw nothing but forest.

The only tracks visible in the snow belonged to rodents, elk, and mule deer. Jake stopped every minute or so to brush away the few inches of fluff and check the ground beneath him for footprints in the frozen dirt below.

*Bingo.* He spotted a new kind of print. Well-defined horse tracks in the hardened muck and boot prints alongside. Their definition meant that they hadn't been through a freeze-thaw cycle. At most, they were a week old—when the last cold front came and went.

"Definitely hunters back here." Jake was crouched over a set of tracks. J.P. turned back to look over his friend's shoulder.

"Whaddya see?"

"Just horses and a footprint here and there. Doesn't mean much." Jake stood and started walking again.

"What sort of stuff should I be looking for?" J.P. hustled to catch up.

"Anything out of the ordinary. A small footprint maybe, piece of clothing, anything like that. If we come across fresh tracks, we'll follow them to their end. I say we head toward the hunting camps atop Mount Baldy. Anything sticks out on the way, we'll check it out."

The clouds eventually parted as the sun came up. The modest warmth was a welcome relief. Still, Mount Baldy wouldn't concede without a fight. As Jake and J.P. approached the last section of the ascent, the slope steepened. The trail that hunters used to access the cabins was littered with downed trees, made slick by the newly fallen snow. They pressed on.

Despite the fire, Esma was freezing. And because of it, she was having some difficulty breathing. Around midnight, the men lit a few pieces of damp tinder and one long four-by-eight on the dirt floor. The smoke from the wet, moldy wood had no way to escape, and they had left her chained fifteen feet away, where the heat from the damp pyre was negligible. She prayed for a painless death from carbon monoxide poisoning.

Was she shivering from the cold or the memory of what the men had done to her the night before? Her body ached, her spirit broken. She fought back at first, but it only made things more miserable for her. The shackles had scraped against her wrists and ankles as the men got angrier.

She'd passed out from pain and fear after about an hour. When she awoke, her body was bruised and beaten. Her clothes were in tatters.

A creak. The sound of the crude wooden door opening. She lay still on her side, the same pose the men had left her in hours ago.

Tinny looked down when he entered. He didn't dare say a word. Despite his passive demeanor, he had been aggressive when he raped her. There was strength in those slim, fibrous muscles.

Now, he played at being gentle. He bent down in front of her and took something out of his pocket. A tube. Tinny pulled Esma's shirt aside and dabbed Neosporin on a tiny wound below her left clavicle. A scratch, likely. A mark of blood not much bigger than a pinhead.

"Up here, I think." J.P. had taken the lead, cigarette hanging from his lips. Jake had to admit that his friend possessed more endurance than predicted, given his generally bad physical condition.

"One to the right and the other to the left?" It was 11 a.m., and they were near the top. At almost nine thousand feet, the snow was deep—seven inches or more.

"Yeah." The trail split. According to the satellite images Jake had printed, one route led to a camp on the northeast shoulder of Mount Baldy, just below a sheer cliff, and the other led to a cabin atop Baldy's western ridge.

"Take the right first." The cabin below the cliff was more difficult to access. Jake wanted to get the more rigorous route over with as early as possible.

He saw the occasional rifle shell and more elk tracks: desperate animals fleeing the snow cover to find food. Jake checked the rounds. All were popular hunting cartridges, nothing overtly suspect about them.

J.P. sped up as the cabin came into view. They had traveled just over a mile from the split. The sun was shining brightly and the snow had become wet. It soaked J.P. up to the knees. The birds were out, chirping and exploring a world that had changed from fall to winter and back again overnight.

Jake whistled, and J.P. stopped. Jake waved him over.

He whispered, "Let's do a walk around the tree line first. Scope things out. Keep yourself hidden."

J.P. pointed one way, counterclockwise around the structure, then pointed for Jake to go clockwise. Jake nodded.

After J.P. started on his way, Jake pulled the Mariner and made sure there was a round in the chamber. Then he clicked the safety back on, hoping it would stay that way.

The log cabin was constructed of native Douglas fir. It was a traditional one-and-a-half story retreat with its loft bedroom visible through large casement windows on either side's gable. Its footprint was no more than 20x30. Woodstove, judging by the narrow chimney. No indoor plumbing—there was an outhouse near the perimeter of the neglected yard, Jake assumed. A summer cottage.

Still, he took his time looking. There was a possibility they had been detected and whoever was in the cabin was waiting in ambush. It was unlikely, but he'd been trained to assume the worst.

Halfway through his walk, when J.P. was directly across the large yard and obscured by the cabin, Jake heard a whooping noise. He scanned the cabin and listened more carefully. Nobody was in sight. Jake bolted for the front of the building, worried about his friend. As he got closer, J.P. started yelling. "Got something! Hurry, man!"

J.P. was fixated on something far away. "C'mon! Get over here! Thought you were in shape!"

Jake struggled to catch his breath after sprinting across the uneven, brushy flat at elevation. "Guess not. What do you see?"

J.P. pointed across a hollow. Jake followed his gesture up to the top of Mount Phelan. There, on a promontory overlooking the river, tiny puffs of smoke popped through the thick grand firs, rising skyward.

"You think it's . . . ?"

Jake deflected. "Only one way to find out."

# 19

Jake's and J.P.'s progress was minuscule in comparison to the scale of the terrain around them. J.P. was exerting himself to keep their pace up, despite Jake's warnings. The duo were already exhausted and sweaty—not a good combination if they ended up spending the night in the backcountry. Exhaustion and moisture led to hypothermia. For now, though, the sun was shining and the temperature was in the fifties.

"Fuckin' moths everywhere!" J.P. waved his hand in front of his face as they crossed a creek.

"*Dicosmoecus*. October caddis. There won't be many once we get away from the water."

"Disco moth!" J.P. lunged out of his way to smack a bug out of the air and almost fell into the creek himself.

"Nice recovery." Jake reached out and caught one of the caddis.

132

He hadn't been fishing in over a week, between Divya's project and winterizing the bed-and-breakfast. This hatch, the October caddis, was the final act of the dry fly season. The bugs were three-quarters of an inch long and meaty—approaching the size of their larger cousin, the stone fly. They would draw big fish to the surface.

Trout, like all living things, have an innate sense of impending hardship. As temperatures began to drop in the fall, the fish responded by stuffing themselves with as many calories as possible—great for fishing. The way things were looking, Jake wouldn't have a chance to capitalize on this reckless behavior.

"How much farther, you think?"

"A ways." Jake looked toward the top of Mount Phelan, then back toward Baldy, where they had come from. He checked the elevation on his watch. Their lack of progress was discouraging. They were back at the same elevation they'd started from early that morning.

Instead of retracing their steps, Jake and J.P. decided to descend Baldy's south face, directly facing Phelan. The route was more direct, but the terrain more challenging. Sharp and uneven volcanic rock rolled and tumbled under their feet. J.P. fell twice, cutting his hand badly between his thumb and forefinger. Rejecting Jake's first aid, he made do with tying a sweaty bandana around the wound.

The north face of Phelan was steep and daunting. After they had crossed the creek and begun their ascent, a thick forest of pines slowed their pace. Downed trees on steep uphill slopes meant lots of work—climbing and scrapping their way over the obstacles. The heavy packs and melting snow wore on them.

\*       \*       \*

Two and a half hours later, the summit was still not within sight. The thick pine forests had given way to steep, wet cliffs and rocky spines. To make matters worse, the cooling afternoon temperatures brought snow showers.

"I don't know but I been told . . ." J.P. hummed the rest of the cadence call, not knowing the words.

"We need to stop soon and eat something." Neither man had taken any sustenance since before sunrise.

J.P. turned around, reached in his pocket, and tossed a Nature Valley granola bar back at Jake. He started walking again.

"Not enough."

J.P.'s shoulders slumped in resignation and he walked back toward his friend.

Jake already had taken off his pack, an old blue Osprey, removed his small stove, and lit the burner. He gathered snow from the shade of a tree, swiped the forest debris from the top layer, and packed it into a pot.

Setting the pot on the stove to boil, Jake sat on a downed tree and motioned for J.P. to join him.

"I'm fine." He lit a smoke.

Jake just shrugged. He pulled off his stiff hiking boots, then his socks, and let his clammy feet dry in the cold air. Satisfied, he reached in the pack and pulled out a fresh pair of hiking socks.

"Always prepared, huh?"

"Who likes wet socks?"

The water was starting to steam, but J.P. was getting antsy. He kicked at the ground and broke dead branches from a surrounding tree, then tossed them at nothing.

"Sit down, J.P. Relax for a minute."

J.P. sauntered over and sat.

Jake gave him a hard look. "We'll find her."

Above them in the canopy, ravens popped from branch to branch, waiting for food scraps. Jake stood and went to the boiling water. He carried it carefully to his pack, where he pulled out his foodstuffs.

"Chinese noodles or Easy Mac?"

"Mix 'em?"

Jake laughed. "Hell yeah. Party time."

The hot food tasted good—not only necessary calories but also a morale booster. Jake cleaned the pot and the backpacking sporks and stashed his kit.

J.P. was still sitting, elbows on his knees, face in hands. Jake sat next to him again.

"What's going on?"

"I just wanna find her. You know, protect her. Remember how protective you were of Noelle after all that shit?"

Jake thought back. He missed Noelle deeply, but there was nothing to be done about it at the moment. Maybe nothing to be done about it at all. But what Divya had done, the whole sloppy mess of it, only reminded Jake of how genuinely he cared for the park ranger. "I know what you mean."

It sounded hollow. He was still distracted, thinking of Noelle. *What a mess.* It had gone from perfect to awful so quickly. As with a fickle trout stream, there was no real explanation for the change in conditions. One day, they were happy. The next, Jake was hinting that maybe things were going too fast.

And Noelle's response had broken his heart. *If you think that's the case, we'll take a break.* How could Jake explain that was not what he meant?

Jake had figured that if she wanted to put their break to an end, she would do so with a phone call. It never came. He wanted to write it off as lack of interest from Noelle, though his better judgment said that wasn't the case.

When he'd seen her around town, she looked happy. Still glowing as she always did, seemingly untroubled. This hurt him. But Jake had feigned normalcy during their interactions—maybe she was doing the same?

His final conclusion was that he wasn't going to take the risk of finding out. *If she wants to, she'll call,* remained his motto.

J.P. interrupted. "Obviously, it is weird, then."

"Huh?"

"To be so paranoid that she doesn't care about me anymore. I mean, half of me thinks we might find her shacked up with someone else."

Jake refocused on his friend, who needed his attention more than his self-imposed problems.

"It's not weird. You care for her. C'mon, we're not going to find her with someone else." Jake looked uphill; he could see the smoke from the cabin's fire again in the distance.

*Really,* he thought, *finding Esma with someone else wouldn't be so bad. At least it probably wouldn't involve a gun fight.* He looked back at J.P.'s distraught face. *Probably.*

"Wanna get moving?" J.P. was still sitting on the log.

"It's just that things like this don't happen to me very often. You know, the beautiful-girl scenario."

They were still two miles or so from the rising smoke. At least a two-hour climb in this terrain, Jake thought. They better get going. He didn't want to be poking around enemy territory in the dark. But J.P.'s face said he needed a moment. Jake joined him again on the log.

"I've gotta say, Jake—seeing you with Noelle was tough, man. I mean, it made me jealous or whatever." J.P. gave his friend a sheep-ish look before looking down again at the forest floor. A few wet snowflakes were shoved around by the wind.

*We should get moving.*

Jake clapped J.P. on the back. "And see how that turned out?" He laughed awkwardly. Heart-to-heart wasn't his strong suit. "What I mean is, the grass is always greener."

"Never happened before," J.P. blurted.

"Sorry?"

"I never had a girl I really liked, okay? Shit, man! Don't make me feel stupid."

"I—"

J.P. interrupted. "I mean, I've had my moments. Tourist chicks, ninety-day wonders, whatever, but, like, I don't know . . ." Jake had heard the stories before. Some of the flings he'd heard first-hand all the way from the trailer.

"It's tough. I mean, I've never had a girl before where people are like 'good for you,' you know? I guess that means she's outta my league."

"Esma's not out of your league. You two are a good match."

Another look. *You mean that?* Jake nodded to affirm his senti-ment.

A cold gust. More snow. *Shit.* Jake had seen this before. Tough conditions and an unknown outcome compounded by emotional breakdown: it was a recipe for disaster. J.P. needed a serious pep talk. He needed to feel the resolve that was necessary to stay focused.

But J.P. was no military man. Not a cop. He was a ski bum from a cozy small town. He hadn't hardened like the people Jake knew from his days at the Office. It was a fine line—push him too far, and maybe he cracks. It was a normal human reaction.

"I just need to find her." J.P. was shaking his head, nearly in tears.

*Goddammit.* It was a long walk back to the vehicle, and night was coming.

J.P. looked up at Jake with cloudy eyes. Jake looked back and saw a broken man. There was far more going on inside J.P.'s head than a missing girlfriend. Unfortunately for Jake, that was the easiest problem to solve.

J.P. cleared his throat. A blink cleared his eyes of the moisture. He was still looking at Jake, but now directly, his focus piercing through the remaining emotion.

*Strength,* Jake thought. *Determination.* Maybe his happy-go-lucky friend was not to be taken lightly.

Jake stood abruptly and pulled J.P. up by his shirt. The two friends were standing face-to-face.

"We're going to get Esma back."

Picking up his pack, Jake started uphill at a reinvigorated pace. J.P. scrambled to follow.

"All right! Do I get a gun?" he shouted through the brush.

"Nope," Jake said, without turning around.

# 20

**TRAM VILLAGE, CHINA.**

In the windowless room, time was a mystery. No clock. Terrell was sure this was intentional. Looking around—the heavy door and sterile, drab interior—he wondered if the entire room had been designed for this very purpose. It wasn't a stretch; this whole damned village was a put-up job.

Xiao seemed harmless thus far—a benevolent kidnapper. But there was no doubt that he was dead set on getting Meirong home. And regardless of his demeanor, there was no way Terrell was going to leave Charlotte unguarded, just in case the giants came back to underscore how serious Xiao was.

She slept, which surprised Terrell. She lay on the olive-green canvas cot, facing the far wall. He couldn't tell whether she was still mad at him or simply exhausted and afraid.

The accommodations were basic but not inhumane, apart from

the chilly air in the room: two military-style cots, old wool bivvy sacks, and the same down pillows used in the hotel. There were a case of water and a few snacks. True to Tram Village's promise, they were American—beef jerky, potato chips, and Red Vines licorice.

For Terrell, sleepless nights were usually spent mulling over work. *Who did what and why?* The prior night had been the same, albeit with higher stakes. He wasn't an outsider looking into a crime anymore. He was living the crime, start to finish, whatever it might be. The who, what, and why were in plain sight.

Instead, he tried to predict Xiao's next move. In his day job, Terrell didn't rely on offender profiling often, but the state required him to attend occasional seminars on the latest science of the criminal mind. The most recent one had been only a year ago.

Criminal profiling focused partly on determining where the offender lived or where he might strike next, which was of no interest to the chief. Terrell wanted to know *what* Xiao would do next. He knew damn well where.

*Right here in this room.*

Now, in what he assumed were the very early morning hours, he was finally painting a picture of Xiao, the man. *Rich, yes. Determined, yes. Insane? Violent?* He wanted his daughter back—that motive was obvious. Or was it? These were the more difficult questions. Was the mogul a normal father whose upbringing told him he could get anything he wanted? Or was he a power-hungry psychopath?

The answers to these questions were the key to getting himself and his wife out of China safely. He looked at Charlotte sleeping. *Or at least my wife.*

If Xiao was merely a wounded father who wanted his daughter back, it made sense for the Terrells to wait it out. *Do what Xiao asks and get the deal done.* On the other hand, if Xiao was a bloodthirsty psychopath, escape was their only option. Even if Meirong was returned safely, they didn't have a chance in hell of getting out alive if that was the case.

Terrell's blurry watercolor was beginning to suggest the scarier of the two options—that Xiao was unstable, at best. All the major signs of a psychopathic personality were there: narcissism, high intelligence, ostensible charm, no remorse for his actions. *Classic.* His poetry infatuation screamed obsession.

The most convincing factor, though, was his desire to have Meirong back, without regard for her own wishes. This was not a man who loved his daughter. A psychopath didn't love. It was ego: to show that no one could abandon him and get away with it. To make up for his wife's death.

*Then how to escape?*

The previous night, the chief had called Layle under the supervision of the giants. It had been a mistake on Xiao's part to be absent; Terrell could talk freely to his deputy without the giants understanding him.

"Look for the girl," he told Layle. "Don't let her know you're there. And don't tell anyone yet—I think there's more to this than Xiao is letting on. I'm sure he will keep us in touch."

Layle understood. He agreed not to contact the embassy or the feds. Once they played that card, things would get ugly: the Chinese government would fabricate some story to justify their imprisonment. Politics would get in the way of a simple transaction. He much preferred to get Meirong to Beijing without that fuss.

Charlotte stirred, and Terrell went to stand by her, but she didn't wake. He bent and ran his fingers through her hair. The toll of the kidnapping was getting to him, even though it had probably been only one night. Instead of succumbing to his emotions, he straightened and took stock of the room.

Two cots with weak aluminum frames. *No good as a clubbing weapon, but maybe potential to sharpen to a point.* A table built with similarly light metals. It would work to stand on and access a window or vent, but there was none. Whoever had set up the cell had thought of that. The chairs were useless, light and cheap. *Damn.* The bedding could be used as a garrote, but that would be useless against the giants. A white painter's bucket for relieving themselves, which Charlotte had refused to use.

The door was flung open. Charlotte startled awake and sat up.

The giants marched in. Tight black mock turtlenecks and baggy military-style pants. Work boots. Their faces were emotionless.

Behind them came Xiao, smiling. He wore a starched sky-blue Oxford and expensive linen pants instead of the full suit. Terrell could see his physique now, compact but muscular. He held a tray of food. American again—eggs and bacon with fresh melon. Coffee. The air from outside the room rushed in, carrying the scent of the food.

Terrell didn't say a word.

"Good morning," Xiao started. "I hope you had a good night's rest." His smile turned into a smirk.

"What do you want?"

"Only to bring breakfast."

Xiao parted the giants, who stepped back and stood on either side of the open door, arms crossed.

"Americans love their coffee, do they not?"

Terrell poured some for himself and his wife.

"I have to use the restroom," Charlotte piped up. Terrell

winced. Xiao waved his hand, and one of the giants pulled her from the room by her arm.

The room was silent. Terrell eyed his captors, now reduced to a single superhuman with his sixtysomething, flamboyant master. Still, Terrell had no weapon, no advantage. He hadn't had time to sharpen a length of aluminum from the cot. When Xiao had turned to allow Charlotte out, Terrell noticed the gleam of a silver revolver tucked into the back of his pants. Intricately etched and polished, it was gaudy and expensive, but still deadly. He could only assume the giant was armed too. This wasn't his opportunity.

"Ah!" Xiao finally spoke, seemingly excited. "I have a gift for you." He reached into his pants pocket and pulled out an old cell phone. Terrell took it. The back was covered in duct tape.

"I've altered it," Xiao said, smiling with satisfaction. "It will call only the number you used last night. Your deputy."

Terrell must have looked confused.

"You may talk to him whenever you'd like. We are conducting transparent business transaction," the old plutocrat said, holding his palms out to Terrell. "You may tell him everything. Your conditions, your treatment. I hope it will convince him that I am reasonable."

"Let Charlotte go. If you want to appear reasonable."

Xiao took a seat and opened the bag of jerky. He held it out to Terrell, who refused, then to the giant, who took a large hunk. The behemoth tore into it like a starved dog.

"I wish I could. A woman should not be subjected to such things." Xiao's attempt at warmth came off as sexism rather than chivalry. He smelled the bag of jerky, then put it down on the table and wiped his hands on his pants. "I mentioned before, I know you well, though we've never met. You are a man of justice, beyond all other concerns." A smirk. "Your cooperation is best when you have a clear head. When you remember what's important. We don't want you making any rash decisions."

"What if I tell Layle to alert the consulate? You'll bring on a hell storm."

"I would advise you against that, Chief Terrell. Do not forget that China is a strong nation, with willpower. Our officials will not simply raid Tram Village on your deputy's word. They will argue with your consulate, draw things out. Maybe move you from here to prison, if I say the right thing."

"And you would start a war for your country."

"I am not afraid of war." Xiao stood, snapped his fingers, and left with the giant.

A minute or so later, Charlotte was shoved back into the room, and the door slammed shut. Terrell was sitting at the table, staring at the cell phone.

# 21

"We really can't have a fire?" It was almost midnight. The flanks of Mount Phelan were covered in snow again. The air was cold but still.

Jake had just fallen sleep. He sighed. "No fire. Go to sleep."

"You don't have any whiskey?" J.P. sounded like a child asking for candy.

"Didn't make the list of necessities."

"I can't fall asleep without a little drink."

"Now's a good time to learn."

Jake and J.P. had summited Phelan at 9 p.m. and confirmed that the hunting camp was occupied. No doubt about it. To J.P.'s dismay, Jake had insisted they wait until morning to make their move. There was no sense in wandering into a potentially volatile situation blind. From a few hundred yards out, all they could see

145

was the smoke and an occasional shadow moving through the main cabin.

They camped a half mile away. A bright waxing crescent moon intermittently shone through snow clouds, giving an eerie feel to the forest. Two saw-whet owls beckoned back and forth.

J.P. wasn't the only one trying to keep his mind from reeling. Jake had plenty to think about too—most pressing, what was the plan for daybreak? He was still holding out hope that if Esma was in the cabin, there was a reasonable explanation. Clearing her head with some friends, whatever. In that case, a knock on the door was all that was necessary.

He wouldn't go in guns blazing; that much was obvious. Approach from downwind—whoever was in the cabin could have dogs. This was something he'd overlooked on an assignment before, and it cost him his target.

More brainstorming: *Be careful not to reveal your intentions too early, in case Esma has been taken by hostiles.*

The lost hunter was his best bet. Play it dumb: *Howdy! Is So-and-So here?* Any name but Esma. Get a feel for the situation. Of course, there was still the chance that she wasn't there at all. The only thing they knew was that Esma's phone had transmitted in the area. And this call—from the River of No Return—was the *only* trace of her in the last several days. Stolen phone, just passing through—there were plenty of possibilities.

Jake flipped over in his sleeping bag, finding the new position equally uncomfortable. Another saw-whet call, like a boiling tea-pot. The tranquility of the woods was a burden, allowing too much space for thought.

He rolled onto his back again and closed his eyes. J.P. was snoring. So much for the whiskey rule. He couldn't get over the name of the mountain. *Phelan. Why does it sound familiar?* It wasn't coming together. His legs were restless, stiff and sore from walking. He did the best he could to clear his mind and find sleep.


Jake woke up before dawn. His arm was numb from sleeping on it. He let J.P. sleep a few extra minutes while he prepared coffee and oatmeal. Another two inches of snow had fallen. He changed socks; his had become sweaty from the down bag. He packed his pad and sleeping bag into their sacks. Then he loaded the Mariner, making sure there was a round in the chamber. The laser sight cut through his foggy breath on its way to an Aspen trunk forty yards out. He put his finger on the trigger, took a deep breath and held it. Just as he was trained. "Bang," he whispered. He exhaled, turned off the sight, and stuffed the Glock into its holster.

J.P. woke up on his own, to Jake's surprise. Without saying a word, he quickly broke down his tent and packed away his sleeping gear. When he was ready, he walked over to Jake and poured himself some coffee.

"Oatmeal?" Jake asked.

He shook his head. "Nervous stomach. How you feeling?"

"Good."

"Confident?"

"Confidence is arrogance. I'm hopeful." Jake was scarfing down some oatmeal, still wearing his headlamp, which he'd turned to its dull-red setting so the light wouldn't carry.

"What's the plan?" J.P. poured himself more coffee.

"Just go observe for a few minutes. If we don't see anything suspicious, I'll approach the camp and see what's what."

"And me?"

"I have experience with this sort of thing. I'd rather you hang back."

J.P. seemed disappointed but didn't protest.

The hike to the perimeter of the camp took twenty minutes. They sat on a snow-covered tree trunk a hundred yards away. Jake held his index finger to his lips to remind J.P. to stay silent. J.P. responded with a series of hand gestures, mimicking a Hollywood FBI agent. In any other circumstance, Jake would've laughed.

After fifteen minutes, there was still no sign of life at the cabin but for the thick, lazy smoke of a dying fire. The sun was struggling to shine through the spotty snow clouds.

Jake gestured for his friend to come close. "I'm gonna go in."

J.P. nodded.

On his way to the front door, Jake took some deep breaths and rolled his neck, trying to settle his nerves. It was a fine line—he didn't want adrenaline to overpower his common sense, but he had to be on edge enough to react quickly if things went south. He made sure the Glock was covered by his pullover before approaching.

The cabin was old and dilapidated, not unusual for a hunting camp. It being so isolated, there was no easy way to bring in materials for a renovation. Jake first looked in the front windows. The woodstove was barely glowing—it hadn't been fed since the night before. A few rifles and a shotgun lay on the kitchen counter. He expected as much, but it still concerned him.

The back windows, presumably bedrooms, were covered with burlap curtains. He continued around the property. An awning extending from one side, walled in with hanging tarpaulins. Jake heard something inside. *Shit.* His heart began to race. *Not good. Relax.* He stayed still for a moment and listened. The noise continued.

Jake spoke quietly so as not to wake anyone inside. "Hello? Who's there?" Silence for a moment, then the noise resumed. He pulled his fleece up over his holster for easy access.

"Hello?"

There was no response. He approached an opening in the tarp, took one more breath and entered.

A loud fracas. Rushing air. Jake's hand went instinctively to the gun. Three or four magpies flushed past him and out the opening. *Jesus.*

Jake looked around—hanging from meat hooks were four cow moose, an illegal take in this area. The men in the cabin were at least poachers, if not much, much worse.

Looking around for any trace of Esma under the awning, Jake found nothing but a few hunting knives and a bone saw. There was an open screen door between the tarped-in area and the cabin. It creaked in the soft wind.

Jake hustled back out before he was heard or seen. Poachers were nothing to shrug at—they could be dangerous and defensive, and there was no doubt they were armed.

As he walked around the last corner of the structure to get back to the front door, he saw J.P. at the tree line, frantically waving his arms. Jake started to jog back toward his friend to see what was the matter.

"Stop right there, motherfucker."

Jake stopped, put his hands up in surrender and started to turn to face his adversary.

"I didn't say turn around!"

Jake glanced over his shoulder.

"Eyes straight ahead, asshole!"

Jake had seen what he suspected. A hunting rifle, likely a 30-06, was aimed squarely between his shoulder blades. The man was thin and weathered.

"The fuck do you want?"

"We got lost." Jake's hands were still up. Soon they would start trembling from the strain. "Looking for a buddy's camp."

"Don't look like hunters! Hey, stay back!" the man warned J.P., who had moved forward from the woods.

"We're not from around here."

"No shit. Did you go around back?"

"I was just looking for the silver ATV our friend rides."

"Find it?" The man laughed.

"No."

"So I guess I'm not your buddy, huh?"

Jake shook his head. *What the hell is his problem?* "Look, we're obviously at the wrong . . ."

"Jake! Listen!" J.P. pointed to the sky. Jake heard the back end of it: the unmistakable scream of a woman.

"The hell was that?" the hunter growled.

"We have to go."

"If someone's in trouble, I'm going with you."

Jake turned and looked him over for a moment. Thought about the poached moose in the back. Then decided extra firepower wouldn't hurt. "Bring your rifle."

The stranger nodded.

The scream had come from the south, at least as far as they knew. It was difficult to figure such things in varying terrain.

"This way!" J.P. had run toward Jake and the stranger, and kept running. "It sounded close."

"There's another camp just a half mile away, overlooking the river." The stranger checked his hunting jacket for shells. "Should do." He had about a dozen. He looked at Jake. "You're not lost, are you?" It wasn't a question.

J.P. turned back to them, now jogging backward. "Wait, shouldn't I get a gun from the cabin?"

"No," Jake and the stranger said simultaneously. His name was Allen, and it turned out he was no hunter.

"Biologist, actually. Wildlife. They send me up here to collect poached animals so we can use them as evidence. This is a no-hunt zone, but there's a crew taking twenty or so animals a year from this area." The intimidating tone had vanished. "So many damn poachers in these hills, I never trust anyone. Sorry."

Jake waved off his apology. "Are you trained in law enforcement with Game and Fish?"

"Once upon a time. Haven't fired a weapon in five years. Used to be pretty good."

"We might be dealing with one or several hostiles. Possibly kidnappers. We don't know."

Allen looked confused but didn't ask. "Up here." He was now leading Jake and J.P. "Okay, through this last stand of pines, then there's the camp."

Jake and Allen went through first, then waved J.P. up. For a few seconds, there was silence. Then, another bloodcurdling scream. And a scuffle.

From behind a shed, two men were dragging a woman to an old F-150. She wasn't going easily. She flailed and screamed.

"Esma!" J.P. said it too loudly.

"Shhhh." Jake glared at J.P., but the men didn't notice them. "Are you sure it's her?" he whispered.

"Pretty sure."

Allen piped up. "Either way, we're going in. There's a bit of a rise there we can use for cover."

They had her in the truck now. The dull knocks of her kicks against the rear windshield were barely audible. The two men were getting in the front seat.

"We gotta go, *now*! No time for cover." Jake pulled the Mariner, but held it at his side as the trio jogged toward the truck.

*Brrrrrrrrmmmm.* The engine came alive. Jake was in the lead, only a hundred yards away and running at a sprint now. Behind him was Allen, rifle slung over his right shoulder. Then finally J.P.

The transmission creaked as the driver put it in gear. Slowly, the truck started pulling away from the cabin.

Fifty yards. While still running hard, Jake took aim with the handgun. It was too dangerous; he couldn't guarantee a shot to the tire from this distance.

The truck accelerated.

"Stop!" Jake yelled in desperation. The men didn't hear him.

Jake stopped running when he got to the cabin. The truck was two-fifty out, at least.

Allen leveled his rifle.

"Can you make it?"

Allen stayed silent, focusing. He waited till the truck started to round a left bend in the road so he had a broadside shot at the tire. Then he took his breath. Jake watched him remain perfectly still and pull the trigger deliberately. The noise was deafening. Allen absorbed the recoil like a pro.

"Get him?" J.P. had caught up.

Allen lowered the rifle and shook his head.

"I don't know."

# 22

Divya came into her office twenty minutes late.

Her assistant looked up. "Everything okay?"

"Fine. Thanks."

"Need a coffee?"

"Haven't touched my first one." She held up a Starbucks grande cup and pulled open the green glass door to her office.

She sighed at the pile of untouched cases on her desk. It was going to be a long day. An endless string of trivial matters. Divya's priority was still the GPSN case, which was starting to come together. The evidence had established a relationship between Xiao and Canart. Whether it was totally hostile or somewhat cooperative wasn't clear, but Divya leaned toward the former, based on the Terrells' abduction.

Her third-story office windows overlooked a manicured lawn.

She looked out briefly before settling into her chair. While her laptop was booting up, she tapped a Mont Blanc nervously on the desk, then checked her BlackBerry. Nothing urgent.

Scrolling through her contacts, she stopped on Jake Trent. She hesitated, then pushed send. The call went straight to voice mail. *Dammit.* Divya hung up. There was no way to explain her behavior with a message. Even a phone call was a stretch. She wished she could clarify things face-to-face. She still respected him. Cared for him. Maybe even loved him.

He'd been the same old Jake when he was in DC, and to her that was an incredible thing.

*What have I become?*

She needed time away. A break. The pressure and deception were getting to her.

She called a cab, not wanting to take the bus as usual.

"Yes, please. As soon as possible."

A pause. "Yes, at Langley. Thank you."

Divya walked out. "Maria, I'm feeling under the weather. I'll see you tomorrow." She smiled weakly.

# 23

"Careful; they could be around any of these bends." Jake still had the Mariner drawn.

"How far could they get if we hit 'em?" J.P. asked.

Allen interjected. "Depends whether it totally blew up or not. If it didn't, they could get to town on a slow leak."

Jake, J.P., and Allen were starting down a two-track that wasn't visible through the canopy on Jake's satellite images.

"Runs the whole way back to the main road," Allen informed them.

The sun was out in full force. The snow would start melting soon.

"Stop." Jake pointed to a tire track in the snow. "Look." The tracks veered to one side and then the other. Then two tracks separated into a full set of four. One of those tracks was a few inches wider than the others. "Must have hit them here." Jake looked back toward the cabin. The distance looked about right.

He talked softly. "They went out of control. They could be around this next bend." J.P. and Allen nodded. Deep drainage ditches on either side would trap even a pickup.

Still, it was a long shot. Unless the blowout forced them off the road, the truck might be able to continue on its rim. Jake started into the woods for cover, then crept parallel to the road, which was beginning to bend to the right. J.P. and Allen followed a few paces back. Jake held up his hand in a fist, telling them to stop. He peered around a thick fir and listened. Two men were only thirty yards ahead, around the curve. They shouted at each other, panicked.

"Gunshot," the skinny one said. "Guaranteed."

"Yeah? You know the difference between backfire and rifle fire? There's no one back there." The chubbier one was messing with the rusty jack.

"Maybe I do." Slim was busting sticks over his knee.

"You can't help?"

"Sorry."

Old Slim started haphazardly tossing logs and rocks—whatever he could—into the ditch to help the truck's traction once the tire was fixed. Jake could see a shape inside the truck. His heart leapt. Head and shoulders. Esma! *Maybe.*

Jake thought about trying to get her attention, but decided against it—she might give them away. He took a deep breath and slowly walked backward, barely lifting his feet.

"Is that them?" J.P. spoke too loudly.

Jake silenced him, giving one stoic nod, then pointed at him and made the fist again. *Stay here.* J.P. started to protest, but Jake grabbed him hard by the shoulder and squeezed.

*"Owwww!"*

Jake gestured to Allen: *Guns up. I'll lead.*

Allen appeared calm to Jake. *Good. No room for nervous mistakes.* The man was a reassuring presence—the polar opposite of J.P. Jake took a deep breath and walked carefully around the bend to his observation point. Allen followed, rifle ready, eyes wide.

The men were still working on the tire. Slim was now down on his knees too, messing with the jack. He faced Jake and Allen at a quartering angle. The larger man had his back to them.

They watched Slim take a big breath as he looked up toward them. Jake feared they'd been discovered. His hand tightened around the Mariner.

Instead, Slim broke into a pitchy "Whistle While You Work."

Chubby slammed the tire iron down. "Would you shut up?"

Jake did the math. Four feet to a weapon in the driver's seat for Slim, if there was one there. One lunge. Three seconds from initial contact before a round was fired. *No. Two, if he's smart and has a round in the chamber.*

More time for Chubby, closer to the rear; he had farther to go. Two big steps. Four, maybe five seconds between contact and shots fired.

These numbers depended on their emotional states, of course. Jake took them in. Reasonably relaxed now, considering they'd just heard what Slim figured might have been a gunshot. Add an extra second for their demeanor.

Four seconds, approximately. Jake hoped Allen and J.P. would hear his voice before getting a visual. His command would take half a second. *Get on the ground! Two. Three. Four.* Then he would fire at Slim if he wasn't still as a stone with his hands on his head in that drainage ditch. A half second to let the sound of gunfire

157

freeze Chubby and force a surrender. If he didn't, Jake would fire the Mariner at him too.

Jake gave Allen a final nod and stepped out. He was twelve feet from the captors—an easy shot.

"GET ON THE GROU—"

A blur in Jake's periphery.

"Esma!" J.P. charged into the chaos. He lost traction in the melting snow and stumbled. *4 . . . 3 . . . 2 . . .* J.P. wasn't moving fast enough. Slim was at the passenger door, fumbling for his weapon. He turned to face J.P., gun drawn.

"NO!"

Jake let a round go. Easy shot to the forehead. Ten yards. Slim was dead before he knew it.

When his ears stopped ringing, Jake heard a groan from below him. Chubby was wrestling with J.P. in the roadside ditch. Jake trained the Mariner on the fracas, but a shot wasn't possible without putting his friend in danger. The commotion moved toward the truck. Chubby was strong, dragging J.P. out of the ditch toward the truck.

*Bang.* Another shot rang out, not from the Mariner. Jake's ears roared again. Allen had fired and missed. Jake heard the man reload, but again there was no safe shot. J.P. had climbed up the big man's body and was trying to wrestle him away from Esma.

Esma clambered into the driver's seat and turned the ignition. She put the truck in drive and floored it, spraying mud toward Jake and Allen. Chubby climbed inside the cab through the passenger door. Two more shots. Deeper than the rifle. Resounding. *Boom. Boom.* Then the whir of tires and bare rim on the road. Smoke poured from the wheel wells.

A few seconds later, a crash. The truck hadn't made it far—forty yards down the two-track. Jake saw only the shape of the vehicle through dense blue smoke. He scanned the landscape, Mariner at the ready. Nothing moving. The woods became silent but for the hiss from the wreckage.

Jake crept toward the debris. His heart was pounding. Adrenaline was drowning reason. He had to be careful not to get trigger-happy.

A sturdy gust of wind cleared the air. A shotgun came into focus—the perfect close-range weapon. Chubby held on to it tightly. It was his lifeline. He faced Jake, backing away. His other lifeline was Esma, whom he held in a headlock with his left arm. J.P. had crawled or slid back into the drainage ditch to Jake's right, where he rested on his back.

"Don't fucking move." The 12-gauge was pointed at Esma's head. The man turned and shuffled off, dragging Esma with him.

"Go after them!" Jake screamed without turning his head. He kept a bead on Esma's captor. Allen didn't respond. Jake ran to the ditch and turned his attention to J.P.

J.P.'s face was bloodied. *Gunshot wound? Where?* Jake patted him down, looking for holes. Nothing. He checked for breath and found it. Then he rolled J.P. over and checked his back. No more blood, just a busted nose. *Thank god.*

Jake stood and glanced at the tree line where the man had taken Esma. They were long gone. He spun around and finally saw where the shotgun rounds had gone.

Allen was sitting up. Blood was streaming from his upper right leg. Jake jogged over to him.

"The radio. Go to the radio in the cabin." Allen was trying to suppress his own bleeding, pushing hard on his femoral with two fingers.

"Everyone okay?" J.P. pulled himself from the ditch. "Did we get 'em?"

"No. I need your T-shirt." Jake's quick-dry was no good as a bandage; it wouldn't stanch as well as cotton.

"Jesus." J.P. had to look away. "Here."

As Jake bandaged the wound, Allen was using his own shirt to tie a tourniquet.

"Loosen it every thirty minutes. Let's try to keep the leg."

Allen nodded. Jake looked at J.P. "Listen to me: if he starts losing consciousness, you wrap that tourniquet tight and leave it."

"I can't . . ." J.P. was trembling.

"I'll be back." Jake took off running back up the dirt road.

Thirty minutes later Jake arrived at the Fish and Game cabin. He was breathing hard and thirsty as hell. The terrain made for difficult running.

"Come in. SOS."

"Go ahead for dispatch." The soft-spoken man sounded bored.

"We need a life flight up here. *Now!*"

"Up where?"

*Fuck.* "I am at a ranger's outpost. First name Allen. Outside Salmon."

"Which outpost? Do you know the site number?"

"I don't know! Mount Phelan. Victim is at three-quarters mile south of outpost. I'll start a fire at the site. Allen's been shot. Another man down."

Finally the dispatcher sounded concerned.

"Okay. I'll send the chopper."

"Police too. Suspect still at large."

Jake dropped the receiver and ran out of the cabin. By the woodpile, there was a green-camouflaged Gator. The keys were in the ignition. Jake fired up the ATV and punched the throttle, then headed south over treacherous terrain.

Fifteen minutes later, Jake arrived back at the scene. He grabbed the reserve gas can from the Gator and doused a small stump.

"Lighter."

J.P. nodded and tossed him one. With the gas, the fire went up quickly. Jake returned to the wounded biologist. "How is he?"

"Okay. Conscious but getting a little goofy."

"I'm fine," Allen mumbled.

His face was pale and his flesh cool. The blood had turned the melting snow a pinkish red.

"When was the last time the tourniquet was loosened?"

"Just fifteen minutes ago. You said every half hour."

"Don't do it again."

"I don't . . . don't wanna lose it. I play volleyball at the Y, you know?" Allen laughed.

"You'll be fine," Jake reassured Allen. "Paramedics are on their way." He pulled the tourniquet as tight as he could. "I'll be back. Keep the fire going."

Jake hopped back on the Gator and sped toward the cabin where the men had held Esma. He spun circles in the open yard, trying to get attention.

Finally, the dull, building murmur of the blades gave way to a visual—the heli was there.

# 24

Jake woke up and called the number for the Steele Memorial Medical Center. Wildlife Biologist Allen Ridley was already gone, transferred to St. John's in Jackson for surgery. He was stable, but hope for the leg was dim.

Jake wandered to the two-story lobby. The coffee was near an old granite fireplace that hadn't been used since its last cleaning. Only the steelhead fishermen were up, waiting for their guides and chatting about the one that got away. Normally he loved soaking in fishing stories, but Jake couldn't bear to listen.

Shock dulled his senses. The gloom he'd tried to forget for nearly a decade had returned overnight. He'd tried to do good but ended up only adding fuel to the fire. Instead of restoring order to chaos, righting a wrong, he exposed an innocent person to forces no one should ever experience. *No more volleyball at*

162

*the YMCA, Allen—all because of my ego. Sorry about that. Keep in touch.*

The fact that J.P. wasn't badly hurt was nothing short of a miracle. The chopper had taken Allen first, leaving Jake and J.P. with one paramedic and the corpse. Fish and Game, with local police in tow, drove up the road on the back side of Mount Phelan an hour later. Jake and J.P. gave their statements and the authorities marked off the scene. A few hours later, they were back in Salmon.

Jake took an extra cup of coffee and headed back down the corridor. One room short of his own, he stopped and knocked.

J.P. came to the door. He was still dressing, his hair wet from the shower.

"Got you some coffee."

His friend took the Styrofoam cup. "Come in. You look like shit," J.P. said, almost smiling at the role reversal.

Jake finished his coffee. He turned on J.P.'s coffeemaker for another.

"You heard from Sergeant Compton?" J.P. asked.

"Not yet this morning. I'm supposed to meet him in an hour."

"You know they found her, right?" J.P. was standing now, futzing with his shirt, looking in the mirror. "Better with or without top button?" He ran his hands through his hair.

Jake was in disbelief. "Esma? They found her? How?"

J.P. finally opened up a big smile. "Dumbass walked right into Steele Medical, they said. Four a.m. Gunshot wound to the abdomen. They called me an hour ago. Didn't want to wake you up. You got him, man."

Jake tried to connect the dots. "I fired only one round."

"Hell, maybe the biologist did it."

Jake thought back. He remembered it now. *Bang.* A rifle shot as he was tending to J.P. The panic of the moment and the ringing in his ears had drowned out the sound.

Allen had fired while sitting on his bottom and nearly bleeding out.

"Anyway, she's okay. A little banged up. I'm going to see her now."

Jake looked at his watch. Still plenty of time before he met with the cops. "Do you mind?"

"She'd love to see you."

# 25

**TRAM VILLAGE, CHINA.**

Chief Terrell and Charlotte had just finished what they assumed was their dinner in their cell. Not bad, really—a lo mein of some sort with flash-fried brussels sprouts on the side. Strange combination, but it tasted good.

They'd decided that evening was their favorite time of day—after dinner. At least there was something to do: sleep. And the giants and Xiao wouldn't be back till morning. But things today had taken a turn for the worse. Xiao was angry and impatient. He had it in his head that finding his daughter would be easy in a small town like Jackson.

He'd brought the phone with lunch and demanded that Terrell call Layle, even though it was the middle of the night in the Tetons. A sleepy Layle had only bad news—still no trace of Meirong. Xiao grabbed the phone and screamed at Layle, frightening Charlotte.

When she began to cry, Left Giant, so dubbed because he always stood on Xiao's left, backhanded her across the face. The chief could barely restrain himself.

It was time for some sort of plan. *What if Layle still has no bead on Meirong by tomorrow? How violent will Xiao get then?*

Terrell looked over the furniture again—his only options for a weapon or tool. He walked to the heavy steel door. The only point of weakness was the knob. It was a traditional pewter bulb-shaped handle, simple key lock in the center. The aluminum flange around the knob was separated from its housing by a couple of millimeters.

Terrell glanced at his wife. Their wedding day had been the best day of his life, until the kids were born. Now their every minor achievement—first birthdays, kindergarten graduations, even making the T-ball team—made him more proud than any-thing he'd done on his own.

"What?" Charlotte asked, sounding irritated.

"Nothing. Excited to get home."

Charlotte huffed, dismissing his optimism.

"I'm getting us out of here," Terrell said flatly. He pulled the thin spring mattress off the cot.

"You're going to get us killed."

"They need us, Charlotte. If we get caught, no harm done."

He flipped the cot over, legs up. Bending down, he tried to wrench the crossbars from the frame. No dice. Heavy bolts secured them to the outer frame. With his fingers, he checked all eight bolts. The four crossbars that he felt every night as he tried to sleep were each connected on either side.

The fifth bolt had a little play. He worked it with his fingers, making a quarter spin of progress every few minutes. From time to time the nut would seize up, and he would tap carefully with the leg of the chair to loosen it.

After forty minutes, his right hand was badly cramped and his fingers were bleeding.

"Stop it," Charlotte blurted. It echoed through the small cell. "You're not going to get it."

The chief didn't even lift his head. He kept trying to loosen the nut, using his left hand to hold his right forefinger and thumb together.

After another half hour passed, Charlotte started to sob. "Just stop! Please!" She sounded as if she was on the fringe of a panic attack.

A few minutes later, her husband, the chief of police and no stranger to trauma, stopped fiddling with the cot, and he too started crying.

Charlotte walked to him, bent down, and hugged him from behind. He was sweating and shaking. Whether it was from the sobs or the exertion wasn't apparent. She closed her eyes and prayed. For several minutes—or maybe it was an hour; after all, they had no clock—they knelt together. Finally, the chief went still, then stood.

"I love you." Charlotte spoke in a resigned tone.

Terrell smiled, then bent and pried the loose end of the crossbar upward, breaking it free from its opposite bolt.

Charlotte laughed and hugged him.

By this point, the chief's right hand was nothing more than a numb, cramped appendage of flesh. Where he had broken off the crossbar from the still-tight bolt, the aluminum had crimped, forming a chisel. He took the bar to the door and fit the chisel end between the door and the knob's flange.

Terrell let it rest for a second and looked around again, hoping for something to act as a hammer. There wasn't much—maybe the chair, but he doubted he could fit it between the top of the cross-bar and the ceiling.

Instead, he reached up, cupped his right hand around the end of the bar, overlaid his left, and used the weight of his body. The bar penetrated farther into the flange.

Blood dripped from his right hand.

Terrell stopped and listened to make sure the giants weren't outside. Silence. He reached as high as he could on the bar and pulled, using it as a lever. With three strong yanks, the flange broke free, sending him backward onto his ass. He reinserted the cross-bar, now much deeper in the mechanism of the knob. Another few pulls.

The knob broke free and rolled across the cement floor, stopping at Charlotte's feet.

Terrell stuck a finger into what remained of the knob and slid the lock open. "Let's go."

As they walked through the unlit kitchen, Terrell shielded Charlotte with his body. In his left hand, he carried the pry bar. The basement was quiet; they struggled to keep the echo of their footsteps to a minimum.

From the bottom of the stairs, they could see the faint yellow glow of a single bulb. A desk lamp or reading light. It could have been left on by accident or on a timer, but Terrell didn't want to take the chance.

"Stay here." Terrell slipped off his shoes and socks, which, like the rest of him, had begun to stink of sweat after three days without a shower or change of clothes. His bare footsteps were unde-tectable as he crept up the stairs.

*       *       *

Charlotte sat on the bottom step. She wrapped her arms around herself, more anxious than cold.

Upstairs, Terrell watched one of the giants read a book at the hostess's podium. *Rather scholarly for a thug.*

Who knew which one he was—Xiao wasn't around, so this giant was indistinguishable from the other. His back faced Terrell. Beyond the giant stood two trivial obstacles: a set of decorative saloon doors, and the automatic glass doors that would someday hold in the scent of maple-infused fatback and cowboy lattes. Beyond that was freedom, or at least a shot at it.

Terrell slowly approached the giant, who was now humming a slow song he couldn't identify. When he got within two steps he paused for a fraction of a second, then pounced.

The book was *The Lexus and the Olive Tree*, in English. *Bastard understands everything we say.*

The man struggled as Terrell expected, but the effectiveness of the rear naked choke wasn't in its strength. It was the technique—the placement of the biceps and the radius bone to stop blood flow to the brain. In ten seconds, the giant was out.

He shouted at Charlotte to hurry upstairs, then quickly dragged the giant across the smooth floor, took his cell phone, and pushed him down the stairs. Charlotte crawled over him and hugged her husband as he reached behind her and locked the stairwell door. The giant would be awake in less than ten seconds.

They slipped out the saloon doors to the accompanying percussion of the giant trying to escape. Terrell knew they didn't have much time. Surely, somewhere in the basement, there was a phone. If not, it wouldn't be long until he broke down the door.

Chief Terrell and Charlotte stayed close to the buildings as they walked down Main Street, Jackson Hole, China. Most were still under construction, and their scaffolding provided cover. There was nothing in the streets. No people, no cars. *It must be late.*

Working their way back to the lodge and the main entrance, they glanced down each phony cross street, hoping to find any type of transportation: a car, a landscaping vehicle, even a golf cart. Still nothing.

The moon was high and full but pale. Nothing brilliant or inspired about its light, just a sentient observer of the night. The stars were similarly dull, veiled by towering smog from cities dozens of miles away. Terrell longed for home and the bright pyrotechnic nights of the high country.

"What do we do if we don't find a car?" Charlotte broke his train of thought.

"We walk."

"Then what?"

"We hope to find a passerby or a home somewhere. Anyone we meet will be less hostile than Xiao."

"You're sure?"

"No, but I don't think the workers knew what he was up to. And there is still the garage under the lodge."

"Are we better off?" Charlotte sounded scared.

Roger stopped walking and turned to her. "Yes. We had to get out."

"Will they kill us if they find us?"

"We're no use to them dead."

With that, Terrell pushed on through the thick night, leading his wife behind him. In a few minutes they were across from the main lodge, where their welcome to China had once seemed warm. Through the window, Terrell noted a single front-desk agent, clipping her nails and watching a movie on a laptop.

"It must be the woman from the first day. She seemed nice."

"Your girlfriend?" Charlotte hadn't lost her spunk.

"You know what I mean. Nice like friendly."

"It's her job to be nice, you know."

"I just mean she might help us if we can't find a way out of here."

Charlotte sighed.

"Let's skirt around the back and check out the garage," Terrell whispered, changing the subject.

The empty village encouraged them. Maybe they could sneak away undetected. They were perhaps a mile from the entrance gate, where, if they were lucky, they might find an escape vehicle.

The ramp into the garage was dark, but a motion detector lit it up as they entered. There was a small black Hyundai on the first level. Terrell jogged to it and pulled the handle. Locked. *Dammit.*

Charlotte joined him. "Can you hot-wire it?"

"Probably not. Too new. If it's valeted, there's gotta be keys somewhere." The chief started toward the stairwell.

"Be *careful*!" Charlotte spat toward him. She shivered and crossed her arms.

The door to the main lobby was tucked behind the elevators in a short corridor. Terrell let it close behind him softly and walked to the end of the hall, where a peek around the corner revealed the striking woman at the front desk.

*What to do?* If she was in the dark with respect to the kidnapping, she could be a major asset. She could get them out. Call the local police. If she wasn't, their gig was up.

Terrell decided to play it safe. He slinked around the corner, out of her view on the other side of the elevators. Outside the business center was a house phone. Terrell picked it up and dialed "0" for the front desk.

"Good evening, front desk."

"Hi, I'm in the Wapiti Suite. We could use some more towels, please."

"No problem, sir."

He hung up and peeked his head around the corner to watch the woman's reaction. She picked up the phone again, dialed, and spoke in what he assumed was Mandarin.

*Was it Housekeeping, or Xiao?*

She put the phone down, grabbed a walkie-talkie from a charger, and headed toward the elevator. Terrell backed off into the business center to stay out of sight.

*Ding.* The elevator door opened, and the front-desk agent was gone. This was Terrell's chance.

He sprinted to the front desk and began rooting through the drawers. Files, paperwork, receipt paper. No keys. Next file cabinet. Stapler, three-hole punch. No keys. *C'mon!* The elevator light board showed that it was still on the top floor.

More time.

Terrell ran into the back office and started searching. In a cedar bureau, he found a small revolver along with an empty 9mm holster. Whether the handguns were for protection or a darker purpose he did not know. Regardless, he checked the revolver's cylinder. Loaded. He tucked it into his waistband.

Leaving the office, he checked the elevator signals. Still on the top floor. Terrell picked up the phone at the front desk and tried frantically to reach an outside line. No dial tone. It occurred to him that he didn't know the number for emergency services in China anyway.

*Stop wasting time,* he thought. The elevator was moving—the fourth floor. Now the third. *Shit!* One last attempt. Again, no keys. Nothing but standard office appurtenances—staplers, hole punch, printer ink. The elevator was on the second floor. He was seconds away from being caught.

*No!* A wave of disappointment swept over him. He'd failed Charlotte. They would be back in the cell in no time. Or worse. He had to run, get out before the agent saw him. They'd go by foot. With the revolver they might have a chance.

Two strong strides and then Terrell was down. He hit the ground hard, nearly knocking the wind out of his lungs. For a moment, he thought he'd been shot. Then he regained his senses and looked toward his feet, where something was constricting him. Still in pain and breathing heavily, he pulled on the straps that wrapped his feet.

Soft purple leather. *A purse!* Terrell reached in while he got to his feet and felt around. Under the various accessories, he felt the loose, cold clink of a key chain.

He turned to run with the keys in his hand and immediately ran into the front-desk agent, bowling her over. She sat on her bottom, confused. Then he saw her reach into her pantsuit. The 9mm.

A shot rang through the serene lobby as Terrell rounded the corner back toward the stairwell.

"Let's go!" Terrell could barely stay on his feet as he raced down the stairs.

Charlotte ran to the passenger side of the Hyundai.

"What was that noise?"

"They're shooting. Get in!" Terrell fumbled with the key chain to find the remote. He unlocked the car. Behind him, he heard the heavy fire door at the top of the stairs swing shut. "Hurry."

The car fired up by start button. Terrell floored it in reverse up and out of the structure. The front-desk agent was running up the ramp, firing. A round hit the windshield, but deflected away.

Slamming the transmission into Drive, Terrell rounded the corner of the building, headed toward Main Street and eventually the ingress road.

As he made the right turn onto Main, Terrell's heart sunk. Blocking the road were the giants and an assortment of other men in quasi-military garb clutching AR-15s.

When Terrell stopped, the men parted to either side and Xiao emerged.

"Get out," they heard through the windows. This was the angriest they had heard or seen their captor.

Terrell took the keys from the ignition. The car beeped like a countdown for their last moments on earth. "Move slowly, honey. Don't do anything rash."

Charlotte nodded.

Terrell looked in her eyes for a second. Here was his life. Everything he had ever cared about. Guilt overwhelmed him. He had no more cards to play. He grabbed his wife's hand and squeezed hard.

"Okay. Let's go."

The giants wrestled Terrell to the ground, giving him several hard pops to the face.

As Terrell writhed on the ground, the giants rushed around the car and restrained Charlotte, who was quickly becoming hysterical.

Xiao walked to the bloodied chief.

"I'm sure you know how the West was won?" Xiao's tone was even now. He tapped the shiny silver revolver on his hip.

Terrell looked at the bright moon and, for the first time in a while, prayed. He reverted to his police-academy persona—unflappable, beyond persuasion.

"My family homesteaded in the American West starting in 1810. *Sir.*"

Charlotte cried out toward Xiao. "Let him be!" Their captor didn't respond.

"A real Buffalo Bill," said Xiao.

"To you, maybe."

Xiao laughed. "Then I am sure you are fastest draw in the West. Are you armed?"

Terrell lifted his shirt to show the stolen revolver in his waistband.

"Ten steps, then draw. Do you understand?"

Terrell nodded, then looked at his wife, trying to convey a lifetime's worth of feeling. He knew there was no chance. If he happened to beat Xiao, the giants would kill him before he knew it. At least he could die in peace, now that he knew it was Charlotte they wanted. Their last bargaining chip. She would have to be kept alive.

"Are you ready?" Xiao interrupted Terrell's thoughts.

"Yes."

"Max, would you be so kind as to start us?" One of the giants nodded in response.

"Three."

"Two."

"One."

The chief tried to count the steps to himself, but it was difficult to stay focused. He must have been off. For the second between what he thought was eight and complete darkness, he wondered: *Did Xiao shoot early? That son of a . . .*

# 26

Jake left the hotel and walked to his 4Runner, which he'd moved back to the hotel late the night before. The wind tossed an array of orange and yellow leaves across the parking lot. Crossing the river at the boat launch above the bridge, anglers were rigging their rods and launching their boats.

The ignition gasped in the bitter morning air. After it fired up, Jake hit the seat heater with a numb finger and gave the engine a moment to warm.

From what he'd overheard on the way to his SUV, the fishing was good. The spawning steelhead had finally decided the temperature, weather, and water level were right. The stars were aligned. Whatever innate switch existed in their tiny brains had turned on; it was time to move upriver and do the deed. Ensure the health of their population. There would be thousands of sea-run fish spread out through the Salmon River system.

Maybe one in a hundred of these fish would decide a properly presented fly deserved a little knock. Nobody knew why. They didn't feed during the spawn, so why the bite? Some compared it to teasing a kitten with a string. When the kitten wanted to play, game on. More often than not, steelhead played the part of the lazy tomcat—uninterested in games, focused on copulation.

Jake's phone buzzed with a text message. Don Hoozler.

Amy says you registered at the hotel last night. Got the day off.

Don was a steelhead guide in Salmon in the fall, and a trout guide on the Snake in the summer. His girlfriend, Amy, was a manager at the hotel. He obviously wanted to go fishing.

Jake wrote back.

Wish I could. Just in town seeing a friend.

An immediate response—a cartoon emoji thumbs-down.

Jake was now waiting to pull out onto the main road, en route to the hospital. He texted Don an apology and turned off his iPhone.

J.P. had already headed out to see Esma. Jake wanted to give them a few minutes alone. Then he would pay his respects, give a statement to the police, jump back in the 4Runner, and head to St. John's in Jackson to see Allen. Bring him some real food. Apologize for ruining his life with shitty decision making.

In her room in the tiny hospital, Esma looked beautiful, but not in her usual way. Instead of seeing strength in her eyes, Jake saw fear, vulnerability. Still, her black hair shimmered under the bright lights, and her face was kind and lovely.

An IV was taped into her arm for hydration. On her bedside table sat uneaten eggs and ham. J.P. knelt next to her, holding her hand. He'd found flowers to bring—quite a feat in a small town in the early morning.

"The hero," Esma said in a raspy, weak voice. "C'mon over." Jake had been standing in the doorway, feeling sheepish.

"He's the hero," Jake said earnestly. "He's the one who heard you scream." Jake winced at his word choice. "He's the one who found you."

"You are both my heroes. C'mon."

Jake left his awkward position at the door and walked to the hospital bed. He bent down and hugged Esma. As he did so, J.P. gave him a few hard slaps on the back. "Love you, buddy," his friend said softly.

It was a lot for Jake to handle. The trauma of a gunfight was taxing enough, and the duress of having had two people close to him in such peril almost sent him over the edge. He stood and took a moment to compose himself.

"Tell me," Esma said with tears welling in her eyes, "how is it that I came to befriend the two most courageous men in the world?"

J.P. blushed. "I'm not courageous, just dumb and in love."

Esma knocked him on the shoulder. "I don't think so, *mi amor*."

Jake stood and kissed her on the forehead. "I should be going. I've got a meeting with the cops to explain all this."

He gave Esma another hug, and then shook J.P.'s hand. "When will you be released?"

Esma shrugged. "Tomorrow. I have everything I need." She tousled J.P.'s already bedraggled hair.

"Take care of yourselves." Jake walked out of the room.

He exhaled. Things were looking up. Esma was safe and happy, and Allen, the true hero, was going to be fine according to Esma's nurse, who had just talked to the folks at St. John's. Fishing with Don was sounding better and better.

Jake parked behind the library and walked into the police station later that morning. The receptionist was a woman who looked to be about a hundred and two.

"Yes?"

"I'm Jake Trent. I have an appointment."

The old woman said nothing, but slowly picked up the phone and mumbled something into the receiver.

A few seconds later, a fortysomething man with broad shoulders strode forcefully toward Jake.

"Mr. Trent." He held out an enormous hand. "Nice to see you again."

"Likewise."

"Follow me."

The detective's office was sterile. No pictures. No desk gnomes.

"We'll make this quick. Have a seat."

Jake shrugged, meaning *Do what you gotta do.*

"First, just a formality. Do you have a Concealed Carry Permit?"

Jake took out his wallet and handed Rapport his card from Wyoming. "Idaho has reciprocity, I assume."

Rapport smirked. "Yep, no problem here."

"I also have this." Jake handed the chief his old Department of Justice identification card. Across the front, it was stamped RETIRED.

An incredulous look from Rapport. After flipping it over a few times, he spoke. "I don't know what this is." He handed it back to Jake, who put it in his wallet.

"I used to work under the Justice Department. Investigations."

"But now you're retired?"

Jake nodded.

"Listen." Rapport leaned over his desk toward Jake. "I got the lowdown already. It doesn't matter who you are. What you did out there was hella impressive."

This reaction was about 180 degrees from what Jake figured he deserved.

"Tell you what, we've got a little award in Lemhi County we call the Spirit of the Grizzly. I'm gonna nominate you this winter."

"That's not necessary. I—"

"I insist." He gave Jake a satisfied smile.

"Is that all? No statement?" Jake was shocked there wasn't more hoop-jumping.

"We got plenty last night. I'll give you a minute to review this for details and then sign the bottom."

Jake looked over the report. It seemed accurate, if vague. He looked up before he inked his name.

"You're satisfied with the amount of detail here?" One of the few specifics was the caliber and type of Jake's sidearm, which the detective had inspected last night. "You'll be able to go after this guy? Kidnapping, everything? Rape?" Jake had guessed the last part from the look in Esma's eyes.

"Oh hell yeah. We get a lot of crazy people in these woods out here. These particular guys have warrants out the ass. A few states." The detective was looking down, clipping his fingernails. "Drugs, robbery, all that. He'll be in for a while."

"What're their names?"

A pause. The detective knew them from memory. "Timothy Corfie is the deceased. Layle Neville is in stable condition."

Jake threw that in the memory bank, grabbed a pen from the desk, and signed the document.

They shook hands, and Rapport gave him a quick salute, probably thinking this was a daily occurrence at the DOJ. Jake awkwardly saluted back.

It was warmer outside when Jake walked out of the station. Sunny, the air smelling of fallen leaves, and rain spitting from a few straggling clouds. Jake was right across from the bronze bear statue in the center of town. On a heap of river rocks, the grizzly stood, watching the salmon and steelhead migrate past his feet, looking for an easy meal.

Jake reached down and touched the nearest fish. It was smooth and ice-cold—not unlike the real thing. The sensation gave him a moment of peace.

He took out his phone and gave Don a ring. "All right, I'm in."

They met at Tower Rock, a few miles downriver from town.

"Still got the Dodge, I see." Jake shook Don's hand. He wasn't a tall man, but the width of his rowing shoulders made him appear bigger than he was. His hair was jet-black, like his scruffy beard.

"Yep, one hundred twenty-one K on her." These were the sorts of things fishing guides liked to talk about. Good, dependable truck, a boat that had withstood years of abuse. It all meant your rod was longer than the typical weekend warrior's.

In this case that was accurate—Don took two thirteen-foot Spey rods from the magnetic holder stuck to the roof of the Ram.

"I can grab something."

Don handed the rods to Jake, who stared at the reels on the outfits. "Old loops?" The reels adorned seven-weight Beulah Classics.

"The originals. Made by Danielsson Innovation. Salmon series."

"Nice. Where'd you find those?"

Jake was walking alongside the truck as Don backed the trailer in.

He shouted back through the window and over the diesel. "An old client. He croaked. Widow called and said he always wanted me to have them." A little laugh.

"Quite a compliment. And you use them with clients?"

Don stopped the truck abruptly and killed the ignition. "Are you outta your mind? Clients get the snickelfritz." Don's term for the cheap gear. "Haven't even had the loops out yet. Just put new line on 'em."

"Wow. Thanks."

Don's old High Side was heavy and the roller bar cranky. It took both of them to push it off the trailer and into the river.

"Be right back." Don accelerated off the ramp to the parking area.

Jake took stock of his surroundings. It had turned into a beautiful day. Tower Rock, the landmark crag where Lewis and Clark once camped, stood behind him, glowing warm orange in the autumn sun. The water was a complementary emerald hue, a little cloudy from the recent precipitation. Sometimes this was a boon; it stirred things up, got the fish going. A steelhead's normal mood was somber and unimpressed. Any change in the conditions might make them happy, mad, annoyed—whatever it was that sparked them to lash out and strike a fly.

Don was back at the ramp. He tossed some loaner waders at Jake.

"Snickelfritz?"

"You'll find out when you get in the water." Which was hovering around forty degrees. Plenty cold enough to feel a leak.

Jake laughed and pulled on the bootfoot waders and carried the rods into the drifter.

Don pulled up the thirty-pound anchor and nudged the craft out into the current.

"Purple on both rods; I know you wanna change to black, so just go ahead." Color was everything—and nothing—in steelhead fishing. In a sport where your odds were so low, people obsessed over minute details: "The one you got last Thursday, did he eat the dark-pink one or the light-red hackled one?" At the same time, logic pointed to the fact that it made no real difference.

Jake was one of the many who subscribed to the notion that any color works for any fish as long as it's black. He took the clippers and the black Hobo-Spey pattern that Don was holding up for him and made the change.

Casting a long Spey rod required a touch more artistic flair than your normal nine-foot fly rod. That, and it brought the fly damned close to the person rowing if you tried to cast from the boat. So the strategy was to use the boat as transportation from likely run to likely run, then anchor and fish thoroughly.

The first few runs were crowded with fishermen. "Bank maggots," Don mused. "Every year I'm amazed that the fish even come back. They run through nine hundred miles of land mines—lures, flies—to get here. This is a mighty strong river to support all the pressure from fishermen."

Jake nodded. He wanted to laugh at the typical frustrated-guide talk, but he'd heard Don do the "mighty strong river" bit before, and he knew his friend took it seriously.

"Mighty strong," Don said again. "Hell of a burden, all these fishermen. 'Course, I'm not helping, I 'spose."

"You act like you actually catch fish."

Don chuckled, and they sat for a few minutes, contemplating the burdens they placed on the land they loved so much.

"This one around the bend is a sleeper hole. Won't be anyone in it."

When they got to the spot, Jake could see why it didn't get fished. "Sandy bottom," Jake said. Steelhead notoriously hated sandy bottoms.

"Looks that way, doesn't it?" Don was pulling the drift boat over into an eddy on river left, working hard. When the boat was in the calm, shallow water close to shore, he dropped anchor. It stuck in the mucky substrate.

"C'mon."

Jake hopped out and handed a rod to Don. Then he followed his friend down the bank.

"The good water is just here at the bottom of the run. That sand and mud give way to three big boulders on the current seam out there." He pointed his rod tip toward the center of the river and swept it downstream. "One, two, three." They were spread out with fifty yards between them.

Jake could see the giant rocks' effect on the current. Three sofa-sized hydraulic swirls along the seam.

Don continued. "That upper part of the run is garbage, but down here if you can send a cast out beyond the rocks and let it swing back through, you've got a good chance. Go ahead and hit it first; I'll jump in behind you."

"Got it." Jake eyed the distance—about seventy feet, not very long for a Spey cast. He walked back into the water and unhooked the black fly from the rod's first eyelet.

"And let that thing swing the whole way to the bank; they'll follow it way in here." One last piece of advice from Don.

It sounded so promising before you fished it, and that was the charm of steelheading.

It was all about covering the water. Since one eager steelhead might be two miles from the next one, the angler presented only one cast from each spot he stood in, then took two steps downriver and repeated. If you got a bite, a pull, a tug, a whack, but didn't connect, you got a free pass to spend an extra five minutes on that spot, changing flies and trying to convince the fish.

After about six cast-and-swing presentations, Jake had seventy feet of line out. Enough to reach the boulders.

Nothing.

Jake stepped downriver two steps. The next cast landed five feet downstream from the first. The fly swung right on top of the rock. No tug. No whack.

Jake stepped down two more. This was the money shot—the fly would be swinging right behind the first boulder, where the river's strong current was momentarily relieved.

Nada. Jake worked his way down, cast by cast, two-stepping to the next boulder.

It didn't take long for the sense of tranquility to come. The waders were holding up, and the air temperature was a pleasant fifty degrees. The repetitive motion of the cast and the swing eased Jake's mind. A smart steelheader was resigned to being unsuccessful, and so could achieve a kind of inner peace. Sometimes the strike of a fish interrupted that Zen moment, but the indignity was quickly forgiven.

By the last boulder, Jake had experienced no lucky interruption. His mind was churning on the previous day's conflict. He walked slowly back toward the boat when he finished, thinking it all through. He had to admit that killing a man was easier than the innocent might imagine. At least the act of it. The aftermath was different. Self-doubt came pouring in like a spring tide. Justification meant nothing in the following days. Over the years, Jake numbed himself to it as best he could. But now, as magpies flitted about in the skeleton trees and ravens' screams echoed through the canyon, he had to strain to keep it from his mind. He was uncertain and regretful. Wondering what he could have done differently to spare a life.

Higher up in the run, Don was still working the second boulder. He didn't need to ask if Jake saw any action—he would have heard the hooting and hollering. "Jump back in behind me if you want. I'll be just ten more minutes."

"I'll wait. I'm enjoying myself."

Jake sat on the bank and admired the guide's cast: efficient, powerful, and graceful. No wasted effort, yet something workmanlike about it. Unfortunately, his proficiency for casting didn't impress the fish. Don finished the run without a take.

"Let's get moving. Plenty of good water before the takeout."

It was 1:30 p.m. now. Back in the drift boat.

"You have heaters in this thing?" Jake had followed a silver tube along the gunwale down to a propane tank.

"People get softer and softer every year. Pretty soon we'll have indoor fishing."

Jake laughed—he was feeling better indeed.

"So what're you doing here anyway, if you didn't come to fish?"

"A friend of mine was having some personal problems—lovelife stuff, bullshit like that." Jake didn't want to get into it. Didn't want to get called a hero again for acting like an idiot. So he spoke in terms a fishing guide would appreciate. It worked.

"Shit, man. Bummer. Anything a bottle of brown water wouldn't fix?" Don had put on jets, rowing powerfully, and glaring at a boat that was trying to pass them.

"Not really."

"Good."

"What's new with you anyway? Still got that hot Smokey-the-Bear chick I met at the fly-fishing film tour?"

Jake looked down. "Not sure if I ever had her, to be honest."

"Man, she seemed pretty taken with you."

"You think?"

"Hold on." Don stood at the rowing station. "Fucking assholes!" he yelled at the fishermen in the other boat, who had successfully cut him off. One held up a silent middle finger and a dry smile. Don laughed at them and yelled, "All right! Well played!"

He turned to Jake again. "Hey, sorry. What the hell do I know? I'm divorced."

Jake wouldn't go there. "You have Amy now."

Don smirked. "True. Best part is Morgan didn't get my boat."

"Or the old Ram," Jake chuckled.

That set the tone for the rest of the afternoon. Jake and Don. Two bachelors out enjoying a damned beautiful afternoon. Fishing. *What could be better?* Jake needed that, considering the gravity of the prior day. Don brought out a bottle of Wyoming Whiskey and it was just like a played-out country song.

Later, at the takeout, Don could say only one thing: "Wasn't your fault, man; he just let go. You did great."

"I lifted my rod tip." Jake appreciated the cheerleading.

"I didn't see it that way." Don had brought an average-sized male, six pounds, to the net on the purple Hobo Spey that Jake had so quickly chopped off. The black fly had turned one fish too, who grabbed excitedly, but came off when Jake tried to set the hook.

"I trout-set him. I've gotta learn to keep that rod tip down when they grab it."

"Everyone screws up the first of the year."

It was getting close to dark by the time Jake arrived back at his vehicle in town. After about fifteen minutes of convincing, he agreed to hit up Bertram's for rib night with Don. Jake was cold and tired, and the offer to spend the night at Don's was accepted as well, after some cajoling. Visiting Allen could wait a day.

At the brewery, Jake's phone lit up with an incoming call. Divya Navaysam. He clicked ignore, and turned back to Don and his plate of ribs.

# 27

**GRAND TETON NATIONAL PARK. OCTOBER 24.**

**7:45 A.M. MOUNTAIN STANDARD TIME.**

Park Ranger Noelle Klimpton was moving up in the ranks. She'd spent her first several years in Grand Teton National Park as an Interpretive Ranger Supervisor, but her role in solving the previous summer's crisis had landed her a full-blown enforcement role. Law Enforcement Ranger Noelle Klimpton. Total police power.

She had more freedom now, which she loved. A new truck too—a gleaming white 2013 GMC Yukon with LED emergency light bars and an oversized engine. Her dilapidated cabin remained largely the same, although the extra $15,000 a year had gone toward some new furnishings—primarily IKEA from the Salt Lake store, the most exciting addition being a cabinet and counter set that she was able to install around the pre-existing sink.

Over the winter, Noelle attended her mandatory SLETP (Seasonal Law Enforcement Training Program) in Rangely, Colorado, and a Search and Rescue course in the Tetons. Getting to know her new sidearm proved both empowering and intimidating. Truth be told, she preferred the laser-sighted taser.

By the end of September, her first high season in law enforcement had begun to wind down. It had been uneventful. Fifty-some DUIs, about a zillion firework citations, warnings for illegal campsites or fires, and a half-dozen marijuana busts. More speeding tickets than she cared to remember—always locals who acted offended to be pulled over. The tourists were too occupied with the wildlife to even approach the speed limit, which was occasionally worth a warning too.

She was parked just south of Deadman's Bar, where the speed limit dropped from fifty-five to forty-five. No speeders yet, but it was only 8 a.m.

Suddenly, her phone buzzed. Jackson police. Odd this early in the morning.

"Hello?"

"Ms. Klimpton?"

"Noelle. Can I help you?"

"Deputy Layle Statler here. Ranger Yowlitz gave me your cell number." Fran Yowlitz was her supervising ranger—a brute of a woman with cropped hair and a Navy Seal demeanor. Noelle got the sense she wasn't Yowlitz's favorite new hire.

Layle waited for her approval.

"Go ahead."

"You're aware of this wolf carcass down here?"

"Sure. The mystery wolf."

"Something like that. Anyway, a lot of the guys that work for Game and Fish like to clean their elk in the big fridge down here. They're running out of room, bugging the hell out of us, and I'm wondering what the park service wants to do with the animal."

"Ranger Yowlitz didn't give you any instructions?"

"Not really. She figured it was good to go . . . be incinerated, but wanted someone to look at it first. She said you were the expert."

*Dammit,* Noelle thought. Old Fran was being sarcastic. Ever since the bear-tooth incident last summer—it turned out to be fake—Noelle's animal-identification skills had been the butt of frequent jokes among the rangers. Now she had to drive thirty miles out of her way and play with a frozen wolf carcass to temporarily satisfy her boss's resentment.

She sighed loud enough for Deputy Layle to hear.

"Is that okay?"

"I'll be there in forty-five."

"Great. I'll see you there."

Noelle flipped on her lights and spun a U-turn. She grabbed her wide-brimmed hat from the passenger seat and put it on—Yowlitz didn't like rangers without hats.

Noelle had altered the unflattering uniform's tan top and green pants to fit her figure. The button-up blouse was always left open two buttons short of the collar, not for the errant sightseer's benefit, but so that she could feel a touch of individualism in the regimented organization. The green work pants were snugger than uniform code, but not in a tawdry way. Her wavy hair was kept up on most days, with just a coil or two peeking out the front of her hat.

She sighed loudly again. *Of course everyone going the speed limit has to slow down to thirty when a cop is behind them.* She flipped on her siren and passed the slow-moving caravan.

Waiting to turn left into the visitor-center parking lot from Cache Street, Noelle ruminated over the wolf carcass. She didn't know much except that a tracker system had detected a radio signal similar to the ones given off by the collars the national park used on moose, wolves, elk, and bear. The Game and Fish department had performed a necropsy, as it sometimes did for research purposes, but instead of finding a collar, the examiners had found a transmitter embedded between the wolf's shoulder blades.

Noelle pulled into a gravel parking lot through the back of the visitors' center. Layle was waiting for her, leaning on his unmarked black Dodge Charger. He was young like Noelle, early thirties probably. He had sandy-blond hair and stood an athletic five feet eleven. His hands fidgeted around, indicating anxiety—something Noelle noticed because of her SLETP training.

The building was a large brick warehouse built in the 1920s. Double-tall garage doors adorned the front. Around the side there was a gray steel door. After introductions, Layle led her inside. Backhoes and graders occupied the cement floor in the front of the building. They walked between them toward the back corner.

Here, there was one small office for the mechanic, and an enormous walk-in cooler. Hanging outside the sealed doors were a few Carhartt insulated jackets and heavy gloves.

The deputy held a jacket out for Noelle, who refused. "We won't be in there for long."

"Sure." Layle was already wearing a navy police-issue sweater. He grabbed two pairs of gloves.

It took a moment for the light to warm up and illuminate the cooler. A scent that reminded Noelle of livestock and a butcher's shop filled the air. She buttoned her shirt up to the collar. Layle took note of this and handed her the gloves.

"In the back. Watch the hooks."

Heavy meat hooks hung from the ceiling, connected to a roller track. All but a few of them were occupied by elk carcasses— Game and Fish employees' trophies, in various stages of butchering. Fifteen or more.

"These guys like to hunt."

"No kidding," Layle replied. "One of the perks of working at Game and Fish, I suppose; free butchering facility."

In the back right corner of the fridge was a stainless lab table on wheels. Its contents were hanging over the edges and covered with a black tarp.

"It's still in fine shape. They're just short on room, as you can see." Layle unwrapped the wolf.

"He's huge."

"Hundred and fifteen, believe it or not."

"Was he in a populated area? What kind of food source would sustain that weight here? That's Alaskan-sized." Noelle actually did know a few facts about wolves.

Layle nodded. "He was up by Moran. Suppose he could've hit the Dumpsters there, but they're all bear-proof, right?"

Noelle nodded and then walked to the table and stroked his fur. She felt his waist, which was hollowed out from the autopsy, but would have been as thick as a keg of beer.

"Did he have a benefactor?" This was the park-service term for a person who fed a specific wild animal.

"Nobody up there admits to it."

"'Course not." Noelle struggled to lift up the front end of the beast. "Anything you wanna point out?"

"Help me flip it over," Layle said. They put the frozen wolf on its side. "Right here between the shoulders is where they found the transmitter."

Noelle ran her fingers over a small patch of shaved skin with an incision across the middle. "What did the biologist say?"

"He consulted with a vet. Blunt force from the vehicle killed him. He did have fluid in the lungs too."

"Pneumonia?"

"I guess."

Noelle felt pity for the animal. A prince of the western high country, second in the pecking order only to the grizzly bear, over-fed and done in by human contact.

"Is there risk of an outbreak in the wolf population?"

"Biologist didn't mention that, no."

"I think I'm finished. Where's the chip?"

"In my cruiser. Let's get out of the cold."

Noelle followed Layle back past the elk carcasses, through the warehouse, and into the parking lot. The sun was up high over Snow King Mountain. Town was starting to bustle, though the commotion didn't approach the chaos of tourist season.

Layle popped the trunk to his cruiser, where there were three file boxes. He grabbed one, closed the trunk, and rested the box on the hood. From among the paperwork, he produced a small Ziploc evidence bag. He pulled on a pair of blue rubber gloves and handed Noelle the same.

"Fingerprints?"

"None. These are more for disease control."

The "chip" looked like a triple-A battery that had been slightly shrunk; a long, thin pill. Layle handed it to Noelle.

"Little different from modern radio tags." She looked up at Layle for confirmation.

He shrugged. "I don't know much about them. The radio spe-cialist from Game and Fish agreed, though. He took the back off here"—Layle pointed to a tiny panel—"and said the antenna apparatus was bigger than usual, and there was an especially powerful battery. Hence the size."

"Radio transmitters don't need much battery life?"

"That's what he said."

"Then what is it?"

"Outdated, he figured."

Noelle handed the silver pill back to Layle, who tucked it into its bag.

"Where does it go from here?"

"It'll live the rest of its life in evidence, along with all this stuff." He motioned to the file box. "Town doesn't have the resources to waste its time pursuing what looks like an illegal-species charge at most."

Noelle thought for a second. Yowlitz seemed to think this thing was open-and-shut, and Noelle had no reason to disagree.

"Go ahead and incinerate the carcass." Noelle pulled off the gloves and tossed them in the can by the garage doors. "Hold on to the chip."

"Don't worry; we can't dispose of it if the case isn't resolved. It'll be in evidence."

"Okay."

"Thanks for coming down."

Noelle put on her Ray-Bans and started toward the car.

Then she stopped and turned. "Oh, how's the chief?"

Layle clammed up, then stuttered. "H-he's good. On vacation as we speak."

"Give him my best." Noelle got in the Yukon and sped out of the lot toward the park.

# 28

"Then call him *again*!" Thomas Wright, assistant director of counter-intelligence, loomed over Divya.

"He doesn't want to be involved, sir."

"Unacceptable. Any word on whether the lobby is going to bring out Shar-Pei as ammo?"

"I convinced them it wouldn't be good for their reputation to leak American secrets."

"Good. Any new info from them?" Wright was pacing, squeezing a stress ball as though he were trying to kill it.

"Not really."

He stopped and shook his head emphatically. "Shit, Divya, he's an agent's dream—a perfectly embedded liaison. Call the man!"

"Isn't there anyone else?"

"They killed that police chief, Divya. Married, couple of kids."

196

"Are you sure?"

"Eighty percent sure. One of the hourly KH-11 transmissions captured the incident."

This filled Divya's mind with questions. "The NRO launched a Kennan Crystal for this? How detailed is the image? Isn't its orbit over two hundred miles?"

"I could tell you when the postman came to your house yesterday."

"Damn." During her preparation, she'd studied Jackson Hole Chief of Police Roger Terrell. She had come to glean that he was not only a solid law enforcement agent, but also a family man. "You said there was no chance of that."

"Things changed. Xiao's more desperate than we thought."

"How hot is the situation there?"

"Wouldn't be too bad for Trent. If he can locate the girl—give us some ideas about her whereabouts. He doesn't need to get any more involved than that."

"So what's the angle?"

"Make something up. You're good at that."

She gave an unconvincing nod. "What about his wife?"

"Alive, we're guessing. She's a good bargaining chip for them. We don't know her condition."

Wright sensed an opening.

"Do it for her, if nothing else. Send me Trent's information by the end of the day." He walked out of Divya's office.

She rubbed her eyes and took a big gulp of coffee. It was her fifth cup of the day. Her heart was pounding but her eyes were tired, her brain a drained battery.

She thought about Jake. His obvious misery in DC and with her. How clearly he'd yearned to be back home.

*What was her next move?* Coming clean was the best route

when dealing with someone as savvy as Jake, but Wright wouldn't allow that. He'd read enough about Trent to know he wouldn't buy into the company line if it contradicted his own sense of justice. According to the assistant director, Jake was too smart for his own good. Which was too bad, because Divya had no doubt that Jake would cooperate if he knew what had happened to Terrell and Charlotte.

*Xiao still has Charlotte, but what is* my *bargaining chip?* She'd been at the agency long enough to know that's what it was all about. A bit more coffee and she signed back into the system. She clicked on the file "Trent, Jake," browsed a bit, and then opened "Internal Affairs (1)," which hadn't even occurred to her before.

*Holy shit.* Her heart sank, but she knew it was her in.

# 29

Jake woke up to Don tying flies in the kitchen and drinking Red Bull on ice. Bacon was sizzling on the range. The smell of burnt toast overpowered the sour aroma of twenty-some empty Rainier cans on the counter, waiting to be recycled.

"No coffee?"

Don didn't look up. "Gave it up." He finished a Purple Peril, size six or so, and put another hook in the vise.

"I'll get some on the way out."

This got Don's attention. "Not fishing today?"

"Time to winterize, I'm afraid. No wood at the house, windows need taping, cover the boat."

"Season's just getting started!"

"Here, maybe. We're about done. Speaking of, don't you ever work?"

Don looked up from his work again. "I could be. Thought you got bitten by the steelhead bug again yesterday. Was gonna tool around with you."

Jake momentarily considered it. He thought of J.P. and Esma. "Nah, wish I could. Maybe next week. I'll call you."

Don shook his head and went back to the vise. "Getting cold out. That water temperature drops much more they won't chase flies so well."

"Right. Getting cold. Gotta winterize. You follow?"

"Asshole," Don jabbed.

Jake grabbed his backpack from the bottom of the stairs and headed for the door. "Go solo!" he shouted back toward the kitchen.

"That's when you know you have a problem!" Don yelled back.

Jake laughed and let the door close.

The weather had improved again overnight, contrary to Don's prediction. It was still early, but already forty degrees. The autumn sun was low but powerful. Nice enough for a light jacket and jeans.

Jake grabbed his Costas from their sunglasses bag and jumped in the SUV. He headed upriver along the Salmon, toward town and Highway 28.

The Exxon had something labeled "Coffee," and since Jake didn't have any alternatives, he filled his stainless travel mug with the hot liquid. It looked inky black and viscous, which was better than amber brown and thin.

He browsed the breakfast aisle for something healthy but came up empty-handed.

"Anywhere you'd recommend for breakfast?" Jake asked the cashier. The slight young man didn't look up.

"Subway."

"Thanks."

Halfway between Salmon and Leadore, Jake spotted a small diner on the right. He pulled into the gravel parking lot.

A bell rang as Jake opened the door, silencing a table of retirees.

"Molly! Someone's here," one of the table's more sprightly occupants yelled into the kitchen.

"Appreciate it." Jake grabbed a newspaper and sat at the counter. Under a clear plastic sheet there were old pictures of game—everything from bighorn sheep to mountain lions—that had been taken by local hunters.

Jake looked toward the group, who were eyeing him back. He sent a friendly smile.

"What's good?"

The same man spoke again, this time begrudgingly. "Corned beef hash. Not on the menu."

"Thanks again." *So much for healthy*, Jake thought.

Finally, Molly emerged from the kitchen and dropped a few plates of hash in front of the old codgers. She was slightly heavy but beautiful. Her demeanor matched. "So sorry to keep you waiting, honey; I do the cooking too."

"No problem at all."

"What can I get you?"

"A good cup of coffee and the corned beef hash."

"Sorry, Molly; Joe told him." A short man with a weak, raspy voice spoke up.

"Oh, you should know better, Joe," Molly teased. "Tellin' our secrets to strangers."

She leaned over the counter toward Jake and whispered, "They think they get the VIP treatment. Really, my printer's just broke and I can't change the menu."

"I won't tell," Jake flirted back.

"They can't hear anyway."

As Molly set his coffee down, Jake spread the paper out in front of him.

### Senator Canart Gains Student Support

Boise, Idaho—Senator Rick Canart is best known for his divisive stance on immigration and support of a bill that would, among other things, provide federal funding to companies who are developing human tracking technology, or nano-GPS.

During the mid-October congressional recess, he's brought his keystone message back home to Boise State.

"Idahoans, like myself, love their privacy and constitutional rights as much as anyone else, yet I have found great support here.

"Idahoans refuse to jump on the opponent's bandwagon, which is built solely on manufactured fear. They understand that we live in a changing world that requires a change in policies. The students here today on the lawn are an indication that even the most freedom-loving Americans understand a need for a revamped immigration policy."

According to the senator's staff, the crowd at the university was six hundred strong.

It all gave Jake the creeps. Not only the thought of a bugged world but also the political process—the deception and the posturing.

"What a mess," Jake mumbled under his breath as Molly clanged down his breakfast.

"What's that, sweetie? Something else?"

"More coffee. Thanks."

Jake turned to the local news, with pleasant headlines like "Wrestler Eric Brighton: This Year's High School State Champion."

His phone buzzed. Divya again. *Dammit. Why did I even go to DC?* He pressed ignore. She hadn't left a voice mail last night. Was she calling to apologize? He doubted it.

The coffee came.

Something had seemed off from the moment he arrived in DC. The party in Divya's apartment, the way the Divya acted, the men and women composing the lobby. It was all canned politics. It didn't fit with his recollections of Divya. Was she faking it just to climb the ladder? It made Jake sick to his stomach.

Or maybe it was the grease-marinated hash.

Jake left twenty bucks on the table, a good tip for a cheap meal. He turned to the breakfast club, but they were arguing over the nutritional values of various cattle feeds.

The drive back to Jackson passed smoothly, save for a slightly slick surface on the top of Teton Pass. Driving into the valley brought on a sense of relief. Here, Jake could live, like the King Cutty, safe and sound but for the occasional stinging ant. The sneaky little devils.

At the bottom of the pass, Jake turned right onto Trout Creek Road, which followed the stream past the back of the bed-and-breakfast and to its confluence with the Snake.

He turned left into the driveway. Chayote showed himself immediately upon Jake's arrival. He had been left out, probably roaming the neighborhood and looking for something smelly to roll in. The cattle dog reacted aggressively at first, guarding his territory, but when Jake rolled down the window and called to him, his tail wagged and he bounded alongside the vehicle.

He reached the guesthouse at the end of the driveway. There was no sign of J.P. The lights were off and his old truck was missing. Jake figured they were still on their way home.

It was 1:15 p.m. Plenty of time left in the afternoon to go collect the wood from the Millers' property below the Wilson faces. It was a good temperature for working outside too. Fifty degrees with intermittent clouds.

Jake opened the tailgate of the 4Runner and folded down the backseats to make room for the cargo. Without beckoning, Chayote hopped up into the back and lay down.

"Fair enough, buddy. You've been alone too long."


As Jake passed the old Stagecoach Bar, a pair of mountain bikers stuck out their thumbs, hoping to hitch a ride back to the top of the pass for another descent. Soon, they would be in ski gear. Jake headed north on the upper portion of Trout Creek Road, on the other side of Highway 22. Chayote joined him up front, sitting on the passenger seat and intently watching the scenery roll by.

Three miles up the road, Jake turned left onto a two-track and stopped. He got out of the vehicle, opened the cattle gate to the Miller ranch, and closed it behind him. He had taken the Millers fishing, and in exchange they offered him access to their woodpile. He switched the truck's transmission to four-wheel drive and proceeded slowly through the ruts, muddy from early season mountain snow.

The Millers' horses wandered over and followed the moving

car, thinking the visitor might be bearing gifts—apples, carrots, or at least some affection. Chayote, true to cattle-dog form, recognized the difference between bovine and equine and didn't yap.

A mile and a half past the gate, the slope of the mountains began and the vegetation changed from sagebrush and the occasional willow to all conifers. In a small pull-off on the right lay stacks of freshly cut wood.

After pulling a pair of gloves from his camping pack, Jake opened the rear hatch. Chayote bounded out and began working his nose. Satisfied they were alone, he walked with Jake to the woodpile.

It was a daunting task. Jake sighed, rolled his neck, and loaded up. Four or five pieces at a time. He loaded the logs first through the rear doors and then progressively worked his way back.

An hour later, the 4Runner was full.

Jake made one more trip in the afternoon and called it quits. He showered, put on clean clothes, and started a fire. It wasn't all that cold in the guesthouse, but it seemed apropos.

He was physically tired, but restless. He played on his laptop for a minute, checked fishing reports, and then lay down on the couch by the fire. Closing his eyes didn't work. His mind wandered. *Shouldn't have had all that diner coffee.* It was only 4:15 p.m., and Jake had nothing to do. With the King Cutty gone from his lair, Jake didn't feel like pursuing small fish.

Sitting up, he grabbed his phone from the side table and flipped it around in his hands a few times. In frustration, he scratched at his head, then unlocked the phone. *What the hell.* He dialed Divya.

"Jake, I'm glad you called." The bubbly tone was gone.

"What's going on?"

"I need you to do something for us."

"Listen, I told you, I'm not interested."

"Jake, please." Her voice sounded stilted—under duress? Jake couldn't tell.

"Look, I'm with you on this; the senator is off his rocker. I just can't commit to anything right now." He didn't mention that the mere thought of being involved made him feel anxious.

"Then why did you come?"

Jake forced a laugh. "I really don't know, Divya. Boredom. Sense of responsibility."

"Listen, Jake, just hear me out." More stress in her tone, almost melancholy.

"I can't. I'm gonna go." He felt relief. Whatever he needed to keep himself busy for the winter, this wasn't it.

Suddenly Divya cut in, blurting something out in a rush of words. But it couldn't have been what he thought.

Jake was silent for several seconds. "Say that again, Divya."

"Paris. 1995."

Jake's mind was racing. "Listen to me, Divya. I have no idea what you think you know—"

"I know it all."

"No." Jake was angry now. "If you knew it all, you wouldn't try to blackmail me with it."

"Then you can explain it to me. After you do one small favor for us."

Jake hung up the phone and slammed it on the table.

# 30

**TRAM VILLAGE, CHINA.**

Catatonic.

*Wait, are you catatonic if you have the ability to recognize that you're catatonic?* Charlotte didn't know. She knew she was trying to tell the giant that yes, she did want a glass of water, but nothing was coming out.

She also suspected that she should have been crying for the last two days, but why cry about something that wasn't real? *It was a dream.* She pinched herself again hard on the back of the arm. The giant scrambled over and pulled her hand away. She looked at her bare arm where he was pointing. Bruises everywhere.

*It's okay,* she tried to tell him. Nothing came out.

She was back in the hotel suite where the crazy dream had started. Just a few blocks from home, she figured. The dream wouldn't end until she got there to see the kids.

The stocky boss man came in again. *Ciao, Shaw, Zhe . . .* Xiao, *that was it.* He'd been sticking around the dream for a while now.

Charlotte could hear him talk, but it was muffled as though he were underwater. "I need you wake up."

*I'd love to wake up,* she thought. *Can you help?*

"Wake up!" This time it was less garbled. Louder. A slap across her face. She didn't feel it, just as she didn't feel the pinches.

"Get the phone!" she heard him say to the giant, who had also been in the dream for too long.

He held it to her ear. "It's the deputy, Charlotte. Talk!"

She must have dreamt that she was older. Her husband—*what was his name?*—was the deputy when they were in their thirties. Maybe she was dreaming the future. Someday he would be the chief. He would love that.

Finally, words came. "Honey?" she called softly into the phone.

"Charlotte? What the hell is going on?"

"Don't be mad."

"This is Layle, Charlotte. What's going on over there?"

*Layle was his name. Oh well.* She thought she remembered something different.

"Nothing. Sleeping."

Xiao yanked the phone from Charlotte's ear. "She's not well."

*Snarky bastard.*

She couldn't hear Layle's response.

Xiao spoke again. "Nothing. She's had some . . . what do you call . . . trauma."

*I'm fine,* Charlotte thought.

"So you've not found my daughter?" Xiao was getting angry. "We'll talk about Terrell when you give better news."

*Terrell,* Charlotte recognized, *is my last name.*

\*　　　\*　　　\*

Layle dropped the phone back in its cradle. It was 6 p.m. but he was nowhere near going home. Keeping the secret was driving him crazy, but Xiao seemed to know everything. If he enlisted help, he had no doubt the man would do something insane. If he hadn't already.

Jess, Layle's fiancée, was calling on his cell again. *Goddammit!*
"Hello?"

"Jesus, what's up your ass?"

"Honey, I . . . nothing, I just can't talk right now. Work is crazy."

"Sure. You better not be with some woman." She was kidding, but it sent him over the edge.

"Why do you always do this? Can't you tell I don't have time for this shit?"

No response.

He looked at the phone's screen. *Call ended.*

Layle cursed and slammed his fist down on the desk. A few files of census data slid off and fell all over the floor. He tilted his head back and sighed, trying to compose himself. In the last few days, he had focused solely on finding Meirong Xiao, except for the brief meeting with Noelle Klimpton to close the wolf case.

He'd searched old county and state cases back to 1980. All arrest records. Census data, phone books, and online. Real estate transactions, old newspapers, business records, articles of incorporation, and civil complaints. Even in surrounding areas. There was no trace of her.

He had run out of resources. Nothing to do but climb up on the roof and yell her damned name.

For the second time that day, Deputy Layle looked through the

FBI contact folder from the chief's desk. He knew what he was looking for: CIRG or Critical Incident Response Group. This was the department that provided emergency assistance for hostage situations, kidnappings, and crises. He dialed the main line but hung up, wondering whether Xiao might intercept the call. Instead, he walked across the hall to the DMV, overrode the network's email password protection with his county-clearance code, and typed up a message to the address listed under "Tips."

Layle filled the email with as much detail as he could without revealing his own identity. He took a deep breath and sent it, then returned to his desk, where he unbuttoned his shirt and hung it on the hook and pulled on a U of Wyoming football sweatshirt. He grabbed the keys to his pickup and locked his office.

Instead of driving back over the pass and home to Victor, Layle headed to the brewpub. The first amber ale and whiskey shot went down too easy, but not as easy as the second round. The dinner crowd filtered in around 7 p.m., filling every available seat. For his third, Layle switched to the pale ale and omitted the whiskey. He started looking around: first, to see if someone fitting Meirong's description might wander by, and second, to make sure there weren't any Chinese henchmen stalking him.

His paranoia grew worse with beers four and five. That was when his phone rang. The caller ID said "Blocked," like every call from Xiao.

"Be right back," he told the bartender.

The sun was setting and it was cold outside. Snow King Mountain was making snow for the upcoming season.

"Hello?"

"Layle Statler?" *Surprise.* It was a pleasant woman's voice, with a mild accent that he couldn't place.

"Yeah?"

"I'm calling about the tip you left on the bureau's website."

Layle was uneasy. He looked around at the locals smoking in the parking lot.

"How'd you get this number?"

The woman sighed. "We're the FBI."

"Yeah, well, I'm a cop; you can't find a personal cell phone number just from an IP address."

"Our resources are extensive, Mr. Statler."

The deputy doubted the woman, but went along. "What's your name?"

"Agent Rachel Vandeleur."

"Hang on, Agent Vandeleur." Layle walked out of the brewpub's parking lot and onto Millward Street, heading south to get away from anyone who might overhear. He stopped between two parked cars, checked his surroundings, and spoke. "Okay, let's talk."

"How have you been in contact with the people holding the chief?"

"Phone. Blocked number. Same as yours."

Vandeleur ignored Layle's suspicion. "We can get around that. Do you have any other information about the captors?"

"His name is Xiao, the one in charge. They are being held at a resort in China. Tram Village, China. That's why the chief went there—to do publicity for this resort based on our town. But it was a ruse, I guess. The guy, Xiao, wants his daughter back; he's totally obsessed. He says she's somewhere here. But I . . ." Guilt washed over him. "I can't find her, and I haven't heard from the chief himself in a while." Layle described the phone calls from China, Xiao's increasing frustration, and the uncertainty of Terrell's condition.

"It's okay, Deputy. We'll get them back safely."

"What should I do?"

"It's important that you don't tell anyone about this. We must be discreet, or we risk creating an international incident. If the chief's stay goes longer than expected, tell your department that the Terrells extended their vacation."

"That's it? What—what are you going to do?"

"Talk to my superior, discuss with Foreign Affairs, verify our jurisdiction, and then act."

*Vague.*

"Can you keep me updated on the progress?" A hiccup from the craft beer.

"Yes, Deputy. We'll be in touch. Call me if you hear from Xiao again." She gave the deputy her number. It had a 202 area code.

The woman hung up. Layle glanced around once more, then headed back to the pub to try to forget about it for now.

# 31

Assistant Director Wright didn't sound pleased to be on the receiving end of Divya's late-night phone call.

"We intercepted a message from Terrell's stand-in, sir. The deputy." Divya and Wright had jumped through a month of bureaucratic hoops over the summer to bug the police station. It hadn't been easy. Since the mid-twentieth century, two congressional subcommittees, the Senate Select Committee for Intelligence (SSCI) and the House Permanent Select Committee on Intelligence (HPSCI), had overseen the actions of the CIA. Neither had been too keen to investigate a fellow lawmaker, let alone bug the office of a state law-enforcement entity. But Wright had swayed them, highlighting the potential ramifications of taking no action.

Divya listened to Wright and cringed, hoping he approved of her intervening and improvising with the deputy.

"Yes, he contacted the FBI," she replied. "CIRG, to be precise." She scratched a few notes onto a pad. "Well, I told him we would get the chief back."

A short rant from Wright, then: "Luckily, both oversight committees—SSCI and HPSCI—are on recess with the rest of Congress. Don't ever tell them about going over the heads of CIRG and the feds. It's between you and me." He went on with a few more questions.

"Right. He has no reason to suspect anything more than a simple quid pro quo. The chief for the daughter."

A few more notes.

"Thank you, sir."

After hanging up, Divya grabbed her notepad and tossed it into her briefcase. Wright was never totally happy with anything, but he sounded relatively approving of her stratagem. She was instructed to carry on with the Agent-Rachel-Vandeleur ruse to see what she could find out.

Divya picked up the desk phone and called her favorite cab driver.

"It is late, Rashi, I know. Thank you."

A few agents were still in various departments of Langley, men and women unfamiliar to her. She threw them weak smiles and nods. The CIA didn't approve of too much socializing between units.


At home in Georgetown, Divya drew a bath. She did some of her best thinking there, although for this case it was really Wright's job to do the thinking.

A simple task had become a mess. Figure out how and why an Idaho senator had come to be familiar with a Chinese technology that was not only top secret but also developed by one of the most elusive and dangerous Chinese spies in history. A spy who had allegedly given up his trade nearly a decade ago.

*An Idaho senator, for God's sake. How did these two individuals find each other?*

How the daughter played into it all was another question, though of secondary importance to the agency. But finding her was paramount, if only because it would help get the chief's widow back. *Poor woman.*

Whether Wright's conjecture that Xiao and Canart had a physical presence around the Greater Yellowstone area was correct didn't matter. There was no way he was going to let Divya go herself. He wasn't keen on using a desk agent who might stick out like a sore thumb. The matter called for someone discreet—a local, who would blend in, wouldn't raise any eyebrows. He wanted Trent. Jake knew the people and the area. And most important, he understood the mechanics of operations like this. He could be trusted.

She had Jake in her pocket now. Everyone in this business had at least one skeleton in the closet. That *one* scar on the Internal Affairs record. And she had found his, buried in a classified government file.

When it was all over, she would apologize and tell him the truth—that she made a mistake in mentioning his name, that she never knew Wright would be interested. That she still cared about him and that she was still the same Divya. Her job just interfered with her personal life sometimes. Often it prevented her from having a personal life at all.

Divya's cell phone rang as she was drying herself off. Number blocked.

"Yes?"

"This is Layle Statler." She'd given him her cell number while posing as the FBI agent. The blocked number meant he didn't trust her totally, but apparently he had nowhere else to go.

"What can I do for you, Deputy?" She was looking at herself in the mirror, at her own curious face.

The man sounded drunk, emotional. "Get me Terrell back. Somebody killed the janitor. I can't deal with all this . . ."

"*What?* Wait, slow down, Deputy." Divya ran to the bedroom to get her tablet of paper and a pen.

# 32

Jake's cell phone rang: unknown local number. He ignored it. They called twice more.

He pushed a snoring Chayote off his lap, marked his place in the John Gierach book he was reading, and picked up.

Before he could say a word, the rambling started. "H-he *trusted* you, you know? Why I'm calling . . ."

"Who is this?"

". . . said you were a good man . . ." Λ long sigh. Thc caller took a moment to compose himself. "I-I need a ride."

"*Who* needs a ride?" Jake was standing, one hand up and open, confused. It sounded like a typical J.P. request, but the voice didn't match. As far as he knew, J.P. and Esma weren't back from Salmon yet.

A deep breath and a push of garbled energy. "Deputy to the chief, Layle Statler! Okay?"

"Layle?" Jake knew him only in passing. "You need a ride? What's going on?"

"I need a ride to—ah, Game and, ah, Fish, you can believe that. F-fast."

"Where are you?"

"Brewpub. The FBI won't help. Somebody just got killed at Game and Fish. Next to the visitor's center."

"FBI? What did you say?"

"Oh yeah. Poor guy."

"I'll be right there. No more beers."

Chayote was up and ready, but Jake told him to stay as he closed the guesthouse door behind him. Jake unlocked the SUV, grabbed the Glock from his camping pack, and tucked it inside the driver's door sleeve.

It was crystal clear in the valley, and cold. The two always went hand in hand. The Milky Way shone as brightly as Jake had ever seen it. As he crossed the Wilson Bridge, the inky Snake reflected its light—a gleaming serpent slithering to its den for the night.

The light at Broadway and 22 seemed to take forever, though few people were out. The road-tripper minivans, campers, and RVs that clogged the streets all summer were gone. Any remaining visitors were staying in the hotels downtown. Retirees, mainly, on tour busses.

Jake turned left on Broadway, drove toward the square, and turned left on Millward. He saw a man on the corner of Millward and Hansen, looking wobbly and holding a cell phone.

Jake parked in a handicapped spot in the pub's lot and jumped out.

"Layle?"

"I didn't have any more to drink."

"Good. What's going on?" Jake did his best to read the man. *Another murder?* "Start from the beginning."

The deputy cleared his throat and spit on the asphalt. "I'll tell you on the way. Can we go?"

They got in the 4Runner and Jake reversed back out onto Millward. "Fill me in. Who's on the scene?"

"Somebody found a body in the warehouse."

Jake was doing his best to be patient. "Any officers on the scene?"

Layle looked at him, dumbfounded. "Paramedics. And, well . . . I'll be there shortly."

*Jesus.* "Call the officer on duty. Who got the dispatch call?"

"I did—I forgot to change the forwarding when I left the station."

"Call the officer on duty *now.*"

Layle did as Jake said. They turned into the Game and Fish parking lot, where an ambulance came into view. The lights were on in the building. Just behind them, a cruiser with flashing lights and sirens screeched to a halt. A uniformed police officer hopped out.

"I'm Jake Trent."

The officer gave him the once-over. No time for a handshake. "I know who you are. The fishing guide who saved Yellowstone. I'm Officer McClelland." He turned to his superior. "He legit?" He was out of breath and got to the point.

Jake answered, to save Layle the effort. "Just here to help the deputy."

"He's good," Layle mumbled.

McClelland pulled Jake aside. "What's with him?"

"Don't know. Few beers, I guess." Jake led the group toward the entrance, deflecting the line of questioning, and held the door for the two policemen.

Inside, a couple of young paramedics were standing over something. One spoke in a panic: "Took you long enough!"

"First homicide for him," the other said.

"Shut up," the first replied.

The quarreling was too much for the deputy. "Stand down!" he growled. Jake responded by pulling Layle back by the collar, then patting him on the back. *Relax.*

"Sorry."

At the paramedics' feet lay the body of a sixtysomething man. It wasn't anyone Jake recognized. He was small statured. Short gray hair, long gray beard.

"Gunshot wound to the chest," the rookie paramedic said.

"Did anybody touch the body?"

"No, sir."

"Who heard the shot?" asked McClelland.

"Nobody. He called in on his own." The young officer shrugged.

Jake and McClelland followed the blood trail to a shop bench where a bloodstained land phone lay, still off the hook. Layle stumbled catching up.

"What's with the deputy?" the paramedic asked his cohort. Layle mean-mugged him, preventing further query.

From the shop bench, the trio followed the spatter to one of the garage doors.

Jake held back, allowing McClelland to do his job. "Was the garage open?"

"Yes, sir."

"Fingerprint this?" McClelland turned to Jake, and pointed to the garage-door button.

"Print the outside keypad too."

"Perp would have to know the code." McClelland said with his pen at the numbers on the pad.

"Yeah." McClelland nodded, knowing Jake was saying, *Inside job?*

"But why leave the garage open?"

"In a hurry, probably." Jake walked outside a few paces, then stopped and pointed to a pile of debris just outside the garage, and then to a broom that rested a few yards away. "Perp didn't know the code, necessarily."

"Shoot. Victim was sweeping out the garage?" Officer McClelland jotted notes on a pad and snapped a few pictures of the broom with his phone.

"Wandered inside to call 911. He moved fast—the blood trail didn't start until he was inside."

"The perp never bothered to make sure he was dead."

"Right." Jake nodded. "Rules out an execution-style killing. It was quick, maybe even shot from the car."

"I need a coffee," Layle blurted, then hiccupped. "I'm going across the street to the gas station."

McClelland nodded at his boss and turned. "What about the body?" he said to Jake.

"Let's take a look."

Jake allowed McClelland to approach the body first, knowing better than to touch anything at the crime scene. The victim had a large section of his torso missing.

"Shotgun," Jake said.

McClelland was holding his hand over his mouth. "No shit," he mumbled.

Jake bent and looked at the damage. "That's not duck shot. Three and a half 12-gauge, at least."

"Goose gun?"

"No. Self-defense gun. Bear gun, whatever. The spread is wide, suggesting a short barrel. Maybe sawed-off. Or a really long shot, but it wouldn't have done this much damage."

"So not a hunting gun."

Jake stood up. "Probably not."

"These his tracks?" McClelland pointed to two bloody footsteps that headed away from the garage door, toward the back of the building. After a few steps, the blood had dried on the victim's shoes, leaving a path to nowhere.

Jake checked the victim's shoes. "No." He'd already noted that the paramedics were wearing the required shoe covers for the crime scene.

McClelland stopped. "Then the shooter did make entry. Why not finish the job?"

"Cause he didn't care whether this guy lived?"

Layle walked back in sipping a twenty-ounce high-octane from the Exxon.

"What you got?" His cadence was slow and even. He was trying his best to get back in the game, focusing.

"Tracks, Dep." McClelland gestured toward the footprints.

"I see. But to where?" Layle followed McClelland's finger in the direction the tracks led. "Son of a *bitch*!" He moved the fastest he had all evening over to the walk-in cooler. The paramedics had drifted off to the open garage door to get some fresh air. The excitement in the deputy's voice got their attention, and they turned back toward the scene.

"What is it?" McClelland was right behind the deputy.

Jake carefully pulled back the sheet that covered the victim from the shoulders down. The janitor's shirt had been torn open after the shooting and his pockets turned inside out. The killer was looking for something, but had never bothered to shoot again.

Layle hollered from the walk-in. "Holy shit!"

Jake hurried over. "What is it?"

Layle and McClelland were standing over an empty lab cart.

"They took the damned wolf."

"What?"

"They killed the janitor and took the wolf carcass."

Jake turned to McClelland for help in deciphering Layle's statement.

"There was a wolf here, alpha male, waiting to be incinerated."

"Incinerated? Why would someone steal it?" Jake asked as the trio left the frigid cooler.

"Dep?" McClelland avoided the question.

"Don't know. Didn't seem right from the beginning," Layle muttered.

"What didn't?"

Layle scratched his head. "We found the wolf with an outdated radio tag in it. Big ol' thing, hit by a car. Must've been someone's pet or something."

"And the driver?"

"Hit-and-run. Nobody wants to admit to something like that, let alone pay the fine."

"And they came back to get it? For a proper burial?" McClelland jumped in.

The deputy was shaking his head. "Guess so."

Jake shook his too—in disbelief. "Kill a man for a carcass? Doesn't add up."

"Yeah, Deputy, I've gotta agree here, I mean . . ."

Layle walked away, on a mission. "Let's check the parking lot."

The medic shouted after them. "What do I do with the body?"

"Leave it," Jake shouted over his shoulder. "Stay here."

The night sky was glowing with starlight. The temperature had dropped further, into the upper twenties. A setting moon left only a sliver of light on the horizon. Jake looked around, just to be doubly sure they weren't in immediate danger. He didn't see anything, and heard nothing but coyotes quarrelling on the National Elk Refuge. Their yips echoed from Saddle Butte back to them. Jake figured they were as confused as he was—howling into the blackness, hearing only an augmented echo of their own questions.

"I'll start here." Layle began slowly walking the perimeter closest to the warehouse.

McClelland was pulling on latex evidence gloves.

Jake headed to the far side, where the lot abutted the southeast corner of the visitor center. He walked slowly, scanning the pavement for candy wrappers, receipts, cigarette butts, or anything else that might have fallen out of the assailant's car.

McClelland had a small bag of evidence going. He joined Jake on the far side of the lot.

"Couple butts over there, that's it."

McClelland went over and picked them up, then returned to Jake's side to show him.

"Where's the chief, anyway?" Jake asked the officer.

"Vacation."

"Figures."

The deputy ambled their way, and they went quiet.

"Find anything?"

"Couple cigarette butts, coffee cup, that's it."

"Shit. No tire marks?" Layle glanced around at the pavement.

"None." McClelland waited for Layle's next cue. The deputy clapped his palms together, trying to think.

Jake was thinking too.

"Does the warehouse have security cameras?"

"Already thought of that. Doesn't look like it." The deputy sounded more sober with every sip of his drink. He and Jake looked skyward, inspecting the roof's eave for a camera.

"How 'bout the visitor center?" McClelland asked.

"Nothing to protect in there. They don't bother with anything other than door and window alarms." Layle waited for a second and started back toward the crime scene.

Jake made him stop in his tracks. "They've got a webcam facing the elk refuge. Hunters watch it to see how the snow affects the movement of the herds. Whether they've started moving to their winter range."

Layle spun to face McClelland. "Get me the director of the Grand Teton Association. Wake her up if need be. And call a detective for the crime scene."

The association ran the visitor center and a few informational kiosks throughout the valley.

"We won't have any view of the lot," the officer objected.

"Get the video."

Currently the only animals in the refuge were a flock of geese resting on the banks of Flat Creek, just thirty yards from the warehouse. The elk would move in sometime in the next month, escaping the heavy snow in the mountains.

A half hour later, a brand new Mercedes SUV pulled into the lot. Out stepped Anne Lowe, the association director, wearing a Patagonia fleece and sweatpants.

"What's going on?"

She met Jake and Layle at the glass front doors of the center, where they'd been waiting since McClelland called. He was off snapping pictures of the crime scene and looking for prints so the medics could get the body to the morgue.

"We need to view the footage from the past several hours on your refuge webcam."

The woman stopped, irked. "How would I have any idea how to do that?"

"We'll figure that out when we get in there. Open the door, please."

"Has there been a crime?"

"Homicide."

"Jesus." She unlocked the door.

"I'll go in first. Just in case." The deputy shined a flashlight he'd commandeered from the medics around the atrium of the center, then waved Jake and Ms. Lowe in.

The building's interior looked eerie in the beam of the flashlight. A mount of a grizzly bear stood to the left of the stairs up the main floor, a black bear to the right.

"Where are the lights?"

"Main lights are on a timer. Let's just go to my office."

They went up the stairs, past the information counter and to the right. Lowe opened a door in the corner and flipped on a light, revealing a stuffy office filled with magazines, books, and newspapers.

"I don't spend much time in here."

"Boot up your computer. Who runs your webcams?"

"A guy named Travis from Idaho Falls does most of the tech work."

"Get him on the phone."

The director looked through a Rolodex and dialed from her desk phone.

"Travis? Anne Lowe at the Grand Teton Association. I have a strange request."

She gave Layle a thumbs-up.

"The police have asked me to bring up webcam footage from a few hours ago. . . . Right. Is that possible?"

She waited, then nodded. "Okay. Thank you." Lowe hung up and turned her desk chair toward Layle and Jake, still looking impatient. "He's going to bring it up remotely." She logged in and then clicked an icon. "What happened?" She seemed keen for new gossip.

"I can't tell you until I have more information myself."

"Oh."

"He's in." Layle pointed to the monitor.

A window to the webcam program had opened, and Travis was inputting commands. He started the video at 6 p.m. and gave control back to the mouse and keyboard in the office.

They reviewed the tape in fast-forward. When the time stamp read 8:50 p.m., Layle slowed the video to real time.

"Headlights," Jake said.

"Look at the geese spook."

"They're dim. Old car?"

"Looks like it," Jake said. "Or just fog lights."

"Right; he could've cut the headlights."

The lights turned off at 8:51 p.m. and came back on just after 8:59.

"Quick strike, if he's our guy."

Jake nodded. "Wait, slow down here."

At 8:59:48, the lights grew dimmer but their beam wider. The car was backing up.

"Where's he going?"

"Looks like he's facing north." Jake pointed to the top left of the screen, where the headlights shone.

# 33

Layle was on McClelland's radio, shouting an all-points to the surrounding law-enforcement agencies. Jake was catching McClelland up on the webcam.

A call came back.

"Ranger Klimpton for Deputy Layle."

Suddenly, despite the cold air, Jake's cheeks felt as though they were burning.

"Go ahead," Layle radioed back.

"I had a beat-up white Toyota Tercel come through a speed trap north of Moose around 9:20 p.m."

"Did you stop him?"

"Wasn't speeding. Driver was a woman."

"Thanks."

"Let's go." Layle tossed the cruiser's keys to McClelland, jumped

228

into the passenger seat, and got back on the horn, updating the other agencies with the car information.

Before he closed the door, he held out a hand, which Jake took and shook.

"Appreciate your help. Discretion would be appreciated."

"Of course. But, Deputy?"

Layle turned back to Jake.

"What was all that about the chief, when you called me?"

"Another time." In the dim light from the cruiser's interior, Jake thought he saw the deputy's face turn ghost white.

It was downright cold. Jake hustled back to the car and headed back toward the west bank of the Snake. On the way, his phone rang for what seemed like the millionth time in the last few days.

*Who is it now?* He hoped it was Noelle—hearing her voice had gotten him all sentimental—but she didn't know he had been with Layle. There was no reason she would call now, or any other time.

Jake flipped the phone over on the dash to see the caller ID. Divya. *Goddammit.*

He answered, intending to put an end to this once and for all.

"Divya. *Enough.* What do you want?"

She got right to the point. "I need you to help me find someone. Someone that lives in your area."

"Why? I've got no reason to cooperate with you."

She sighed. "We went over this."

"That information won't hurt me now."

"I'm not trying to hurt you. But do you really want the Paris story public?"

"Nobody here would listen. They wouldn't care."

"I bet Noelle Klimpton would be astonished."

"Is that what this is about? Jealousy?"

"*Sure.*"

Jake weighed his options.

"What's the name?"

"Meirong Xiao. I'll email you a description."

"Never heard the name. How did she end up in your sights?"

"We think we can use her to discredit the senator."

"Woman on the side?"

"Exactly."

"Jesus, Divya! What are you *doing*?" Jake was fuming.

"Check your email." Divya hung up.

Jake pulled in to the bed-and-breakfast at 11:10 p.m. The light in the guesthouse's living room was on, exactly as he left it. J.P.'s truck was still missing. Inside, Chayote was running in his sleep on the rug next to the fire, being chased or chasing in a dog dream.

Jake emptied his pockets onto the side table and sat down. He bent forward with his elbows on his knees and took a deep breath. Restless and annoyed, he went to the fireplace and added another log, which spooked Chayote. He hopped up and ran to the front door, barking the whole way.

"You're okay. C'mon."

Jake lay down on the couch and Chayote jumped up with him, settling down by his feet.

"I should've gone fishing today, Chayote." He closed his eyes. *Why was Divya so hell-bent on involving him in her political games? He knew now that she had been manipulating him from the start, but to what end? And why* him? *How the hell had she learned about Paris?*

He shifted his legs, numb from Chayote's weight. The dog grumbled his disapproval, repositioned himself, and got back to snoring. Jake followed soon after.

# 34

Susan was loading the white Tercel with her clothes and toiletries.

"You're going to stay with *him*?" her partner asked. He tried to put up some resistance. He stood near the door to the house, arms crossed.

"What does it matter? I can't stay around here."

Dr. Eric Youst didn't know what to say. She was right, he knew. "What do I do with Alfie?"

"Bury him on the Buffalo Fork. That was always our plan."

"I can't believe you did this. We're fucked." He threw his hands up in the air and let them fall to his sides, clapping against his painter's jeans.

Susan stopped packing. "They were going to incinerate him. Sweep him up like garbage and put him in a Dumpster."

"Where's my money?"

231

Susan resumed packing and pretended not to hear. Eric approached her and grabbed her by the arm.

"Hey! When is my money coming?"

"It'll be here!"

"You don't need me anymore, I guess? You have him."

"Fuck you. I'll bring the money. Then you can do whatever you want."

"They'll catch you trying to get out of here."

"I'm not going through town."

"Good luck." Eric didn't mean it. He slammed the door and walked back inside the warm house.


Susan tried to shake it, but she was scared. Unfortunately, there still weren't any other options. She had to go, *now*. From what the senator had told her, she assumed it wasn't just the police that were after her. The safest place was anywhere but home.

She opened the garage from the pad near the door, looked briefly at the warm light coming under the door from the main house, blew a kiss in Eric's general direction, and got in the Toyota.

The headlights were off, in case someone was watching the cabin from afar. She leaned over to the passenger seat to make sure the shotgun was within reach should anyone try to stop her.

When she hit the highway, she turned on the headlights. At Moran, she went north through the Grand Teton National Park gates, unmanned at that late hour. Going the speed limit through national-park land was frustrating; she wanted badly to push the little four-cylinder to its limit and get the hell out of Jackson Hole as soon as possible. But that was asking for trouble.

A herd of elk crossed right before she went through the Yellowstone gates, miles farther down the road. Thirty head or more. They seemed to move in slow motion.

Another unmanned gate. *Thank God.* Susan had taken one man's life. She wasn't interested in taking another. A thirty-two-year-old murderess. She had been so close to starting over, finding peace after a youth of chaos, manipulation, and abandonment.

The park was quiet, eerily so. She half expected to round a bend and find a roadblock waiting. She turned left onto Grand Loop Road toward West Yellowstone. Almost there.

When she made it through West Yellowstone and was headed south on Idaho Route 20, she called the senator.

"Hi." She knew she sounded like a schoolgirl, but she couldn't help it. She was in awe of him. From nothing, he'd transformed himself into a presidential hopeful.

"Susan? We're in bed here." Meaning he and his wife.

"Baby, you said you were leaving her."

"*You* said that."

"Let's not argue."

"Okay." A hissing sigh that cut through Susan like a knife. "What is it?"

*Why did he sound so disappointed?* "I'm coming there. I had to get away from Jackson."

He was walking, getting out of the bedroom so he could talk business. "I told you to stay."

"You said I was in danger."

"*Shit.* I said you needed to be aware that he was looking for you. Wanted you back. I've got nowhere for you to stay, and it's definitely not safe here."

Things were falling apart. *Why is he acting this way?* "You tell my goddamned father to come and get me, if he can. You can protect me, can't you?"

Another sigh. "Where are you?"

"I can be there in an hour."

"I'll meet you at the lab."


Senator Canart went back into the bedroom, where his wife was now awake.

"What is it?"

"Nothing. Just heard that CNN is going to tear me apart next week. I need to go meet with the boys."

"This late?"

"It will all be worth it when this thing gets approved." He gave her a peck on the cheek, got dressed, and headed downstairs.

There was coffee left in the pot, which he drank cold. He took the keys to the Lincoln from the basket and went to the garage.

Rick Canart was sixty-four years old, bald on the top with a ring of Just For Men "Real Black" hair cut short. He was shorter than he would have liked, and bigger around the waist. His tone was most often quiet and intelligent, but his speeches could become impassioned, almost fiery, when discussing immigration.

His father, Rick Sr., was a self-made man, who by all public accounts had lived the American dream. Starting young, he created a lumber empire in Coeur D'Alene, without attending college. Later in life, he took the privileged family east to Idaho Falls and set up shop. There, Rick Sr. occupied various county political offices.

Young Rick attended Washington State, where he studied mechanical engineering. After graduating in three years, he went back to Idaho to take over the logging business from his ailing father. It was then that he discovered his family's involvement with members of the Christian Identity Church, who had helped form the Aryan Nation in the early '70s.

The twenty-one-year-old was enraged at his father, having taken his cues from a liberal state institution during the height of the social revolution. But by the time his father died in 1980, Rick Jr. had come to embrace many of the teachings of the Christian Identity Church—including the belief that European-descended Americans were the chosen race of God. In his young career, he'd already seen thousands of jobs taken by immigrants in the agriculture and logging industries.

When the logging boom breathed its last breath, Rick Jr. sold off the business and seeded a technology firm, Catalyst Technologies, to take advantage of a growing industry. During the early years, Rick Jr. focused his mechanical-engineering knowledge on downsizing electronics for use in new consumer products such as the Walkman and the personal computer.

Political aspirations took him away from the helm of the company off and on, and in turn the company veered away from consumer products to government contracts for various technologies, including Radio Frequency Identification (RFID). A predecessor to GPSN, RFID became mainstream by the early '90s, and Rick Jr. was at the forefront of its introduction.

As a public servant, Rick Canart Jr. grasped early on that a heavy-handed approach was counterproductive. With the advice of party mentors, his career arched along a path less extreme than his father's. He found great success in Idaho running on a more moderate platform, at least on its face. He worked his Christian Identity message into his platform only in the most diluted way possible, and never directly, because he was a smart politician.

Now, he was in the biggest mess of his life. The development of the nano-GPS was a quagmire of political and personal entanglements. It had been a simple transaction in theory. Canart would get the savant Meirong so he could complete his project. Xiao would be paid licensing fees for life. A cool million every quarter.

The problems arose when the brilliant Meirong took a liking to Senator Canart that bordered on obsession. And the senator had been flattered by the exotic young woman's fixation. Canart enjoyed her company. His desire was heightened by how wrong it all was. A married, xenophobic senator sneaking away to make love to a young Chinese woman. If he got caught, he knew his marriage and career would be over. Somehow, it added to thrill.

Unfortunately, after a stupid argument with Meirong, she had informed her father of their tryst. His political survival was now at risk, and with it the fortune he would make from the GPSN technology.

Now, Xiao wanted to take Meirong back and call off the whole deal. Luckily, his ability to do so was limited. As a former cyber-spy for the Chinese, Xiao wouldn't dare show his face in the United States.

The trouble now was what to do with Meirong. Canart needed her to complete his project and get the technology off the ground, but he couldn't have her so close that she was threatening his personal life and public image.

Indeed, the girl *was* something special to Canart—not because of the nights they'd spent together, but because of her intellect. After failing school the year her mother died, she became a prodigy. When she was eighteen, her father sold the technology she'd helped develop to the Chinese government for what amounted to just over fifteen million in US dollars. They called it Shar-Pei. Technology that would protect the herd—the Chinese population—from destroying itself.

The senator went to the front office of the electronics laboratory and switched on the light. He cleared off the couch in the corner and tidied up the desk. Dim headlights shone through the window. It was her. She looked around in her normal paranoid way, then hurried to the door. Canart was there before she knocked. She met him with an embrace.

"Get inside." Though he was an hour from home, he didn't know who might be watching. He walked her through the small lobby and to the office.

"You need to stay here for a while. I'll go over to Walmart and get bedding. You can't leave, okay?"

She smiled. "What are we going to do tonight?"

"You're not understanding what's going on, Meirong."

"Don't call me that."

*Jesus.* "Susan. You don't understand. We need to get the proto-type down to size and move on. Couple of weeks, max. That's all you have. I'm back to DC in a week or so."

"What about us?" The smile had faded.

"We can talk about that later." He brushed his hand against her hair to placate her. "I'm going to get you some stuff so you can sleep, okay?"

She kissed him on the cheek.

Back in his Lincoln, Canart dialed Xiao. There was one card left to play.

He got Xiao's voice mail. "Listen," the senator said, "let us finish what we started, and I'll get you the information about your wife's shooting. Be in touch."

For now, he would keep Meirong in the lab, working as much as she could to get the chip down to the size where investors would take him seriously. It would take all that and the public funds he was pursuing to get the chips into production.

Once that was done, he would ride out another term to assure implementation of the program, and then resume his role as CEO of Catalyst Technologies.

# 35

Jake woke up and checked his email, where Divya's description was waiting. He read it with disgust. Then deleted it, feeling nothing but hatred toward Divya now. *What the hell am I supposed to do? Wander around Jackson Hole looking for an Asian woman in her early thirties? To hell with that. She can tell Noelle all she wants.*

He opened a new message and addressed it to Divya, letting his frustration out and informing her that he wasn't going to be blackmailed. Send.

Next was the Deputy Layle Statler situation. Jake was intrigued by his comments on Chief Terrell. *What did he mean, the chief trusted me? Why doesn't he trust me now? Where is he?* He phoned the police station and asked for Layle, who was out. Then he asked the secretary about the chief.

"Vacation," she said. "With his wife. They finagled a free trip to China." There wasn't an inkling of concern in her voice.

*China?*

Unsatisfied with the answer, Jake resigned himself to starting the coffee, then went upstairs to change clothes and brush his teeth. When he got back downstairs, Chayote was yipping at the window as J.P.'s pickup finally rolled in.

"What up?" J.P. looked happy to be home, but exhausted. Esma was behind him. "You just getting up?"

Jake looked at the clock on the oven. It was almost 10 a.m. "Wow. Yeah, I guess I slept in. Everything okay?" He glanced from one to the other.

"I'm going to run to the restroom." Esma excused herself.

"You good?" Jake asked again.

"Yeah, man. We're recovering. They, uh . . ." J.P. looked around to make sure Esma was out of earshot. "They treated her like shit, man. Those rednecks."

This confirmed to Jake what he'd already figured. "Jesus," he said. "I'm sorry." A quick embrace.

"But, you know, we're good." He nodded to convince himself. "We're alive. How you been?"

"Ah, crazy. I'll tell you some other time."

Esma returned and gave Jake a big hug.

"Welcome back," he said.

"We're gonna head to breakfast. Wanna join?"

"You guys go and have fun."

Jake sipped the black coffee from an old yellow mug with a faded message on it. Noelle had given it to him. *Do what you love. Love what you do.*

A wet snow fell on J.P. and Esma as they hurried back to the truck. Jake smiled, feeling comforted that things were at least normal on that front.

"These mug folks really make it sound easy, Chayote."

The dog barked.

"Breakfast. How could I forget?"

After feeding time, Jake pulled on some Muck Boots and an old Orvis raincoat that hung near the back door. He walked out through a quarter-inch of slush to look for the King Cutty.

A few modest-sized fish sipped blue-winged olives in the middle of the current, but the castle was vacant. The fish had moved elsewhere, as Jake suspected.

Throwing sopping snowballs to Chayote occupied Jake for another ten minutes, until his hands froze. He heard the grumble of gravel that meant they had a visitor. Chayote was two steps ahead, already running full speed toward the front.

Walk-ins were rare at the bed-and-breakfast, but not totally unheard of. Jake hoped the guard dog wouldn't deter the guests.

"C'mere! Leave it!"

The snow came harder. Firm little spheres, not friendly flakes. It blew up from the ground and around, irritating Jake's eyes.

In the driveway, there was a park ranger's Yukon.

Jake called Chayote over and stood near the front door, waiting. The heeler could barely contain his excitement.

"It's not her, buddy. Relax."

The engine turned off and the driver's-side door opened, which was facing away from the house. A figure came around the back of the SUV, but Jake couldn't make out who it was through the veil of snow. He tried to shield his eyes from the precipitation, but it was no use.

He stood there, frozen for half a second, wondering if Chayote was right. The snow had covered his short hair, and he realized he was freezing. He wiped the snow off his head and shoulders with his hand and walked toward the ranger.

"Hello?" he shouted. The figure, which he could now deduce was female, stood about twenty-five yards out.

"Jake? J.P.?"

That voice. *Goddammit, that voice.* About sixteen hundred emotions welled up inside him. *It* is *her, Chayote.*

"Yeah, it's Jake. Come in."

Jake held the door for Noelle as he had a hundred times before. When she walked by him into the entryway, he sensed her presence in the personal way that he used to—the smell and the warmth.

But she didn't take off her coat.

Jake was almost afraid to make eye contact with her, feeling that he would immediately be able to tell what she was thinking. He wasn't sure he wanted to know.

"We're fine here. Thanks. Just wanted to get out of the snow."

"Coffee?"

"No."

He made the eye contact he'd dreaded, but it didn't give him a hint either way. Her normal warmth wasn't hiding, but neither was that sad, distant look she sometimes had in the mornings after they'd fought.

"I was just driving by. Doing a loop down Moose-Wilson and back up to the highway."

"Oh?"

"I got a strange call as I made the turn there at 22."

*Paris.* Divya had done as she promised.

Jake looked down, ashamed.

"A woman who says she knows you called and told me an unbelievable story. I wanted to talk to you about it."

"Let's sit down."

Noelle started to resist. "Please," Jake added.

She followed him into the kitchen, where she opted to sit on one of the high bar stools at the counter.

"We can sit at the table."

"This is perfect."

Jake remained standing.

"Do you know where Chief Terrell is?" Noelle was looking around as if to make sure no one was listening.

"Only by chance. He's on vacation."

"That's what I heard." She blinked too long. She was struggling with something. She pulled her dark hair back behind her ears, as if what she had to say would've been diluted by the wisps. "But the call I got from your anonymous friend . . . they . . . *she* said Terrell has been killed."

"What?" Jake's mind reeled.

"That's not all. She said if I didn't get you to help, his wife would die, too."

"Noelle, that doesn't . . ."

"She said you knew what you had to do."

"I don't . . . she didn't say anything else?"

"Jake. *Stop.* Why would she say that?" Back in Noelle's eyes was the uncertainty, the fear from last summer. "What's going on?"

"Lemme get you a coffee." He was buying time to think.

She protested. "This isn't a social meeting."

He ignored that. "Sugar only, if I remember."

"Very funny."

Jake dumped in the generous pour of half-and-half that he knew she preferred. No sugar. Sweet 'N Low only. He put the mug in front of her on the granite. Now she was the one avoiding eye contact. "Thanks," she mumbled to the counter.

"Can I be honest?"

Noelle nodded and finished her sip. "If it's about the chief, yes."

"I don't have any idea what's going on."

She leaned in, expecting more—a hypothesis, something. But Jake wasn't quick to reveal his recent interactions with Divya; there was no way it could make things better.

"You know someone was killed last night? There was an APB for a connected vehicle going north in the evening. I think I may have seen it."

"That I do know. The deputy needed my help. I was at the scene."

She didn't let this distract her. "And now your friend says the chief is dead."

"Now I know that, yes." Why hadn't Divya shared this with him? And why hadn't she gone through with her blackmail? "What kind of proof did she offer?"

"She said to ask Layle about the chief."

"I just saw him last night. He was the one who told me the chief was on vacation." *Damn. This explains Layle's comments about Terrell.* "Something was wrong, though. The way Layle acted."

"Maybe something's changed." Noelle stood up and headed toward the door. "We've got to get to the bottom of this. I'll meet you at the police station?"

"I've gotta get dressed."

Noelle gave Chayote a quick pat on the head and took off. Jake jogged upstairs to take a shower and put on some respectable clothes. As the water heated up, he called Divya, who didn't answer her phone. *Shit.*

One more cup of coffee in a to-go mug and he grabbed the keys to the 4Runner and went after Noelle, Chayote following him. The snow was still coming hard with the wind, and visibility was just a few hundred yards. A guide Jake didn't know was launching with his clients at Wilson boat ramp. *Poor guy.*

Jake pumped the heat and thought of Noelle, Divya, Layle, Terrell, and the murder—or was it murders? *What in the world is Divya wrapped up in?* Why hadn't she followed through with her threat? Was Roger Terrell dead? If so, why?

The police station was just past the town square and one block south. Noelle parked in the Law Enforcement Only lot. Jake cruised Willow and King Streets looking for a parallel spot. Near Shade's Café a minivan was leaving. Jake slid the SUV in.

There was nobody at the front desk when Jake walked in. He grabbed the white phone and pressed "0" according to the instructions. Before there was an answer, Noelle came strolling back out past him, putting her hat on and thanking the receptionist for checking.

"He's out," Noelle said. "Let's go."

"Still?"

Jake acknowledged the receptionist with a nod and followed Ranger Klimpton.

"Where is he?" Jake shouted through the blustery snow.

"Don't know for sure, but I think we both have a pretty good idea. On scene at Game and Fish. Or up north, wherever that car was going."

They got in the Yukon together, leaving the 4Runner behind. Noelle took off her ranger hat and set it in the backseat. Her hair was in a tight ponytail, as per park rules. Her tan uniform shirt was buttoned up tight against the cold.

"Did you ask where Terrell is?"

"Of course." The question irked her. "Vacation."

"You didn't tell them what you . . ."

"No. We'll talk to Layle first."

That was it for conversation until they arrived at the Game and Fish warehouse. Two cop cars were parked on either side of the tall garage doors, which were wide open.

Police tape was strung across the opening and around the parking spots in the area where Jake assumed the murderer must have parked, based on the webcam footage.

A detective Jake didn't recognize was outside in the lot. Layle was inside. Noelle dipped down to go under the tape, but Jake stopped her.

"Not your crime scene."

Jake hollered over the tape. "Deputy Layle, can we have a minute?"

He looked up from the lab cart, where the missing wolf once rested.

"Meet you around the side." He didn't look surprised to see them.

At the side door, Layle pulled off his evidence gloves and tossed them. "Tons of prints on that thing. We'll take it to the lab for sure."

"Can we talk to you out back? Somewhere private?" Noelle asked him. He looked wary.

"Give me one minute." Layle walked back around the front near the garage doors and shouted to another officer to watch the door.

In the back of the building, there were a few benches facing Flat Creek and the National Elk Refuge. The geese from the night before were still there, unmoving in the water with their heads tucked in, trying to stay warm.

"What's going on?" His wariness still evident.

Noelle got to the point. "Where is Terrell?"

The question caught Layle off guard. "What? He's on vacation—"

"Where, exactly?" Jake interrupted.

"China. They were invited by some billionaire to represent Jackson Hole at a resort opening. That's all I know." He started back toward the warehouse, which raised Jake's hackles.

"Hey!" Noelle called after him. "He's dead, isn't he?"

Layle turned and hurried back over. His tone was hushed. "*I don't know what the hell you're talking about.*"

"A woman called me today. She said the chief is dead. She said you know something about it."

Layle took a seat on one of the benches and brought his hands to his head. "A woman?"

"An anonymous woman, yes."

Layle immediately took his cell phone from his pocket and dialed the number of the FBI agent he'd spoken to the day before.

When he hung up, he looked straight across the refuge with cloudy eyes. He didn't say a word.

"Deputy Statler?" Noelle asked.

"We all need to go somewhere and talk," he said.

# 36

"No more injection," Xiao told the giants. "We all must face music eventually."

Charlotte was in a drugged slumber in the Wapiti Suite. Copious amounts of chlordiazepoxide had been injected into her system at regular intervals for the last thirty-six hours.

When the door slammed shut behind Xiao, Charlotte awoke. She was still foggy, but the light from the lamp seemed unfairly harsh. Too bright for a dream. She stirred a little and closed her eyes again but couldn't fall back asleep. She took a glass of water from the bed stand and downed it.

Objects in the distance came into focus for the first time in what seemed like forever. A man was in the corner, sitting on a leather ottoman and playing on his phone. She tried to ask where she was, but only a grunt came out. The man stood up as if to stop

248

her from doing something, so she laid her head back down and closed her eyes.

Memories came filtering back—she remembered a flight, an airport, and a big truck with a valet. *But where am I?* She felt tired and sad in a way she'd never experienced before. As if her will to live had been gutted out. There was still some sense of sleepy-numb tranquility in her mind, but it faded with each passing thought.

She felt the urge to get up, to go somewhere. She tried to sit up, but she felt nauseated. *Take a little rest.*

*1 . . . 2 . . . 3.* She was sitting up now. The man in the corner was looking at her in a peculiar way. She looked right back at him.

Charlotte took a minute to get steady on her feet, then walked to the bathroom. All the while the man watched. *Who was he?* Her clothes smelled old and sweaty, so she shed them and turned the shower on. The warm water rejuvenated her.

She was in China, she remembered. *Vacation?* She shampooed her greasy hair. She looked around. *Too nice for a hospital.* Definitely a hotel. But wasn't she sick? She didn't know.

She recalled his face, the man in the corner, and she knew he wasn't a friend. The way he looked at her when she woke up. *He's not going to let me leave.*

She washed her body with a sage-and-ginger body bar. The smell reminded her of home. *Where is home?* Somewhere beautiful. Sunny and clear and clean.

*Was she dead?* That didn't make sense. Who dies and goes to a hotel? She laughed at the idea. The noise startled her. Her lips and tongue felt numb. She thought hard for a minute, then said aloud, "I can speak."

A sense of identity came back as she dried herself off. *Charlotte.* She heard a kind man's voice say it. Sweet and loving.

She put on the robe hanging on the rack and walked back to the main room.

"This will help." The man was enormous. *A giant.* She took the cup from him. *Coffee.* She knew the smell.

She sat on the bed for a while, sipping the coffee and letting details come back. Mountains, weddings, family: panoramas of exquisite countryside and close-ups of heartfelt smiles. She just lacked the big picture. How did it all connect? After the coffee was gone, she got up for another walk. The giant stood again.

She eased along the perimeter of the room, observing the paintings, looking for clues. She walked by the giant, who didn't move as she inspected him. Past the giant was the window. It was dark outside, but there was a pale light emanating from the streetlamps. She looked far-off first, hoping to see the landscapes from her visions. Nothing. Then to the surrounding buildings, where something seemed oddly familiar, but not quite right.

Finally she looked at the ground. *The dust.* It was where she'd gone to sleep. A familiar place.

"No!" she shouted. The giant walked toward her. "Stay back! Oh my god!" Reality came flooding in.

# 37

Jake, Noelle, and Layle were stuffed into a little corner booth at the Bunnery. They had ordered lunch, but no one was eating much.

"What did the feds tell you?" Jake asked when the waitress was out of earshot.

"Nothing, really," Layle explained. "They said they were on it. That they would turn it over to their international department, jump through the hoops, and get back to me. It was a short call. They told me to keep quiet."

"How short?"

"I don't know—a few minutes."

"Doesn't that seem strange?" Noelle piped up. "You report an international kidnapping and they don't have much to say?"

"She said she'd be back in touch."

"But she didn't call back?"

251

"We didn't talk until just now, no."

"What did she say now?"

"That . . . she said that Terrell had been shot and killed by his captors. That a team was on the way, and that since this may be an issue of national security, we have to stay quiet."

"How did this happen?" Jake was asking rhetorically.

"I should have tried harder to find her," Layle mumbled.

"What?" Jake asked, intrigued now. "Find who?"

"To hell with it, I figure I'm getting canned after this anyway. The kidnapper called me—made the chief call me—and told me I had to find out where some woman's house was in Jackson."

"An Asian woman?" Jake asked.

Layle nodded. "The daughter."

*"Jesus."*

"What is it?" Noelle was playing catch-up.

"The woman who called you. She wants me to look for the same person."

"So put out an APB." Noelle had turned to the deputy.

"Hold on. Did the FBI contact mention any daughter? Any woman?" Jake asked.

"No."

"I need to make a call." Jake stood up. "Your FBI agent, the woman who called Noelle, my . . . acquaintance. They're all the same person."

Jake headed out the swinging doors, took a quick look around, and headed to the back alley. Voice mail again. "Jesus Christ, Divya. If you don't call me and let me know what's going on . . . someone is dead, for God's sake." He hung up.

*Check that. Two people are dead.* Jake hurried back into the café. Layle was gone, on the phone.

"Noelle. The car. Did you find the car from last night?"

"The Tercel? No trace of it."

"We need to find that car."

Jake left a fifty-dollar bill on the table, and they rushed out.

Noelle motioned to Layle that they were leaving; he was leaning against the bannister of a wooden boardwalk. He hung up, put his cell in his pocket, and followed them back toward the Game and Fish warehouse, just two hundred yards north.

"What is it?"

Jake turned. "Until we hear something, the only thing we can do is try to find that Tercel."

"Agent V-v . . . whoever she is . . . said we should keep our eyes open for the girl. She said they were looking too."

"Right," Noelle said. "And the only lead we have in any direction is the murder last night."

"I'm not sure you should believe anything that agent says," Jake added.

At the Yukon, Jake paused for a second. It was still cold out. "Can I bring Chayote?" he asked. The heeler was scratching at the passenger window of the 4Runner and whining. "I can't leave him to freeze."

"Fine."

Jake jogged over and opened the door. Chayote bolted to the back door Noelle was holding open.

"I'll follow in my cruiser," Layle shouted across the lot.

Noelle switched her light bar on, but left the siren off. The traffic headed north on Cache yielded, and she punched it toward Moose Junction, Layle in tow.

"Where did you see the Tercel?"

"Between Moose and Moran. Crest of the hill above Deadman's

253

Bar." Noelle checked her speed. She didn't want Fran Yowlitz to catch word that she was up to something.

"Everyone speeds there," Jake said.

Noelle laughed. "That's our most productive trap."

"How often do you stop someone?"

"I'd say ninety percent don't slow down to forty-five by the sign, but we let most slide."

"And the Tercel was doing the speed limit at the sign?"

"Right under."

"Being cautious at a known speed trap," Jake guessed.

"A *local* being cautious. Tourists, if there are any around, wouldn't know it's a speed trap."

"You think she lives somewhere up there? Somewhere she would encounter the trap on the way to or from work?"

"Possible, yeah."

Jake let his gaze on Noelle linger a second too long. Behind her perfect profile was the cloud-hazed outline of the Tetons. The two most beautiful things Jake had ever seen, all wrapped up into one convenient package.

"What?" she said. She brushed her hair behind her ear so she could keep an eye on him.

"Nothing."

He continued with his postulation. "Not many places to live up here. One of the dude ranches, or up by Moran."

Noelle nodded. She slowed down slightly at Moose so as not to attract attention from the park service.

At Circle Y Ranch, a few miles past Deadman's Bar, Noelle slowed and turned right. "Good a place as any. They've got quite a few employees living here. Maybe one drives a Tercel."

She put the Yukon into four-wheel drive to climb the winding hill toward the main lodge. Chayote was anxiously hopping between rear windows, looking for cows to bark at.

"I need to get one of these." Jake pointed to the Plexiglas divider between the front and back seats. "He always has to be up front, causing trouble."

"I haven't forgotten," Noelle said.

Jake thought he detected a slight upturn in her lips.

Noelle turned off the light bar before the lodge so she didn't alarm anyone. A rusty Dodge Ram was parked outside, turquoise and tan with longhorns bolted to the front grill.

An old man came out. He wore old Ariat boots and a heavy wool sweater.

Before Noelle could talk, he burst into a rant. "If you're here to bother me about that culvert there at the road, I told ya I'd be on it when I can afford it."

She disarmed him when she took off her hat.

"I'll do it, is all I'm saying." He spit tobacco onto the fresh snow.

"We're not here for that, but if you keep flooding the shoulder of the park road there, I'm coming back with handcuffs." She shot him a smile.

*Good police work*, Jake thought. *Keep 'em on your side as long as you can.*

"Reckon I'll keep flooding it, then. C'mon in."

Chayote sniffed at a few bull-elk heads wrapped up on the porch waiting for the taxidermist. "Tags for all those, I'm sure?"

"'Course. Y'all gotta start checking the wolves for permits. Twelve of 'em back here chasing mules around this morning."

Noelle knew better than to go there.

The mudroom was littered with dirty cowboy boots and horse

blankets. The rancher kicked them out of the way. "We're just packing up for winter."

Layle opened the door and entered the already crowded entryway, drawing a glare from the old man.

"Howdy," Layle said.

"Cavalry's here, I see." The rancher rolled his eyes.

"Anyway." Noelle got to the point. "We're wondering if any of your hands might drive an old white Toyota Tercel that could have been involved in a crime last night."

"I don't think any of those weenies are capable of committing a crime." He wasn't protecting his employees, which was good. "'Sides, they're all gone."

"Done for the season?"

"Yes, ma'am."

"Do you know of any cars like that?"

"Never seen one around."

Jake took a look around as Noelle finished up with the rancher. Nothing suspicious, as far as he could tell.

"Do you mind if we take a look in the barn?" Noelle asked. Jake figured it unnecessary; there was nothing in the old man's tone suggesting a lie.

"Do what you want. I gotta go get these horses ready for transport."

"I'll leave a card here on your desk in case you see that Tercel around."

He shrugged at Noelle.

Layle laid his card on top of Noelle's.

"Doubt it's here," Jake said as they walked behind the lodge toward the rickety prairie barn.

"Agreed." Noelle didn't look up. "But the Ram had a flat tire.

Been sitting there a while, looks like. Gotta wonder how he gets around."

"Nice." Layle was impressed.

As was Jake. "Didn't notice" was all he said.

Jake held the door to the barn open. Layle entered first, then Noelle. Jake swept the landscape for the rancher, just to keep the man within sight. He was a few hundred feet down the driveway, putting a head collar on a calico mare.

"Well, shit." Jake heard Noelle from inside. "It's a Toyota, all right."

Jake's eyes adjusted to the darkness as he walked in. By the high door sat a brand new pearl-white Prius.

"*Nice.*" Layle said again, then laughed.

On the way back down the driveway, Noelle slowed down by the old man and lowered the window. "Get that culvert fixed." He didn't look up from his work. "Cute truck you got in there."

"Yeah, yeah." He waved them away.

"Moran?" Jake asked as she put the window up.

"Think so. Not much between here and there."

They rode in silence to Moran Junction. Noelle pretended to take interest in whatever chatter came over her radio—turning it up, then rolling her eyes or shrugging and turning it back down.

Bearing right at Moran Junction toward Togwotee Pass reminded Jake of a day hike he and Noelle had once taken to Heart Lake. He gave her a sideways glance, wondering if she was thinking the same thing. She didn't show her cards.

Noelle pulled onto Buffalo Valley Road on the left and stopped the Yukon. Layle pulled up alongside them and opened his passenger's-side window. "What's the program?"

"I say we split up. Check as many driveways as possible before word gets around that we're here."

"Sounds like a plan."

Layle pulled forward and sped down the country road. Jake and Noelle were only a few car lengths behind.

The deputy's cruiser was pulled over on the left where a large A-frame sat in a stand of pines. Jake and Noelle continued past to a small hunting camp on the right. The Buffalo Fork flowed through the shanty's backyard.

They slowed down. The driveway was empty—no Tercel. The yard was a cluttered mess of old farm equipment and vehicles, waiting in vain for repair. A large vegetable garden was starting to rot from fall moisture.

Along the Buffalo Fork, a bony, tall man was walking back toward the structure. He looked to be in his early forties, with tan, wrinkled skin. He wore the rags of a drifter.

"What's he carrying?" Noelle asked, stopping the car just past the driveway.

Jake squinted through a growing squall of blowing snow. "Looks like a rake or a shovel."

"Gardening's done for the year." Noelle put the Yukon in reverse.

"Yep."

Chayote was going nuts again in the backseat, anticipating a chance to be free from his cell. He scratched at the window.

The man continued to walk home, looking more uneasy, or at least curious, now that he noticed the ranger's vehicle. He didn't wear a jacket, but the snow didn't seem to bother him. Jake and Noelle parked the Yukon a hundred feet from the cabin and got out, hollering a *hello there* through the building storm.

The scrawny man didn't react, neither coming nor going. He simply rested the shovel against the north wall of the camp and stood still, staring at them.

Before Jake could get far, Chayote started barking, so he went back and opened the rear passenger door. The dog bounded toward the river, stopping once to mark his new territory.

Noelle was identifying herself to the man as Jake walked up. He got a glare from the landowner.

"You can't just let him sniff around, can you? Not that I care." The man had crossed his arms around his scarecrow body.

Noelle spoke up before Jake could explain. "He's not a police dog."

"Still."

"Planting?" Jake motioned at the shovel, enticing him to lie.

"No. It's October," the man said flatly, but didn't bother to explain the shovel.

*Fair enough.*

"We're looking for a certain vehicle. Do you keep a car here?" Jake went on, figuring he was already the bad cop—he might as well push it.

"I don't have to answer that, do I?" It worked. The scarecrow turned to Noelle. "And how come he doesn't wear a uniform?"

She jumped in. "We're just curious. We're looking for an old Toyota Tercel hatchback that we think might be connected to a crime."

Jake watched his face, but it remained emotionless.

"I don't have a car. I use the old Gator four-by back there when I need to go to the convenience store. Anything farther, I hitch."

They gave him a second to see if he would offer anything else. No dice.

"Do you mind if we look in the garage?"

"Go ahead."

Noelle and Jake peered through the tiny window. It was empty.

"I'll leave my card in case you see it around." Noelle held it out, and the scarecrow took it hesitantly. "Thanks for your time."

Jake gave the man a head nod, and they headed back toward the Yukon. The wind was up again, now in short gusts. Jake whistled for Chayote, then waited by the truck for him. He didn't come.

Another whistle and a loud shout. "Chayote! Come!" Nothing. Noelle joined in the beckoning.

The ruckus attracted the scarecrow, who wandered back toward the Yukon. "Some dog you got there."

Jake didn't respond. He turned to Noelle. "I'm gonna go get him." She was starting the car. He headed off through the blowing snow and behind the house. The scarecrow was following him at a distance.

"Hey! Chayote! C'mon!" No sign of the heeler. Jake turned around. The man, if he was still there, was concealed by the storm.

"Let's go!" The visibility was such that Jake realized he was at the riverbank only a few steps before tumbling over. He gave another few whistles here, since Chayote, like his owner, had a soft spot for rivers.

Jake started upstream along the Buffalo Fork, whistling the whole way. His hands were freezing; he'd left his gloves back at the house.

"Dammit, Chayote!" He checked again for the scarecrow—a vague gray outline behind him on the bank.

Chayote rarely wandered this far. Thinking he might have returned to Noelle and the truck, Jake turned around. The dog hit him from behind in his usual style—paws up and hard. "Hey! Let's go." Chayote bounced in circles around him, excited.

"Get over here!" Chayote calmed down slightly and pranced to his owner. "Where the hell were you?" Jake swatted the dirty paw prints off his backside, then grabbed the heeler and cleaned off his paws and muzzle, which were covered in loose dirt and mud.

"What'd you find?" *A dead wolf, maybe?* The heeler only bucked back onto his rear haunches, begging, *Play with me!*

When Jake didn't, Chayote took off back in the direction of the Yukon, looking for a more compliant friend. Jake followed. He had no authority to investigate Chayote's treasure without Noelle. The scarecrow was already onto him; Jake didn't want to push his luck.

Back at the truck, Noelle was wiping Chayote down with an old towel. "Sorry 'bout that," Jake said.

"It's okay. He's too adorable to be mad at."

"Where'd Señor Creepy go?"

"Don't know. He followed you out there, but didn't come back out front."

Jake checked Chayote for mud one last time and gave him a pat on the head. There was a tiny tuft of fur sticking out from his jowl.

# 38

WEST BANK, SNAKE RIVER. OCTOBER 25.
3:45 P.M. MOUNTAIN STANDARD TIME.

After they wrapped up their search with no more answers and filled in Deputy Statler as to Chayote's behavior, Noelle dropped Jake off. The good-bye was stilted. Jake wanted to ask her to come in, talk about what was going on, have a drink, dinner, whatever, but he knew it wasn't the right time. He also knew she would have declined, no matter what she felt in her heart.

As it stood, the day was just a chance encounter. No indication of anything to come. Noelle would pursue the leads as her job required her to, including taking the fur to the park biologist, as Layle suggested. If it was wolf fur, a search warrant would be issued, and she and Layle would go from there. Jake didn't need to be involved.

She was "sure he was busy." *What the hell did that mean?*

With respect to their information about Terrell's alleged mur-

262

der, neither Jake nor Noelle knew the correct path to take. Divya, Jake knew, was not who she said she was. Who she was, he didn't know. For some reason, she'd posed as an FBI agent and insisted they keep the chief's death quiet. They'd agreed implicitly to keep it to themselves until something more came to light or their investigation came to a standstill. The chief was still MIA.

*But why did Divya try to play me in DC? To what end?*

She was still not answering her phone.

J.P. walked in as Jake was taking the Bialetti espresso maker off the burner. He tossed his keys on the counter and slumped into the couch.

"Coffee?" Jake asked, making himself a robust Americano.

"Anything stronger?"

"Too early for that. What's going on?"

"Ah, nothing, man. Esma's not doing great."

"I can imagine."

"No, I mean she's back in the hospital. Mild sepsis. They've got a handle on it with antibiotics and fluids, but she'll stay for another three days at least."

Jake joined his friend on the couch. "She's gonna be okay."

It was both a question and a statement.

"Yeah. Just more shit to deal with."

"Can I get you something to eat?"

"Nah, gonna take a shower and head back over there. My stomach's torn up."

"Gotta eat something."

J.P. shrugged, then looked up. "Maybe you could keep me company? I'll buy you dinner over there. They say the cafeteria's fantastic." He was smirking.

"Yeah, of course, buddy. Let me change my clothes."

"Take your time."

Jake put on khakis and a Mountain Hardwear flannel shirt, which he tucked in.

J.P. had just started the shower, so Jake wandered into his fly-tying den.

The small room had been underutilized for the last few months, but at least that meant it was spotless. He sat down on the office chair and reached down to his right, where the bins of hooks were stacked. He kept them organized under three broad categories: freshwater, saltwater, and salmon/steelhead.

Out of the steelhead bin, he selected a size 3 Alec Jackson design, standard weight Spey hook. He clamped it in his vise and let his fly-tying imagination run wild for a moment, which you could get away with for steelhead. There was no need to imitate a specific insect; garish patterns were often the recipe for success.

He grabbed a bobbin of red-wine-colored 3/0 thread and wrapped the shank of the hook from eye to bend. Then he selected a sparse bunch of wine-colored hackle tail fibers and fastened them to the back of the shank with two quick wraps.

Comparing two pieces of purplish-colored chenille, he chose the thinner of the two. *Less is more.* Before tying in the chenille, he secured a four-inch-long piece of silver tinsel, to garnish the body. After wrapping both materials forward, tinsel on the outside, he picked a piece of dyed-purple guinea fowl from its skin and hackled it around the shank near the eye, creating a fan of fibers around the body that would undulate in the water.

Jake finished the head of the fly just as the shower faucet turned off. He dabbed the final wraps with head cement, then took the fly from the vise and carefully inspected it from all angles. Not a piece of art compared with what many other tyers could do, but functional.

He laid it down on the table and stood up. J.P. was in the doorway, drying his wild, scraggly hair with a towel.

"Pretty."

"Thanks. You too."

"I'm trying. Can I borrow a shirt?" J.P. looked enviously at Jake's attire.

"Take whatever you want."

He returned downstairs wearing a blue oxford-style button-down that was too snug to be tucked in. He complemented it with Jake's best pair of blue jeans and gray leather Wallabees.

J.P.'s sullen mood on the way to the hospital was punctuated by angry rants aimed at Esma's captor. "I'd like a few minutes with that son of a bitch!"

Jake assured his friend that it wasn't worth it. "He's going to rot in prison. No worse punishment than that."

"How long?"

Jake had checked the Idaho criminal code to quench his own curiosity. "It's first-degree kidnapping, where there's intent to . . . uh . . ."

"Yeah. Go on."

"Well, depends on the circumstances." Jake looked at his friend, who stared eagerly back from the passenger seat.

He decided to err toward a longer sentence. "Thirty years, maybe."

J.P. pondered this for a moment. "Seems short."

Jake had to agree.

The sun was peeking through intermittent clouds as they pulled into the visitor parking at St. John's.

Inside, the lobby was empty. Jake and J.P. went straight to the reception desk. The nurse minding the desk looked up awkwardly. He was tense.

"Can I help you?"

"Checking in to see Esma," J.P. said anxiously.

"Of course." The nurse picked up the phone and spoke quietly into the mouthpiece. "Visitors for Esma." A pause for an explanation. "Okay. Thank you."

"A doctor will be right out," the man said.

"No," J.P. said faintly, his nerves more obvious now. He shook his head. "I know where the room is, I'll go myself." He started toward the far end of the desk, where a corridor led to the ICU.

The nurse stepped out from behind the counter, hands up, to stop him. Jake jogged toward his friend and restrained him from behind.

J.P. tried to pull away. "Why? What the fuck is going on?"

"Everything's okay," Jake said. "The doctor is on his way out."

"Got him?" the nurse asked Jake, who nodded and eased his writhing friend down into one of the waiting room's chairs, where he held him by the shoulders. J.P. continued to make a fuss. Jake eyed the red security button on the counter's edge and prayed the nurse didn't press it.

"What the fuck, Jake?" He was nearly hyperventilating, and still trying to get up.

Jake wondered the same thing. Sepsis was dangerous. *But she couldn't be gone.* Jake had seen Esma just a day ago.

"It's okay." Jake was bent over his friend, keeping him planted in the chair.

"Get someone out here!" Jake shouted.

The nurse got on the phone again. *"I'm telling you to hurry, please! It's her boyfriend."* When he hung up, he mustered a calm smile toward Jake and J.P.

"Jake, why won't they let me in?"

"They will. Hold on." J.P. was out of breath from the struggle and close to tears.

The doctor was a slight woman, barely over five feet. She looked to be in her early forties. She walked fast, which Jake didn't like the looks of. When she got to them, she held her hand out for J.P., who was too fretful to notice.

"Dr. Antol," she said, tucking her hand back to her side. She showed the apparent ambivalence that doctors could sometimes summon in the face of trauma.

"What the hell is going on?" J.P. was trying to get around her to the corridor. Jake struggled to hold him back, and the nurse started coming around the corner.

She turned to the reception desk. "Danny, it's okay. I'm just going to take them back."

She walked at a deliberate pace toward the ICU and talked calmly. Jake figured she was trying to work on J.P., manage his emotions before she broke whatever horrible news she had.

They arrived at a large window looking into a room, where Esma lay unconscious, surrounded by computers and tubes.

Dr. Antol stood in front of the door, blocking their way for a moment.

"Esma suffered a fibrillation of the heart."

J.P. was distracted; he stared through the window at Esma's inert body.

"Hey, do you know what that means?" The doctor reached for his shoulder. It startled him.

J.P. looked up and shook his head. "No." His face was ghost white. Another nurse went into the room, checked the monitors and the IVs, and left.

"An hour ago, Esma's heart rhythm became dangerously weak

267

and inconsistent, which is called a fibrillation. We revived her with CPR and the defibrillator. She is stable now."

"How?"

"It's not always clear why it happens. We think in this case the sepsis may have been the cause."

"The infection?"

"Yes," the doctor answered. "Or possibly stress from the incident, or some combination of both."

"Is she going to . . . ?"

"Her heart is functioning normally. The sepsis is still an issue. She is on a heavy dose of antibiotics."

Jake could tell that J.P. wanted to fight back, tell them to work harder, save Esma no matter what, but an air of resignation washed over him.

"So there's a chance she'll be okay? When can I see her?"

"Tomorrow."

Jake did his best to comfort J.P. in the lobby, where he insisted on staying until they kicked him out at 9:00 p.m. When his friend was calm, Jake stepped up to the desk.

"I'd like to see another patient, please. Allen Ridley."

"I'll have to have someone come and take you back." The nurse was unwilling to leave J.P. alone.

Allen's room, outside the Radiology wing, was a brighter scene. The man was awake, watching a late-night show, and eating flavored ice out of a plastic cup.

Jake knocked as he entered. "There's our hero."

"Hardly." He chuckled. "Like my outfit?" Allen nodded down at his gown.

"Armani? Hey, you've still got your leg though. That's a nice accessory."

"Couldn't let the volleyball team down."

Jake collapsed into the chair beside the biologist, rested his elbows on his knees, and leaned forward. Words came pouring out.

"We're in a mess here."

Allen listened for a long time—about Esma and the chief, Divya, and the murder at the Game and Fish warehouse. It was a rare occasion that Jake confided in someone like this.

"That's not a mess," Allen said when Jake finished. "That's a goddamned train wreck."

This made Jake laugh. "You saved our asses, you know, Allen. Saved Esma."

"That remains to be seen, sounds like."

"What do I do?" Jake was tired now. At his wit's end.

"You do what I did when you needed my help. Trust yourself. You were made for this."

Jake scratched at the stubble on his face.

"Now get out of here. I haven't been able to relax and watch TV since they put me in that damned cabin."

# 39

The senator was pacing behind the desk in the front office of the lab. He'd released his aides and staff for the recess, citing a need for personal time. Meirong sat still, turning her head only to watch him.

He was thinking hard.

"And she survived, the Mexican? Or we don't know?"

Meirong nodded first, unsure whether talking would enrage him further. She chanced it. "Don't know."

Instead, he reset himself. "Okay. Where do we go from here?"

"I think the fibrillator is good, I . . ."

"*No*. What's our exposure?"

"What?"

Canart raised his voice again. "Can they find this place?"

Meirong spoke confidently now. "No. Materials are sourced

from all over. Some handcrafted. They won't be able to find the origin of the tracker or the fibrillator."

"Can they somehow reverse-trace the signal?"

Meirong let out a little laugh, which drew a glare from Canart. Her face became serious again. "No. Our software is better than that."

Canart moved on. "Any luck on microsizing?"

"Just a matter of getting the battery smaller, but still strong enough."

"And?"

"We have some ideas."

"Fine. Keep me up-to-date. I have to get home for dinner."

The senator checked his phone, muttered something in frustration, and put on his suit jacket.

"You're leaving?"

"I have a family and a career, Meirong. What we did was a mistake. The result of too much time working together, that's all." He hustled out of the building.

The Lincoln peeled out of the lot. Meirong slammed the door to the office that was serving as her makeshift sleeping quarters and headed back into the lab.

It was a skeleton staff: herself and three other researchers. They all had engineering or software degrees, even PhDs, which made communication between her and the group challenging. Communicating had never been easy for Meirong growing up. She understood *things*—computers, machines, and numbers—but not people. They were too capricious and volatile.

"Smaller!" she yelled at the men. The goal was to make the device so small as to be nearly undetectable. Her accent exposed itself when she was angry. "Is that so complicated?"

The energy density of the lithium-limited battery was slowing them down. They had to find a way to pack enough punch into the fibrillator to cause a fatal arrhythmia while downsizing the whole package size *and* maintaining a steady power source for the GPS unit. *How?* As it stood, the prototype measured eleven millimeters long and had to be implanted with a large syringe. Ideally, the device would be small enough to be hidden in smaller needles, implanted with vaccines, without detection.

But the senator's demand that the entire package measure 20 percent of its current size was outrageous. Impossible.

"What time is it?" She walked by a man inspecting something under a jewelry scope.

He pulled up his sleeve. Then tapped the face of his watch. "Dunno. Battery's dead, I guess."

Meirong took one more step and stopped. "How many hours have you been working?"

He continued working. "Eighteen a day, like the senator said."

"All in this seat? Let me see your watch."

The man huffed and then obliged, peeling it off his arm and handing it to her.

"Get up," she said, and took his seat. "Your battery isn't dead, idiot."

Meirong searched a tool tray for a small file, then grabbed a ball-peen hammer. She laid the timepiece on its bezel and inserted the tip of the file between two layers of steel.

"Hey, that was a gift! It's a TAG Heuer!"

*Pnnnk!* She hit the file hard with the hammer, and the watch broke apart. With nervous hands, she quickly sorted through the innards.

*"Where are you? Where are you?"* She was mumbling. The

PhD was wringing his hands—overworked and now witnessing the gory demise of his fine possession.

"Here!" She held up a damaged string of tiny metal parts, and rushed over to another lab table, where her laptop rested.

"I'm stupid." She pounded her fist against her forehead a few times.

"Wha . . ." The man wasn't keeping up with her.

"It's perpetual motion." She was typing fast, researching the technology. "The power comes from the movement of your hand as you walk, clap, shake hands, whatever."

"So?"

"It's the solution to our battery problem."

The PhD was on track now. "The torso doesn't move enough. Our signal would be inconsistent at best. The hand, it swings like a pendulum . . ."

"I'm not talking about the torso generally moving. The chest—I'm talking about the heart beating and lungs expanding. It's the most consistent power source in the body. I can't believe I over-looked it . . ."

"Will it generate enough power?"

"Plenty for the GPS, considering its efficiency." She cracked her knuckles and typed some more, flying through science-journal articles online.

In the meantime, the other two men left their stations and gathered behind Meirong, transfixed by her breakthrough. They were amazed at the speed with which she scrolled through complicated microcircuit schematics, all the while talking to herself, noting God-knows-what in her head.

"If we have the right capacitor," she finally said. Then closed the laptop.

"Huh?"

The little ducklings followed her to the front office but she shooed them out, wanting to talk to the senator alone.

"It's me." She took a deep breath. "I think we can get the packet down to size."

"Yes." She nodded. "Ten days, max."

# 40

Xiao sat in his office perched above Main Street and tapped a pen on the rough cedar desk. How had he let Canart outmaneuver him? If the whole transaction blew up, he could face extradition to the United States. He couldn't let that happen.

He hadn't been in direct contact with Meirong for months. *Falling for the American senator. Foolish child.* That was the moment he'd lost control of the situation. It wasn't that he particularly cared with whom his daughter slept, but he had to be certain where her loyalty lay.

He'd tried to call the whole thing off. Get her home, find someone else he could trust to develop the chip. Someone with better resources, who could assure him that he would make the money he deserved.

They had made quite the team—the savvy, powerful father and

275

the brilliant-but-unpredictable daughter. Xiao had long known his daughter's intellect was his most valuable asset. Alone, she wasn't capable of using it to her best advantage, but he could help. Win, win.

With Meirong's new lust-driven allegiance to the senator, Xiao risked losing her, but there was no other way to play it. Ever since his wife's death, he'd longed for closure. Along with his will to survive—to *flourish*—solving his wife's murder was one of the things that drove him. He would never be satisfied until he knew who killed her, and why. And that was information Senator Canart said he possessed.

So he'd let the deal play out, at least for a reasonable amount of time.

The last remaining issue was what to do with Charlotte Terrell.

When Xiao entered the Wapiti Suite, Charlotte was at the window, watching trucks roll in from the main gate. He waved at the giant, dismissing him. Charlotte didn't acknowledge her captor.

"There is television, you know." Xiao sat on the bed. Charlotte didn't respond. "What you looking for, Ms. Terrell?"

Charlotte walked over to the bed and stood over him defiantly. "What the hell is this place?"

Xiao stood, walked past her, and went to the window. "Do you see this?"

"The food trucks, yes."

He chuckled. "Beyond the trucks."

"Clouds." Charlotte joined him.

"No clouds. Smog. The city. Do you know population of China?"

Charlotte shook her head, not following.

"Something like one and a half billion."

"That's a lot of people."

"True. But that's not the worst part. In the late eighteenth century, the entire world's population was less than that. Yet one scientist was horrified at the power of population. Do you know why?"

"No."

"Because population growth is geometric, while sustenance is finite. Meaning, in a matter of time, any population outlives its welcome, so to speak."

"And then?"

"Then we don't know. Chaos. Some say the strongest survive. But I am realist. And what do realists do?" A smile came to his face. "They buy insurance."

"So, what are you saying? Tram Village is a colony?"

"When my daughter was fourteen, she showed me a calculation. A prediction. It has been spot-on. It won't be long before this country collapses. Man running like wild dog looking for a carcass. People killing one another, God only knows. But when it does collapse, I will be prepared."

"Good for you." Charlotte left him at the window.

Xiao turned to face her. "And so will you, should you remain prisoner."

"You think you and your daughter will survive the end of the world in a country club?"

"It's only insurance, should we fail."

"How do you plan to do that?"

"Meirong has her ways, but the public finds them hard to swallow."

"Why don't you just kill me?" Charlotte was sitting on the corner of the bed with her head in her hands.

"The same reason I built this very place we sit."

"Insurance."

"Now you're starting to understand."

"But you are from a family of politicians—important men. Won't your government protect you?"

"It's a convenient story." Xiao laughed. "Your husband told me he grew up in cow shit. I grew up in much worse than that."

# 41

Jake was pounding his fist on the fly-tying table and muttering profanities into his phone. *Pick up, pick up!* J.P. was just outside the front door smoking, so when he heard the beep, Jake tried to hush his infuriated tone.

"Divya, what the hell is going on? Two people are dead. I'll do whatever you want, but you have to tell me what's going on!"

"What a fucking week, man." J.P. stepped back inside.

Jake hurried and ended the call. "Yeah. You doing okay?"

J.P. shrugged and looked at his phone, and Jake knew why. "When's next visiting hours?"

"Two hours for ICU." J.P. plunked down on the couch and switched on the TV. Animal Planet was on, and Chayote came over to see what sort of prey might be flitting about on the magic window.

"I hate these commercials," J.P. said at the break.

279

*"Help support the ASPCA. Call now,"* urged a dried-up C-list celebrity. *"They need your help."*

Chayote was barking at the still shots of flea-ridden dogs, accompanied by a Sarah McLachlan tune.

"I'd bark too, buddy," J.P sympathized. "Those shih tzus are snobbish little bastards, even with flies on their faces."

Jake was deep in thought about Esma, the chief, and the dead janitor, but J.P.'s comment got his attention. He looked up at the TV.

"That's not a shih tzu," he said, standing up and hurrying to the kitchen counter where the laptop was charging. "That's a shar-pei."

*Shar-Pei. The code name for the Chinese social-control experiment in 1999. The GPSN experiment.*

Jake opened the computer. J.P. joined him at the counter, peering over his left shoulder. He typed "Detective Tim Rapport Rick Canart" into Google.

"Son of a bitch." Jake didn't even need to open any of the results. The two names appeared together in multiple contexts. High school football recaps, articles of incorporation for various businesses, and Idaho state and county legislation.

Jake fumbled through his wallet to find Rapport's card. He took his phone from his pocket and dialed the station in Salmon, Idaho.

"Police, nonemergency. How can I help you?" It was the ancient secretary.

"I need Detective Rapport, please."

"One moment." Hold music. Billy Joel, elevator-style.

*C'mon.*

"Sir?" The centenarian was back. "May I ask who's calling?"

*Shit.* "It's Jake Trent."

A pause. "Regarding?"

"I think I left a jacket in the detective's office."

"I'll be right with you."

Billy Joel again. J.P. gave an inquisitive face. Jake held up his forefinger, telling him to be patient.

"He's out of the office," the woman said. "And I didn't see any jacket."

"Thanks." Jake pressed End.

"We've got a problem," he said to J.P. He dialed another number.

"Layle. Tell me about the wolf."

Jake stood there listening to the deputy chief with an astonished look on his face.

"*What?*" J.P. whispered.

"Right," Jake said into the phone, "we need to get ahold of Noelle right away and see what the biologist said." A pause. "But I think it'd be better if you called."

Jake ended the call and walked with the laptop back to the couch. J.P. followed. Chayote sensed the excitement and jumped up to join them.

Jake searched for pictures of wolf fur but didn't find a detailed enough picture. The general coloration looked similar to what he remembered—banded segments that ranged from light to dark. Black tips.

He was getting antsy, tapping on the armrest of the couch, thinking of what else he could do from home. *Nothing.*

"What?" J.P. asked again.

"Feel like playing sidekick again? I'll bring you up to speed in the car."

J.P. stood up. "Hell yeah. That is, if you tell me what's going on."

"Bring Chayote."

\*     \*     \*

On the ride, Jake filled J.P. in with enough information to stop him from asking more questions. Or so he thought. The Mariner was still in the driver's-side door sleeve. When they hit Moran Junction, Jake pulled it out, loaded a round in the chamber, put the safety back on, and tucked it into the space between the driver's seat and the center console.

"What's with the gun these days?"

"Better safe than sorry."

"So do all retired lawyers carry limited-edition Glocks?" J.P. was pushing Jake further than he had in all the time they'd known each other.

"Only the ones who own bed-and-breakfasts."

J.P. stayed quiet for a moment, hoping for an elaboration. When it didn't come, he spoke again. "C'mon, man."

They still had twelve miles before the turn up the Buffalo Fork. Jake decided to give him a bone. "You know the story, basically."

"The Office of Special Investigations? I've googled it."

"Ninety percent of the job description was finding and prosecuting those who had committed crimes against humanity— Nazis first, and then as they died off, Bosnian Serbs and Hutus in Rwanda. People like that."

"People who committed genocide."

Jake nodded. "A lot of paperwork and negotiating with the International Criminal Courts to root them out."

"And the other ten percent?" J.P. was looking at the Glock.

Jake took a deep breath. "As civilian experts on war crimes— academics, really—we could get into places the US military couldn't. We consulted foreign governments, attended diplomatic summits, things like that."

"Summits? With a Glock?"

Jake let out a forced laugh. "That's where my story becomes classified."

J.P. turned and looked Jake in the eye. "Hit me with it."

"When the US government lost hope that its courts or the ICC would be able to prosecute one of these criminals using the formal legal process, we occasionally . . . A select few of the prosecutors, including me, were tasked to carry out the legal process ourselves. In an informal way."

"Judge, jury, and executioner."

*Goddamn, he put that succinctly.* "Yeah," Jake said. It was the first time he'd revealed the true nature of his prosecutorial career to anyone outside the Big Office.

"What about in Philly?" Apparently J.P. wasn't satisfied.

"Different deal in the small office. We were investigating domestic organized crime, police and political corruption, things like that."

"But you needed a gun."

"In that office, prosecutors are trained law-enforcement offi- cers. We can't always trust the local authorities on the ground."

They made the left turn up Buffalo Fork Road. The scarecrow's decrepit hunting camp was only a mile or so ahead, on the right.

"And you're carrying it now because you know something?"

"I'm carrying it now because I *don't* know something."

A few hundred yards before the driveway, Chayote started whin- ing and scratching at the window. "Hold on, buddy," Jake said.

Jake eased the 4Runner toward the house, all the while scanning the property, looking for the tall man. Visibility was good—Jake could see the whole way past the house and to the riverbank—and there was no sign of him.

"Shut up, Chayote." J.P. blew in the dog's face, which made him sneeze.

"Let him be," Jake said. He left the 4Runner forty yards out from the ramshackle camp. "Wait here."

Jake had the Mariner drawn, but at his side, concealed. He approached the shack carefully, looking through the makeshift tarpaulin windows, front and back. Next, he checked the garage—still no white Tercel. Walking back to the vehicle, he tucked the Mariner into the back of his pants and pulled his shirt over it.

He opened the passenger door. "We're good." Before J.P. could exit, Chayote jumped over his lap and bounded off, headed upstream of the structure.

"Hey!" J.P. shouted. "Get back here!"

"Let him go," Jake said. "I know where he's going." Chayote showed no intention of listening anyway.

"Come with me." J.P. followed Jake around the side of the shack, toward the riverbank. The ground in the shade of the building was still frozen from the night before, crunching under their footfalls.

Around back, Jake stopped and muttered, "Of course."

"What?"

"I should have known." Jake stooped down and looked at a narrow pair of tire tracks that went around the other side of the camp. "He's gone. Let's go find Chayote."

"Who's gone?" J.P. hurried to catch Jake, who was walking fast upstream.

"I don't know him, or exactly what his role is. But he was a person of interest, and we missed it at first. And now he's gone. He had an old ATV back there that he uses to get around."

Up in the distance, Chayote was furiously digging, pausing occasionally to wolf down whatever scraps he deemed edible.

"What's he up to?"

"I'll show you."

284

When they arrived at the burial site, Jake sternly called off Chayote, who reluctantly slunk away with his crimson-red muzzle to chase mergansers in the river.

Chayote had dug a hole only six inches deep, but the carcass of the animal was becoming exposed. Jake took a rock from beside the grave site and unearthed a broad shoulder of tan, brown, and black fur.

"The wolf?"

Jake stood. "Let's go see what we can find in the cabin."

They beckoned Chayote and he tromped along below them in the river shallows.

Jake tried the back door, where they could enter without any neighbors or passersby noticing, but it was locked. So was the front entrance, but the door featured a small window.

"Got it," J.P. said, and gladly plowed his elbow through the glass.

"Nice one." Jake reached through and unlocked the door.

The smell of mildew filled the air. The interior was spartan. No TV, no computer or microwave. The kitchen consisted only of a Coleman propane range and a Tupperware washbasin. No running water. In the living area, nothing but a long couch, a cheap sleeping bag, and a few dog beds scattered on the floor.

Jake bent down. The dog beds were coated in fur similar to that of the carcass. But was it wolf, or a heavy-coated breed like a husky?

Along the south wall was a long desk with two mismatched chairs. The lack of dust in spots suggested things had been recently moved from the desk's surface. Jake opened a large drawer, filled mainly with disorganized letters and maps. From the bottom, he pried an 11x16-inch framed document, set it on the desk, and wiped the dust off. It was a diploma.

*The University of California, proudly confers upon ERIC WIL-
LIAM YOUST the degree of Philosophiae Doctor in Applied Science and Technology*

Jake took a picture with his phone to note the name and put the
framed document back in the drawer.

"Look at this." J.P. crossed the dingy hardwood floor toward
Jake. He handed him a framed picture of the cabin on a snowy
day. A slim Asian woman stood near the front door, flanked by
two large wolves with grizzled gray coats. *The woman Divya and
Layle are after.*

He handed it back to J.P. "Bring it with us."

The place was mostly bare—cleaned out by the scarecrow upon
his quick exit. Jake took a few pictures of the interior and opened
the rough wooden door to the garage.

The light in the garage was dim—a single fluorescent bulb illu-
minated a workbench in the very back. As they made their way in
that direction, a series of hurried clicks carried through the garage
doorway from the main cabin. The latch on the front door was
being tested against the strike plate.

"Hell was that?" J.P. stopped dead in his tracks.

*"Quiet!"*

Jake cautiously turned to face whatever might be coming. He
reached behind his back and gripped the Glock. Another series of
frantic jiggles, then a hard push. Jake pulled the gun and silently
moved back into the main cabin, squaring himself to the front
entrance.

The visitor made a few more weak attempts. *Click. Click. Click.*
Jake peered through a roughly shaped Plexiglas window. No vehicle in sight.

*Scratch. Scratch.* J.P. began to chuckle from the garage. Jake replaced the weapon in his waistband, stepped forward to the door, and opened it.

Chayote rushed in, ignoring Jake, more eager to sniff every piece of furniture and floor that had been touched by the canines of unfamiliar scent. Jake took a quick look around outside and shut the door.

"Shoulda shot him," Jake muttered as he came through to the garage. "Let's make this quick."

Jake and J.P. combed through boxes of old clothes, records, and broken electronics under the workbench. Jake noted a crate of 10W-30 motor oil, wondering whether the ATV was a four-stroke. If it was, the scarecrow had no need for regular synthetic and had lied about owning a car—possibly an old Tercel.

"What's all this?"

J.P. was crouched down, inspecting his fingertips. Tiny flecks of bronze glimmered in the vague light. Jake took a closer look.

"Copper wire ends, looks like." Jake looked around the bench, which he now noticed was littered with similar scraps.

"Your boy is a real handyman."

"Looks like it. Let's get out of here."

Jake left the cabin dragging the heeler, who was preoccupied growling at an especially furry corner of the couch.

There was a dried-up mud puddle where the driveway met the road. Jake put the 4Runner in park, jumped out, and snapped a picture of a set of skinny tire tracks.

When he got reception near Moran, he dialed a phone number for only the second time in a decade.

"Human Rights and Special Prosecutions."

"Nancy, it's Jake. I need Schue again."

"Jake? He told me specifically not to put you through ever again."

*That son of a bitch.*

"Nancy, I need his help. People's lives are at risk."

"Dammit, Jake." The line went dead momentarily, then started ringing again.

"How did I know you'd call again?" He seemed more entertained than angry.

"Thanks for taking the call." Maybe he'd read Schue wrong.

"What do you want?"

"I need research. Things that would take me too long to find without help."

"Like?"

Maybe Jake wouldn't have to figure this whole mess out on his own. "I need you to check out a Chinese research project called Shar-Pei—see if a US Senator, Senator Canart of Idaho, had any involvement—and I need you to get me a full bio on an individual."

"Name?"

"Divya Navaysam." He spelled the last name.

"What type of project are we talking?"

"Not totally sure. Population control, maybe. The Chinese flirted with a project that would identify every citizen and immigrant electronically."

"Is that it?"

Jake thought a moment. "No, I need any information on a woman named Charlotte Terrell—her whereabouts, if she traveled recently, where she is now."

"What's the timeline?"

"As soon as possible."

"You owe me," Schue said and hung up.

# 42

Divya took a moment to compose herself and then knocked on Wright's door. He was in a heated discussion on the phone, but he finished abruptly and motioned for her to come in.

"Have a seat. Is it already time for an update on this fucking mess? I have to say, not my favorite time of day."

"Me neither, sir."

"What do you have for me?"

"Some new information from the tapes." Divya had spent the morning poring over the transcripts from the phone tap on Canart.

"Anything important?"

"I'm not sure. Canart has promised Xiao to fill him in on who killed his wife and why."

Wright laughed.

"Sir?"

"That's fine with me. We didn't do it. The Chinese killed her."

"Why?"

Wright ignored the question. "Is Trent looking for the girl?"

"He's cooperating, yes. Why is she so important?"

"Have you been briefed on Shar-Pei in its entirety?"

"Of course."

Wright chuckled. "Then tell me when Shar-Pei was dreamed up."

"Mid-1990s. Shortly after the one-child policy was put in effect. A response to overcrowding."

"You're a hundred years off."

Divya's jaw dropped. "The technology wasn't even available . . ."

"Shar-Pei wasn't about technology in the beginning, Divya. It was about growing a superpower."

"How?"

"Selective breeding."

"What?"

"The dog breed shar-pei dates back to as early as 200 BC. The dogs were bred by the Chinese for their intelligence and dominance. By selecting animals with strong positive traits and mating them, the gene pool steadily improved. Basic heredity. In 1881, a Chinese geneticist proposed a long-term plan for China to create a superior race, or at least a ruling class superior to that of other nations. Shar-Pei, named for the nation's proudest dog breed."

Divya jumped in. "Xiao named it Shar-Pei for his daughter's pet."

"Wrong. When the Chinese expat leaked information about the killer GPS chip to the US, the United States threatened to expose the program to the world."

"Blackmail?"

"Run-of-the-mill foreign relations. We wanted information about Iran's purchase of North Korean Scud missiles."

"So, China made up a backstory to placate the US?"

"Exactly. But the Department of Justice continued investigating, claiming sole jurisdiction on grounds that it was a crime against humanity."

"The Office of Special Investigations." Divya was shaking her head.

"And they found mention of a covert operation called Shar-Pei well before the 1990s."

"What did they do with the information?"

"We've monitored the situation jointly ever since."

"That's why I got this assignment—only because you need Jake Trent?"

"We need the girl and her father, and quietly. Any commotion around her and Xiao disappears. We didn't have the necessary information to coordinate a pinpointed mission to take her. The Office suggested Jake could help."

"Why do we need them?"

"Xiao and Meirong are the only two remaining intentional Shar-Peis, the superior breed. Meirong was an accident, but she in particular has an intellect as dangerous as a nuclear weapon. The operation stalled after Xiao and Mei Li proved too difficult to control. With their intelligence came unpredictable, rebellious personality characteristics. They believed themselves too smart to be used as pawns. Meirong is the vessel of that bloodline."

"The Holy Grail. Jake would have cooperated, had he known."

"You read about Paris. He couldn't be trusted."

"C'mon, that man was dying, stage-four lung cancer. Jake let him say good-bye to his family."

"Regardless, he was a war criminal. Jake's orders were to get him into custody."

"You didn't think he would finish the job?"

"I wasn't sure if you would either."

Divya stood up and paced. When she sat back down, she was still thinking. "Xiao sent Meirong here, in part, to save her from her own government."

Wright nodded.

"Will we even try to get the chief's wife home safely?"

"Of course."

She looked into her superior's eyes. She had to believe him. It was Charlotte's only shot. "Then I need a real briefing on the whole story. And I need the name of the point man for the Office. I can convince Jake."

# 43

Jake was in Esma's room. It was almost lunchtime. J.P. had spent a sleepless night in the uncomfortable cot the nurses provided, and he was now passed out in a chair with his head resting on Esma's bed. She was sleeping too, although she'd been conscious for nearly two hours straight in the morning—an encouraging sign.

His phone vibrated in his pocket. It was Schue. Jake walked quickly down the hallway and through the waiting room. Once outside the hospital, he answered the call.

"Hello?"

"Jake, we need to talk."

"You have the information I need?"

"That and more. Are you sitting down?"

Schue's explanation bowled him over. Jake retreated to a seat in the waiting room to process the facts.

293

A Chinese prodigy was helping a US senator develop an inject-able chip that could track and exterminate a person.

Divya Navaysam was a CIA analyst, charged with enticing him to cooperate in an international investigation into a hundred-year-old Chinese experiment that US intelligence had been monitoring since the mid-1990s.

Not only was Meirong Xiao living under his nose in the Greater Yellowstone Region, but his former employer, the Office of Special Investigations, had been the first US government entity to become aware of the true nature of the Chinese program.

Once again, Jake's simple existence in Jackson Hole had spun into pandemonium. Restlessness? Meet chaos.

His phone buzzed once more. He was so deep in thought it made him jump up from the seat. Back through the automatic doors to the parking lot.

"Divya?"

"Jake, I'm sorry about all this."

It didn't matter whether he believed her now. "What's going on?"

"Terrell is dead."

"Jesus." Jake's heart sank.

"I know you knew him, and I'm sorry, but his wife is still alive and, it seems to me, the only thing that can be salvaged from this mess."

"How do we get her back?"

"We get the daughter, and give Xiao the information he's expecting from Canart."

"Which is?"

"His wife was assassinated in '99. He wants to know who and why."

"And you know?"

"The CIA does, yes. It was the Chinese."

"Why would they kill their own prized creation? Will Xiao believe that?"

A deep breath. "The birth of Meirong rendered Mei Li sterile. She tried to keep it a secret, but her doctors reported it to the government. When she started socializing with dissidents, they deemed her a liability, and she was no longer of use to them owing to her infertility. All that's left is the daughter."

"And I need to find her?"

"Before local authorities dig too deep and spook everyone. The relationship between Xiao and Canart is tenuous, at best."

"Tell me how to do it."

"We have a recording of a call between Meirong and the senator. They were intimate. We believe she may have retreated to him for help."

"After she killed the janitor."

"That's what we believe, yes."

"Why? To get the technology back?"

"Probably not. We think she had some emotional connection to the wolf. With her high IQ comes a degree of social and developmental disability, Asperger's-like."

"I need you to send me information about Canart. Where he lives, what he likes to do, where he takes his family to dinner. Everything. Do we have her vehicle information?"

"None registered in her name. Canart has only two vehicles registered, his Lincoln and a BMW in his wife's name. I'll email you the rest."

"Wait," Jake said. "What will happen to Xiao and his daughter?"

"They'll probably be detained and used as bargaining chips for information on Korea, or maybe be prosecuted by the Office for the raid on rural villages."

"I won't kill them," he said quietly, though there was no one around.

Divya paused. "I already told my chain of command. Surveillance only."

Jake went back into the ICU and wandered down the mazelike corridors looking for the break room. Dr. Antol was there, pouring a cup of coffee.

"Mind if I join you?"

"There's a waiting room just past reception."

"I know. I wanted to pick your brain."

Dr. Antol looked around, apparently deciding there was no harm in it.

"Go ahead."

"This is going to sound far-fetched, but I don't think Esma's heart attack was natural."

She took off her bifocals and rubbed her eyes.

"Meaning?"

"I can't say exactly. Were any foreign objects found in her? Maybe her chest?"

"Like a pacemaker?"

"Something like that, yeah."

"No. And our defibrillator would've let us know."

"How?"

"All the newer models scan for any device like that. It could interfere."

"Okay." Jake paused for a second to think. "Where did you go to medical school?"

"You're questioning the merit of my diagnosis? My education?"

"No, it's not that. Just curious."

The woman looked troubled by his line of questioning, but she went along. "Fine. Arizona. Is that all?"

*Wasn't Idaho, at least.* "Can you keep a special eye on her?"

"I treat all of my patients as my oath requires, I—"

Jake cut her off. "I trust you. Please just watch her closely."

He walked out, hoping his instincts were right.

On the way back to the west bank, he stopped at Shirle's Auto and asked for Craig, who had done plenty of good work on the 4Runner. Jake trusted him. A young man with a ponytail came through the door from the garage, wiping his hands with an old blue rag. They shook hands when he was finished.

"How's the fishing?"

"Haven't been out. Look, I need a favor, Craig."

"Shoot."

"If I show you a picture of a tire track, can you surmise the vehicle?"

"Narrow down maybe, not much more than that. What's going on?"

"Someone coming in the driveway at night, casing the house maybe."

Craig looked enthralled by this notion, though he tried to hide it. "Whoa. Lemme see."

Jake took out his phone and zoomed in on the track.

"Small wheel."

"ATV-sized?"

The mechanic looked again. "Don't think so; they have a rougher tread pattern. Compact, though—Civic, old Corolla, Geo Metro, something like that."

"Toyota Tercel?"

"Sure."

"That's all I need."

"Good luck. That's creepy stuff."

Jake got back in the 4Runner, turned right up Broadway, and then left at the big light on Highway 22. A mass of mule deer were hustling up the butte at Spring Creek Ranch, spooked by either car or coyote.

At the Wilson Bridge, Jake looked downstream toward Crescent H, wishing he and Chayote could spend the day walking down the levee, looking for late-season risers. The river was low—four hundred cubic feet per second, last he checked—which meant the river was mostly fast shallows, and habitable holes were few and far between. When you came across one, the action was fast and furious. Small blue-winged olive mayflies, genus *Baetis,* blanketed the water, especially on overcast days. In preparation for winter, the trout fed on them recklessly.

There was a police officer stationed at Wilson to catch speeders through town. Jake gave a wave, in case it was Layle or McClelland, then turned left at the gas station. He wondered whether Layle knew any more details of the situation. He doubted it, considering the secrecy that Divya and the CIA had found necessary. She might still be playing him as an FBI agent, instead. Either way, Layle wouldn't be of any help to Jake. He knew he had to go it alone this time.

The drive to Idaho Falls would take ninety minutes, but there was no reason to leave before he had all the information from Divya. He got home, let Chayote out, and went upstairs to start organizing the gear he would need for the trip.

From the small safe in his closet, Jake retrieved the leftover items from the trip to Salmon to find Esma. The extra ten-round clip for the Mariner would be useful in case he needed to change on the fly. There were also two Gerber five-inch tactical knives, Steiner binoculars, and a pair of thin black synthetic gloves, similar to the ones worn by wide receivers. The last item was a fake driver's-license set, complete with corresponding credit card and passport. Useful souvenirs from his days at the Office. Satisfied, Jake locked the safe and slid it to the back of the closet floor.

Jake was picky about his attire for the first time in a decade. Everything he selected was dark and dull, not only to conceal him in the shadows and darkness, but also to ensure he didn't stick out. Patterns and lettering attracted the human eye. On the bench next to the bed, he set a short-sleeved synthetic tee, a solid black Barbour button-down, and a gray Filson sweater. Grim but functional.

Jake moved to the oak dresser, where he picked out a light gray pair of Mountain Khaki work pants. His gray and pale-blue Merrell trail-running shoes would be the most recognizable piece of garb.

From the dryer downstairs, he took three pairs of boxers and socks, a navy-blue hoodie, and an extra T-shirt. Who knew how long this task could take?

He stepped outside the guesthouse with Chayote in tow to retrieve the Mariner. Uncharacteristically, he'd neglected to clean it after its last use.

The afternoon was in its full glory—the auburn autumn sun was still high enough to peek above the lodgepoles and cottonwoods, lighting up the remaining fall foliage. The open angle of the sunlight cast long, dark shadows on the property.

Chayote ran frantically around, sniffing his favorite spots and marking them carefully. Jake took the Glock from the 4Runner, allowed himself a few seconds to enjoy the fleeting tranquility, and whistled for the heeler.

On his way through the guesthouse door, Jake was struck by a sudden thought, and he set the gun down on the kitchen counter and picked up the laptop.

Had he overlooked something obvious? Jake entered the name from the diploma, Dr. Eric William Youst, into Google. The results were few. A couple of pages referencing the PhD's time at Berkeley, a newspaper article for a high school technology award, and a personal website, advertising his technology consulting business.

Jake clicked on Youst's personal page. Useless. The page looked years out-of-date, suggesting that Dr. Youst had moved on.

Jake called Divya and asked her to find vehicles registered to Eric William Youst.

"Who is he?"

Jake was surprised she didn't know, given the agency's resources. "Person of interest in the murder at Game and Fish. No info online tying him to Jackson."

"He certainly flew under our radar. Our surveillance has been limited up there, though. Meirong is too smart, and wary."

"Any satellite images that might help find her? Or a Toyota Tercel?"

"There's a KH-11 up as we speak, but it's aimed at the Chinese compound, to try to track the hostages."

"I'll be in touch."


It was 4:30 p.m. on the East Coast. Divya assured Jake she would have the registration information to him before the end of the day.

There was one other phone call that Jake felt obliged to make, but he knew he couldn't. Noelle would want to know about the wolf—that it was in fact buried up there by the camp along the

Buffalo Fork. Divya had ordered him to steer clear of local authorities. If he shared his findings with Noelle, Charlotte's life could be in jeopardy. *What would she do if she found out I kept her in the dark?* She could, in theory, get him in a load of trouble for withholding evidence.

He kept the gun-cleaning kit in a small cedar cigar box in the fly-tying room. He turned on the light at the desk and went to retrieve the Mariner.

# 44

The sun appeared a dull reddish planet through the heavy smog. The smog, Charlotte had begun to realize, was commonplace—the clear sky on the first day she and the chief had spent in China was just the result of some lucky wind. A lull before the tempest.

The village was bustling. Trucks rolled down the dusty road, filled with workers, lumber, and building materials. The carpenters and electricians started early, preceding the smoky crimson sun by an hour or more.

Since she'd regained her mental clarity and memory, Charlotte had bounced from gloom to anger. The only consistent feeling she had was best described as *adrift*. Out at sea with nothing to cling to. Blank horizons in all directions.

If and when she got home, what would she tell her children? How would she find the strength to support them when she could

302

barely keep herself sane? Her mother was dead, her father in an old-folks' home in Laramie. She shuddered at the thought of burdening her friends.

*You know what doesn't mind being adrift in the ocean? A buoy. An inert entity that rolls with the waves and the storms. No emotion. No tears. A hard shell and a buoyant core.*

The giant walked into the Wapiti Suite earlier than normal that morning. It caught Charlotte by surprise. She moved quickly away from the window and lay down on the bed.

The giant just sighed.

"Asshole." She spit the word in his direction.

"I know what you doing." He spoke in a quiet, even tone. "He will hurt you for it."

"Worth a shot." She flipped on the TV to tell him the conversation was over.

"If you survive the fall, we will be waiting. Nowhere to go."

"Are you on the list?" She changed the subject, still staring at the television. A reporter in a crowded slum. "Do you get to live if all this crazy talk comes true?" She pointed to the screen.

He shrugged. "Maybe."

"He told me it was only family."

"Family?" the giant asked, laughing. "Is that what he said?"

Charlotte muted the TV and turned toward the giant. "Who, then?"

Like the television, the giant was silent. Charlotte closed her eyes and imagined herself at home, walking the trail from their house up to the neighboring pasture, where they used to take the kids to feed the horses carrots and apples.

# 45

Jake hadn't been able to fall asleep the night before. He thought a drink might help. In a cabinet he found a bottle of Chateau Montelena cabernet sauvignon he'd bought the prior winter to share with Noelle. It hurt him to drink it. Another slap in the face—closure—as if her total dismissal of him two days ago weren't enough.

He contemplated calling her. Instead, he bundled up and sat on the back patio, listening to the nighttime secrets of Trout Run, and throwing a glow-in-the-dark Frisbee to Chayote.

In the past, he'd never let himself obsess too much before an assignment. If he did, he knew he would never find sleep. So he'd shut his brain down as much as he could.

When his fingers started to hurt from holding the stemware in the night air and the heeler was panting heavy clouds, he wandered back inside and tied up a few more steelhead patterns, until he noticed a decline in their quality from the cab.

Then it was the couch and Chayote, who did his best to snuggle with Jake and comfort him through an anxious and sentimental evening.

Jake awoke at daybreak.

He dressed in worn blue jeans, a black T-shirt, and a light synthetic down hoodie. He took his coffee to the back, as he often did, and watched Trout Run slip by. The cobalt sky matched the inky flow—cold and mysterious. No trout rising. No sign of activity. The stream wasn't giving away any secrets.

Like a sea-run *Oncorhynchus mykiss*, the impossible steelhead, Meirong Xiao was elusive and abstract. A whisper on the wind. Like finding an eight-pound anadromous rainbow trout in a 425-mile current with countless veins of tributaries and innumerable lairs. The River of No Return.

When he finished his coffee, he went inside to print the information from Divya on Senator Rick Canart. Chayote was entranced by the sound of the laser printer, tilting his head back and forth and yelping. Jake folded the pages and slid them into a manila envelope. He ran up the wooden stairs to the loft and got his gear.

But what to do with Chayote? He texted his neighbor once again so as not to burden J.P. Then texted J.P.:

Going out of town to see a friend.

Jake went out to defrost the 4Runner. He loaded his duffel and laptop and put the Mariner back in the driver's-side door pocket. He tossed a glance at his skiff, which had accumulated not only water from precipitation, but also detritus from the

305

autumn wind. He needed to cover and stow it for the winter. *Not today.*

The sun was rising over Snow King as Jake ascended the Teton Pass, lighting up the bowls and chutes so popular with backcountry skiers. It was early in the season, though, and obstructions protruding from the mountain snowpack kept the skiers at home. The only traffic was early morning commuters.

Thirty minutes later, in Victor, Idaho, Jake turned left toward Pine Creek Pass and Idaho Falls. He drove carefully—the road was windy and sheathed in a light blanket of snow. He descended the pass into Swan Valley around 9:30 a.m., at which point he found cell reception and called a hotel in Idaho Falls. Gave them an old alias, just to be safe.

The drive took Jake just under two hours. Idaho Falls was a sprawling little city, population around sixty thousand. The outskirts claimed a few big-box stores, car dealerships, and taquerias.

Jake's hotel, The Falls Lodge, was located on the corner of Broadway and the river, overlooking Sportsman's Park, in the heart of the old town. The clerk allowed him to check in early. His room had a good view of the waterfall, an angular twenty-foot man-made diversion dam. Looking upriver, a gleaming white church stood in the middle of the river's horizon.

The city's greenbelt, a corridor of parkland and pathways along the Snake, was filled with strolling workers on their lunch breaks. The temperature here, where the elevation was only 4,700 feet, had climbed into the upper forties. Scattered clouds were pushing through on a gusty wind.

His room was basic—one double bed—but clean and smartly decorated. He put the Mariner and its clips in the safe and spent a few minutes organizing what would be his home base for the foreseeable future. With his gear in place, he sat down at the small table to examine Divya's notes.

The senator's mansion was in the foothills east of the city, an area called Ammon. 117 Sagebrush Court. Jake took out his laptop and looked up the address on Google Earth to get a sense of the surroundings. The enormous houses on Sagebrush Court were separated by ample space. The road extended for only a mile or so, with three houses on either side. Each was set back on what he estimated were two-acre tracts. This meant two things—first, he couldn't possibly get close enough from the street to make any meaningful observations, and second, the residents of such an exclusive neighborhood would immediately notice the presence of an outsider.

Jake scanned the map to the east. Eagle Point Park abutted the back side of the Canart residence. *Perfect.* His military-grade Steiner binoculars would put him within easy sight range from the tree line.

He flipped to the second page of printouts. The Canarts' vehicle information. The senator himself drove a 2011 Lincoln MKZ in sterling gray. His wife apparently preferred German engineering, with a mineral-white 2010 BMW 535i. Such cars would stick out in Idaho Falls, a town of blue-collar workers and ranchers turned small-business owners. Jake entered the license-plate numbers in the notes on his phone.

The next page offered physical descriptions and photos of Canart and Meirong Xiao. Canart stood five-foot-seven and weighed a meaty two hundred pounds. The excess was stashed mainly in his midsection, where a dense belly drooped over his belt line. He was well dressed in the three provided photos. His hair was a black wreath around an otherwise bald head. His small nose hooked sharply downward; his eyes were beady and dark.

Next was Canart's political bio. Jake read this thoroughly, having somewhat disengaged from politics after his move to Jackson.

This was Canart's first term as a senator. Main office in Idaho Falls on Business Route 20 near Liberty Park. Branch offices in Coeur d'Alene and Boise. His chief of staff, Frances Gilleny, was born in Utah and attended Harvard's Kennedy School. She was a sharp-looking woman, short and proper, who preferred dark pantsuits and no heels. Canart employed only sixteen other staff members, many fewer than the average of thirty-four. *Easier to keep secrets,* Jake figured. Idaho was a good place for a senator who liked his privacy or had something to hide.

The senator split his time between Idaho Falls and Washington, choosing to return home during breaks rather than travel. His political views were heavily influenced by his self-described "struggle to succeed in the changing landscape of my forefathers' land." He was ardently against free-flowing immigration and believed the world's burgeoning population was leading to a day of reckoning.

*How does a nutjob like this get elected?*

Jake read on. During his campaign for senator, Canart had played a game of smoke and mirrors, dodging and explaining away questions about his personal beliefs. Instead, he gained Idaho's support by rallying against the "deliberate degradation of American Ideals."

Meirong's images—CIA photos taken from a distance and outdated by a few years—gave the opposite impression: graceful and light. Waiflike. An avian creature with chestnut eyes that revealed a kind of tortured cleverness. Dark, straight hair to her lower back. Light skin. She stood five-foot-two and weighed one hundred pounds, at most. *Good.* Her size would stick out, especially if she was being toted around by a two-hundred-pound man in a $2,000 suit with a Lincoln.

The last two pages consisted of a "location profile," detailing Canart's known stomping grounds. There wasn't much: when he wasn't in DC, the senator liked to go to the Elks Lodge in downtown Idaho Falls on Tuesdays to play poker for charity and glad-hand the locals. Otherwise, his habits were fairly unsystematic. He liked fine dining, but anyone could have predicted that.

Meirong didn't have a location profile, because the CIA had been unable to track her in the United States. She was too shrewd for that. Jake knew she would be considerably more difficult to find than the senator.

When Jake was finished, he searched for car-rental agencies on his iPhone, in case Canart's people had somehow come to know his vehicle. There was a Hertz three miles west on Route 26.

On the way out Jake locked the safe—he wouldn't need the Glock for his initial reconnaissance. He pulled the blue nano-puff hoodie from its hanger and put it on.

Jake got out of the 4Runner and slid the Costas down over his eyes before approaching the rental counter. He had no idea how extensive Canart's or Xiao's intelligence was, and there was no excuse for being sloppy.

The clerk was tall and lanky with a pimply face. No older than eighteen. Jake gave him the name Mike Keller, using the corresponding driver's license and credit card from his safe at home.

"Car trouble?" The kid was looking around Jake at the 4Runner.

"Yeah. Not sure how long I'll need it."

The kid shrugged. "Pick whatever you want."

Jake walked the lot and found a new Dodge Charger in black. It was a little showy, but the extra horsepower could come in handy.

"Ninety-nine dollars a day," the clerk said. "You want insurance?"

*Ninety-nine dollars? CIA better reimburse me.* "No. Can I leave mine here?"

"Sure, but we can meet you at the mechanic's."

"Thanks, but I'll do the work myself when I get home."

Jake parked the 4Runner so that its license plate wasn't visible from the highway. He drove the Charger back east, past the old town and toward Ammon and Sagebrush Court.

The neighborhood was a typical suburban McMansion hamlet— out of place in the high plains. Small community parks dotted the landscape, with handsome wooden jungle gyms and paved bike paths. Sagebrush Court was the gemstone. A painted sign marked the entrance, where the road split around an island of small land-scaped hillocks.

Jake turned in for a quick look. He figured the residents of Sagebrush Court were used to wide-eyed wannabes cruising the street, wondering where their American Dream went wrong. The ostentatious-but-affordable Charger fit the part perfectly.

Number 117 was the last house on the left, set back from a wide cul-de-sac with its own island of shrubbery. Jake took the circle slowly for observation's sake. The Canart residence was redbrick, with occasional façades of taupe stucco framed by timber beams. Dormers and gables garnished the expansive roof. A three-story windowed turret dominated the right side of the home, and on the left, a large arcade window looked into a library or den.

The driveway wound its way up a gentle grade and back behind the tower on the right. Jake saw no sign of anyone.

He left Sagebrush Court and turned back onto the neighborhood's main street, then made two more quick rights and entered Eagle Point Park. It too was empty. Jake walked past a gazebo and playground and went into the woods on the western edge of the park. It was a thin strip of willows and planted aspens along a tiny creek. After a short stroll, Jake could see the back of the Canarts' home behind two or three hundred yards of lawn. A large stone patio with a dining set and outdoor fireplace abutted the back door. The garage doors faced left, and his position allowed him a clear view of the driveway.

*Good enough.* The trees would provide Jake cover to look into the rear windows using the binoculars. If the senator came or went, Jake would know.


Jake drove back to the hotel and responded to an email from Divya, informing her of his location. He opted for an early meal so that he could be in position at the park when the Canarts would potentially eat dinner themselves.

He walked along the river path a few blocks before turning toward town and its strip of bars and restaurants. The wind was blowing harder now, whisking away the heat from the Indian summer sun. He sat down in the back corner of a tapas joint, where he could watch the entrance. It was a small city, and a chance encounter with his mark was a distinct possibility.

His phone buzzed as the food arrived. Text from Noelle. *Why not a call?* Jake shook it off.

The park biologist had confirmed that the piece of fur came from a wolf. Jake already knew this, and thought for a moment about how to respond. He didn't want to blow her off, but he couldn't tell her where he was and why. He wrote back:

Interesting. What's your next move?

Buzz.

Going back to cabin this evening with county detectives.

He took another bite of chorizo and waited for Noelle to send another message. Nothing came.

Jake paid his bill and walked back to the hotel, taking in faces. The Friday happy hour filled the strip with workers, jackets slung over their shoulders, soaking in the fleeting sunshine.

It was 5 p.m. when Jake arrived back at the hotel. He flipped on the news and changed his clothes, adding layers in anticipation of a cold evening in the park. On the way out, he ordered a coffee from the café in the lobby.

The sun was slipping toward the Sawtooth Mountains to the west as Jake fired up the Charger. His nerves were heightened now. He had the Mariner in the center console and one of the tactical knives clipped to his belt. The binoculars rested in their case on the passenger seat. If Divya was right—that he might encounter interlopers from Canart's side *and* Xiao's side—he had good reason for extra caution.

Eagle Point Park came quicker than he remembered from earlier, but that was because his mind was racing. The swing sets and slides were empty and the walking paths barren, save for a woman in a fur coat walking a similarly attired poodle.

Empty was good. Jake parked the car as far from the road as he could get, and in the shadow of a large cottonwood. He allowed time for the two poodles to walk out of view and then followed the tree line to the entry point he'd noted earlier.

In the woods the light was dimmer, and with it came a feeling of isolation. He crossed over the small creek and positioned himself so he could see into the kitchen and living room. He rested his back against the trunk of a tree and waited.

It didn't take long. At exactly 6:21 p.m. Senator Rick Canart pulled into the garage. Jake watched through the Steiners as the mark washed his hands at the kitchen sink.

# 46

"What's our endgame?" Divya was pushing Wright more than she should have.

He noticed. "How long have you been here?"

"With the agency? Six years."

"Then you should know better than to be concerned with endgames."

"With all due respect, sir, this affects a friend of mine."

They were sitting in a coffee shop near the Library of Congress, debriefing after a meeting with Schue. The bustle of lunch hour concealed the subject of their discussion.

"The Office wants Xiao and the daughter for prosecution."

Divya already knew this. "And what do we want?"

Wright was slowly spinning his espresso cup on its saucer. "Information, as always," he finally said.

"The technology?"

He shook his head. "We have no real use for it. But for our national security, we need to be on top of developments like this."

"Why not send in a team and take Meirong by force?"

"We need to stay abreast of *all* developments here, not just foreign. And we can't find her."

"You mean, we need to know Canart's endgame?"

"Stop saying endgame. It attracts attention." Wright smiled at a young busser who was observing the pair while he cleared the next table. The boy moved on.

"Is that it?" Divya hadn't touched her salad or coffee.

"We have to let this play out a bit."

"Why?"

"Because Canart may indeed garner enough support to make this a reality. We want to know his true intentions."

"Since when is it up to the CIA to influence domestic politics?"

"Look, if someone is a little misguided, we let him live his life. If he is a threat to national security, we intervene. It would've taken one well-placed bullet in 1933 to prevent World War II."

Divya was silent for a moment. "That was Germany. This is the United States."

"Either way, it takes only one rotten egg to spoil the carton."

"What about Jake?"

"He can handle himself."

"So we're just throwing him to the wolves?"

Wright shook his head and finished his espresso. "I've gotta run. Squash. Ladder." He rose and walked to the door.

A minute later, Divya followed and hailed a cab.

"Langley, please." The light-haired driver stubbed out his cigarette. She wished it were Rashi; she could have used some of his wisdom.

\*       \*       \*

Divya was back at her desk by 1 p.m. She pulled up the information on Jake Trent that the Office of Special Investigation had emailed upon her request.

Well equipped was an understatement. *Jesus Christ.* She'd never seen the real story until now. *Jake has seven hits to his name?* The Office, like all government entities, sterilized its dirty work, dubbing these killings "ad hoc" prosecutions.

*Judge, jury, and executioner. No wonder he got out of the business.*

Divya suddenly felt sorry for him. The hidden beauty of any justice system was its complexity—the discrete layers of the process that allowed the executioner to sleep at night, the prosecutor to shrug off pushing for a death sentence, the judge to go home and forget his decision over a glass of wine.

The blame for a state-sanctioned execution was all about perspective. It was shifting, transient. The justification—the offender's crime—satisfied the executioner's guilt only theoretically. The real panacea was to blame it on the judge, who could blame the jury and the lawyers, who in turn could blame the criminal himself—what was it to them? They didn't take a person's life; they merely advocated for it.

Jake's job at the Office had no such insulation. When he found his mark, every role of the justice system was in his right hand. A cold metal fistful of justice.

To a thinking man like Jake, it must have been hell. Erased were pretty notions like due process. There was no way his diligent mind could forgive him for his "ad hocs." How could a moral man unwind from a job like that?

Wyoming, fishing, separation—suddenly his trajectory made perfect sense. He was finished with it. And rightfully so.

# 47

Jake jogged up the stairs instead of taking the elevator. He'd just finished his workout: twenty reps of one-legged squats, ten butter-flies, ten bench presses, ten shoulder shrugs, ten curls, and ten tri-cep extensions, all with forty-pound dumbbells. He cycled through five sets as fast as he could.

He wasn't as vigilant in his fitness as he had been when he was younger. The weightlifting taxed him. He shed his clothes, turned on the shower, and went to the bureau to check his cell phone, still panting.

Divya had called again. He didn't have much to report; the prior night's watch yielded nothing—the senator and his wife had chicken, heirloom potatoes, and asparagus with a bottle of Char-donnay. After dinner they watched TV for an hour before Mrs. Canart went to bed. The senator followed shortly after.

317

This morning, things had gotten only slightly more interesting: the senator left the house around 9 a.m., drove toward town, and pulled into his main office near Liberty Park.

Jake watched the door for an hour before he gave up. There was no way to hear what was going on inside, and the receptionist had started to look up curiously at the Charger. He stopped on the way back and grabbed a late breakfast, let it digest, and hit the gym.

He called Divya back as the shower water warmed.

"Nothing yet, except I can verify that the senator is here."

"Good." A pause. "Jake, I want you to be careful out there. You know how the feds can be."

"No. Tell me."

"The CIA is very interested in what's going on out there, but they can't overtly support you. They're worried about spooking Meirong and Canart back into the woodwork."

"I've been on my own before."

"I know that, Jake. Call me when you find the girl."

Jake hung up. *How much danger am I in?*

He jumped in the shower. Divya's warning didn't sound like general advice. She must have had reason to believe that the relationship between Xiao and Canart had eroded to the point that either side might be trigger-happy.

Jake dried off. He dressed warmly again, not knowing where he might end up or for how long.

He drove past the office building where he'd seen the senator just a couple of hours prior. The Lincoln was gone.

Jake made a U-turn into a gas station and drove back toward Ammon and the senator's residence. On the highway, a dull gray Ford Taurus peeled abruptly from the left lane into the right and settled in behind him. Jake eyeballed the sedan in the rearview mirror. When Jake took a left off Route 20 at the Ammon exit, the car followed.

Adjusting the mirror, Jake took note of the license plate, typing the number into his phone. He pushed the accelerator and passed an old minivan. The Taurus did the same.

*Shit. So much for not spooking anyone.*

The right turn for Sagebrush Court was coming up quickly. Instead of taking it, Jake continued straight, past the turn for Eagle Point Park and into the foothills on Sunnyside. The road straightened out and climbed out of the artificial verdure of Ammon and into rolling slopes of silver sage and rabbitbrush. He accelerated until the Taurus was out of view.

At the intersection with Bone Road, Jake pulled over and waited. He opened the center console, took out the Mariner, and set it on his lap.

The Taurus never came. After thirty minutes, Jake, confident he was alone again, spun the Charger around in the dust and headed back to the park.

Throngs of children frolicked through the playground, bundled up against the chilly air. Their days outside were numbered with the approaching winter. The weather shifted; the gusty wind from the prior afternoon brought with it low cloud cover and occasional snow flurries. A front was parked squarely over eastern Idaho. Jake parked and took a look around using his mirrors—plenty of SUVs and minivans, but no Ford Taurus. He opened the door.

Jake concealed the Mariner in his waistband but draped the binoculars around his neck. If anyone asked, he was spotting sandhill cranes. He walked slowly through the woods to his surveillance point.

Canart arrived at the residence at 2:30 p.m., leaving the Lincoln in the turnaround. He spent a few minutes discussing something in the backyard with a gardener, then went into the house. He changed clothes and returned to the sedan.

Before the senator could get in the car, Jake was in a full-blown sprint back to the Charger. He ran through the strip of trees, ignoring the path for a more direct route. He had his hands out in front of him, deflecting low branches that aimed to sting his half-frozen face.

His pace coming out of the woods attracted the attention of the mothers at the park. He gave them a quick wave, hoping to quell their suspicion with a gesture of normalcy. They sent back puzzled looks.

Jake squealed out of the lot, taking a left out of the park to the stop sign. At his next left, he could see the terminus of Sagebrush Court. Jake waited a few seconds. No Lincoln. Had Canart beat him? *He must have.* Jake accelerated toward the main artery.

On Sunnyside Avenue, Jake passed slower traffic until the Lincoln was within view. He slowed to the speed limit, keeping a buffer between himself and Canart. No Taurus. So far, so good.

At the Idaho Falls city limits, traffic picked up. A procession of Saturday afternoon traffic, moviegoers, and early-bird diners. Jake lost the Lincoln in the snarl. All he could do now was watch the turning lanes and hope.

The intersection at Highway 26 was crowded with vehicles. The perfect place to lose his target. Sunnyside spread out into four lanes at the light and the highway was six lanes, both ways. If Jake guessed the wrong lane, it would be impossible to get back on Canart without giving himself away.

Luckily, it didn't come to that. At South Hitt Road, Jake watched the Lincoln turn north toward Grand Teton's mall and movie theatre. The seven or eight cars between them did the same. Wind was gusting head-on at the Charger from the north, which usually meant an encroaching cold front from British Columbia or Washington, and a second wave of weather was fighting its way across the west.

Canart continued past the shopping center and took a left onto East Seventeenth, toward South Holmes. When he got there, he turned right at the light toward the highway again.

The Holmes intersection didn't concern Jake. The senator had to go right or straight—he would've taken Sunnyside the whole way out to access the highway between there and South Holmes— and the intersection was smaller, only three lanes.

Two cars stood between Jake and the senator when they hit the highway. The Lincoln went right and accelerated briskly back the way Jake had come the day before, east toward Teton Pass and Jackson.

The afternoon was increasingly dull and moody to the east, where the elevation rose. Only small, opaque windows of light shone through thin spots in the clouds. A grainy snow began to fall.

The Lincoln was some four hundred yards ahead, and Jake maintained that distance. Traffic lightened as they left town. A few miles out they passed Iona, and then Ririe. The speed limit was sixty-five now, but the Lincoln was beating that easily, making Jake wonder if the senator was headed the whole way into Jackson.

Ten miles east of Idaho Falls, the senator slowed and merged into the left turn lane toward Heise Hot Springs.

Jake stayed in the main lane of traffic. Following the senator here, when there were no other cars around, would raise eyebrows. In his rearview mirror, he watched the silver sedan make the turn, then flip on its right turn signal.

*Got ya.* Canart was turning into a small commercial complex.

Jake continued on 26 until a rest stop perched above the South Fork of the Snake, where he made a U-turn. He got on his cell phone and called Divya as he accelerated back toward Heise.

"Were the three offices the only real estate in the senator's name?"

"That and the house. I sent you all four."

"You did. There's nothing else?"

Jake was eyeing an abandoned industrial park set back a quarter-mile from the highway.

"No."

"Where is his research team located?"

"We don't know."

"Okay. I might be onto something." Jake pressed End. *A shady senator visiting an unoccupied commercial park.*

Jake slowed to make the right turn at Heise, but quickly got back on the accelerator. *The Taurus.* He exchanged momentary eye contact with the driver of the dull gray Taurus, a meatball of a man with military-cut gray hair. A bodyguard. He turned left toward Canart and the industrial park.

*Shit.*

Jake had no choice but to continue straight. He pulled off at a small diner on the right and parked in the back of the stone building, where the Charger wasn't visible from the highway.

He went inside and got a cup of coffee to go. Jake settled in, standing in the sharp, pelting snow at the back corner of the restaurant, looking west, where he could see Route 26. His gray and black attire matched the atmosphere. He was hoping to see a Taurus headed back toward town, and a Lincoln too, so that he could investigate the industrial park.

After three hours, Jake's hands and feet were frozen and his face battered by the early season storm. He got back in the Charger, again putting the loaded Glock on his lap, and pulled out of the lot toward Heise and the industrial park.

The main building looked recently built—the last five or ten years. Plain vertical aluminum siding adorned an exterior with few windows and zero frills. Taupe colored, with a dark roof. The Lincoln and the Taurus were side-by-side in the back corner of the lot.

Jake parked the Charger down the road a ways and across the street. The evening light was leaden, dulled by the cold front. He left the binoculars, opting for the Glock and the tactical knives.

There were three entrances to the building: one facing the highway, and one on either side. The entrance closest to the senator's sedan was lit up by a single incandescent bulb. On the right side of the heavy steel door, one of the building's few windows was lit from within. Jake concealed himself behind a hedge just a few yards away from the two parked cars and watched. Slat blinds made details difficult, but Jake could make out figures: One was surely Canart, with his small head and ballooned abdomen. The other had the rounded muscular shape of the man who drove the Taurus.

After a few moments, the security man left the room with the window and came outside to have a smoke and to check the perimeter. He looked agitated, on high alert. Jake was well hidden in the landscaping, though, and the guard seemed satisfied with his patrol.

Jake put his attention back on the window. The senator's shadow was perched atop a desk on the right. He was looking left, where the door toward the entryway must have been. He was gesturing excitedly, either on speakerphone or talking to someone just out of view. A third figure.

The gesturing turned to yelling, and Jake struggled to make out the words. They were too muffled. The security guard noticed the commotion too. He stayed outside, but shifted the revolver in his belt line, preparing for action.

The ruckus was coming to a crescendo. The senator's bellowing, though loud, was still indistinct. Looking anxious, the security man opened the door, peered in, and listened. He must have deemed his services unnecessary, because he resumed his post and lit another cigarette.

Silence. The senator had apparently said his piece. After a few quiet moments, a sobbing escaped through the walls. A woman. Jake's eyes were glued to the window, looking for Meirong's slight silhouette.

Movement. The senator was up and walking toward the middle of the window. His hand was out in front of him.

Canart's shouting resumed and the object revealed itself. A petite shadow. The two figures collided in the window in a tangled melee. The mass stumbled toward the window, knocking the slats of the blinds in every direction.

There were muted grunts and cries. The security guard had had enough. He flicked his cigarette into the halo cast by the outdoor fixture.

Jake saw the guard's form join the tangle, doubling its size. He stood up and drew the Mariner, then resumed his crouch.

*Crack!*

A blast of gunfire. The gathering fell to the ground. After a short moment the hullabaloo resumed, rowdier than ever. Pieces separated from the group. One was rushing to the exit. The door to the building was flung wide open. Jake dropped flat to the ground.

He spun and wormed his way behind the cement base of a light post. *Crack! Crack!* The concrete disintegrated, leaving a curtain of dust. Jake couldn't see his assailant, though he had a guess. He relayed a few shots back at the bodyguard, who had no choice but to retreat toward the car.

Jake heard a car door open and close. He stood and fired. The engine turned over and the transmission thumped into reverse, followed by the screech of rubber on asphalt.

*Damn.*

Jake waited for a few seconds to make sure the attacker was gone. When he checked, the Taurus was missing.

He peered through the dust back into the senator's office. There were no figures visible. Whoever was left wasn't standing.

Jake backed off out of view, and ran to the Charger to call Divya.

# 48

At dusk the skies were spitting a granular snow. Jake had moved the Charger even farther down the dark country road, but where he could still see the intersection with the highway. The Lincoln hadn't left the complex.

"Just another minute," Divya said. "I'll try Wright's land line."

Jake was still catching his breath from the adrenaline and the run.

"Yes?" Wright was nonplussed.

"Sir, I have Jake Trent on the line. We have a development."

"Go ahead."

Jake spoke up. "Less than ten minutes ago, I witnessed a shooting among Canart, his security guard, and a person I believe to be Meirong Xiao."

"Casualties?"

"I don't know. I believe the security guard fled."

Divya took over. "I think it's time to activate a team out there. I'd be willing . . ."

Wright didn't let her finish. "Jake, what's the current situation?"

"Two of the three appear to remain in the building. I still have visual of one of their vehicles."

"Are they armed?"

"Safe to assume so."

"Are you armed?"

"Yes."

"You believe the senator and Meirong remain in the office?"

"That's my best guess."

Wright took a moment to think. "Are you comfortable resuming surveillance?"

Jake thought, *Whoever is left inside heard the shots in the lot and knows they are being watched.* "If it will help to get Charlotte Terrell home, absolutely."

"We're working on that as we speak."

Jake wondered if this was true. "What do you want me to do?"

"You need to find out who was hit in the shootout. If Meirong is dead, we have to make sure her father doesn't find out. If he does, he has no reason to give us Charlotte Terrell."

Jake hung up the phone, made sure it was on silent, and worked his way back to the building. He hunkered down for a few moments in the same bush, hoping to see Meirong. The light in the office was still on, but no silhouettes appeared in the window.

He had to get closer. If he could get to the window without being noticed, he might be able to catch a glimpse of the office through the cracks in the window shade.

It was now a quarter after seven. The arctic air had started to settle in. High, mired clouds emancipated swollen flakes—the largest yet from the early season crop of storms. The plains above the South Fork of the Snake were slowly filling in, obscuring the crop rows and tractor paths.

Still no movement from within the office. The building was silent. The wind that came in with the front had died off, and Jake could see tracks from the office door toward the spot where the Taurus had been parked. They were large—a man's foot for sure, but Jake couldn't be sure whether it was the guard or Canart himself who'd taken the Taurus. He preferred to encounter the senator, if it came to that. He was less physically imposing.

Jake crept closer until his back was against the building's aluminum exterior. He was shielded from the falling snow by a small awning. He looked out to the parking lot and then right toward the highway to make sure the Taurus wasn't returning.

*I should be so lucky.*

The building blocked his view of the Taurus, but Jake could hear the new snow betraying the guard's intentions. It squeaked and cried under his tires. The car was reappearing slowly, lights off.

Jake shuffled along with his back against the cold metal toward the far corner, where he could hide. The Taurus came into view around the opposite corner and made a sweeping turn to face the battered concrete where Jake had hid only a few minutes before.

The security guard stopped the car and flicked on the high beams. The big flakes came heavier, immobilizing his senses; he couldn't see much beyond thirty feet out.

The guard got out of the car, his back to Jake. He was checking the landscaping, looking for confirmation that Jake was dead. Jake knew the man wasn't going anywhere. It was his duty to stay between the senator and whoever had been in the bushes. He was an obstacle Jake would have to go through, not around.

Jake was creeping up behind the figure before he knew it. Pure instinct. The man crouched just at the end of the high beams' reach, looking for blood on the snow.

FUBAR, the military called it. Canart and Meirong knew there was a threat just outside. The security guard was on to him too. Tactical measures were a thing of the past. For the first time in many years, Jake was forced to be something other than human—a machine on a mission.

"For the chief!" Jake shouted.

The man startled and turned.

*Crack!*

When Jake approached the body, the look of surprise still showed on his face. He appeared perfectly lifelike, but for the tiny entry wound between his eyes.

# 49

Jake took a deep breath. He was just a short counterclockwise spin away from being able to see inside the office, where he would take a quick glance, and then spin back, in case of gunfire.

Jake started to move, the Mariner enveloped by both hands and held low, inches from his belt buckle.

"Drop it."

A voice from behind. The doorway. A *female* voice. Pleasant except for its mandate. His target had turned the tables. She'd hidden elsewhere in the lab after the first spate of gunfire, explaining why Jake hadn't seen any more figures in the office.

*Stupid.* He was rusty.

"Drop it." Again. The soft air of a Chinese accent. "Don't turn around."

Jake did as she asked, bending down and placing the Glock on the carpet.

330

"Keep your hands up and walk backward."

Again Jake submitted, slowly walking toward her with his hands up. He knew better than to mount a counterattack. There would be better opportunities when his captor's adrenaline had flushed through her system. For the next ten minutes or so, she would have a hair trigger—a shoot first, ask questions later attitude.

Meirong led Jake into the office, the room with the window. She'd killed the lights. Jake couldn't see inside, but he could hear labored breathing. A wounded man.

She was gathering some items from the desk's drawer with the light of her phone. Jake heard the jangle of a key set.

If she was going to lock him in somewhere—a closet or a store-room—his chances of escape were slim.

"C'mon." She pushed Jake from behind down a short hallway that opened up into a workshop of sorts. *Ground zero? Was this where they were developing the GPSN?* The space was empty, and only the dim auxiliary fluorescent lights were on.

She steered Jake along the left wall of the laboratory to a door in the far corner. Meirong ordered him to sit on a cluttered desk and went to unlock the closet.

She was smaller than he'd realized, probably under ninety pounds. Her dress was plain, a white blouse and black dress pants. She made brief eye contact with him as she spun around from unlocking the door. He tried to detect something, anything that would give him an idea of her mental state, so that he could use it to his advantage. Her face was apathetic and her breathing nor-mal. She didn't seem afraid.

"Stay there." Meirong pointed the gun squarely at Jake's fore-head and then quickly turned to pull a stack of boxes from the electrical closet to make room for her prisoner. He wanted to sack her, make his move while she had her back turned, but she was still on edge. It was too dangerous.

"Get in."

Jake's window of opportunity was closing. He walked into the tiny room.

Meirong didn't slam the door shut. Instead, she sat back on the desk where Jake had just been and relaxed a bit but kept the barrel of the gun trained on him.

"Who are you?"

Jake had to think quickly. "I'm here to protect you."

She laughed. "Did my father send you?"

Jake sensed hostility in her voice. "No. Canart was going to hurt you. Take advantage of you."

Another chuckle. "Everyone takes advantage of me."

"We are trying to set you free."

"And you are who? The American government?"

It seemed to Jake she knew a hell of a lot more than the CIA was aware of.

Before Jake could speak again, she affirmed his suspicion. "I know what I am worth. To any country, not just China."

"I am here to help you, not enslave you."

"The senator did not have me enslaved."

She was loyal to Canart. Jake could use that to his advantage. "I can help him, you know. I am a trained medic"—which was a lie.

"Stay here." She was up quickly and slammed the closet door.

He'd missed his chance. Now, Jake's only company was the buzzing electricity. Modems, circuit breakers, and phone routers. There was no ceiling fixture in the room, but the various pieces of equipment in the closet emitted thin beams of colored light from their power buttons.

Jake took a seat on the floor and felt a tug in his pocket. His phone. Meirong had neglected to confiscate it. He texted Divya.

Meirong has me captive. I'm okay. Believe Canart was the one shot.

Her response came quickly.

Stay safe. Calling Wright.

Jake used the phone's flashlight app to look around the closet for anything useful. There wasn't much. Two cases of printer paper, a mop, and a spool of Cat 5 internet cable.

He held the phone up to examine the doorknob. It was a traditional lever knob with a simple key lock from the inside. Unusual, but not unheard of—key locks were considerably cheaper than the inside toggle-lock variety.

He turned and inspected the rear wall where the electronics were mounted. The circuit breaker was centered on the wall. Jake opened the gray steel swing. The top switch was marked MAIN.

The flashlight on the phone turned off as a text arrived from Divya.

If you are not in danger, stay put for now. We are tracing your cell location.

Jake shook his head in frustration. They were using him to find Meirong.

I am in the big building on the northeast corner of Heise Road and 26.
Stay with her. Wright's orders

was all Divya responded.

*Dammit.*

Jake looked back up at the circuit breaker and decided it couldn't hurt. At the very least, it would improve his chances to interact with Meirong again and disarm her.

He pulled the switch from left to right, killing the power to the entire building. An unnerving silence replaced the buzz of technology.

It took a few minutes longer than he expected. When Meirong finally opened the door, there was blood on her hands. She slipped past Jake, gun trained on him, and flipped the switch back to the left. When she came back past him, he could hear her breath, shaky and fearful. She was losing her cool.

The equipment on the wall beeped and blinked as it started up.

"Don't do that again."

"I told you I can help. He's losing too much blood."

Had the prodigy shed a tear? Maybe it was sweat. Her face was ashen, her eyes desperate and vacant.

"Get up." She led Jake at gunpoint back through the laboratory and into the front office.

Senator Rick Canart was on his side with his knees drawn toward his chest, almost into a fetal position. He was holding his breath now, clearly in pain, and letting it escape in a swift huff that was half-exhale, half-moan. He didn't regard Jake or Meirong.

"Left side," she said, going to him.

"I have to move you again." Meirong grimaced with him. She was more focused on her lover's condition than she was on Jake. He was going to use that to his advantage.

Jake helped Meirong move the portly politician to his back. His breath came shallow and fast now. Rapid breathing and heart rate.

Hypovolemic shock. His organs were dying. The pooling blood around him hadn't spread into an expansive tarn as it did in the movies. Instead, it absorbed into his clothes and rested in small clotted puddles on the laminate floor.

Estimating his blood loss at more than two liters, Jake didn't give the senator any real chance of surviving the gunshot, but he kept that to himself. The wound was several inches below his heart, in the left middle of the abdomen. Canart couldn't speak or move on his own, other than occasional winces of pain.

"I need clean water and some clean towels," Jake said

Meirong was still too sharp to leave him alone in the room. "Let's go." She walked him at gunpoint to one of the lab tables, under which sat a file cabinet with two drawers.

"In there."

Jake bent down and opened the drawer and grabbed a roll of paper towels. "This won't be enough."

"It's all we have."

"He needs a hospital."

"No." She gestured for Jake to stand up, and then led him back into the office. From behind the desk, Meirong pulled several bottles of drinking water.

Jake opened the senator's dress shirt and began wiping around the wound. If Canart could feel the pressure, he didn't show it. His eyes were only slightly open on their upper halves, and they stared up toward the ceiling.

"I need to apply pressure to the wound. Do you have anything we can wrap?"

Meirong silently backed off, the gun aimed at Jake, and pulled a sleeping bag off the couch adjacent to the desk.

"I need a knife."

She shook her head.

"Then I need you to cut strips from the bag, four inches wide and long enough to tie around his torso."

She went back to the desk, grabbed a pair of scissors, and did as Jake asked.

"Bring it to me."

Finished, Meirong brought the first tether over.

"When I lift him, slide it under." After she did as he asked, Jake tied the compress of wadded paper towels in place with the strip of nylon from the sleeping bag.

"Good. Now go cut some more."

The senator moaned and closed his eyes.

"He's dying!" Meirong pleaded, and moved toward them.

Jake stopped her. "Keep cutting."

The life was seeping out of the embattled senator. Not that it mattered to Jake. He was still a machine with one goal in mind: saving Charlotte Terrell.

When she came back with two more strips from the bag, Jake made his move. He reached up to take the makeshift bandages but instead grabbed the prodigy's left hand, which held the pistol. He forced the barrel up and away, where it harmlessly discharged into the drop ceiling. A flurry of mineral fibers fell down on them.

The scuffle lasted no more than a couple of seconds. Jake stood up and aimed the pistol at Meirong, who was on her knees beside the senator.

She bent over him and let out a cry. "He's not breathing!"

"I'm sorry." Jake caught his breath, bent down next to the hysterical woman, and grabbed the nylon, which he repurposed as constraints.

"You need to stand up."

Meirong was disconsolate, hands trembling with adrenaline and the emotional shock of her lover's death. Jake put her hands behind her back and tied them. Then he walked her over to the departed senator's swivel chair and tied her to it by her waist.

"Goddammit!" He didn't mean to say it aloud. *How the hell did I get here?* Adrenaline waning, the human was creeping back into him.

He wiped the blood from his hands on the remaining paper towels and took out his phone. He was surprised to find his own hands trembling.

"Divya. I have Meirong. The senator is dead." The prodigy whimpered at Jake's words.

As Jake listened to Divya's instructions, he pulled aside the blinds and checked the parking lot.

"Got it." Jake ended the call.

He turned and untied Meirong. "We're leaving."

"Let me stay here with him."

Jake didn't respond. He led Meirong around Senator Canart's body and through the office door to the hallway, opened the door to the parking lot, and looked around once more. Still empty. The senator's secrets had worked against him. His staff and family, all in the dark, weren't able to save him. He scrambled out and grabbed his Mariner from the carpet and returned to Meirong.

"Let's go." Jake hurried her through the lot, around the corner of the building, and to the street where the Charger was parked. He loaded Meirong into the passenger seat and took off south toward the highway.

337

# 50

The Office of Human Rights and Special Prosecutions looked like an ordinary workplace. It was located on the fourth floor of an Indiana limestone structure on Pennsylvania Avenue, a couple of blocks from the White House and next to Freedom Plaza.

The staff was small—six attorneys, who, like Jake Trent, were also law-enforcement-trained special agents. Others were located throughout the Eastern Seaboard in various branch locations.

Each special prosecutor had an assistant, a cream-of-the-crop graduate from a top law school.

Barry Schue, early forties, of average height but athletic, was still at his desk, to his wife's chagrin, along with his assistant. It was another late night at work, but his understudy probably cherished the opportunity to impress his superiors. At least that's how Schue rationalized it. He would have felt that way in his younger days.

They were seated inside Schue's office poring over pages of documentation on the rural ransack organized by Xiao and his young daughter. The evidence was sufficient to prosecute both of them. The question was whether, after the judgment, it would be possible to impose a sentence. This was a part of the business for which Schue couldn't sufficiently train the assistant. It was the last hurdle in closing a case. Getting your man into custody.

Wright had hinted all along that Meirong's prosecution might become a casualty of foreign relations—spy business, really—and that irked Schue. The job of the Office was to pursue justice, not make concessions and play political games.

*Why the hell did Wright object to her prosecution anyway?* At the very least, she was an accomplice to crimes against humanity. At worst, she was the mastermind. *What was in it for Wright and the CIA?*

"Justin?"

The young assistant looked up from the pile of paperwork spread on the carpet.

"I'll look through the rest of this. Can you get me a quick bio on the point man for the agency on this?"

"Assistant Director Wright?"

"Yes."

Divya had returned to Langley, where she had access to all her contacts and the full resources of the agency. The building was dim and cool. She started up her laptop, put some coffee on in the break room, and called Wright.

"I'll fly out and pick up Meirong," Wright told her. "As soon as we get her, we'll begin the process to get Charlotte Terrell back."

"I'd like to stay on. I'd really like to be out there myself. He's a friend."

Wright became incensed. "You have a serious problem with authority, Divya. Do not question my command." He hung up before she could say anything more.

*Asshole.*

Divya went to the break room, poured a cup of coffee, and sat back down at her desk. She was anxious, tapping her fingers on her desk, feeling idle. She called Jake and told him the plan.

"Lie low until Wright contacts you tomorrow."

*Be careful,* she forgot to say. *Don't get yourself killed.*

She anxiously plied through the Canart/Xiao file for a few minutes before turning back to her computer. She went to a flight search engine and typed "Idaho Falls" in the destination field. "Dulles to Idaho Falls. Depart 5:18 am EST, arrive 8:48 MST." She supplied her credit-card information and clicked purchase.

On her way home her cell phone rang.

"Divya? It's Schue."

"Yes?"

"You need to stay away from Wright. Tell Jake the same."

# 51

Jake perched the Charger on a high, sandy shoulder above the dirt road to Ririe Reservoir, where he could see any vehicles coming or going from the highway. Back to the west, he could see the glow of Idaho Falls, and to the east the scattered outposts that sat along the southern fork of the Snake.

The reception was spotty, but he checked his phone often. Nothing since Divya had called half an hour ago.

Heavy snow continued to fall. There were four or more inches on the ground. The night was gray rather than black—the thick clouds reflected light pollution back onto the snow-covered high plains, which returned the favor, lending a dull glow to the atmosphere.

To keep Meirong comfortable he'd left her in the car, out of the snow. Jake sat on the hood. He needed the fresh air.

Around 11 p.m., Jake got back into the Charger and turned the heat on. Meirong was shivering from the cold, but her emotional state seemed to have calmed.

"Thank you."

"No problem." Jake was playing good cop. "I need some information. There is a woman in Jackson. A friend of mine. Did you put a GPSN chip in her?"

"I haven't put a chip in anyone."

Her face looked as though she was telling the truth. "Did the senator?"

"I don't know."

"This friend is not unlike you." Jake let his words sink in. "Very special. Very smart. She had a heart attack that nearly killed her. Is that how your wolf died?" Jake guessed.

"Fibrillation. Ventricular fibrillation. What's her name?"

"Esma. How does it kill?"

"Like a pacemaker resets the heart. Electrical pulses," the prodigy said. "They can remove it. It was just a prototype. A trial." She touched her left shoulder with her right hand. "It won't activate during the procedure."

"You're sure?"

She nodded but appeared disappointed. "The technology isn't there yet." A frown.

"Thank you."

Jake took the keys out of the ignition, grabbed an extra shirt from his pack in the backseat, and draped it over Meirong.

"I'll be right back."

Jake walked through the ankle-deep snow, uphill from the Charger. To the west, a rock promontory jutted out into the night. Jake carefully climbed its slippery face, found stronger reception, and called the hospital.

Dr. Antol was on the night shift.

"It's Jake Trent."

The woman took a moment to place the name. "The cardiology expert?"

"How is Esma?"

"Fine. Doing better."

"Good. I need you to listen to me carefully."

Jake explained, and the doctor seemed to listen, intrigued by the bizarre story.

"We'll take a look," she promised.

After he got off the phone with the hospital, he called J.P. and filled him in. "If Dr. Antol doesn't find anything, you need to get a second opinion." Jake was still concerned about whether Dr. Antol would take him seriously. J.P. sounded confused, but compliant.

It was a few minutes before midnight. The moon was rising to the east. It glowed through the foggy shroud of clouds.

Jake arrived back at the car to find Meirong asleep. He started the car again and ran the heat for a few minutes before returning to his watch outside. His view from within the Charger was limited, and he didn't want anyone sneaking up on them. He went into the car only to thaw his hands and run the heat for Meirong.

Around 1 a.m., the snow intensified to whiteout conditions—a squall within a storm. The driving flakes weaseled into Jake's collar and cuffs, wetting his under layers and chilling him to the bone. The watch was useless in the blizzard; visibility was less than a car's length. He retreated to the driver's side.

Meirong was still asleep. The heavy sheets of blowing snow tested the windshield. They arrived in short runs of rhythmic gusts, occasionally strong enough to shift the body of the car on its struts. He fought off fatigue, but the cadence of the storm eventually made Jake's eyes close.

He woke up at 3:45 a.m. The wind had decided to take a break—the storm was again dropping large swollen flakes into a still night sky.

He got out to have a look around. The squall had drifted nearly a foot of snow against the passenger side. Jake kicked at it to test its consistency. It was wind-buffed into a dense slab. Getting back out on the road in the rear-wheel-drive car would be difficult, but he would deal with that when the time came.

He walked back up to the promontory and his phone hummed. Voice mail. It was from Divya. Jake pressed play.

Voice mail unavailable.

Jake trudged farther uphill, beyond the rocks. Still no reception. The weather had only made it worse.

*Dammit.* Why was Divya contacting him? As far as he knew, Wright was making the morning pickup.

The moon was setting now, and if Jake looked hard enough, he thought he could see the glow of the arriving sun over the southern Snake River Range to the east. He checked his phone. Only a few minutes had passed. 4:01.

On the way back to the car, Jake stopped, urinated, and checked his phone again on the unlikely chance he had reception between the rocky perch and the car. Still nothing.

He would have to move the car. Find a place to hide with a good vantage of the road and some reception. He didn't want to miss his chance to get rid of Meirong, get Charlotte back, and end this whole mess. The sudden plunge back into his old life had been cold and unwelcoming.

The snow was uniformly six inches deep, except for the deeper drifts on the lee side of rocks and brush. The squall had scoured all the precipitation that wasn't anchored down by the prairie short-grass. Once Jake could dig around the drift against the Charger's passenger side, the car should be able to get back on the road easily.

He continued down the slope to assess the situation and start digging.

Something was wrong. The light in the cabin of the Charger was on. He jogged the last thirty feet to the vehicle.

"You'll freeze to death!" he shouted into the storm. He whipped around, scanning the tiny area where he could see through the darkness.

Meirong was gone. Somehow she had wiggled free from her restraints, scooted across the center console, and exited through the driver's door. A nylon strip of sleeping bag rested on the pas-senger's seat.

Jake got down on all fours and started clearing the drifted snow by sweeping his arm under the car. The snow was dense, its par-ticles jammed together by the force of the wind. Jake was work-ing up a sweat, but his hands were cold and wet. He pulled them into his coat sleeves and sat on his ass, using his legs to sweep the remaining snow.

*How could I let his happen?* A grim mood washed over him. He might have just blown the whole thing. Cost Charlotte her life because he was out of practice. *Get it together.* There wasn't time to brood over his mistakes.

When the passenger side was adequately cleared, Jake tore

dead branches from the surrounding sagebrush and stamped them down behind the rear wheels for traction.

He got in. Pressing the gas pedal softly, so as not to allow the Charger's V8 to rip the tires free from their moorings, he eased back onto the 4x4 track. Then he carefully idled down the steep hill back to Ririe Reservoir Road.

Back toward the reservoir, there was nothing but expanses of sage flats and potato farms. Fleeing in that direction was a death wish if you were unprepared for the cold. A right turn had him pointed back toward the highway. Chances were Meirong was headed in that direction. Two miles lay between Jake and the intersection, where, if she were lucky enough to encounter a late-night driver, she would have no problem hitching a ride in such a storm.

Jake pushed the Charger as much as he could without risking fishtailing into a roadside ditch. The high beams cast a wide swath of yellow light into the bordering fields.

He got to the intersection with the highway, stopped the car, turned off the headlights, and searched the snowy ground for tracks. He found nothing but the footprints of a curious raven, pecking around for roadkill.

Jake turned the car around in the empty intersection. As he did so, a beep emanated from somewhere in the dash. Jake scrolled through the menu on the Charger's computer. *Twenty-five miles until empty.*

*Dammit. Shouldn't have gotten the V8.* It wasn't enough if the search lasted a few hours. He threw the car into reverse, made a three-point turn, and accelerated back toward Idaho Falls to find a gas station.

On the way, he was finally able to retrieve his voice mail.

Jake. Divya. Not sure Wright can be trusted. I'm on my way.

# 52

Charlotte Terrell gazed out onto empty streets. She went to the bed and flipped on the TV, but didn't pay much attention. On the nightstand beside her, there was an uneaten hunk of meatloaf with a side of potatoes.

The giant was in the corner leafing through a magazine. A knock on the door startled him from his post. He swiped his hand over his face to wash the exhaustion off and went to answer it.

It was Xiao. Charlotte made no effort to acknowledge him. He walked between her and the television she was pretending to watch.

He was unusually chipper. "Get your things."

Even the giant showed surprise.

"Pack your things. You are going home." With that, he started toward the door.

She called after him. "What's going on?"

He stopped, but didn't turn around. "Daughter is coming home. Now, I am free."

"What does that mean?"

Xiao was out the door.

The giant resumed his post at the desk in the corner and flipped through the same old magazine. Charlotte detected a slight smile on his lips.

"That's it?"

He put the magazine down. "Nightmare is almost over."

"My nightmare will never end."

"Sorry for your husband."

Charlotte let her thoughts spiral down that dangerous path—telling the children that their father was gone, making a living on her own to support them, keeping herself sane enough to be a good mother.

The giant got up. "What is it? You look ill."

"You took my husband away. My children's father."

"A cruel world."

"Not for you."

"You know nothing." Charlotte wasn't interested in hearing her captor's sob story. "What did he mean, *free*?"

"Xiao?"

"Yes. He said he is free now."

The giant sighed, apparently figuring there was no use in secrets anymore. "It was always about his daughter. When he used Meirong for his own gain—to help the Americans, no less—it angered our government. Shortly after he sent her to the States, he became aware of the colony here at Tram Village. He promised to get Meirong back if they would hold a place."

"Couldn't he buy his way in?"

The giant laughed. "A place at Tram Village can't be purchased. People are chosen."

"How?"

"Genes. Intelligence. Physical strength. Any exceptional trait."

"*Breeders?* And Meirong?"

"She is exceptionally intelligent."

"Why Jackson Hole, why Tram Village?"

"Some Chinese officials attended an economic summit in your town, and found its sense of liberty and sovereignty appealing."

"The last of the Wild West."

"New face for a new world."

"What if it doesn't happen? What if Xiao's daughter is wrong?"

"It's as certain and unstoppable as the Yellow River."

Packing proved to be an especially emotional task for Charlotte. From the three drawers on the right side of the bureau below the TV, she gathered her clothes. She tried not to glance at the left drawers, where Roger's clothes still lay, folded and organized as if nothing had ever happened. Her heart told her to indulge—grab a T-shirt and smell and smell until he came back to life—but her better sense resisted.

The chief's leather duffel bag, with the Jackson Hole Police Department tag, lay at the bottom of the closet. She didn't dare move it. Its deep wrinkles drew in her gaze though, reminding her of the sun-browned furrows beneath her husband's loving eyes.

The giant, noticing her state, got up out of the chair.

"I will pack his things. You would regret not having them."

She nodded and fought back the urge to cry. In silence, the giant carefully placed the chief's clothes and personal items into the duffel. Charlotte couldn't bear to look at them.

# 53

"We'll split up and go look by the reservoir." Wright was pouring copious amounts of sugar into his coffee.

"Good plan."

Jake had met the assistant director at the diner near the industrial park, where Senator Canart's body still lay.

"What do we do about him?"

"Leave him for now. We have more important things to do."

*A senator left rotting in his own office,* Jake thought. *Not good publicity for the CIA, but if anyone can hide the truth, it's the agency.*

In the bathroom, Jake surreptitiously read another text from Divya. Her flight had been delayed in Salt Lake, so she rented a car and was navigating through the snow on what was usually a four-hour drive.

Of course, Jake didn't reveal that to Wright. He hadn't revealed anything that Divya or Schue told him. He could tell Wright was on edge and wondered whether it was normal work stress or something else.

And Divya's suspicion? *What had she come across?*

He figured Wright needed him for the search. As long as that was the case, he posed little danger to Jake. If and when they found Meirong, that dynamic could change, if Divya was right.

They drove toward Ririe Reservoir separately, which suited Jake just fine. The lake was another two miles beyond where Meirong had escaped. The landscape was wide-open and the visibility reasonable—high storm clouds were still hanging in the hills, but the snowfall was sputtering out.

They found no trace of their target between the parking pull-off near the promontory and the state park at the reservoir. It was feasible that Meirong had broken into one of the park's summer cabins to stay warm. Without a coat or shelter, she didn't stand much chance.

Jake pulled over at the boundary to the park and lowered his window. Wright pulled up alongside in his rental Jeep.

"I'll drive the east loop," Jake said. "The west loop is just through there. Meet back here?"

Wright nodded and spun around to enter the west loop, in the direction of tent campsites and the visitor center. Jake headed toward the summer cabins.

The blank canvas of snow was marred by occasional animal tracks—mule deer, mainly—a few of which Jake stopped to inspect in case they proved to be shoe prints. No dice.

Cabins dotted the east loop, where the road formed a ring and came back onto itself. The austere cedar lodgings looked spartan even from outside. They had been winterized—inch-thick plywood was nailed over the windows and doors. It would take quite a bit of muscle to remove the barriers. Not an easy task for most people, much less a petite woman.

Still, Jake made the circle slowly, inspecting each small building for any sign of an overnight occupant. In the middle of the oval, a dim light shone on the side of the restrooms. No barriers blocked the doors.

Jake killed the engine and got out, tucking the Mariner into the back of his waistband. He followed the snow-covered path from the road to the concrete building. He didn't notice any tracks, but given the wind and precipitation that meant little.

On the front of the restroom, between the men's and women's doors, hung a park bulletin: ATTENTION ICE FISHERMEN: DO NOT CLEAN YOUR CATCH IN THE RESTROOMS.

The bathroom was open for the winter.

Jake reached for the door to the ladies' room. He entered to find a nestlike pile of unspooled toilet paper beneath the hand dryer. A bed?

Leaving the bathroom, Jake looked more closely for tracks and found slight indentations covered with fresh snow leading through the cluster of cabins. Two sets. Coming and going. He followed them until the path of the traveler was apparent. Back toward the main entrance and the intersection of the east and west loops.

Jake jogged back to the Charger and drove to the meeting point. Wright wasn't there. He looked around for Meirong. Finding no sign of her, he parked and waited.

A few minutes passed. Anxious, he started the engine and steered the Charger onto the two-mile west loop, where Wright had been searching.

He found the Jeep, running and with its driver's-side door open, parked in tent site 132. The sites were surrounded with dense grand firs, and beneath them was a layer of willowy brush.

Jake could see Wright's tracks leading from the Jeep into the quagmire of vegetation.

*What the hell?* He parked the Charger, Glock in hand. He heard the crunch of frozen twigs near Wright's entry point into the forest.

"Wright!" Jake yelled. The noise subsided.

Jake was thirty yards from the Jeep. A burst of motion flew from the shady trees. Someone running through the snow. A woman. Meirong.

"Stop!" Jake shouted louder this time, hoping to frighten her. Instead she moved faster—into the Jeep, slamming the door as he closed in on her. She nearly ran him over backing up. In the mirror, Jake glimpsed her horrified eyes before she slammed the Jeep into drive and sped off.

Where was Wright? Jake had no time to stop and search for him. With a vehicle, Meirong would become considerably harder to track.

Jake ran back to the Charger. He fishtailed through the campground's S-turn and slid onto Ririe Road.

Meirong had a good lead—an eighth of a mile or more. She pushed the Jeep to its limit as she descended toward the highway. Jake matched her on the narrow, frozen road.

Near the intersection, the snow was changing to slush. Meirong took a right, almost colliding with an eighteen-wheeler, and sped east toward the laboratory.

*　　*　　*

As he had expected, Wright's rental Jeep was parked at the laboratory. Jake drove the Charger into a space but didn't get out. He watched through the slats of the blinds, where he could see Meirong rushing about. She was aware of Jake following her, but it didn't matter. She had nowhere else to go.

The gun that killed the senator was safely in the trunk of the Charger. It was possible that Meirong had another weapon somewhere inside, or the shotgun that killed the janitor at Game and Fish, and given her acumen with firearms—now having killed two men, the senator and the janitor—Jake didn't want to risk an up-close encounter.

It was senseless for him to go into the building anyway. His target was isolated, and Divya was on her way.

Whether Divya could be fully trusted was another question. Jake had no idea where anyone's allegiances lay, except his own. *Charlotte Terrell. Esma.*

*Shit.* Meirong had been looking for a way to communicate, not a weapon. She pushed aside the blinds and held up a newspaper, marked up with black Sharpie in block print. LEAVE ME ALONE OR I WILL KILL ESMA.

He started to get out of the car to plead with her, but she retreated from the window.

*Goddammit.*

Jake dialed the hospital. He discovered it was Dr. Antol's day off. Jake did his best to impress the gravity of the situation on the new attending doctor, but the man didn't buy it. Jake demanded Dr. Antol's home number.

"You know I can't do that."

Jake tried to explain, told the young doctor about the chip, the Chinese, and the kidnapping in Idaho. The details didn't have the desired effect of persuasion.

"I'll keep a close watch on her, like all patients" was all he would promise.

Jake hung up.

*Deputy Statler.* His next-best bet.

"Jake, where have you been? I've been trying to reach you."

"I can't really say. But I need your help."

"What's going on? Is Charlotte safe?"

"I'm working on that. I need a favor."

Where he failed with the doctor, Jake succeeded with Layle.

He remembered Meirong reaching to her left shoulder when she explained the device. "It's above Esma's heart somewhere. Left clavicle."

"A month ago, if I'd heard that story, I would have said you're crazy. But I believe you."

"Go to the hospital now and help Esma. Don't take no for an answer."

# 54

The storm had moved east, over the Tetons, and the sun was out by the time Divya arrived at the laboratory. She looked severe in black twill dress pants and a heavy peacoat with oversized Tom Ford sunglasses.

"Where's Wright?" she said instead of greeting him.

Jake gave her a play-by-play of Meirong's escape and Wright's disappearance. "My guess is he's still up by the reservoir, looking to hitch a ride out."

"He's got some history with Xiao, Jake. Going back a ways. They *know* each other."

"In what capacity?"

"I don't know yet."

"Jesus."

Jake apprised Divya of the situation with Esma.

356

"I'm sorry, Jake. I had no idea what we were getting into."

To Jake, she sounded sincere. But all that stuff would have to wait. His priority remained the safety of the two imperiled women, Charlotte and Esma.

"What's the plan?" Divya asked.

"I'm hoping the deputy can persuade the doctor to open Esma up and remove the chip. It was the best I could do."

"You're sure Meirong's not bluffing about the implant?" Divya asked.

"I'm giving her the benefit of the doubt."

He glanced toward the window. Meirong was peering at them through the blinds.

"Look." Jake pointed.

"What's she doing?"

"I don't know." Jake felt useless. Was she tinkering with whatever device controlled Esma's fate? Moreover, how had Divya's phone call a week earlier led to this chaos? Now the lives of two good people were in his hands, and he had little notion of whom to trust.

Meirong moved to the desk, where she appeared to be writing something again. When she finished, she brought the newspaper to the window and held it up for Jake and Divya to see. Jake walked through the sopping snow toward the window, until Meirong shook her head and waved him off.

He returned to Divya's side, near the concrete abutment where he'd sought cover from the firefight the night before.

"What does it say?" she asked.

"Ten minutes."

"Damn."

"We need to get out of her view for the time being. Keep watch, but from farther out. If she knows we're still around, she'll kill Esma."

Divya nodded. "Disable the Jeep?"

"No. Not worth it."

It was an unnerving balance; an innocent woman's life lay on each side of the scale.


Jake and Divya left the parking lot separately and crossed the highway, where they parked Divya's rental and regrouped in the Charger. A service road continued up a gentle grade to a potato farm.

"We can see the intersection from here, and she won't be able to see us."

Divya didn't seem convinced. "What if she goes the other way?"

"There's nothing there but the river."

Jake took the Steiner binoculars from the car, but there was no clear view of the building itself. A cluster of tall cottonwoods blocked his view. He took out his phone and checked for a voice mail or text from Layle. Nothing.

He was desperate to know that Esma was okay, that the chip had been removed and the threat was gone. When that happened, he could pursue Meirong without hesitation. And get Charlotte home to her family, where she belonged.

"You okay?"

Jake realized his hands were shaking. He tossed the binoculars to the backseat and grabbed another layer.

"Why did you involve me?" He didn't make eye contact with her. He was watching the intersection. The wind gusted against their backs. Divya's long, dark hair blew out from her collar and swam in the wind.

"Wright asked me to."

"Why didn't the Office come to me first?"

"He was skeptical of their plans. Now we know why—he's got other plans."

"You could've said no. You didn't have to lie."

"Hindsight . . ." Another gust toyed with Divya's silky hair.

Jake made eye contact. Her face was flushed, maybe from the cold breeze.

"I needed you." She blurted it out, trying to get it over with—throw it into the wind, where it would go away. "This job. The agency. It's so bursting with deceit."

Jake understood.

"And you were always . . ." She stopped. "You know. It seemed like you always had direction. The proverbial moral compass."

Jake stared at the highway intersection.

"Jake?" Divya put her hand on his arm.

"Hold on. What's that?" He pointed.

An old cherry-red pickup was slowing down. It pulled onto the shoulder and deposited a well-dressed man. Jake grabbed the Steiners, his hands as steady as rocks now.

"It's Wright."

Jake got into the driver's seat and floored it down the dirt road, taking the car's suspension to its limit. The Charger slid out onto the highway. Jake corrected the wheel slightly to the left, and then accelerated to the right onto Heise Road.

Jake slowed down and looked for Wright. He was already around the corner of the building, on the side where Meirong had been positioned at the window.

"No!" Jake shouted in futility.

Wright was up against the window with his gun drawn, shouting orders at Meirong, who had retreated behind the deceased senator's desk.

"Wright! Back off!" Jake rushed the assistant director, who out-matched him physically. He pushed Jake aside.

"Leave her alone!" Jake yelled.

"She's locked herself in. We need to break it down."

"Listen, she's not stable. All she wants is to be free of all the chaos. Live her life without being used and betrayed. We have to make her feel comfortable, at least until everyone is safe."

Wright's face was all confusion. He turned and started to tell Jake to back off, but spun back to the window as Meirong started pounding her fist on the glass.

She was holding the newspaper again. Black Sharpie. 1 MIN. ESMA.

"We have to go. She's going to kill someone with the chip. Innocent lives are in her hands."

Wright wasn't affected by this.

Jake tried another angle. "There's only so much that can be swept under the carpet. If she kills again, this whole thing blows up—there will be no containing it. This will all get out. Including what your role is."

"Back up, Trent. You don't know what you're doing."

Through the window, Jake saw Meirong take a seat at the desk. She reached for the keyboard. Jake went for the Mariner. It was in the Charger.

Jake slammed into the glass with his elbow to break it, but Wright grabbed him by the shoulder and sent him crashing to the ground. When Jake tried to stand he was met with a hard pistol whip to the nose.

The world started to dim, but Jake fought off the darkness. He clutched at Divya, now by his side.

Meirong was standing again, away from the computer. She'd

done it. When Jake looked at her she showed no remorse. She started scrawling on a piece of newspaper again.

THERE ARE MORE. 5 MINS.

Jake wiped away the blood from his face with his sleeve.

"What does she mean?" Wright asked.

"He told you!" Divya said, helping Jake.

Jake packed a handful of melting snow and held it against his broken nose.

As the snow reddened, he took out his phone.

J.P. hadn't called yet, but Jake knew it was coming.

# 55

Esma was still. It was over.

*Who designed this cruel machine?* J.P. thought.

Her blood was on the bed, but her body was not. A tangle of cords remained in a nest by her pillow. J.P. stared at it, still in shock. Then he let out a sigh of relief and looked to the corner of the room, where Layle was helping soothe Esma while the doctor stitched up her incision.

On the floor next to the bed lay an unusual looking device. Small like a pill and shiny chrome. It hadn't buzzed or sparked or done anything movie-worthy. Instead, it clicked softly every thirty seconds or so, and continued doing so now on the linoleum.

Layle must have noticed J.P. staring. "Don't touch it."

J.P. walked over and crushed it like a bug with his size 12 Timberlands. Then he sat on the bed to catch his breath.

It had been a blur to J.P. Deputy Layle had raced into the hospital room, hollering about Esma's heart attack and threatening to "take the damn thing out myself!"

The doctor then resisted, while J.P. looked on in horror.

Layle took out his phone and called Jake. No answer. He left a short voice mail. "Jake! They won't listen!"

"I'll call security if I have to!" the doctor shouted.

Layle had finally seen enough; he pinned the MD against the wall and spoke calmly but sternly. Their faces were only an inch apart. "Listen to me. That woman right there is going to die. You can choose to be either a hero or a hindrance." He tossed the man to the ground and approached Esma.

"Fine! Don't touch her!" The doctor stood up and shouted into the hallway for local anesthetics and an extra hand.

A careful incision was then made four inches above her left breast while J.P. and Layle held her down. With the help of a surgical assistant, a thoracoscope was inserted into Esma's chest cavity.

"No history of heart disease?" the doctor asked the assistant.

"None."

"Okay, there's something here. Confirm, please, that she doesn't have a pacemaker."

"No pacemaker."

"Oh my God." The doctor was frozen for a second. "You're right. It's something . . . I don't know . . . man-made."

"Hurry!" J.P. shouted.

The doctor startled and got back to his task. He reached in carefully with his hemostats and removed the device. For a second, he held it in front of his eyes in amazement.

*Click. Click.*

"Shit!" The doctor dropped the chip, hemostats and all, into a surgical tray. "Thing shocked me!"

"Nobody touch it!" Layle kicked the whole tray to the ground.

It was a peculiar-looking object, like something from a sci-fi film. Two short nodes on one end, and two tiny wires leaving the other.

"Pretty sure it's dead," the doctor said. J.P. was still standing over the crushed mess of tiny wires. "We're going to take her to a clean room. Give us ten minutes."

J.P. only nodded. He walked out to the waiting area with Layle, who, after helping him sit, brought over a Styrofoam cup of ice water. J.P. gulped it down.

"You're okay." Layle was kneeling on the tile in front of J.P. "Look at me. You're okay. We did it."

"Fucking nightmare," was all J.P. said, and Layle laughed.

"No shit."

Dr. Antol bustled through the waiting room in street clothes, saying, "I'll be right back with you," and headed back toward the ICU. The surgical assistant had called for her.

The color started to return to J.P.'s face. "How did you know?"

"Jake called me."

A few minutes later, Dr. Antol returned to the waiting room.

"C'mon back," she said in a soothing voice.

Esma's new room was only a few doors down. Layle waited outside while Dr. Antol took J.P. in.

"We gave her an injection for the pain, so she's sleeping now. She'll still have to be treated with antibiotics. A two-day course, at least."

"And?"

"I'd be lying if I said we've ever experienced something like this." She looked into his desperate eyes. "But, I'd assume with that thing gone, she's not at risk anymore. How did this happen?"

"Some other time."

The doctor left J.P. alone with Esma.

He slid a chair over from the window and sat. He leaned forward, rested his head on the bed at Esma's side, and started to cry.

# 56

Wright crossed Heise Road, to where Jake and Divya had gathered out of Meirong's view.

"You all right?"

Jake had another snowball to his nose and was listening to the voice mail from Deputy Layle. He still stared toward the industrial park, keeping an eye on Meirong without her getting wind of it. That would cost more lives.

"I need your help to go get her." Wrong timing by Wright.

Jake growled back at him. "We backed off to stop her from killing an innocent person. Isn't one enough? She's too volatile to aggravate at this point." Jake glared at the assistant director. His menacing gaze and twisted nose made Wright look down. There was silence for a moment.

Jake put the phone back in his pocket and spoke up. "You got

366

what you wanted, right? She's trapped—can't leave that compound without us knowing."

"I'm sorry for anyone who died and their families, Jake."

"Bullshit."

"You don't know what my orders are."

"You're not acting on orders. There's something in this for you."

The towering Wright shook his head. "You think this makes me happy?"

Jake gave him a puzzled look.

"I can't get Charlotte Terrell back, Jake. I'm sorry. My orders are to keep Meirong."

"Keep her?" Divya was intrigued too.

"I was charged with making sure she didn't disappear again, or worse, escape back to China. There was no way I could stop Xiao from taking the Terrells, and your friend . . . I didn't even know about your friend, Jake."

"But you worked with Xiao? Schue told me everything."

Wright chuckled. "I was a UC, Divya, a plant. I spent a few years in China getting as much information as I could on the technology and the Shar-Pei program. You know we can't share that information with other agencies."

Jake didn't know whether to believe the man or not, but it didn't really matter. "So Xiao will just end up killing Charlotte, like he did the chief?"

"Probably not. If he kills her, he loses his bargaining power for Meirong, and the Chinese government rains hell upon him for losing her."

"So Charlotte's a prisoner, indefinitely."

"That's my guess." Wright was taking intermittent glances back toward the building.

"What if more people are implanted, like she said?" Divya's voice waivered. Jake realized they were all in over their heads.

Wright just shrugged. He turned back to the laboratory building, where the crown jewel of Shar-Pei was unraveling.

"Why?" Jake shouted into the breeze.

Wright looked over his shoulder. "Because she's a threat to us if she goes home and an asset if she's here. Cold logic. I have to detain her now, Jake. With or without your help."

"I'm not one of your kind anymore."

Wright got in his car and went back down the hill to complete his mission, by force.

Jake got out of the shower at 5 p.m. Divya was gone.

He found her at the lobby bar, where she was having a gin and tonic.

"I could use something too."

"Let's finish our drinks and get somewhere private." She drained her cocktail.

Back in the room, Jake listened intently to Divya's explanation of Shar-Pei, Xiao, and Tram Village. He was focused now on Charlotte.

"What about a precision strike, a few men go in and get her?"

"We would never get the green light with Wright in charge. Besides, it would be way too risky. As soon as Xiao saw American forces, he would hole up with her or kill her."

Jake agreed with Divya, especially on the latter point, but let his thoughts develop.

He stood up from the bed, a focused look on his face. "What if it wasn't Americans who were striking?"

"What, like a Trojan horse?"

"Not exactly. Let's go get my truck."

# 57

IDAHO FALLS, IDAHO. THE SAME EVENING.
5:45 P.M. MOUNTAIN STANDARD TIME.

Assistant Director Wright was on his way to Salt Lake City, where there were facilities to detain and question Meirong, who was cuffed in the backseat. Jake and Divya were in the 4Runner a hundred miles behind him. As much as Jake despised Wright, he was their only chance to save Charlotte.

The drive from Idaho Falls was just over two hundred miles—the first few dozen of which followed the meandering Snake River on its way to the American Falls Reservoir. Farms eventually gave way to rolling sage slopes and mountain ranges south of Pocatello. Except for the highest mountain passes, the roads were dry. Easy driving.

Northern Utah was much the same until Tremont and Brigham City, where hay, corn, and barley farms dominated the landscape.

A text lit up the dark cabin of the SUV. Divya picked up Jake's phone.

"From J.P.," she said.

Jake panicked, swerving over the rumble strips. "Lemme see."

"She's okay." Divya held the phone in front of her. Astonished. "Lemme see."

Jake had slowed to twenty-five miles per hour.

"She's alive, J.P. says. They got to her just in time."

Jake exhaled loudly. "How did . . ." He stopped, overwhelmed.

Divya reached over and put her hand on his shoulder. "I don't know. But Esma's okay. You have missed calls from both J.P. and Layle. Must've been when we were in one of those deep valleys. You did it."

"Thank God." Jake went quiet for the next thirty miles. Then, out of nowhere: "Thank God." Again.


They stopped just outside a small town in the Bear River area to refresh.

"You think it will work?" Divya had just returned to the parked 4Runner from a Conoco, where they stopped to get trail mix and coffee.

"I do." Jake took one of the steaming cups from her and opened the door. "Thanks for the coffee."

He pulled back onto Highway 15, headed south. They were approaching Ogden, where the northern reaches of the mountains that laid claim to Utah's most famous powder snow began to rise to their left. The grayish outline of the peaks was visible against the dark eastern sky. The snow line here was higher than up north, and the weather in the valley, where the road ran, was warmer—in the upper forties, even though the sun had set.

They arrived in Salt Lake City at 10:30 p.m. It had taken some wheedling to get Wright to agree to let them come, and that was accomplished by Jake's threatening to take the thing public.

The hectic nature of a city always caught Jake by surprise. The roads were wide and full of cars, even at night. The inky-black darkness of the western sky was polluted by glowing signs and parking-lot streetlamps. Businesses, mostly big-box stores and megagroceries, were still open and bustling.

The small detention center for women where Meirong was being kept was located between the famous Temple and Capitol Hill, on West 300 North, a dreadfully unimaginative moniker.

Jake pulled in to the campus after receiving a visitor pass for himself and Divya at the front gate. The building was low—just three stories—and its landscaping surprisingly elaborate, reminiscent more of a suburban hotel than a prison. The only giveaways were the high fence around the perimeter and the powerful xenon flood lamps.

On the way inside, Jake pondered his chances. He had no viable avenue other than to appeal to Wright's sense of decency. That and his ego. The plan was reasonable, Jake thought, and would allow the assistant director to bury Terrell's death with one last heroic act.


They were buzzed in by an imposing Latina woman in her early forties who wasn't happy to be there.

"Thanks," Jake said.

The woman responded only, "Follow me."

Wright was sitting in an interrogation room—bright but austere. A place that might make you reconsider your decision not to cooperate.

A metal table sat in the middle of the room. Wright sat on an orange padded desk chair on one end and gestured for Jake and Divya to take a seat at the other, where there were two unpadded stools.

"So," Wright started, "Divya says you have a plan to get Chief Terrell's wife out of China." He too was sipping on a large coffee.

Jake cleared his throat. "What do you know about Tiananmen Square?"

The assistant director frowned and took a swig of coffee. "I was there from early April to the middle of May, when things got too hot."

Jake tried to hide his surprise. "And how would you describe it?"

"Chaotic. Hell, scary. I don't know. What are you getting at?"

"The Chinese have a history of political protests. Riots, really, for social equality. I think we can use that to our advantage."

He swallowed a gulp of coffee. "How?"

*At least he's hearing me out.*

"I think if we could leak information regarding Tram Village and the plan to perpetuate a dynasty of Shar-Peis, we could set off a chain reaction that might topple the place—a localized social revolution that would allow us to sneak in with as few as four or five men to get Charlotte out."

Wright was rubbing his stubble, looking unconvinced. "And when you say men, you mean who? You're not going to go. I'm not going to go."

"CIA with Special Forces."

"And we'd need a heli or two?"

"Yes, sir."

A long sigh. "What about recoil? We can't destroy our relations with China for one woman's life."

This was why Jake hated the CIA, and politics in general. "Blame the dead senator. He leaked it, and the US had to respond to a citizen in danger. No choice."

Wright was quiet. Jake and Divya exchanged looks. She mouthed something that might have been *Good* in his direction. Jake shrugged, thinking: *Worth a shot.*

Wright cleared his throat. "Impossible."

Jake's shoulders slumped, the last bit of hope starting to escape.

"You've been with the agency too long," Divya blurted at Wright, who betrayed no emotion. "Let's go, Jake." Divya stood up.

"Do you have a family, sir?" Jake was still sitting.

"A wife and one son."

"What if her life was at risk? What if your son were to grow up without a mother? Would you want CIA hard-liners to dictate her fate?"

Wright shook his head. "I would want you to dictate her fate, but no man is bigger than the machine, Jake."

Jake stood, but maintained glacial eye contact as he started to the door.

"I do appreciate everything. Both of you. But I've got a huge mess to clean up."

Jake heard Wright's words as the door to the interrogation room slipped closed behind him.

They were silent until Jake started the car.

"What do we do now?" he asked Divya. He didn't look at her.

"I don't know."

Divya returned her rental car and opted to fly out of Salt Lake. She called United, but there wasn't a flight available for twenty-four hours.

Jake felt guilty leaving her alone. "You can keep me company on the ride if you want. Fly out of Jackson."

She agreed, hugging him and saying over and over again, "I'm sorry."

"Are you going to stay with the agency?" he asked on the long ride home.

"I don't know. Might take a little break." A pause. "Jake, I tried to do it right."

"It's okay." From his days at the Office, Jake knew how it felt.

# 58

Jake called Layle in the morning to inquire about the Terrell children.

"Not yet. They don't know yet. Still in Victor with their aunt."

"Does she know?"

"I've told her that things got tangled up in China, and their return is delayed. What's going on at your end?"

"It's over as far as we go. Keep me updated on the kids."

Chayote's enthusiasm at his master's arrival lightened Jake's mood somewhat—he'd received attention from the neighbor only for feeding and bathroom breaks. The same storm that barreled through Idaho Falls had spread through the tall spires of the Tetons, leaving two new feet in the mountains and seven or eight inches at the bed-and-breakfast. When Jake let him out, the heeler galloped through the snow, eating big scoops of it until he was shivering.

Jake made a small fire and sat down by it to drink his coffee.

375

The sixty-year-old guesthouse wasn't airtight, and drafts haunted the downstairs. He didn't like turning on the electric heat until the first night below zero.

J.P. was with Esma at the hospital. She was doing well. The sepsis was in check, and she was likely to be released the next day.

Jake's plans for the day were basic—he needed to cover and store his boat, tape some of the especially leaky window frames, and deal with Divya. She still didn't have a flight. The airport was behind because of the weather.

Jake's plans changed when she came racing down the stairs at 8:45 a.m.

"Meirong is dead," she blurted. "Hanged herself in the cell by her jumpsuit."

Thoughts flooded Jake's head. "Where does that leave us?" An epiphany. *Can we go get Charlotte?*

"Wright is in. He's on the phone as we speak, trying to sell the agency higher-ups on your idea."

Jake jogged upstairs to get dressed and brush his teeth. "What can I do?" he shouted back down at her.

"Nothing but wait."

He took a seat on his bed and aired a big sigh of relief. All was not lost. Meirong was gone, and with her the biggest bargaining chip for Charlotte. But Xiao didn't know that yet, and if they acted quickly, he wouldn't find out until Charlotte was safe.


Jake was shoveling snow out of his skiff with a small shovel from his backcountry ski pack when Divya came outside. He had retrieved the canvas cover from its place in the garage and spread it out beside the boat.

Divya looked like Jake felt: reinvigorated and optimistic. Still beautifully severe in a dark outfit and her mirrored sunglasses.

"Any word?" he asked her.

"Not yet."

Jake looked at his watch, wondering what was taking so long. *Bureaucracy,* he figured. Hopefully not so much as to derail the effort entirely.

"Hey, do me a favor and grab the other end of that cover and pull it over the stern."

When the cover was attached, Jake pushed the trailer a few dozen feet back off the driveway, under the shelter of a large pine.

"This guy yours?" Divya was crouched, rubbing Chayote's ears.

"Yeah. Kind of forced his way into the family here."

"I love the place. Get much business?"

"Not really. Let's go inside; I'll show you around."

The main house was cold; there hadn't been any guests since the weather changed, and thus no need for heat. The large interior—thirty-five hundred square feet or so—was decorated in a combination of brawny fishing lodge furniture and contemporary western art.

Divya stopped in front of a tangerine rendition of an American bison in the main gathering room.

"Interesting." A smile peeked through.

"Hey, we're in Wyoming."

"I've never been to Wyoming."

"Then don't dis my orange buffalo."

After the brief tour, they settled in by the fire in the guesthouse to get down to business. Chayote, with no such aspirations, snored loudly from the hearth.

"What's the timetable?" Jake was feeling anxious.

"Hopefully quick. We need to move before Xiao learns that Canart and Meirong are dead. We've informed Canart's wife only that her husband is missing and that revealing such information to anyone else at this stage could jeopardize his life. Not a perfect plan, but it buys us a few days."

Shortly after noon, Wright called and asked to speak with Jake. Divya handed her phone over.

"Jake. It's a go. We're gonna try to get out of this mess with some semblance of a positive result."

# 59

Charlotte Terrell turned over in her bed. She'd been trying to spend as much time as possible asleep, where reality was diluted, but her body was restless. She flipped onto her back and opened her eyes, blankly staring at the stucco ceiling for a few moments.

"Funny seeing you here," she said toward the giant in the corner, who didn't say anything in response.

Charlotte sat up and looked at the clock. *Holy shit!* She got out of bed, used the restroom, and washed her face. Looking in the mirror, she could swear she'd added a few wrinkles since this nightmare started.

"Food?" she asked the giant as she walked back to the main room and plopped down on the corner of the bed. He got on the phone and ordered some.

"Ask him when I am leaving."

The giant hung up. "It wasn't Xiao."

Charlotte's bags sat neatly packed in the center of the room. Her late husband's bags were pushed into the corner, where they didn't catch her eye as often. The TV had become more of an annoyance than a luxury; there were very few programs in English, and she hadn't even begun to understand the local dialect. Instead, she reread the *Western Home* magazine that was in the room.

Her body was sore from being idle. "I need exercise if I'm staying for a while." She'd said it hoping the giant would reassure her that it wouldn't be long.

All he said was, "I'll ask Xiao."

The food arrived, brought by the front-desk woman, and Charlotte ate as much as she could despite a weak appetite. She wanted to stay as healthy as possible—physically and mentally.

The room was starting to smell lived-in. The hot food coming and going had stuck around too, bringing a cafeteria aroma to the carpet and upholstery. The sheets had been changed only once since their arrival, and not at all since her daylong drug-induced sleep, from which she had woken up clammy and sweating.

She showered frequently, but she preferred to wear the same clothes—a white pajama outfit with holly leaves and berries.

"I'm going to clean up," she said to herself. The giant didn't bother looking up from his phone. She washed her face and put on makeup and body lotion, thinking the ritual might induce a sense of normalcy. When she was finished, she walked to the window.

"What's that?"

Nothing from the giant.

"Hey, who are *they*?"

The giant sighed and stood, joining her at the window. Charlotte had a forefinger pressed to it, pointing to the front gate, where a crowd of a few dozen people was gathered on the outside.

"Just workers."

But before he could sit back down, his phone rang. The giant spoke fast in Mandarin, then hung up and turned to her.

"I'll be right back."


In groups of three and four, more and more people were accumulating. Half the distance to the formation, the giant from the room was standing with Xiao in the dusty road, looking on.

She was still watching when the giant came back.

He walked to his post in the corner without saying a word.

"What's going on?"

"Nothing. Villagers."

Charlotte returned to the window. It looked as though the crowd was approaching fifty or sixty.

"What do they want?"

"Probably money."

As more and more villagers gathered, the mass began a procession toward Main Street.

"They're coming in." The group was pushing and pulling on the gate, using leverage to break it down.

The giant joined Charlotte at the window, then abruptly headed for the door.

The mob reached the middle of Main Street in short order. It was made up of men, mainly, early teenagers to fortysomethings. They moved about without direction, an uneasy throng looking around curiously. A few held picket signs, but Charlotte couldn't decipher the characters. Every few moments a new group of five or six would pour in from the broken front gate.

That silly white bison was their first target, and Charlotte watched it tumble over with some satisfaction. A few minutes later, a very young demonstrator wandered over to the fallen beast and tried to light it on fire.

The men became more unruly as their numbers multiplied. River rocks from the ornate landscaping were tossed at windows. Doors in various buildings were being tested and broken down.

The giant came hustling in, calling for Charlotte. When she followed him into the hall, Xiao was there too, and she looked at him.

"We're moving. Leave your bags."

The giant gripped Charlotte by the upper arm. He led her down to the parking garage, where they got in a silver luxury sedan. With the giant behind the wheel, he pulled out of the garage that faced the opposite direction from the mob.

He drove fast around the back side of Main Street and stopped behind the restaurant where Charlotte had been imprisoned with her husband. He jumped out, grabbed Charlotte from the backseat, and with Xiao, led her into through the back door, down the stairs and into the stark-looking kitchen.

"Sit down," the giant ordered.

"What's going on?"

Xiao fielded this one. "Local farmers, here to steal. Scavenger dogs." Uncharacteristically, he sounded unsure of himself. "It will pass." He walked up the stairs and disappeared.

Even in the bunkerlike basement of the restaurant, Charlotte could sporadically hear the crowd shouting in unison. "What are they saying?"

"I can't tell." The giant, like Xiao, seemed concerned.

The noise from outside grew louder. It sounded now as though the crowd was just outside the restaurant. "Are they trying to get in?"

The giant didn't respond. He was busy listening.

Xiao returned with a handgun for the giant. He was visibly shaken. They spoke to each other in Mandarin for a moment and Xiao left again, up the stairs.

Charlotte sat in silence, until she noticed the smell. "Smoke. They're trying to burn the building." Her uneasiness morphed into full-on fear. Not because she was afraid of her own demise, but for her children.

The giant left Charlotte's side and looked up the stairwell. When he came back he said, "Something outside burning," but didn't look convinced.

More ruckus. The structure of the building itself seemed to be emitting a low buzz; the crowd was here. Testing windows, doors, and walls.

"Come with me." The giant grabbed Charlotte by the arm again and led her to the dry-storage room where she'd shared her last days with her husband. The broken cot still sat near the door, a memorial to Roger's courage.

Both Charlotte and the giant were breathing heavily now—uncertain of what awaited them. The din of voices was followed by the clamoring of pots and pans hitting the tile floor. The mob was in the kitchen.

The lock still hadn't been repaired, so the giant leaned his mass up against the door, attempting to barricade it. The sharp ping of shattering wine glasses and dinnerware knifed under the door, coming from a much nearer source than the initial racket. They were closing in.

Neither Charlotte nor the giant uttered a word. The chaos was just outside the door. Charlotte knelt in the corner, hands over her head, glancing up only from time to time. She prayed for her family.

The banging subsided after a few moments, the gang apparently satisfied with their destruction. Their voices still echoed through the basement kitchen.

"What are they saying?" Charlotte whispered in the now quiet room.

"Looking for things of value."

"Thank God."

The voices soon yielded to silence too. The giant slumped down onto his behind and took a deep breath, still leaning against the door.

"We need to get out of here." Charlotte couldn't stand the confines of the cell any longer.

"No." The giant was adamant. "We'll wait until we know they are gone."

For what seemed like an eternity, Charlotte remained in the corner, recovering. She didn't weep for her husband or family or fret about her own fate. The giant didn't speak either.

Twenty minutes later, the cautious steps of someone whispered through the door.

"Xiao," the giant mouthed.

The volume of the padding steps increased until they came to a stop right outside the door.

The giant started to stand and turn as the heavy door burst open. He was hurled backward onto the table. A thick smoke filled the room. Charlotte heard him struggle to free himself, but another force was keeping him down.

Charlotte's wrist was pulled through the fog, and when she

resisted, her assailant threw her onto his shoulders. She grabbed for the doorjamb but couldn't hold on. She was being carried through the kitchen and up the stairs, taken.

Her eyes burned from the smoke and she couldn't open them. A rush of cool air told her she'd been taken outside, where a hectic drumming noise overwhelmed her senses. Sand and dust flew in a stiff wind, stinging her face.

She was laid on a cold metal floor. She tried to see, but the fiery stinging forced her eyelids shut again.

# 60

It was midmorning when Jake's phone buzzed. Divya had spent the night in Jake's bed again, while he took the cold leather couch downstairs. Her flight was at 3 p.m.

They had coffee and a quick breakfast in Wilson, all the while making sure their cell reception remained strong. The mood grew tenser with each passing hour.

When the message finally came, Jake opened it and immediately stood from his seat at the bay window overlooking the creek.

Divya popped up from the couch and walked toward him.

"She's safe," he blurted.

A wide smile came across Divya's face. "I got it too."

\*     \*     \*

The roads were slick from the blowing snow on the way to the airport. Traffic from canceled flights moved at a snail's pace, and by the time Jake pulled up to the curb Divya had to rush for her flight.

"Call me if you get canceled."

"Will do." The winter storm brought out a rosiness in Divya's dark skin. She looked content. And gorgeous.

"I'm sorry, Jake. For putting you through all this."

He waved it off.

"Gimme a hug."

Jake waited in the 4Runner, sipping coffee and watching the weather until Divya's 747 took off eastward. He pulled out onto 89 toward town and put the wipers on high to deflect the incessant flakes.

A few elk had moved into the refuge during the night, hounded by the even more perilous weather in the mountains. He pulled over to observe a herd of mature males and called Deputy Layle.

"Charlotte is safe."

"Thank God. I'll go over the hill and tell the family."

"That's a tough job. Thank you. Looks like we have a new chief in town."

Layle chuckled. "I've got a wedding to plan and a fiancée who says I don't spend enough time with her. I have half a mind to put your name forward for the job."

Jake looked south toward the town of Jackson, barely visible through the storm.

"Not a snowball's chance in hell." He wasn't sure whether he meant it. "Do me a favor and tell Noelle that Charlotte's okay."

"Of course."

# ACKNOWLEDGMENTS

Enormous thanks to all those who helped along the way; I couldn't have done it without you: Margaret Riley, Paul Whitlatch, Kyle Radler, David Lamb, Tom Bair, Molly Lindley, Benjamin Holmes, Dr. Jeff Dreyer, Dr. Arwind Koimattur, Dr. Rahul Tendulkar, and Lara Bertsch.